Beneath the Love of a Woman

P.D Lorde

P.D Lorde

ISBN:-10:1508431469
ISBN-13:978-1508431466

DEDICATION

I dedicate this book to my beloved mother, who taught me how to be me. Some days we have to stand in our moment and shine.

Also To my Daddy, my rock, best friend and confidant. Always. When you are no longer here to give me your wise counsel, I shall find the most prominent tree to talk to, as you will hear me through the rustling of the leaves. Mine lips to your ears only. For Eternity!

CONTENTS

ACKNOWLEDGMENTS

Sitting in this moment I have to acknowledge God and the universe. I am a firm believer that 'nothing happens before its time'. God has made this winding path straight for me, and for that I am grateful. This project has been a decade in the making. I am consumed with emotion and am joyous about the fact that this story is complete and successive tales have just begun.

Nothing brings me more joy than writing. To my supporters in this life and the next whom has made this book possible, I thank you from the bottom of my heart. I acknowledge my mother, Auntie Gloria, and my Uncle Verly, you are the best story tellers on this planet. To the rest of my family, both the Moore's, the Lorde's and the Innes', thank you for the love, support and continued assistance. My adorable husband Richard, my sons Aaron, Richard Junior and Joshua. My Swan Sisters. We are the toughest Mudders on Constitutional Hill! I love you and thank you all. Adonica Simmons, Victoria Reynold Jones, and Beverly Allen. I would like to send out a special thank you to Melanie Newland Harse, who encouraged me to be my best self, and has contributed to me 'getting over the line', with this project. I am a firm believer that people come into your life for a reason, season or lifetime. I can do and be anything, it's taken me forty years to realise that. We all can all you have to do is dream and believe. To the formidable Dr. Mayo Angerlou, who told me that my story needed to be told. May your spirit and words continue to enlighten and lift me.

Book One

Chapter One

The Journey

January 13th 2005 10AM

"H-e-l-p   m-e-e-e!" Jonathan screamed down the corridor, his baritone voice ricocheting off the walls. The three Macmillan nurses on duty all looked up and without pause started to sprint towards his mother Edwina Mallard's room.

Nurse Alice Mckee was the Lead Macmillan Nurse for Edwina.

"Please Alice – SOB - Please –SOB- ... Alice I am not ready! It's not her time yet." Jonathan could feel himself losing composure and was trying desperately to keep his emotions in check. "*How dare you! How bloody dare you! This is the last thing that mum needs ..... her sniveling middle aged son losing all composure.*" I am the mature dependable one, not this gushing river about to burst its banks. "*Get it together Jon*".

Alice looked at this man with complete empathy. He looked and smelt like he was in need of a long hot shower. He was unshaven, his clothes were disheveled, his beard over grown and he was visibly exhausted; the poor love had been at his mother's side for the past 17 hours. It was an effort for him to keep his body upright. Every muscle was screaming for him to sleep, but he just couldn't. He was not going to leave his mummy. Alice could feel her heart swelling with emotion; she knew what this moment felt like. Despite this emotional machine gun discharging its ammunition into her chest she pushed herself back to the here and now. She did what she was trained for. Alice got to work and started to review Edwina's vital signs. She looked up and noticed that Jonathan hadn't moved from his position.

4

Alice walked towards him and gently ushered Jonathan out of the room. Every muscle clenched in his body; he was not leaving.

"Jon... Jon look at me" slowly he took his eyes away from his mother who lay helpless gasping for any oxygen she could snatch from the room.

"Jon you are going to have to give us a minute, we just need to assess your mum and I will come out and let you know how she is doing." She held his gaze squeezed his arm.

"Okay Jon?" Alice made the point of speaking slowly and looking directly into his eyes, she patiently waited for an acknowledgement. Reluctantly Jon nodded.

Unable to contain his grief, heavy prominent tears began falling uncontrollably from his large almond shaped brown eyes, his lips quivering, nose running, he threw his palms to his eyes, snapped his head back towards the ceiling and inhaled deeply. "

Okay" he began to sob. *Keep it together Jon he told himself.*

Alice automatically started to stroke his forearms horizontally, "I will be back shortly Jon, but it's time to call the family, your mum is getting close my love."

"How long Alice?"

"Not long Jon, not long at all..... Call them in."

Slowly, Jon withdrew his hands from his face, and watched Alice close the door behind her. He walked through the corridor and down the stairs, once in the fresh air, he realised it was a beautiful sunny morning. He retrieved his mobile phone looked up at the clear blue sky and dialed his sister Phoebe, she picked up on the first ring, which was amazing as his sister was such a slob and usually either never had her phone or was fumbling for it in one of her many over sized designer bags.

"Hello", she whispered, "What is it Jon?" Phoebe's demeanor took him by surprise, his sister's voice which was usually so confident and strong was frightened and weak.

Hi Phoebes, it's me…. it's time to call Maddy….." He took many deep breaths before he could continue. His voice strained and cracking with sorrow. "She's close Phoebes, she's real close."

"Where's dad?", Phoebe asked sharply.

"He's in the family room. I am going to wake him now."

"Ok see you in 30 minutes. I'll pick Maddy up and I will be there real soon. Hold on brov. Love you."

Phoebe suddenly felt chilled to the bone. Goose bumps appeared all over her body. She slumped back on her bed, closed her eyes shut, and released one solitary tear from her left eye. This was the call that she was dreading. Not because her mum was dying. As upsetting and terrifying as it was, she had accepted that fact weeks ago. She could deal with that. She now had to face her elder sister, the ostracized one, the embarrassment. The Drunk!

"It's time", she allowed herself to say it out loud.

"What was that Edwina, did you say something?" Alice asked

"I am dying, I feel it, my body is betraying me."

Alice looked down at Edwina and squeezed her hand. "We both knew that this day was coming", she said quietly.

Edwina lay weak and helpless in her hospital bed. She looked out her window and smiled at the crisp blue sky and winter sun, how she enjoyed those winter days. The radiating heat of the sun on her cheek warmed her face. "I really love England I will miss it", she told herself. In particular Islington, London, where she'd settled with her husband Harold nearly 48 years ago.

Her room was beautiful, and that made a difference to how she felt, it was significantly larger than the average hospital room, then again she was in a hospice, the least it should be was comfortable. Her peach soft furnishings and perfumed crisp linen and lilac room plug in lingered in her nostrils, she was happy that her room did not smell of a clinical disinfected ward at a hospital, nor did it have the thick aroma of death. Without warning Edwina's body reacted and thrashed against the familiar burning sensation and stab like pain as it began to spread across her whole body; Dr Alcock at Middlesex Hospital had informed her 25 days previously that her lung cancer had spread to her bones. She could not believe the news and took some time to process the information; she had begun to feel better up until that moment. How strange life can be?

"Today is my birthday, but this wretched disease does not care about that, it continues to wreak havoc with my body, in particular all my vital organs, everything feels slower."

"Arrrrrhhhhhh" …… the pain is precise and vengeful. Perspiration is washing over my body again. Oh that's hot. There it goes. Oh no. I cannot take it. its starting at the tip of my right toe and its spreading, oh Lord come soon I cannot deal with this anymore, it's unbearable Oh Lord, it's everywhere spreading across my body like an uncontrollable bush fire.

Alice was in the corner of the room washing her hands and saw Edwina writhing and moaning in her bed. This woman had the endurance of an ox, she thought. She rarely made a fuss when she was in pain. "Edwina press the morphine pump my love. I know it makes you sleepy but it will take the pain away." Without hesitation Edwina administered her pain relief.

-CLICK-

-CLICK – CLICK –CLICK…

My morphine pump, my savior and new best friend, the relief you bring is like a fireman trained to extinguish a burning inferno. With the soothing of the fire comes the self-induced dreamlike hallucination. The burning is still here but my mind is far away, the fire does not touch my senses. I love morphine, I really do. The irony of it, after 69 years of a drug free existence I truly wish that I had experimented with drugs in my lifetime. I smile to myself I must be dying. After all the self-righteous talks I have given to my three children about the perils of drugs and addiction. If they could read my thoughts now?

I am not sure if it is the drugs or the cancer but I sometimes hallucinate and it's heavenly, even sexual at times. I cannot tell anyone, I mean, I should be dying, not having drug induced orgasms. That's not right, is it? I will take these experiences to the grave. I did think of telling Alice but she has bonded too well with Jonathan. The obvious fear is that she'll tell him, the last thing I need is that during my last moments of me leaving this world I will be preoccupied by the thoughts that my own son thinks that I am having morphine induced pornographic experiences. As I am shaking my head at this thought, I see Alice eyeing me from the sink from the corner of my room. I smile wryly at her to reassure her that I am alright. She must think I am having some sort of breakdown.

I look over to the digital clock and I cannot believe that it is only 10.05AM. Why do I feel like the day has already passed? Because you have cancer dear and every waking minute is filled with pain and discomfort, minutes pass like hours and hours like days, so shut up and deal with it.

Oh gosh it's happening again. Embrace it Edwina, come on you can do it, I sternly tell myself. Just think you may meet that lovely man whom you had much pleasure with last time you drifted off. My body has lost its sense of gravity, slowly my head becomes adrift, "come on don't be scared, this is what it will be like … death, being dead, passing over to the spirit world, being able to drift from one place to the next. It will be fine", all of this has to be worth something. As my shoulders and torso float towards the ceiling, that's it, my stomach is going to flip again, oh no, no, no, there goes the yogurt that I had this morning.

"Edwina love is the morphine making you feel sick again?" Alice pressed a button for assistance. By this point I am on the ceiling watching the activity in the room. I am just not sure if this is my spirit or my drug induced self is on the ceiling, but whatever it is, I feel exhilarated.

Maybe when I am dead I will understand why I feel so well. Not just my mind but also my body. When I take the morphine there is such clarity and lots of it. The energy that I feel is another story, I gave that sexy hot rod a run for his money the other day. Although I cannot see myself, I feel myself and I feel that I look good, I mean really good. "I l-o-o-o-o-v-e-e-e-e-e m-o-r-p-h-i-n-e". The pain and suffering is parked into a underground garage, just look at me. I am laughing and nothing hurts. Death will not be the end, it cannot be. Well I hope that it's not. Look at me I am free of that body.

"Jonathan I am sorry", I blurt out

"What was that Edwina love?" Alice asked leaning over the bed, whilst she starts to take my blood pressure.

"Tell Jon that I am sorry I need to sleep I am sooo tired",
I whisper.

"That's the morphine my love, just rest I will tell him that
you asked for him."

I am floating, oh I love the sensation it gives me.
Whheeeeeee- Whoooaa Oh look that was New Year's
1979 now that was messy. My body is horizontal as I
float backwards in time. This is such a surreal
experience. I have never floated through time before, of
course you haven't you stupid woman, you were never
dying before. I smile with myself. I loved the 70s, with
that I try and throw my head back to see some other 70s
years but the vortex of pressure tunneling me through
time restrains me. Wow we are moving faster by each
second it feels. This is new; I have only experienced
slow floating, time must be running out for me. The
upshot is that I am out of the bed and moving it feels
magical. I open my eyes and there is a beautiful ocean
beneath me. I turn to my left and see these plush green
mountains, thick with vegetation and tropical foliage, it's
magnificent and reminds me of Trinidad and Tobago. A
blink of the eye, more mountains more oceans, the sun
is now burning my face and chest. Enjoy it Edwina, I
order myself. I release all the tension from my body and
surrender to the vortex.

A few more blinks of the eye, oh good we seem to be
slowing down, the fresh sea air fills my lungs, the sun is
no longer burning but is warming my body. I feel myself
glow, how I love to sun bathe. I close my eyes and
throw my head back and stretch out my arms with grace
and precision, directing my legs in the air like I am a
ballerina in Swan Lake, wait we have stopped, the smell
is very familiar. My body reacts to the scenery before my
head is able to engage itself. I feel my body tensing; I
blink my eyes open violently. I am frozen. I try to vomit
but there is nothing. I am no longer floating on my back,
I am facing the ground and fall to my hands and knees

heavily; there is someone in front of me. It cannot be. I raise my head and It is me - my six year old self standing in front of me.

The year is 1941, how can this be? "No No No" I scream. Am I to live my life again – what is this?

I am back. Back to the land of my birth, Jamaica. The little girl giggles and starts running through the sugar cane fields barefoot and care free on the plantation that her grandmother owned; wearing nothing other than her pink sleeveless summer dress, with white lacy trim.

She ran through one aisle and came back towards me in the other. Still in shock on all fours I just watched the little girl running towards me. Her energetic sprint slowed down to a cautious walk as she eyed me up and down suspiciously. This little girl stopped abruptly and squinted, wiped both her eyes with the back of her hands and squarely focused on her adult self, me, free from disease, beautiful and in my prime.

"Why are you here, it is time for me to die?" the little girl asked.

Completely taken aback by this, I sharply inform her "No it's not".

I could see the annoyance in my tiny face, and could not help the smile which crept across my face. That expression had not changed over the years, ask Harold and the children. I must say my younger self was less impressed and angrily spat out the words, "then why are you here?"

I giggled, I just could not help it, "I am not sure."

My younger self walked closer to me and sat next down on the warm grass. She looked at me for some time, which was funny as I was drinking in every element of my younger face. Staring at each other with the intensity

11

of young lovers, my younger self clearly had had enough and stood up abruptly, she then slowly stretched out her hand and stroked my cheek, with the tenderness of a prize gardener tenderly stroking his petunias. This truly touched me. I have not been touched with that level of tenderness for years. I forgot what it felt like. My little self-focused on me as if she was searching my face for a particular answer. Such concentration. Her right arm touched her face, and with her left hand she held my right cheek. I dare not say a word; I just wanted to drink in this innocent me. It's been a long time since I have felt innocent. Pure. Neither of us said a word, yet a deep and meaningful conversation took place.

After quite a while she whispered "It's not fair". Without warning she threw her arms around my neck, her grip so tight that I could feel the bones crunching in my neck. I tried to pull my neck away with no success. *Yikes I am a strong little thing aren't I?* I pull both her arms to adjust her pressure for fear of strangulation. I could feel her trembling, I am scared, I just held her close in the middle of the sugar cane field for what seemed an eternity. It's no use, I cannot keep it together it's all too much being here. The silent tears started to roll down my cheeks uncontrollably, instantly being evaporating by the tropical sunshine.

"You look just like her", the little girl said.

"Who?", I quizzed .

"Grandma Lucy", the little girl said grinning from ear to ear.

It was as if a sledge hammer hit me in my chest. A switch turned on in my brain and a lifetime of memories flooded through me like a violent tsunami. I put my head in my hands, embarrassed by my emotional nakedness. It was here that I was happy, safe and loved, and more important to me was that I was able to give love.

"Mima." I gasped. The air felt very thick and I was having trouble breathing.

I close my eyes to regulate my breathing, the scent of lilac fills my nostrils. I was back in the hospital fighting for oxygen; the pain was ravaging me like a mad angry dog. The memory of my grandmother has sent my body into some sort of shock. What is happening am I dying? I am full of perspiration and can hear my six year old self screaming. Harold's large hands are over mine and I can hear my Jonathan and Alice calling my name.

"Nooooooo," I moan with what little energy my body permits me to have "not here there is no pain in this place."

"What is that mum?" Harold whispers.

I want to open my eyes but I can't. I just want to go back to 1941; I need to know why I went back. My six year old self is starting to disappear and get smaller, panicked she screamed "touch the machine"

"What?" I say, barely able to breathe

"Touch the machine, it will take it all away.... QUICKLY!!!!".

CLICK ...... CLICK.....CLICK

I close my eyes praying that I have more time. Oxygen populates my lungs and I open my eyes, I am back in the safety of the sugar cane fields.

"Hhmmmmmm, Huh, huh, huh Hhmmmmmm.

"That's better" I say, the silent tears flowing at their own pace. "I have not thought of Mima Lucy in so long. It has been a lifetime. It's as if I have blocked her out.

"I know" said the little girl, "she still loves you and she wants me to tell you that she is waiting for you".

13

"Waiting for me, where? I bark.   I see my younger self wince, I recoil my temperament and gain a little composure "where is she?" I question quietly.

The little girl folded her arms and starred at me. "Edwina, she has been with you every day" she says annoyed, and looks through the sugar cane to my grandmother's house.

Chapter Two

Jonathan

13th January 2005 12.32 pm

Jonathan over the past four nights had formed a bond with his mother's Macmillan nurse, Alice McKee. She was a delightful bubbly woman who originated from Edinburgh Scotland. Jonathan, coincidently studied Geography at Edinburgh university; within minutes of discussing Alice's hometown, it became apparent that they'd attended the same venues, for instance they'd both frequented the Bongo Club, one of the hippest clubs in Edinburgh. They both adored the Winter Wonderland held each year at Princess Street Garden. Each year and without fail Jonathan always made the effort to go back with his partner, Jack. This was Alice's favorite place in the world for more sentimental reasons. Her father used to take her there as a child. Also, this was the place where Daniel had proposed to her. He'd passed away twelve years ago from a brain tumor. It was this life changing event that inspired her to care for the dying.

"Did you call your sisters Jon?" Alice asked almost in a whisper as she routinely checked Edwina's vital signs.

"Yes...thanks for asking", Jon replied without looking at her.

"Are they on her way?", Alice asked glancing at her watch.

"Any moment now thanks".

"Ok, I will be doing my rounds just use the buzzer if you need anything." Alice replaced Edwina's chart and left the room. As the door was about to close he heard her greet Phoebe in the corridor. Her shrill voice seemed to bounce of the corridor walls.

"Hi Phoebe, I was just asking after you". She chirped.

"How is mum?" Phoebe asked, her words sounded like they had been dragged out of her mouth. She sounded different, than her usual self.

"As well as could be expected as this time love", again Alice's voice and tone resorted to a half whisper

Highly strung and ready to explode I could not contain my anger. "What time do you call this, half an hour you said? *I am furious; I have been sat by my mums side the majority of the morning waiting for my sisters to make an appearance.*

Taken aback by my eruption, I see that Phoebe physically had to steady herself and pause for a few seconds before she replied. Already an emotional wreck, her eyes immediately sprung tears, she inhaled too deeply for her lungs and looked towards the ceiling, "Jon, I got here as fast as I could". She snapped

"Where is Maddy?".

"That's why I'm late. I went everywhere I thought she'd be ..." Phoebe let out a huge sigh. " I left a message on all phones. I just did not know where else to look". With that her reassured voice broke.

"Can't you see that I am under it here?" my voice grew louder with his rage "I ask you to do one thing. One thing, and you turn up empty handed! Did you get bored and go shopping instead?"

No sooner than those spiteful words came out of my mouth I wanted to take them back. My sister looked like she'd been kicked in the face by that last comment. I need to get this under control. It's not her fault. That was a low blow even for me.

Calm down Jon, stop taking this out on everyone else.

"WHAT!!!!" Phoebe was wide eyed and furious.

Oops too late..

Phoebe threw her bag to the floor, she looked ready for war. "Just hold your horses Saint Jude, I did what you asked. Maddy is out there with god knows who, doing god knows what. Open your eyes Jon I'm here where I'm supposed to be. Where I am bloody needed and you cannot be seriously tearing strips of MMMEEEE for that." Not realising she was now shouting at her brother "ARE YOU JON?"

I lower my eyes, embarrassed by my cruel attack, she was right. I should not have taken out my frustrations on her. "All I am saying is …."

Alice flew into the room. "NOW - I don't know what this is about and I don't care, pipe down or get out" Alice looked at both of us with complete and utter disgust.

"May I remind you why you are both here". With that she glared at my mother in her bed. "Do I need to point out that your mother is N-O-T the only dying patient on this floor!", again that look. We both lower our head, the embarrassment and guilt sting my face.

Alice tutted very loudly as she left the room.

I reluctantly raise my head and look at my sister, her tears are already in free flow. She has backed herself up against the far wall and turned her head towards it, her shaking shoulders give her away. I feel even worse.

Phoebe turned around with multiple tear streaks down each eye, "Look Jon if you want to play Dempsey and Makepeace be my guests go find her. I just need to be here". She pointed adamantly towards the floor.

"Dempsey and Makepeace?", I stare at her, she registers my amusement and we both fall about laughing.

"What so funny?" Harold enquired as he entered the room.

"Dad" I uncomfortably shift my body weight from foot to the other. The temperature in the room went from a hot day in Sudan to the freezing conditions of that Antarctic. in a blink of the eye. Phoebe gave our father a stony stare

"Coffee Jon?" she asks icily

"Errr no thanks," I looked from Phoebe to my father to Phoebe again. *Not today phoebes please not today, I pray.*

Phoebe picked her bag to head towards the door, *she is not going to blank him, not now. Jon watched in complete horror. That's when she stopped as if she read my mind and turned around.*

"Dad"

"Yes Phoebe", I swear I thought Dad was about to breakdown.

"Coffee?"

"No thank you PP I have just had some tea, thank you ..... for asking that is".

Phoebe looked at the floor like an errant child then rushed out the room.

"Well at least she is talking to you dad?" I said.

"You know as well as I do son that she did that for Edwina, not me". Harold sat down next to his wife, and took the perfectly folded white starched handkerchief out of his right breast pocket from his navy blue blazer and dabbed his eyes. He took hold of my mother's hand and whispered to his wife "You win babes, you win", he started to chuckle and cry at the same time.

"What dad?"

My father looked at me searching my face for clues to his riddle, "We had a bet when we were sixteen years old which one of us would die first"

"Really" I sound surprised. To think of my parents as young and invincible that they would bet or even joke about death seemed strange, especially in this moment.

"Your mother always said that she would go first as she could not bear to be left behind" with that dad threw his head back and closed his eyes.

"You'll be ok dad".

"How do you know?" he snapped.

"Sorry" I sound confused.

"How do you know that I will be alright?

"I just meant".

He cut me off "Let's face it, my children do not care for me." With that the neatly dressed old man rested his head in his hands.

We lock stares and suddenly both felt an unwelcome spectator at the doorway, we both turn around and Phoebe was standing there with a coffee cup in hand, "Whose fault is that Dad, Eh? Eh?" she sniped loudly

"Phoebe", I bark at her, wide eyed and ready to pounce on my sister if required. "Not now", I growled. She stares at me, then slowly lowered her eyes to our mother. My body language is unmistakably not playing with her. She senses this, she feels the warning and silently sat down sulking at the other side of the bed.

"Where is Maddy?, any one seen her" Harold enquired

"You noticed then did you? That she's not here." Phoebe scolded.

"Phoebe, this is your last warning". I shot off my chair. Wide eyes, tense from the hair on my head to my toes I had never slapped his sister yet but today might be the beginning of many firsts.

"Really Jon…. W-a-r-n-i-n-g." She could feel the anger swelling in her chest. "What you going to do? Beat me to a pulp?", she shot dad a scolding look.

Harold stood up and walked to the window, "Maybe you and I need to talk PP"

"No dad, I need to sit here and be with my mum. You need to stop calling me PP, you lost that right a long time ago".

Harold walked to his dying wife, kissed her on her head and walked towards the door.

"Where are YOU going?", Phoebe looked hurt and shocked all at the same time.

"I need some time alone" he answered crestfallen; he looked like he was going to cry.

"Oh here we go; it's all about you, isn't it?". Phoebe started to laugh hysterically.

"Phoebe", I am shouting again. "For the love of god, put your differences aside and let's at least try and show a united front for mum. I look at my mum and feel my legs go weak, I fall back into the chair exhausted. "Please Phoebe for mum" I plead.

Nurse McKee charged into the room. "Right I told you once, I am n-o-t telling you again, there will not be a third discussion. Shape up or get out! If you cannot respect your mother and all the other patients on this floor then you will be asked to leave. RESPECT THIS SITUATION!. Maybe if you spent less time fighting amongst yourselves and more time focusing on your poor mum, she will be able to die in peace. Did you hear me?.... I said.... die in peace". With that Nurse Mckee started to check Edwina's vital signs.

"Oh Edwina," She looked at all three of us with unfiltered hatred. . "It's alright". She lovingly stroked her head and reached over to the side table for a tissue.

"Mum..... Alice is she alright, what is it? I plead with her.

"Jon", Alice said icily, she lowered her voice but that did not regain the temperature in the room. "you were all so busy arguing with one another, you forgot why you were here, Look, she's been crying. She obviously can hear you".

You could have heard a pin drop. The realisation of what had occurred was overwhelming for all of us. This was a first for Alice. She wiped the tears dry from mothers eyes and cheeks. "Not another cross word … I mean it". The glare that she us reminded Jon of a lion protecting her cubs. He knew that she really meant business.

Hurt, embarrassed and ashamed of our conduct, all we can do is nod our heads.

Disgusted by her behavior, Phoebe whispered, "She's right, can we please just focus on mum, please?"

 "No problem love", with that Dad walked around mums bed and kissed me on my forehead. He started to walk towards my sister, she sat frozen to her seat. She looked uneasy. Dad hesitated and slowly lowered himself. He put his hands in front of his chest to reassure Phoebe that it was going to be ok, and slowly planted a kiss on her forehead. She closed her eyes and cried silently. He tried to hug her, she shrugs him off, it's too soon.

"Please dad, don't" she whispered. He nodded, now visibly crying, he walked quickly around the bed and grabbed his wife's hand. Squeezing and rubbing it, terrified at what the future meant for him. Edwina was the glue, she kept them stuck together. Without her, where would his family be?

Chapter Three

I am Home

Lying on my back with eyes closed my nostrils are delighted by smell and the sweetness of the sugar cane. I wonder how much time I have here. I shudder reminiscing briefly of the hospital room. I inhale as deep as I could, I look to the sky. It's a miracle I am pain free. Wiping the tears from her eyes, I study my younger self who is crouched over me. We stare at one another for a short while.

"Oh baby girl I am so tired" I moan.

"We have to go" she whispers.

"Where Winnie?" I ask.

Winnie giggled loudly, "only Mima calls me that" she informs me completely amused.

"I know" I whisper, "So Winnie it is" I smile

Winnies face became very serious "We have to go?"

"Why, where?"

"Home, Mima will be worried. We have to go; she doesn't like me out too late"

It cannot be, this makes no sense. I follow this child through the cane field, although wading through the field was making me exhausted, the long canes offered excellent protection from the sun's intensity. It was calm, cool and serine in there. The therapeutic howls of the slight breeze rustling through the cane is mesmerizing.

"Edwina,"

"Yes Winnie", my little self automatically giggled again. Clearly still amused by the nick name for her.

"Why did you forget us?" she asked her face serious.

"What?"

"You said, back there that you had forgotten Mima? How did you forget?"

Embarrassed by my admission "I am not sure how, but somehow I forgot her.

"Mima is hard to forget?" Winnie said looking at the floor. Without warning, she threw her body to the floor with a thud, laced her fingers together and wrapped them behind her head. "What do you remember?" she asked excitingly.

"Not much". I lower my eyes from Winnie's intense stare. "Being back here I remembered how kind and loving Mima is.   All I got was kisses and love here".   My mini me was smiling towards the sky. "Mima used to sing to me lots, and she make the best "Pineapple upside cake", we both said and giggled.

"What do you remember about Mima? You know her dying" I ask and immediately am met with sheer confusion.

"Grandma Mima is not dead" Winnie almost spat the words out at me.

What?

"Grandma is still alive". Winnie was clearly cross at such an unforgiveable mistake.

"W-I-N-N-I-E ......W-I-N-N-I-E. It's lunch time.   Come and get washed up P-L-E-A-S-E.

"Coming Mima" Winnie shouted as loud as her miniature

voice box would allow.

I stopped. I did not blink, breathe, move or swallow. Eyes wide, my head spinning. I was back!

Back on the land of my fore parents and their fore parents. I was back with Mima, and the place where at six years old my world made sense. Tears sailed down my cheeks, I have an opportunity to see Mima, smell her, love her and have her love me again. My chest swells, goose bumps are all over me.

"Are you coming?", Winnie asked.

"Me", I whisper afraid she will see me through my haze.

"Yes". Winnie replied, most annoyed at her older self.

"Well, honey I am nearly seventy, Mima will not recognise me. She may even think I am a wicked person that does horrible things to little children" I retort.

"What horrible things?", Winnie was truly intrigued.

"Well she may think that I am a child molester" I blurted out absently and innocently

"What's one of those?" she asks innocently.

Stunned by her response. I could then have kicked myself. This was the 1940s, pedophiles were not part of the global landscape.

"Never mind sweetheart, just forget I said anything. Mima will not be happy to see me" I say all very matter of fact.

"Is a mal – mal o-s-t-e r, like the man at the orphanage in town?" Winnie looked puzzled.

I choose to ignore her.

"Mima can't see you". Winnie whispered as if divulging a very important secret.

I whisper back and smile at Winnie "really?" grateful that she had forgotten the child molester conversation.

"Only I can see and hear you, you're my friend" she smiles.

I just stood starring at Winnie, surprised by her revelation. After all I had travelled back in time so maybe I was dead. Or half dead? I still wasn't sure what this was.

"Hurry Edwina, Mima will be cross if my lunch gets cold", with that Winnie ran like the wind "Coming Mima, I'm coming"

"Alright Winnie, it's on the table, Mima yelled. "Wash your hands"

"O – o – o –o K – a – a –a –y", she responded mid-flight through the cane fields.

For the first time in a long while, I could breathe. I mean really breathe, inhaling and exhaling without pain, no pressure on my chest. Just fresh fragrant air. I webbed my fingers and threw my body on the rich earth, then immediately crossed my legs, "Arhhh", I inhale, and it felt like an eternity since I stretched. Each muscle was relaxing, and the afternoon sun continued to warm my face and body. Fatigued and overwhelmed an unwelcome heavy sleep is upon me. I close my eyes and reluctantly drift to sleep.

The breeze blowing on my face is cool and wakes me up, it must be after 5 o'clock ,the sun is setting as the night insects awake. I brush the mosquito from the end of my nose. Once on my feet I am blown away by the spectacular architecture and design of the plantation house. Encapsulated by the setting sun, it was a sight to behold. I suddenly felt proud that Mima, and my Grandpa Vincent built this plantation house from nothing. I walk, heart in mouth to the house. My skin still radiating with warmth, tingling under the surface from the evening sun. I felt good, my body feels warm and nourished. "If this is death, then I welcome it", I mutter to myself. Walking towards the house, the sun continued to soak into me. I couldn't help but overhear the conversation which was taking place not more than five feet either side of where I was walking. The cool evening breeze whistles through the sugar cane and creates loud whispers. I smile.

I sense I am not alone, I look behind me. Nothing. The intensity of feeling is stronger as I get closer to the house. "Oh no", I freeze, my dog, which Mima named "Daaag". It's my black and white border collie, she was my best friend as a little girl, but right now she is eyeing me suspiciously. I was the enemy and she was looking directly at me. I slowly walk towards the veranda. Daag is not taking any chances. Her beautiful black coat surrounds her ears, eyes and chubby cheeks. Her nose throat, chest and two front legs were white. I want to cry. I want to run and hug my dog but I can't. I am a stranger, and she will not be petted by strangers. That much I remember. I cannot believe she has not barked her head off. She is just standing still staring at me, as I start to walk up the steps, Daag, slowly steps backwards,

"Woof.. Woof woof woooooooof

"Daag whose there?" Mima yells behind the door

Woooooof Woof woof woof

"Daag, what is going on over there?"

I am rooted to the spot which is in the middle of the veranda, my heart starts pounding. I have nowhere to run as Mima would see me. I am going to bloody wring

Winnie's neck, invisible my eye. Before I could do anything Mima swung open the screen doors, shot gun underneath her left arm, lantern in the right.

"Daag, what is all this noise?" She swings the lantern and it nearly takes off my head"

"Mima I can explain", I say panicked.

Mima, grabs my dog by its collar, as she was barking at me. She looks straight through me, Daag, there no one here. You old fool."

Woof Woof Wooof ….. Grrrrrr" She parades up and down the veranda like a soldier of war, her eyes not once deviating from my presence.

"Stop this foolishness" Irritated by Daag's outburst, she drags my dog curtly by her collar into the house." Winnie needs her sleep". With that she slams the doors shut.

Realization of my presence engulfs me. "She could not see me." I wait and wait then open the door; I walk through the main hall. My nostrils explode with the scent of citrus. It must be a Friday, it's cleaning and washing day. I smile the polished hard wood floors are gleaming. I stand by the main reception room. Mima is sat with Winnie on her lap; they are both reading the bible.

 "God Bless Lucy" I say.

"Shhhhhhhh" Winnie puts her hands to her lips.

"Winnie why are you being so rude as to tell Mima to be quiet?" she says crossly, my grandmother was not impressed.

"No Mima", Winnie shot me filthy look.

"Then who are you telling to Shussh?" quite annoyed that the Book of Exodus was interrupted. Mima turned Winnie right around so that she could look at her insolent

28

granddaughter's square in the eye.

"Mima, my friend is back." Winnie mumbled positioning her head to the floor to avert her grandmothers annoyed glare.

Desperately trying not to laugh, "Winnie, you best warn your friend not to mess about as you who I can see and hear will have to pay the price with a spanking". Mima said curtly.

Winnie's eyes immediately sprang to tears; she lowered her head to the floor, "Yes Mima". Mima picked Winnie up and took her to her room. Still annoyed with my outburst which got her scolded, Winnie stuck her tongue out at me as she passed me in the doorway. I smile. I was a gutsy one.

I observed my grandmother's quiet demeanour as she encouraged Winnie to a tranquil state of sleep. Before she fell deep in to that restful place that all six year olds crave after a long and arduous day playing in the field, my grandmother spoke to her only grandchild, her companion with fondness and love.

"Mima, can I p-l-e-a-s-e- have one more coconut cake?" Winnie asked pleadingly knowing the answer. "Please Mima, please, please,please, please" she smiled.

"Baby you have just brushed your teeth. Mima sighed very loudly. "Okay you can have one more but no more", she tried to contain her smile. Go on to the kitchen and get take one." My little face lit up like a bright flame. Winnie dashes to the kitchen, retrieved one cake from where they were cooling and shoved it whole in her mouth, she ran back to her room, her mouth, chin and fingers engulfed in sugar and pieces of coconut. She flung her little arms around Mima's neck and whispered "You are my best friend and I love you very very very much". She squeezed her grandmother and jumped in bed "Night Night Mima"

Mima blinked back the tears. "You are more like your mother than you know my sweet darling. I love you too, very very very much". Lucy kissed her grand-daughter many times all over her face and neck, sat quietly by her side until she fell asleep.

Unable to contain my own emotion I leave the room. Although I am not visible I had not quite worked out if Mima could hear me. I retreated to the kitchen and sat in Grandpa Vin's chair, which was situated by the east wall of their kitchen.

I do remember Mima telling me this was the very spot that Grandpa Vin would sit each evening and watch my grandmother cook. It was for a time, the place that my grandfather sat with my mother when she was a child until she fell asleep. As my mother grew older this was her favourite chair and she and my grandfather would jokingly squabble over that seat most evening. Just the thought made me feel very joyous and exuberant regarding my family.

With Winnie was sound asleep, I watched my beloved Mima enter her most favourite room. In need of a warm beverage she lit the stove and filled her kettle with water. Whilst she waited for her water to boil, she started to knead her rested dough as she was baking bread for the next day. Completely engrossed in her own thoughts she began to talk to him.

"Vin, I know that you are there, I feel you", Mima looked around the kitchen.

I immediately jump out of the chair and look behind the door. "Granddad" I whisper looking underneath the kitchen table.

"I love you Vin and miss you more with each passing day. Mavis told Rene that Barrington was enquiring about me...... Lord I hope that he is still as ignorant as ever. If they know about Winnie I will have to send her to school in America. Rene told me about a good school for coloured girls in Chicago. This year's harvest will be good. We have sold more cane than ever so by the end of the harvest I can afford it."

Mima looked straight through me. "I know you're proud of me Vin and I am proud of you....wherever you are. This was your dream" She smiles to herself then hums quietly a sad tune that I had never heard before.

Watching Mima work and listening to her, made me miss her more than I ever remembered. This lapse in my memory is a wrong doing that I cannot shake or forgive. Drinking in every movement, I notice now as I did as a child how she struggled with her right arm. An accident she had once explained after relentless pressure from me.

Pride swells by belly when I look at this beautifully proportioned petite, small, brown skinned woman. She was intensely powerful, articulate and had the stamina and work ethic of ten experienced male plantation owners. Being female in a male dominated world is no simple task, let alone in the1940s on top of all that she has a disability, and that did not stop her. My grandparents were respected in the village, there was always some farmer sending his son or daughter to help out at harvest time. They loved Mima and Grandpa Vincent, although he had been dead some years, I knew they loved him by the way they always spoke highly of him.

"Warrior Lucy" I say quietly. I cannot help it I just stare at her, slowly I pluck the courage up to shadow her around her chores, looking at her face, pushing my nose into her neck and smelling her coconut infused hair oil.

I could have watched her all night, whilst she was cleaning her stove. Mima poured the washing crystals in a bucket let them dissolve and went to work. I remember when she bought her AP Simmons Wilson

Coal and Wood burning Stove. Mima had saved for half the year and it arrived after being on order for three months from the United States of America. Although I did not know it at the time, this was quite a milestone. Only the affluent houses could afford such luxuries. Saying that, my grandmothers baking skills were legendary, so if anyone deserved a luxury stove from the United States in our village it was Mima. We all benefited, and I mean everyone.

I reluctantly leave her in the kitchen and explore my old home. Walking into my grandmother's bedroom set all my hairs on edge. In here I am reintroduced to her personal scent. I stand in the middle of the room, close my eyes and inhale. I slowly open my eyes and turn three hundred and sixty degrees, to take in the sights that surround me. Mima's bedroom was like something out of an upmarket house and garden magazine. I look at the handmade blankets, with Hibiscus Sabdariffa flowers patiently hand stitched on them. Hibiscus was Mima's favourite flower, it grows naturally around the Red Sorrel trees on the plantation. The cross-stitched image in the centre of the fabrics looked very professional. The white to pale yellow flowers with a dark red spot at the base of each petal was mirrored on the handmade curtains, accompanying fluffy cushions and blankets. I just did not remember my life being this prosperous as a small child, later on definitely; this house, my early home was exquisite.

Something was happening to me physically, I am starting to feel very tired as I had earlier in the day. My eyelids are starting to betray me, my bodies urgent request for sleep is as vital as oxygen. Quietly I take off my shoes. I do not care that Mima cannot see me, just in case this spell breaks, and she returns to her room to witness an old woman on her bed with shoes on. I am well aware disability or no disability I am going to get a beating! I fall into a deep sleep, its peaceful and free from suffering.

What the hell is that noise, I open one eye. Merciful Jesus I have not heard that sound in decades. I jump up and rush to the window. It's Buster, Mima's rooster. He was on time that's for sure. He crowed every morning at 5.30am and every evening at 6pm.

I return to the bed that I lay peacefully in all night. Mima is laying on the other side looking at me, I am unnerved, has my spell broken, can she see me?

Her hair brown with a few unruly grey strands is draped across her forehead and delicately framing her face. Her piercing dark brown eyes were something to behold in the morning.

"Vin is that you? She whispers, "I feel something and I like to think it's you. Good morning Vin I love you, help me today and give me strength to carry on. Lord knows I am tired".   Mima stretched over and picked up my grandfather's picture on her side table, she kissed it repeatedly and stood up, opened the closet and there was a closet full of clothes, of my grandfather's clothes. She leant in and pulled as many of the garments she required to her face. She stood there in his moment as if reawakening from her sleep she inhaled deeply, then turned to face her day. She turned around to pin up her hair I noticed that there was a solitary tear rolling down her cheek. How I wanted and needed to comfort her and be comforted. Watching my beloved Mima in her grief made me think of Harold. How will he cope, I pray that he can move on.

November 24th 1941

The sun was hiding through the clouds, it was the perfect afternoon, hot but not scorching, "The sun was manageable" as Mima would say. Winnie was playing a skipping game with her best friend Cora from the adjacent farm. Cora was Aunty Rene's niece. All the farm staff had gone to the Morant May shipping docks to deliver the sugar cane and coffee beans to their supplier's handler from England and America

Mima was in a happy mood. After today the harvest was over. The smell of freshly grated ginger interlocked with sugary coconut and caramel trickled through the house out into the yard. Her mission that afternoon was to make fresh ginger beer and coconut cakes for the girls. Relaxing playful afternoons like these reminded Mima of her own delightful childhood with her best friend and sister Rene, and beloved daughter Angeline. Listening to her granddaughter and her friend squeal with delight was heaven in a bottle. That's what Vin used to say, when Angeline was a young child giggling and squealing with joy over nothing.

Enjoying the atmosphere I lay like a lazy cat sunning its breast on the veranda when I saw the dust cloud approaching.

"Winnie what's that? I point at the road approaching the plantation.

"Mima, Mima it's a motor car". Winnie and Cora squealed excitedly. It was the 1940s only Doctor Barnet and other rich white families in the next parish owned cars.

Mima ran outside on the veranda, she took one look at the Master DeLux 1939 Chevy, recognition and fear crept into her face. "Winnie inside" she barked

"But M-i-m-a", Winnie tried to protest

I said inside" Mima screamed, Winnie instantly became scared.

"Cora run home as fast as you can and tell your auntie that I have trouble. Quick Cora. Move" Mima voiced hit an unbearable high pitch. Without hesitation Cora sprinted through the cane fields, Mima ran into her house, heart pounding in her chest, she slammed and bolted the door. Once inside she leaned on the door and tightly squinted her eyes shut for a few seconds. Once composed, she jolted back to the presence of her situation.

Grabbing Winnie's right arm, with immense strength she tipped her to an angle and dragged her helplessly like a rag doll up the stairs to her room. Her poor little feet barely touched those perfectly polished wooden floors.

"Winnie darling", Mima's voice was shaking "I need you to jump in the trunk at the end of your bed, once inside cover yourself with the blanket" Desperately trying to sound normal, Lucy could not contain her cracking voice..

"Mima I'm scared", Winnie stated to cry.

My grandmother was not wasting any time she grabbed Winnie and shook her hard, once, Winnie's head snapped back and Mima knew she had her attention. "Baby," her voice broke again "Let's play hide and seek. Remember that game".

Winnie nods and looks directly at me. She senses my fear. I stood by the wall, petrified and tearful. Although I cannot remember what occurred I remember t-h-i-s feeling. I could hear the car engine roar as if the driver had flat footed the accelerator, the engine screaming louder and louder as it approached the house

"Now go hide, quickly. QUICKLY" Mima instructed, trying desperately to keep her voice even.

Winnie ran as fast as she could. She could tell that Mima was scared. She jumped in the trunk and covered herself;

Desperate to know who Mima was so scared off, I run to the window and immediately recognised the car. It was my fathers. Mima is beside me and is frantic. She ran to the kitchen and returned with her shot gun. I can see that her hands are shaking.

"Quickly Mima", I scream, forgetting that she could not hear me.

The brakes screech the car to a standstill and we both hear the heavy clunk of the car door slamming. He is here, running towards the front door, and I could feel his rage.

"L----u-------c---------y" Daddy screams "I will give you one opportunity to G-I-V-E ME MY

D-A-U-G-H-T-E-R……"

-Bang- -Bang-

It sounded like he was using a large stick to knock the door rather than his oversized fist; How I had forgotten his goliath strength.

"L----u---c----y…… did you think I would not find out? You Listen to me…".

"Nooooo you listen to me you son of a whore. Mima spat the words out with such venom as she cut off my father. "Leave my property or I swear to god I will finish what my Vincent started".

I awake from my paralysis "Oh my god Mima, Son of a "Whore", I had never heard Mima speak that way to anyone; Daddy was not the only one in rage. She was furious. This was not a side that I had seen to my grandmother. She was always kind and loving, not a personality trait I could label my father with.

Bang – You old bitch give me my daughter now!!!!!! She belongs to me you hear. You have five minutes."

Mima ran to Winnies room and opened the chest. "Listen Sweetie Mima is going to start counting and when I get to five hundred I want you to come out"

""Ok" with that my grandmother raised me up and kissed me so hard on the lips and hugged me like it was the last time we would ever embrace. She covered me up with the blanket to my chest and made sure my head was adequately supported. "See you soon Winnie.... alright baby love"

"Ok Mima, see you soon". Winnie lets rip one of her delectable smiles, parading all her teeth, including her wobbly bottom tooth.

"If we don't see each other after today, I will be with you always, you hear?"

Winnie nods terrified of what Mima was trying to explain to her.

Mima ran into the drawing room.

"-Bang- -Bang- "Three minutes Lucy"

I start to shout "Mima .... run. Mima please take Winnie and go". The feeling in my chest is tighter than before.

Oblivious to my pleas, Mima ran to the window, smashed the glass, and pushed the shot gun through the hole created. Every tendon and muscle around her right shoulder was screaming, she raised the gun as high as she could with her left arm, and took aim.

"Today I am going to finish you." she muttered.

Barrington heard the smash of broken glass and turned around, He was confronted with the barrel of a shot gun, and instinctively he threw himself to the left of the veranda behind the big oak chair.   Within that split second he saw a bright yellow flash, and was pushed backwards, cracking his head on the hard oak veranda. Momentarily dazed, he lay seething on the floor. "Stupid old bitch missed". Grateful that she no longer possessed a competent aim, he jumped up. Something was wrong. Feeling weak in the legs and slightly giddy, he looked down and witnessed warm red liquid running down his waist. What! She d-i-d shoot me. Panicked he stood up and examined himself; there were two bullet holes to his abdomen and at least 6 on his right waist and thigh.

"Think... Barrington..... Think", Adrenalin racing around his body like a prized fighter. "*The car, get to the car, assess your wounds, get your revolver and go kill that told hag"*. He tried to run to his car, his right leg buckled underneath him "Arrgghhhhhhhh" He steadied himself and locked his knee and ran awkwardly back to his car, praying that Lucy would not finish him off.

This is not happening. It cannot be happening. Although I have watched events unfold before me, it seems so very unreal. The frustrating truth is that I am a bystander to my life, and am totally ineffectual as to how my path will develop.

"Why?" I scream out of pure frustration. I look out of the window at my wounded father and I view my beautiful Mima, "

This is the last time I will see you". I cry "Lord why did you do this to me". I run to Mima and franticly dance and wave my hands in front of her, she felt me once so she can feel my presence again.

 "Mima Run", I scream. Every turn, every move I am

screaming at her, "Pllleeaaassse Mima run he is going to kill you" Please I sob "Just go". Defeated and weak I fall to the floor on all fours.

Mima for the first time during my visit looks old and tired, breathing heavily, and I am not sure whether it's the adrenalin or exhaustion. She checks the barrel of her shotgun and wipes her brow. As she watches my father in the car she prays loudly and franticly. "Lord Stand with me today against this devil. If this is where my journey ends then lord guide and protect my granddaughter I beg you".

Barrington sat in the passenger side of his car and was ripping the bottom of his shirt into strips. Half naked bound his thighs and was relieved that all bullets holes appear to be flesh wounds. Shaking his head in disbelief, he could not believe that Lucy George shot him. He had underestimated her husband once, and that nearly cost him his life. Today, he'd underestimated the ease with which he could take his daughter, he was not about to make a third mistake with Lucy. He opened his glove compartment and pulled out a black velvet purse. In it was a lavishly gold engraved Colt 45 single action army revolver. In fact, it was a departing present from his creole lover Margerita Salido. How he wished he was there wrapped in her loins, rather than here about to do what he thought he would have to.

Loading the gun, he appreciated craftsmanship of his revolver. Barrington drew a long breath, looked to the house, kissed his crucifix, rubbed his abdomen, opened the car door and stormed to the house shooting directly at the exposed shotgun.

In her drawing room peering out of the broken glass window Lucy felt nothing but pure hatred for Barrington and his mother. It was hard enough being a good Christian and accepting that she and the Barnet family were inhabitants of the same earth, let alone country and district. That vile sick dog anf his mother had caused her so much pain, so much suffering, but most of all, what she would never forgive was that they had murdered her husband, and her only daughter Angelina was dead to her because of him, he was pure evil.

In one move he was out of the car and shooting at her. The first bullet kissed the left side of her head; her left ear was ringing from the sensation. Lucy threw herself to the floor and took the impact of her full body weight on her right shoulder. She felt and heard something pop and tear within her. The pain ripped through her body like the unrelenting machete attack. She screamed out loud then inwardly. She could not scare Winnie. Tears ran from her eyes, she knew that if she had any chance of survival she had to get to her feet. Her chest heaving she let out a cry from deep within her throat.

Through the crippling pain Lucy stood up and took aim and cocked the shotgun into her shoulder, this time her left arm buckled under the strain. "Steady" she told herself. "Finish him….Do not get weak now" she winced at the pain that ripped through her collarbone and down her right side. Fresh tears sprang to her eyes. "This is for you Vincent", with that she pulled the trigger; the flash of light momentarily blinded her. She missed ... damn; their eyes lock, he was ready for war and now he was running with his injured leg to the house. Barrington was heading to the rear of the property. "Old Woman you forgot to lock the side door". Cursing her forgetfulness and disabled by the pain in her shoulder and right side, Lucy ran as fast as she could, as she arrived to the side door in the kitchen, it was too late. Barrington was running up the steps. Shot and injured he was still quicker than she was.

She attempted to raise the shot gun again, this time her right arm failed her, "Noooooooooo" she screamed in sheer frustration. She looked at the counter her knives were laying there, she ran for the long sharp kitchen knife. She was not fast enough.

Daddy was running straight for Mima, I jump in front of daddy to try and head him off, "Mima runnnnnn" I screamed. Daddy ran straight through me. I run in front of him again, filled with terror " Daddy please …. It's me… S-T-O-P"

Mima attempted to raise the shotgun one last time, the muscles around her shoulder and collar bone resisted this action and failed her, panicked, she put her finger on trigger, it was too late, Barrington was running through the door, gun aimed. Mima saw the flash of light, and then she heard –CRACK-. The force of the revolver catapulted her limp body from the floor and violently pushed her against her stove, she winced as the immediate pain in her chest far outweighed the pain in her shoulder. .

"Nooooo Daddy Noooooooooooooooooooooo", I scream. I am on bended knees. Head in hands eyes screwed shut. "No daddy", I SOB.

Breathing heavily, Mima tried to gain her breath and sit up. It was fruitless. Her left lung is filling with blood and she knows that she is slowly drowning. This is it.

"Lay down Mima…. " I say trying to cradle my Grandma in what I know are her last moments. "Please don't move" I sob.

My beloved Mima is looking at me through her glassy eyes. She is responsive as if she can hear me. She knew she was dying, Tears in her eyes she starts to mutter a prayer.

"Yea through I walk through the shadow of death I….", her breathing is labored. "I know you're here Vin I feel you. Forgive me for failing you. I just could not protect her"

"Where is my daughter" Daddy growls over her. Gun pointed to her head.

"No daddy", I scream. I try to push him but it's no use, I just fly through him. "Leave her alone"

"Go to hell", Mima is amused by this situation as she giggles.

Barrington leant over and dragged Lucy to her feet. He pushed her to the wall and shoved his face in hers. "Where is she???"

With sheer defiance Mima just looks my father square in the eye, she smiles the broadest smile I have seen.

Daddy could not contain his anger; he punches Mima hard in the stomach, twice. She falls to the floor "arrrrrrggggh". She coughs and splutters blood violently as she tried to negotiate air through her blood filled lungs.

I feel as if I am suffocating, the air has been sucked out of my lungs, this beautiful kitchen has become my furnace, sweat is pouring from me, my skin feels like it is on fire. I know what is coming. My throat is dry, I cannot speak. Rooted to the spot I attempt to cover my eyes through open fingers. I watch the man known to me as my Daddy conduct himself without mercy or compassion. It's hard to believe that I am a product of this animal. Daddy grabs the lapel of Mima's shirt and drags her blood-soaked body to her feet like a ragdoll. She has lost the use of her limbs, but still holds the fire in her eyes. Her deadweight body is too heavy for him; he throws her to the floor like foul smelling rubbish.

His wounds start to affect his breathing, he is panting loudly and struggles to say "Where is she?" with his usual gruff tone.

Blood is voluntarily trickling out of her mouth, Mima spits out her words with the last venom she has left. "You may be Winnies daddy, but who is yours?"

"What?" Daddy's screams his eyes wild with fear.

Mima is sat with her back against the wall, her head tilted to the ceiling as she is gasping for oxygen. Her blood soaked teeth and mouth are smiling through the pain. She steadies herself and looks Daddy straight in his eyes and pronounces each word slowly, "Winnie is not the only bastard in this house"

"Shut your filthy mouth!!" I saw the vein in Daddy's head pop out from its hiding place, his eyes wide and ready to pop out of their sockets from the strain.

Although he was always adamant with himself about hs southern bloodline, he knew deep down that she was right. He never quite felt connected to his father. This could explain why. Incensed by the revelation, the moment completely overwhelmed him. Flashbacks of memories flooded to the forefront of his mind. The painful rejection of his father dismissive attitude towards him. Never feeling that he could make his father proud. His father's obvious absence at all major events in his life to date. His first nativity play, piano recitals, football games to name a few. She was right, and she knew that he knew that what she was telling him was the truth, but she was gloating at him, reveling in his pain.

Unable to contain the volcanic eruption within him. He felt his conscious spirit leave his body, it was as if it was ashamed to a part of what he was about to do. Without the feelings of emotion and responsibility Barrington raised his pistol to Mima's head. My beautiful grandmother looked into my fathers eyes, not with anger or fear, but with acceptance. She closed her eyes with a huge smile on her face and said, "Vin I am coming home".

-CRACK- -CRACK- -CRACK –CRACK – CRACK-

My father shot Mima in the head twice. He stared at her for a few seconds, raised his pistol and shot my beloved

Mima a further three times randomly around her body. A bullet lodged in her elbow, knee and groin. Momentarily stunned by his madness, he looked at the dead old woman's corpse for what seemed like an eternity. Finally as if his spirit had returned to him, he looked around the room and was repulsed by himself. He ran out of the back door, the contents of his stomach refused to remain in it after his behavior, Once outside he promptly vomited in the perfectly manicured herb bushes in the yard.

Memories of my father's irrational, violent and unreasonable behaviour started to flood my memory. Through my own tears I saw her standing still like a statue staring at Mima. What the hell do you say to a child who witnesses this? I immediately run towards Winnie and attempt to cuddle her. It's no use, she is transfixed by Mima's corpse, and she looks at me with wide eyes and whispers, "What happened to Mima?"

"Don't look Winnie .... Winnie look at me", I beg.

"What happened to Mima?" she asked quietly.

Neither of us noticed that Daddy was standing in the doorway. "Mima had an accident sweetheart you are coming to live with me" he said without emotion or consideration he was talking to his estranged daughter who has never met him.

Winnie ran to Lucy and threw herself on her blood soaked corpse. "Mima" Winnie shook her grandmother. "Mima wake up," she shook her as hard as she could "Mima wake up" she screamed.

"Mima, Mima, please wake up" Winnie cried. She looked at me "Mima won't wake up Edwina, why won't she wake up"

"Come on little girl daddy has to go", my father had his irritated stance on.

"Daddy? My daddy and mummy are dead" Winnie spat the words out with venom through her cracked voice. The emotion of grief not quite realised in her tiny self.

Barrington looked up and starred at Winnie "What did you say?", he asked quietly.

"Winnie" I scream. "Winnie say nothing". Winnie looks at me confused.

"You're not my daddy My daddy is dead, just like my grandpa Vincent", she shouted through the tears. She was angry at him and he could tell.

I look on realising that my younger self's ill-considered comment will cost her dearly. "Winnie, I know you're upset, PLLLEEEAASSSSE listen to me, say nothing, he is a dangerous man and HE IS YOUR DADDY", I scream. "Be quiet please Winnie" as the little girl turned to look at me she was met with a hard unprovoked punch to middle of her face. Winnie fell off her grandmother on to the kitchen floor with a thud. Bouncing across the floor in the other direction was her wobbly tooth, with a friend to accompany it.

"Daddy", I cry. "Daddy, No"

Winnie lay flat on her back, legs apart, both hands holding her nose and mouth. She did not utter a word or make a sound; she just held her face which was bleeding heavily through her fingers. That one punch was all it took to strike fear into this young vulnerable human being. He leant over her and dragged her by her hair to her feet. Winnie yelped in such a high pitch tone it had Daag barking. "I am your daddy do you hear?" he asked through gritted teeth.

"Say yes Winnie" I scream feeling completely helpless "please say yes. If you can't speak nod"

My little self was in no mood to toy with this animal, she

nodded. He picked her up and threw her over his shoulder and moved towards the car. Daag started to growl and bark viciously. He jumped up and sunk his teeth in Barrington's backside, she swung round forcing his flesh to depart his body, he yelped, cocked the gun and shit Daag dead.

Once in the back of the car I consoled my younger self. "Winnie lay your head back and pinch your nose like this", I showed her how to control the bleed.

Confused and shell shock, she lay her head back, squeezed her nose, and tried to push the tears from her eyes by squinting tightly every few seconds. I sat next to her holding her thigh rubbing the bump in the centre of my nose, sixty years later paralysed by the realisation of how it became so. I am filled with such grief; I look at my little self and start to cry for her, for me! I hold her thigh tighter; she looks at me I smile through the tears. I cannot even tell her that everything is going to be OK. I know that it's not. Physically battered and emotionally crushed I see myself for the first time. I am petrified. Covered from head to toe in my grandmother's and my own blood, wearing my favorite yellow dress, that is no longer yellow but a muddy brown. I wonder how the hell I made it. No wonder I blocked this out. No wonder I became who I am.

Chapter 4

Harold's Time

13TH January 2005 18.42pm

The mood and atmosphere in Edwina Mallard's room had changed from a volcanic eruption earlier, to sorrowful and quiet reflection. Harold had not moved from his wife's side, he couldn't, watching his wife's life slip away was more than his spirit could bear. The last two and a half weeks had been emotional. In fact, it was sheer hell. When Doctor Alcock delivered the news, it was me that crumbled like a sand castle. Edwina, even now, when she needed me to be her rock ended up comforting me. She was always the backbone out of the two of us, and always put me first, especially at the times I had deserved to be last on her list. Maybe Phoebe is right "it's all about me, always has been".

Harold inhaled deeply. Jon and Phoebe looked up.

"You ok dad", Phoebe asked

"I'm fine love", he looked pained, *Don't lie not now just tell them how you're feeling* ..... Harold took off his glasses and looked directly at his children. "Actually I'm not!!!! .... I still can't believe that this is happening. When Doctor Alcock gave us the diagnosis I've been numb. At first, I told myself that it's the wrong results. Not my Eddie, not now, we just reconnected again". Harold wiped a tear from his eye. "Then I was angry, angry with your mother"

"Typical..... you all over, it had to HER fault", Phoebe snapped

"Just shut up girl, you're so angry that you don't even listen to what is being said", I barked.

Jon looked at Phoebe with a childish smirk, "Good for you dad"

"I admit it", I sniffed "I blamed your mother. I was angry. After her breast cancer fifteen years ago she should have been more insistent with her GP about her health. She had a cough, a persistent one, and would not do anything about it. She was in denial, and I allowed her to be comfortable there. When I dragged her to the doctor's she played it down .... I should have insisted that she keep going back. Your mother just blew me off like I was having one of my moans. I was furious"

Phoebe tutted very loudly.

"With myself Phoebe"

"What Dad?"

Harold's voice broke, tears streaming down his face, "With myself are you deaf? I was angry with me for not being able to 'insist' that she go and take care of herself". Harold started to cry.

"Dad, no one blames you" Jon said quietly

"I blame me Jon. I blame me..... I have bargained with god and every one of Jesus disciples, NOTHING!!!!." They all chuckled quietly as Harold was very resistant to religion. "She'd gotten worse. Even after all that prayer your mother is still dying........ Then it hit me, and that's why I had to stay away. I will be a widower very soon and I could not cope with that prospect. We have been together since we were fourteen years old. Do you know this morning, when showering I cried like a baby. I'm not ashamed to admit it. You know why? I used the last of your mother's shower gel, and knew", his voice broke again, "and knew that I would not be replacing it. My beautiful wife will never shower again in our bathroom. We will not have dinner together at the table. I will not make her omelettes for breakfast. There will be no-one to shout at me when I ruin the whites in the washing machine. She will not kiss me goodnight or rub my back when it aches. You may not believe me when I say this, but I loved your mother, truly, madly, deeply loved her, and am still in love with her, and will always love her. She ...... she was ... is my best friend, my warrior, the mother of my children, my biggest fan. My lover. She made me feel like a man, even when there were times I did not act like one". Harold could not contain his emotion. He let the tears flow freely, and through the emotion and the pain, he lay back in his chair, looked lovingly at his wife and muttered "You can go my love. I will be ok".

Not wanting to infringe any further on her father's transparent intimate thoughts, Phoebe thought that she would go for a comfort break.

"Jon, dad I'm going to the loo and stretch my legs" Phoebe whispered.

"Good idea Hun I will do the same I need to call Jack and give him an update, it's been a while", Jon said quietly. He was still reeling from his father's recent disclosure. His mother's terminal condition had promoted a more revealing and communicative side to his father. He loved it, but wished he'd found his voice twenty years ago. His whole existence might have been different.

"Kids take your time .... If anything happens I will call you. There's an Italian down the road, go eat. I'm here. Jon if I am honest you look like you need a break." Harold smiled.

"You sure?", Phoebe asked concerned.

"I'm sure".

"Thanks dad, we won't be long one hour tops", Jon reassured his dad.

"Take your time .... It will be nice to have her to myself for a bit .... Oh can someone bring me back a coffee on the way back?"

"Sure", Jon replied.

Once the children had left, Harold stood up and kissed his wife on the lips. She was starting to develop a grey tint to her skin. Whatever that was he knew it was not good. He stretched his legs, walked over to the sink in the corner of the room and washed his hands and face. He smiled to his wife through the mirror. "Look, I know that you will cuss me if I don't keep myself looking presentable. You know what you're like," he smiled at her. "Harold you must always maintain a certain standard when you go out," he mimicked her in a high pitched voice. He wanted to laugh, but couldn't. He wanted to cry but wouldn't. "You're not dead yet Eddie I will have plenty of time to cry when you're dead".

He laughed to himself, when you're dead he thought. Edwina was full of such energy, to see her like this was an abomination to her spirit. "You love me, our children and music so If Eddie is not the life of the party" Harold had to wipe his eyes " I will be the life of the party for Eddie". His wife's favourite song of all time was My boy lollipop, by the Jamaican teenager Millie Small. This was released in 1964, which was the year that Jonathan was born; laughing to himself Harold remembers how she danced to this tune even when heavily pregnant. He started to hear the harmonica solo is his head, it was too late. He started shaking his legs like he was in his mid-twenties again.

Da um dum dum dum

My boy Lollipop

Da dum dum dum dum
You make my heart go giddy up

Beneath the Love of a Woman

Da dum dum dum dum
You are as sweet as candy

Da dum dum dum dum
You're my sugar dandy

Whoa oh, my boy Lollipop
Never ever leave me
Because it would grieve me
My heart told me so

Edwina opened her eyes and fixed them on her dancing husband. Harold's heart leapt and he put both palms across his heart and continued to sing to his wife.

I love you, I love you, I love you so
But I don't want you to know
I need you, I need you, I need you so
And I'll never let you go
My boy Lollipop....

Da dum dum dum dum

It was a long time since Harold had sung to his wife, it felt good. He felt young again. Sharing this moment with her was precious and priceless. She watched him and smiled, and the smile reached her eyes. She was happy he was here she could tell. They held on to this moment, and with utter reluctance she closed her eyes, with the smile on her face.

The hair on his neck stood up to attention, someone watching him. He swung around to the door and there was Jack, that homosexual person that'd corrupted his only son. The moment, his moment was over"

"Umm Ummmm Good evening Mr George. I came to see Eddie and to check on Jon. I didn't mean to intrude" completely embarrassed by his arrival Jack's cheeks went crimson.

"Well you did and he's not here," I snapped

Jack's eyes shot to the floor. He knew that Harold could not stand him.

"How is she?" Jack whispered looking at Edwina, desperately trying to manoeuvre himself out of this awkward situation.

"She's dying .... we're not sure how close, but we're close if that makes sense", he whispered back. Harold felt momentarily ashamed of the way he'd treated Jack.

"Take a seat, she'd be happy that you came" I pointed to the chair. "Sit".

Not wanting to cause any further distress Jack followed the order and sat down. He smiled at Harold and picked up a magazine.

"How are you Mr. George?" Jack enquired.

"Why do you *still* call me Mr. George?".

"Because with you I cannot presume that I can call you Harold" Jack said as a matter of fact.

"Please call me Harold. I may not ... not approve of what you and my son do, but that does not mean you can't call me Harold".

Jack was staring at me as if confused. He started to nod his head "Ok" he said. "Thank you ... Harold". I saw a smile creep across his face.

"How long have you been together?" Jack asked

"Over 50 years" I responded "Why?"

"Oh I knew it was a long time, but could not remember if it was fifty or sixty years" Jack responded.

"And you?" I asked looking squarely into the eyes of the man who had sex with my *only* son.

"I'm sorry" Jack look confused.

"How long have you been in a .... a you know.... thing with Jon?" I asked frustrated that he was pretending to not understand me.

"Thing" Jack snarled doing the inverted commas sign with his hands, "by thing" do you mean a relationship?"

"To you it's a relationship to me it's a "thing"", I repeated his sign

"It will be twenty two years next month", Jack said sarcastically.

"Really .... that long", I say back with the same amount of sarcasm.

"Harold don't you think that it's time that you accept the situation?" Jack asked quietly.

I cannot believe this impertinent homosexual. Who does he think he is? He is lucky my wife is in that bed or else I would let him have it.

 "Accept the situation. A-c-c-e-p-t the situation" Harold whispered loudly looking at his wife, who he could have sworn was smiling. "Jack I do not like what you do. Full Stop. I cannot understand why you do what you do, and I will not apologies nor accept you or the way that I feel about you."

"And what exactly do you feel about me," Jacked was clearly annoyed.

"I feel disgust. There I said it. It's nasty, and your homosexuality generation, you gays, you batty men, queers ...... you, to me are all dirty. That is just how I feel and there is nothing more to be said". Harold pulled his lips in to his nose and scrunched his nose as if he smelt something foul.

"On the contrary Harold you have said enough. Something wrong with your face". Jack asked in his overtly polite British accent. He started to unnerve Harold.

"Yes. When I think of the acts that you perform on my son I cannot stomach it. Eddie always said that my face is my window to my soul and she is right. I cannot pretend. I find it so ... so ... repugnant"

"Harold, why have you not considered the acts that you son's does to me? He is just as willing a participant", as soon as Jack said it he knew he had crossed the line.

"*I cannot believe you said that*", Harold thought, wide eyed hurt, angered and stunned, He looked at his wife then back to Jack. A horrific memory which occurred over twenty years ago sprang to mind.

"Harold, look I'm am so very sorry I did not mean to upset you"

"Yes you did" Harold snarled. "May I remind you that I have never witnessed my son doing anything to you". He starred at Jack so intensely Jack removed his gaze.

Jack did not want to anger Harold as he had previously been on the receiving end of his rage which left him in hospital. "Ok maybe a little ... It's just that you have never engaged with me in any way"

"After the way you have just spoken to me is there any wonder?"

"I'm sorry", Jack mumbled quietly with humbled eyes.

"Didn't your family teach you any manners... no respect for your elders". I stared him down.

"Harold Er Um.... I'm sorry.... I love your son very much. The fact that we have been together for over twenty years, does that not count for anything?" Jack pleaded.

"It does I suppose, but I don't have to like it. Jack I am entitled to my opinion".

"As I am entitled to mine".

"Meaning?" I snap.

"Meaning that when you came to England you experienced severe racial abuse. We, that is Jon and I have to deal with prejudice and discrimination all the time, just because we are a couple. We are more similar than you think."

This homosexual must be smoking weed in his spare time. "We are not similar and it's not the same. I c-a-n-n-o-t help being black"

"But I can help being gay. That is so ignorant."

"Ignorant .... No it's not ignorant. It's a fact. You have a choice with whom you sleep. I am black, no choice, end of story." Harold was very dismissive.

"Unbelievable" Jack threw his hands up in the air.

The silence was deafening. "When did you know?" I ask with obvious annoyance

"What? Know what, that I liked men" Jack asked astonished. This was the most dialogue that he had with Harold in twenty years, and the most direct that he'd had with anyone about his sexuality.

"Of course, that's what I mean, when?" I snapped

"I think 4 or 5 years old?"

"Were you abused?"

"I beg your pardon, was Jonathan abused?" Jack retorted angrily.

"I've asked him and he keeps saying no. What are you so indignant about, according to you less than five minutes ago, I was the ignorant one, now I am asking questions of you, you're acting as if I am offending you. Is this what your relationship is like with my son?"

"What?", Jack felt defensive

"Contradictory. Abrasive. Look at the situation that we are in." He pointed to his wife. You do not appear to have any real compassion for your surroundings. You are an angry man, aren't you Jack? With that Harold took the time to observe this young man.

"That was like a sledge hammer to the head "Err No". Jack thought about Harold's words and observations.

"I love him Harold. That may be hard for you to hear, but I do. He is the love of my life and I do want to spend the rest of my life with him"

"What exactly do you love about my son?"

"I'm sorry? I don't understand", Jack asked

"Yes you do. What do you love about him? He is the love of your life after all". Harold turned his whole body so that he could review Jack's complete response

"Well he's erm funny, Umm Um... er....a really good cook.......He's smart.....We have a great time together, he's generous ...."Jack continued to talk about his son but Harold surprisingly zoned out.

Poor poor Jonathan, this man was not the person for him. I'm not convinced that he is as genuine as he makes out. Eddie always said he was a snake in the grass and having spoken to him maybe she is right. I

just wish that I could go back in time, had I spoken to him twenty, fifteen years ago I would have told Jonathan to find another man.

"Jack... Jack stop. Let me make myself clear to you. If you hurt my son, you will experience more of your fair share of drama, from me" I said.

Stunned Jacks jaw dropped "What did you say?" he asked quietly

"You heard me," Harold was in no mood to joke and he was looking deep into Jack's soul

"It's a bit late to start doing the concerned father routine DON'T YOU THINK?"

I leaned over the bed "Keeping your F-ing voice down, it may be late in your eyes, but as long as I draw breath in my body Jonathan George is still my son. My wife always knew there was something suspect about you. Now I know too. Hurt him, in any way and I will hurt you. Now if you don't mind I would like to spend some time with my wife".

Jack looked at Harold's opened mouth. "Right then. That's it. Tell Jon I popped in".

Jonathan walked through the door as Jack stood up. "Hello love" he looked at Jack and his dad. This was a surprise. There was clear tension, "Everything alright?"

"Just fine" I said. "Jack and I have been having a lovely chat, son. He was telling me how much he loves you".

"R-E-A-L-LY!" Jon asked, practically floored by this information

"Really " Jack said dryly.

"I'm going to go", Jack said. Harold observed this man with his son and saw that his body language was abrasive and bullish.

"No stay", Jon begged. He gently tugged Jacks elbow, but he shrugged it off. He turned his whole body round towards Harold and puffed up his chest like a penguin.

"No", he drooled in an over exaggerated camp way purely for Harold's benefit. He threw Harold a filthy look "I must, this is a family time and I have taken up too much of that time already"

Jack kissed Jon, then threw Harold another filthy look. "Walk me to the door babes".

"Bitch, I can tell he's the woman, Harold thought to himself, then chuckled aloud at his own joke.

Jonathan looked at his father "Dad you ok?"

"Yes son" I replied quietly "Erm where's PP?"

"Getting your coffee, she will up shortly", I nodded, "Take your time don't rush back." As he was out of earshot, he looked at his wife, his thoughts filled with worrying prospects for his son

"Oh Eddie", Harold Stroked his wife's cheek with his forefinger, "What did I do all those years ago, Had I killed him, Jonathan would never have forgiven me, but right now I wish I had, something has made me uneasy about that man. I just cannot put my finger on it" My heart felt heavy and all I could do was sigh.

Eddie's eyes opened again. I could tell that she wanted to say something, I leaned in closer, she whispered angrily "You should have killed him"

I jerk back, *What…* "What Eddie?...." I gently nudge her as she had closed her eyes. *Woman you cannot fall off somewhere now without explaining this to me, Why should I have killed him? My heart is racing as I am starting to feel sick. My spirit never liked that homosexual toff and now I detested him. If Eddie, my precious loving wife who loves all things, including beatles is telling me this, It is with good reason.*

"Eddie" I gently prod her. Nothing.

"Eddie" I squeeze her hand.

Damn it woman wake up.

My mind is racing, and as I am staring at my wife who has frustrated the hell out of me, dying of cancer or not, I need answers. I close my eyes and am confronted with a memory that I have been trying to erase for twenty two years.

23rd December 1983.07.35am

"Harold I am so happy that Jonathan is coming home. I will give him a piece of my mind regarding how long he is coming home for, four days what kind of vacation time is that?

"What for?" I scolded my wife

"What for? She moans sarcastically at me "Are you serious Mr. George?" Eddie eyeballed me so hard I averted my gaze. She knew that I knew all too well why she was annoyed with our son.

"Eddie, give the young man a break. He is in his first term at university and he is finding his feet."

"Doing what? Term finished last week. What could he be doing?"

We both looked at each other and smiled.

"Studying" I chuckle. Now leave my only son alone, after all, without practice how can we expect grandchildren". I walked over to Eddie and cuddled her, she felt good and

smelt even better. I planted a wet kiss firmly on her luscious lips.

Hmmmm Mr. George, that feels nice, now what is that for", my wife asked in a flirtatious manner that made me tingle in places that reminded me why I have three children.

"Nothing baby, but give him a break, he most probably has a young woman stashed away somewhere".

"Crumbs ....That reminds me Harold; he asked to bring a friend home for the holidays. That's OK is'nt it?

"Of course", I chuckle " see that explains it, he has a special friend who he is spending time with. Relax woman. I bet she is pretty".

23 December 1983 2.46pm

"He said lunchtime" Eddie moaned at me whilst we ate the lovely prepared rice and peas, curried chicken and fresh salad that my wife has spent all morning preparing.

"Eddie, I know he's acting selfish, but there will be a credible explanation, you'll see."

Phoebe bounds in, "Hi Mum"

"Hello Love, where have you been?" Eddie asks.

"Woolworths", she throws up five bags filled with Christmas goodies. "It's madness on the high street, but I am done done done", her voice echoes like an opera singer.

"Anything for me PP", I grab a bag like a school boy giggling and run across the room with it.

"Dad" Phoebe squeals, "You'll ruin the surprise" and grabs the bag back. "I am going upstairs and yes I will be wrapping presents so please keep Inspector George

downstairs mum".

"No problem" Eddie says smiling.

As Phoebe opened the dining room door she squealed again, this time twelve octaves higher than last time "Jonathan", I jump out of my chair. Tears momentarily spring to my eyes, I am so proud of him; he was the first George ever to make it to University.

"Alright PP let my son go so that we can have a go" I snap. My daughter looked at me disapprovingly but I couldn't help it I had missed him so. I embrace my son, the only way a father can. I bear hug him close, kiss his ear. He feels thin but smells the same. Old spice aftershave fused together with Coconut oil and I sniff a couple of times then push Jonathan away "You smoking now?" I asked accusingly.

"Er …. Well yes. I am just trying something new"

I look at my son, he looks different. His hair is longer; his face is well sort of smoother. His clothes were grungier. I shrug off the feeling. He's a student. This is how they are; they look like peasants, smoke too much and drink even more.

"Oh …… well make sure it's a short lived habit, anything else your trying that you want to tell me about?"

Like what, Jonathan chimed in with an exasperated expression on his face

Like ….. Drugs, marijuana, heroin"

"Dad! I'm at Uni and I like to smoke a few fags with my beer ok, don't start I've been back all of five minutes"

"Alright so, where's this girl that your bringing home"

"Girl"

"Yes your friend", I ask frustrated of his innocence

"Oh you mean Jack"

"What is that short for Jackie, Jacqueline I ask obviously confused"

"No sir, its short for Jack", a young white posh man in his early twenties appeared from behind my son. He looked like a student but a lot more stylish. His long blond hair has every strand strategically placed and scooped off his brow. He had piercing grey blue eyes, square jaw, and a dimple in his chin. He reminded me of a young Kirk Douglas. He looked like one of those male models in Phoebe's "Jackie magazine" Perfectly manicured. Too perfect.

"Oh hello", I was visibly surprised, which embarrassed me. "I just presumed Jon was bringing home a girl"

"Well I hope that you are not too disappointed"

I blushed.

"Hello Jack", my wife stretched out her hand. "I am Edwina, but everyone calls me Eddie"

Jack shook Eddie hand then gently raised it to his lips and kissed the back of her hand very gently, whilst maintaining eye contact.

"You are definitely charming", Eddie said and blushed. "Harold stick with him you might learn something", my wife joked

Flash git I thought to myself. I look at Jack for a few seconds longer than is necessary and he feels my stare.

"Mr. George, is it OK that I am here?"

"Yes son, of course, any friend of Jacks is a friend of mine". I stretch out my hand, and both men glance at

one another, Jack shakes my hand firmly.

"It's a pleasure to finally meet you. Jon talks very highly of you". I blush. It makes me proud that my son speaks of me to his new posh uni friends.

"Ok Harold", Eddie started to direct the situation, she looks at Jonathan and holds his square shoulders " you must be starving lads, come and eat. Jon get the plates off the side and tuck in".

Jon did what he was instructed. Jack was served a healthy helping of the rice and peas and curry chicken.

"Mrs George, this is absolutely gorgeous, is that coconut in the rice and beans"

"Please call me Eddie and yes it is coconut, we call this dish Rice and Peas."

"Its lovely Eddie, Jack said licking his lips.

So Jon, how come Jack is not going home to his people for Christmas?" I enquire.

Jon turned to me, "His folks are in the Caribbean, his parents have a villa in West Moreland Barbados that is where they holiday every year.

"Lovely" Eddie chimes in, eyebrows raised clearly impressed "Why didn't you go?" My wife asks suspiciously. " I mean Islington - Barbados no contest".

"I had an assignment that's due in the New Year. I just wanted a head start Eddie. When I am in Bados I just don't do anything but sunbathe". Jack responded shyly.

"I have never been to Barbados but I hear that it's beautiful. What are you studying Jack?"

"Yes it is and Law and Philosophy", he announced proudly.

"Do you like it?" I chimed in

"I love it sir" Jack smiled.

I drink in the atmosphere and embrace this feeling that I have. My family. It's just perfect. I look at my son filled with pride. Both Maddie and Phoebe are on top form completely embarrassing their brother for his love of clubbing and brit pop bands Wham and Pet shop boys. I don't get it myself but he's young. This is his time. I have to say I am taken aback by Jack, he is a nice fella; clearly well to do, but very down to earth. He even has a healthy appreciation of cricket, which makes him every West Indians best friend. I see my son, my daughters and wife all smiling at me. I know what they are thinking, and its true I am making an effort. I want to. This is my son's friend from University; he must think a lot of him to bring him home. Also, Jack will be the type of people he will be mixing with in the future so I need to put aside my class prejudice and get over myself. This is for my boy.

4.06am

I wake at the same time every night. It's so frustrating, but after twenty three years its irritatingly reassuring. I turn and kiss Eddie, sound asleep like an angel. I swear this woman could sleep through a hurricane.

Hmmmmmm Huh Huh Hmmmmmmmm I blink myself awake.

Hmmmmmmm Huh Huh Hmmmmmmm

My heart is pounding. There it is again.

"Ummh"

I sit up. thud thud. Lord we are being burgled. This cannot be happening, whoever it is is going to get a pounding. "Ummh"

I jump out of bed and pick up the hockey stick that lives behind the door. "Ummh". That's a muffled sound, Mercy the girls. I panic.

"Eddie.. Eddie "

Hmmmmm. I shake her violently awake.

"Wake up love, we're being burgled". My wife jumps out of bed disorientated.

"Stay here" I order. "and call the police" I start to feel sick as it sounds like some pervert is taking advantage of my daughters, both of them. I run out to the landing, Nothing. I wait looking around. Both girls door are closed. I put my ear next to Phoebe' door. Nothing, all I can hear is my own heartbeat. I slowly open the door, she is sound asleep. A wave of relief sweeps over me. I then creep next door and open Maddies door, she too is asleep.

Thud…. Thud, there it is again. I am less panicked, my girls are safe. I open Jon doors as I could do with reinforcements. His bed is empty. "Maybe the boys went clubbing" I think to myself. I take the slow approach down the stairs. My heart is racing, but I have the advantage. I know where every creaky floorboard is. I take my time as the element of surprise is going to help me break some bones.

"I hear whispers in my living room". I burst in, the sight before me weakens my core. I must be in shock as I cannot move. My stomach falls to the bottom of my ankles and my mouth starts to water like I am going to be sick. I open my eyes as wide as they could stretch as I need to see the full picture, my mind must be playing tricks on me. The TV is on, and in front of my tv, on my rug is my son and Jack naked. Jack is lying on top of my son, and moving his hips in a motion that I only know a man should move on top of a woman when naked.

P.D Lorde

"Mr George" Jack shrieks fear in his eyes. "We were … we were just"

"I know what you were doing" I scold. I stare at my son who face is buried in his hands, he is on all fours and his backside is still in the air.

"My son look at me. L-----o-o---k a-t m-e-e-e-e I scream at him.

Jon turns his head, tears swell and burst their banks and roll down my face. I cannot help it, I kick him hard in the side of his arse that is still in the air.

"You let this batty man fuck you." Jon looked to the floor ashamed. I could feel the bile and rage in my stomach rising. "Boy ….. answer me. I start to shout at the top of my voice " You let this dirty batty man fuck you? Hmmm hmmm? You bring this abomination to God and man in my h-o-u-s-e". I bellowed

Jon face was streaked with tears and snot. He was shaking I did not know whether it was from cold or fear, but he was visibly shaking. He nodded and lowered his head.

That admission was the welcome mat my bile needed. It rose without warning and lurched out of my mouth onto the Christmas tree and presents. I kneel to try and focus the vomit, when Eddie walked in. She did not speak. She whispered to Jon, "Jon what is going on here?" Jon lowered his head.

"You are not a homosexual are you?" she said her voice cracking. She moved slowly towards me and knelt on the floor and put her arm around my shoulder.

"Why" Eddie snapped

"Mum I am just discovering who I am", Jon croaked

66

Discovering who you are, Discovering who you are. Your my son and you are not Gay." Eddie snapped and shook her head vigorously. Her eyes were screwed tight as if to try and push the image out of her head. "No, not you"

"Mum", Jon tried to interject quietly.

Eddie's voice changed, she was furious. "why would you disrespect us like this?. Jonathan. Jonathan I have just asked you a question. You bring this nasty ungodly act to my home. You introduce your lover to us as if he is your friend and do this. Look at your father. Look at him. Is this what you wanted?" Eddie screamed.

"Eddie" Jack pleaded, he look worried about his situation. He was red in the face, I wasn't sure whether that was from embarrassment or that was his flushed just got fucked face.

"Shut your filthy mouth" I screamed.

"Dad…. mum, what's going on?" Phoebe asked, as she bounced through the door like a care free teenager who has just been expectantly woken up. Maddie was behind her. Both girls once they entered the room just fell silent. There was no giggles or jibes. Just shock

"Jon why are you both naked?" Maddie whispered eerily.

"Because he's gay" Phoebe informed the room. With that she walked out the room, "Come on Maddie, I think mum and dad need to have a chat with Jonathan", she shouted disapprovingly as she stomped up the stairs.

I could see Jack putting on his clothes in such a rush, so much so he nearly fell over getting his jeans on. I just sat in shock looking at my only son. It was as if my life had ended, I was having flash backs to when he was a young boy, his teenage years, all our father and son chats. Jonathan George likes women, I know this, he told me so. No this is not him. He is being influenced by that posh twat. I am sure of it. I bet he went to some private school and was buggered to kingdom come, and he meets my fine young buck of a boy and convinces him that he's gay.

"Mr. George, Mr. George, err sir", I hear that filthy homosexual voice pulling me back to this disgusting scene. My body erupts with heat as if I had a litre of hot pepper sauce poured all over me.

"Mr. George", he walks over to me and puts his hand on my shoulder. Oops too late Jack, the vein in my forehead pops out for all to see.

"Take your hands off me", I scream. I am trying to control the rage but he is now in my face.

"If I could just explain" Jack said pleadingly.

"Explain, Explain what?, that you were raping my son in my living room" I screamed.

"Dad …. No I'm ..", Jonathan tried to explain.

I push my hand in the air so hard I am sure he felt a breeze on his face. "Noooooo son, please so not say it. Please"

"Look Mr. George, this is not the way that Jon wanted you to find out, but its better in the open. Earlier, we were all friends, we are still the same people we.

I grabbed him by the shirt and threw him into the Christmas tree. Christmas balls, tinsel and lights were strewn across the living room floor.

"Harold", Eddie screams "Please Harold don't. I know that you have been provoked but please Harold" Eddie was crying, "Please" she whispered.

Jonathan get you're your friend out of my house" Eddie

scolded her son

Jonathan cautiously walked towards his lover, without taking his eyes of his father. He gently pulled Jack off the flattened tree. He walked towards the door and came back "Dad I am soo sorry", he sobbed.

I couldn't say anything. Tears were streaming down my face uncontrollably

"Dad, its not"

What?"

"Its not nasty, its natural"

"Then why is the government informing the country that batty man has spread the capital letters? Why is it that if you are a batty man, you will contract Aid and they are showing tombstones everywhere? Hmmm? Why?" I stare at them both

Have you lost your mind Jon, you must be taking cocaine to backside, it is not natural. A man poking his penis into another man is arsehole is not a natural act. If it was god would not be punishing you all. How can you get satisfaction from that? Hmmm? Hmmmm? The bible says its abhorrent. If we lived in another country you too dirty batty man would be dead for "I point at the floor violently, "for this".

"Dad"

"Don't dad me. You have that battyman disease, HIV AIDS, do you have it?

No Dad, Jon whispered.

"We really care"

"Shut up – SHUT UP…. I did not raise no b-a-t-t-y m-a-n!!!!" I bellowed. I could see my wife wincing in the

corner of my eye. Jon physically stepped back.

"Well actually Mr. George you did", Jack said with his arrogant posh accent, stepping forward and looping his fingers in my sons. The vein in my head popped. I grab Jon with both hands by his afro and pull him as hard as I could from Jack. I straighten him up and slap him across the face so hard his body tumbles into a half summersault before his lands on the floor.

Jack charges towards me, everything slows down, I hear Eddie scream "Nooooo Harold", the living room door opens, Maddie and Phoebe run towards me, its too late I push through them and connect with Jack. I pick him up mid movement and throw him to the ground, I am kneeling in his chest, my hands are wrapped around his throat, I close my eyes and have my first flashback in years, his penis is entering my sons anal passage, I squeeze as hard as I can. I feel the bones in his neck crunch, I start to retreat into that place, it's getting dark and the volume in the room is getting quieter and quieter.

My wife hits me in the face with her fists, she is franticly screaming at me to let him go. I cannot hear her but I know what she is saying. I look at the batty man rapist under my hands and see his lips are turning blue. Good, I'm gonna choke the life out of you. The cheek of him. I did not raise a batty man. I am a man. My son is a man.

Something cold and hard strikes me in the back of my head. Pain cripples the right side of my head and I lose the feelings in my arms. I topple over like a bag of heavy rocks. Dazed and momentarily confused I lay on the floor. I see Maddie with her mother's dutch pot in hand. I cannot believe she hit me with that. I say to myself before I black out.

I must have been out a few moments. I wake up to find Eddie over me with a cold cloth on my head. She looks terrified. I turn and see Jack in the corner. He is sat up drinking water holding his throat and staring at me wild eyed. I see the fear in his eyes when he realises I am awake. I try to move but the room starts to spin and I realise that my legs do not appear to be working as well as they should be.

Phoebe and Maddie are sat behind me, when they see my eyes open.

"Alright dad" Phoebe asks I nod.

"You should have killed him dad", Maddie whispers and winks at me before she plants a huge kiss on my head.

Eddie bends down and kisses me "You old fool" she whispers. Tears of relief grace her cheeks. "I thought you were going to kill him"

"Get them out of here Eddie. Please. Get them out" I moan, I roll to the opposite end of the room so that I do not have to look at my son. My head is banging, and my face is started to swell from the pounding that Eddie gave it a few minutes earlier.

I weep like a child, uncontrollable. I am inconsolable. My heart and spirit are broken. My son is gone.

13th January 2005 21.44pm

As the day languishes into night, my thoughts take hold of me. I am struck between two valleys. This first is that I want Eddie to stay like this for as long as possible. At least she will be alive, maybe not well, but with me. The thought of facing the rest of my life alone was not part of the deal. My second valley, is where and I feel ashamed to admit this, I want her to die, quickly, pain free and with dignity. Seeing her like this makes me sick to my stomach. This suffering happens to other people. Not us. Not Eddie. I am not sure why I think that she is immune from the evils of the world and disease, but I do, although history tells me different, somehow this was never our story. My wife was as strong as an ox, healthy and energetic. Only a few weeks ago she was so full of life and energy. Today, this sick, decrepit old woman is alien to me. I start to question my own mortality. My failing as a man, her man, her husband and father to our children. All in all we made it through some pretty rough years. To be more accurate, she made it. She had to dig deep, I did not make it easy for her, but she stuck by me. The lord only knows why, but she did.

She is so peaceful now, her honey tone has a slight ashy tint to it. She's leaving me, I feel it and now I can see it. My Eddie looks as she did as a young woman whilst asleep. Free from all the pain and suffering any human being can endure. I look at her lovely white nightgown and straighten her collar for her. I want to cry but can't. I need to holla and scream out like my life depended on it and won't. The lump in my throat is larger than any rock I could carry, and my sorrow heavier than a clunky old chest on my back. I stand over my wife, my Eddie and cup her face in my hands as gently as I could, her eyes reluctantly open, she looks at me confused, then she smiles. I smile back.

"I should have behaved better than I did and for that darling I am sorry. I disparaged you when I should have loved you without fear of regret. I attacked you when I should have celebrated you, and just for the record I did love you. Through my own failings, I loved you, and over the years I have learned to adore you. I know I was never …..him. I tried and I hope that you are not sitting here now with regrets. If you are its ok, I just want to say that I am sorry for not living up to your expectation of what and who I can be. I acknowledge daily that I was not good enough for you. We both know this. When I finally learnt how to be a man, your man and do better I did. That's what I hope that you take with you. I loved you enough to change"

Eddie eyes smiled at me, "It's alright baby, you did ok and I was happy" she croaked. Eddie looked straight through me "I need you to promise me something?"

"Anything darling"

"I need you to move on, meet someone else and find happiness quickly. It's hard being alone and you will find it excruciating" she said weakly. "Find love and be happy Harold you deserve it". She inhaled deeply and fell asleep.

Still hunched over I cup her face tighter than before, my tears run down my face and wet hers.

"Oh how I love you". My chest feel tight. I feel nothing but regret. How I wished I can turn the clock back. Its fruitless these thoughts I know this. They change nothing. I still wish things were different. I sit back and close my eyes, my heart breaking and my soul glum, I reluctantly close my eyes. I am so exhausted, that as I close them they burn. My body relaxes and I fall quickly into a deep sleep.

I wake to abruptly alarmed that there are people in the room. I bolt upright attempting to regain my visual focus, my eyes are blurry from the interrupted respite. The room is in darkness, the monitors and low lamps are the only source of light. She is sat there holding her hand, stroking her forearm. Angela McDermott was the closet figure to a mother that Edwina had. They had been firm friends for over fifty years. There were only two black families that lived on our street, ours and Angela was the other. She was petite, do not let her size fool you, she was like a warrior, I felt for poor Niall, he was dragged around by his eyelids most days. Her small frame was muscular, she was always jogging, and until her 70th birthday she ran the marathon every year. Proceeds went to some orphanage in Jamaica. She moved to Islington with her Irish husband Niall in 1955, she had a son Phillip who was in his fifties now, living in New Zealand. They were like family. In fact, they were family. Angela was stone faced, she has visibly lost weight.

"Angela what are you doing here" I whisper concerned for my elderly friend..

I just could stay at home not doing anything. I wanted to be here. I didn't like the thought of here alone. I just can't think of anything else right now" she whispered

"She has me" I say more curtly than I mean.

"You know what I mean", she tells me exasperated by my childishness.

"Look" I look to my shoes embarrassed by my behavior. "I am exhausted. The kids are in the family room and I want them to sleep, especially Jon he is dead on his feet. "Are you ok to sit with her?"

She looks at me as if I am crazy "Of course …. go"

I walk through the door, as I turn to close it I see Angela bending over and stroking Edwina's face. "My precious child how are you?" she holding it together, kissing Eddie on the forehead, cheek lips, hand, she sat down next to her and put her cheek to Eddies hand and held it there. She turns to look at me. I close the door as I can sense that I am intruding.

I walk through the corridor. The night staff nod at me. I go down the stairs out of the main doors, the crisp January night recoups my spirit and I am now awake. I decide to walk around the gardens. I recall the last time I was out this late, it was when Angela tore me a new backside for being an arse to Eddie.

31st December 1983 6.24pm

Harold I think you need to sleep Hun. You have not had a decent night sleep since ….. Jon came home" Eddie tells me in her quiet voice.

"I'm fine. It's a new year and a new start. I need to look ahead. I cannot be stuck in 1983 forever. I want to forget it and the year that he was born".

"Stop it" she snapped.

"What?"

"You heard me, you talk such gibberish when you are drunk. He's gay Harold, not the Yorkshire ripper" she barked at me clearly annoyed at my stance."

"It's just as bad Eddie", I shout. "And in my house, on my carpet"

"Is that what this is about? Would you be happy that he is gay and had sex outside your house? Would that please you? Hmmmm so you would prefer that he was not being gay in here with you" she laughed at me.

"That's not what I mean. I'm not like you I just can't cut him off like that. He's my son, I love him, I miss him. I have to help him maybe he is just confused"?

"You think? I don't want you conversing with him. I forbid it. Not in my house".

My wife who was dressing for her party, suddenly stopped. She looked at with her steely eyes. "You do not have the authority to forbid anything" she instructed me slowly and precisely. "You do not own me. I am not your property. You do not dictate to me Harold. Understand? Her quiet yet very serious voice was back.

"Understand? Who the hell are you talking to?" I was furious.

"You. He's my so". She screamed at me

"Not anymore" I shout, as soon as the words leave my mouth they sound stupid.

I will not lose him.

"This is my house, Harold shouted. "I should be able to comfortable in my own home"

Her quiet voice returned "Actually Harold it's not your house. It's mine. My grandfather brought this for mmmeeeeeeee. He is my son and if I choose to see him I will in my hoooouuuusssee. You do not own me. I will not be dictated to. I will not be ordered. If you don't like it, you leave". With that she walked to our en-suite.

What? I say stupefied by her response.

You heard me, you leave. I will not have you treating me like your chattel.

"Your taking his side?"

It's not about sides, she yells. "I am not going to lose my son, you may want to throw him away but I cannot do it. He's my flesh and blood.

"So what am I?"

"Your Harold" She realised what she said. "Harold look I'm sorry I didn't mean that" she touches my arm. I

punch her hand hard and she falls into the bed frame.

"Argghh" she moans. "What are you doing?" She spins around and is in front of me

"Woman get out of my way", I snarl

"No", she says defiantly. Her eyes were wide and she was angry and ready for war.

"What is going on" Angela yells at both of us.

"What are you doing here? I ask embarrassed and annoyed that my neighbor is in my house again, and at a time when I need my privacy the most.

"Maddie came and got me" she says, she looks at Eddie rubbing her wrist. "You ok? She shoots me a death glare.

No no…… Ange I am fine" Eddie tried to reassure her.

Angela Mc Dermott looks at me "Leave" she said quietly. I could see that her usual happy go lucky disposition has left the room, what was left unnerved me.

"What?" I asked

"Don't let me ask you again. Your upset, she is upset. Leave"

I look at Eddie who is sat in her bed. "Eddie I didn't mean to…" I stop myself as I don't want Angerla to get the wrong idea. I look at her, it's too late she thinks I am a prized shit and now I feel like one.

"You never do that's the bloody problem. Ange is right. Gooo" Eddie screams at me.

I storm out, the girls are downstairs in the kitchen with uncle Niall. He looks at me "Get your coat mate, you and I are going to the pub"

One sec" Angerla shouts. Niall slowly closes his eyes. "Harold can I speak with you outside for a quick min?". Angela asks sweetly. She was smiling the whole time, that was for the children's benefit. I knew this was not going well. I followed her to the cloakroom situated by the front door.

"Inside please" she says nicely

"Look Angerla I am not sure what this is but"

Not sure, are you sure about that?

I was about to say something

Shut up" she interrupted my thoughts.

I look at her completely stunned. "What is with you today?"

With me… with meeee you're the one hitting on your wife.

I never hit her, it was more of a reflex reaction.

Do you hear how that sounds" she yells "She is your wife, treat her like your wife and not some scratch you pick up from the gully. You are screwing your marriage up."

"What do you know about it"? I mumble as my neighbor chastises me.

"More than you by the look of it Stop being this man who over reacts, becomes a bully and a pig. That's not you", she looks at me with concern.

My ego becomes bigger than my rational mind. "I don't need to listen to this", and turn to leave the room, as I grab the handle to open the door. I see a flash in the corner of my right eye. Angela then grabs my right arm and pulls me back into the room. I look at her as its inconceivable that this little woman has the strength of a man. "Sit down" she barks. Naturally I listen.

"If you listen to nothing else hear me now. Take care of her. Love your family, you just never know when it's going to be gone. She is a rare and precious jewel your wife, so if you hurt her I will hurt you Harold. Man Up she shouts. This is your one and only warning.

My ego rears its ugly head again and tells me that I have had enough of this. My ego who has no manners pushes what I can only describe next as Bruce instructing Kung Fu teacher out of the way, very hard and attempts to walk out. All I remember is that I got to the door handle and attempted to walk out. Bruce Lees helper grabs my shirt collar and wrenches me backwards, as I am hurtling back to the floor she karate chops me in the side of the head. I am not kidding the force of that crack makes my bloody head snap back. Not only do I go crashing towards the floor as I have lost all sensation in my legs. I try and regain all sense of self, buts it's no good, As I careen to the floor I feel her bony knee in my ribs hard. I hear a crunch, then feel the burning sensation in my left side. I am winded really really… really badly. I look at this 5 ft bony Bruce Lee impersonator, and slide down the door to my knees. I hold up my hands in surrender.

Angela kneels down in front of me, I am breathing very hard and am sweating, everywhere. She eyeballs me for a few seconds.

"Harold I love her. She is so very dear to me and I will do anything to protect her. Now" she says quietly "get it together. After our little chat I think we understand one another now. Sweetheart If you are foolish enough to touch me again, I am not going to leave you with the use of your legs understand"

I nod repeatedly. She opened the door, even with my body weight behind it and stepped over me. Niall was waiting outside the closet. His hand were behind his back, he looked at me crumpled on the floor then to his wife.

"Night dear", he leans in to kiss her. He looks at me "It's going to be a long night darling"

Niall watches me trying to console myself. My left hand is holding me head and my right hand is clutching my ribs.

"Harold I think you going to need more than a beer mate, she says in his thick Irish accent, he cannot help it he laughs hard. "She kicked your arse mate, and by the looks of you, she did it well.

Chapter 5

Doctor Barrington Barnet

November *24th 1941*

My life on days like these is just perfect, the sun is embedded deep into the blue sky, bouldering its heat like a functioning furnace. It's lazy afternoons like these that fill me with excessive joy. It reminds me of home. How I yearn for my southern roots, my people, my Mother, Father and older brother Mason, most of all I miss my Black Mammy Viola. Can you believe that she is still alive. She is 76 years old and I never miss a birthday. She taught me everything I know about life.

If I could turn back time I would still be in Madison County Mississippi. I look out onto the plantation and see all the field workers picking coffee. The grief of losing them all stills cuts deep. I was young, impulsive and stupid. Even though I go back it's not the same. Loss, the feeling of loss is a funny thing. The deprivation of one's family, and all that they hold dear, changes a person. That loss shrinks you to become insignificant. It makes you consider the "What ifs" in life which is always a dangerous road to travel, It turns a loving man in to a hateful one, and honest man into a criminal. A kind man into a mean son of a bitch. When you are in depravity, what little you have you hold on to it, even when it sickens you to the pit of your stomach.

"Hmmmmm" I roll backwards in my rocking chair with my pipe attached to my mouth. I am going to enjoy the haze of the sunshine and good old fashioned Louisiana tobacco. I take the deepest breath that my lungs could muster, the fragrant scent of my plantation, the sweet perfumed smell of the ripe mango bulging from the fragile bulbs that keeps ii in place transforms the aroma of my yard.

I smile to myself. I may be lonely and alone, but look at all this. I have achieved it all.

I hear the clicking of her heels on the highly polished wooden veranda. My wife Phyllis glides around this place giving instructions to the yard boy, about tidying something or the other. I quietly contemplate as I have on many occasions before, that my wife is sure one beautiful specimen of a woman. Born and raised in New Orleans. A product of two worlds that is her Spanish father and a mulatto mother. In the United States of America she is described as a "Quadroon". To my white southern family she is a 'nigger". Her pale olive skin and thick black wavy hair to her waist made her a vision to behold, then when we first met over twenty years ago and now. There is a saying "Beauty is only skin deep" and I do believe that the longer I am with her, the more I believe this saying. I gave up my distinguished southern family and prestigious life for this woman. I was far too inexperienced to realise it, but I have surrendered to the fact that the worst day of my life was the 24th July 1915, it was this day that I married Phyllis DuBois.

What I know now as a middle aged man is that my wife, as stunning and beautiful as she is, is the most deceitful, manipulative, lying, two faced wretched cheating whore I have ever had the misfortune of gracing my presence with. I despise the way she walks, talks and even breathes. The very oxygen that I breathe is wasted in her wretched soul. If I could find a way to kill her without this sin staining my soul for all eternity then so help me god I would do it in an instance.

I chuckle to myself as I would be left with that bastard the whole village and districts knows is not my son. My mother always knew that she was no good. "It's nigga blood you can't trust son", she said in her silky south Madison County of Mississippi drool.

I hear the Chevy screaming up the drive, Barrington, my spoilt jacket, is hitting the horn like a drunken fool.

"BARRINGTON" I hear Phyllis shriek.

"What now woman" I shout back. Jolted out of my own thoughts. "I swear if he's drunk again I will take that car away from him.

I mutter under my breath "Spoilt selfish SOB". I make my way to the south of the veranda reluctantly. I better go and see what he has done this time.

As I get to the veranda I see Phyllis running to the stalled Chevy. The thought of my wife running makes me smile. The field hands run over to the car, and stop dead. Something is wrong. Why are they stopping, is he dead? *If only the Lord would grant me that one wish. I smile to myself, insisting that I behave.* Why won't they help him? Phyllis is dumb struck by something. She appears dazed by the contents of the car, as I get closer I see that he is not alone, but can't quite make out what or who it is.

"What have you done?" What have you done? Phyllis screams.

A knot the size of Alabama starts to form in my gut. I start to sprint and say a prayer, whatever it is is not good as the field hands are getting het up.

Barrington groans and his eyes roll back in his head.

"Miss Phyllis, one of the field hands punches the air. He repeatedly points to the back of the car accusingly. "That's Miss Lucy's granddaughter, why is the little girl bleeding?" Hmmmm

Another field hand pushes his head in the car, "You hurt Winnie?"

As news spread amongst the field hands, Phyllis sensed anger starting to rise, "Where is Miss Lucy, they start to shout?"

Phyllis calmly walked to the passenger side and pulled Barrington with all her might out of the driver seat, she needed to get him to the house quickly.

The same insistent field hand pushed his way through the crowd in the car, he tenderly rubbed Winnie's knee, she recognised Rex from church, "Where's Mama baby?"

Lucy let go her face and blood sprouted out of her nose like a fountain. Started Rex jumped back.

"Baby love", he wailed pushing his hand in her face.

Winnie looked at limp father's body "He did it..... He did it ...... He did it" she screwed her eyes shut as if remembering a horrible memory. she held her nose and pushed her head back to stem the flow of her blood with little success.

Transfixed on the young child in the rear view mirror, Phyllis put the car into drive. She looked at her son and wondered, *"Am I to blame for all of this*?" *Blinking back the tears she wished that she had kept quiet about Winnie. Oh Barrington what have you done this time.*

I cannot see my wife as there is a lot of people crowding the car. Phyllis is driving towards me, stop my sprint and run back to the house, my field hands are in hot pursuit. *Whatever has happened this is not good. My wife's haste to get out of the car motions me to my professional demeanor.* I look in the car and see a blood soaked Barrington Junior. I run to the car as she stopped in front of the house. "What happened?", I enquire curtly. For a split second I am concerned for him.

*"*Not sure" Phyllis said quickly, I look in the back of the car and my heart sank, it cannot be. In the back whimpering and terrified is Lucy and Vincent's granddaughter covered in blood. My pulse quickens and the heat within my body is rising out of control. I look at Phyllis with cold steely eyes and she immediately throws her eyes to the floor. "If you have had anything to do with this I will deal with you so help me, you will holler for mercy"

Phyllis steps backs eyes averted everywhere anywhere but mine. I have my answer.

I forget Barrington and immediately open the back door. "Hello Sweetie, My name is Doctor Barnett and I am going to help you" I stretch out my hand, but this poor child is petrified.

"Come on darling. Its Ok. You're safe". I glance over to Barrington who has lost a lot of blood, I don't care about him he is not my concern right now. This little girl by the looks of it had been to the gates of hell, and once again that boy is responsible for another human being's suffering.

Winnie is in shock, and unsure who to trust, she just stares at me, willing me to be kind to her. Her nose is broken, I can tell that without even getting close, her eyes are closing, she must be in agony, and nothing, nit a sound.

"Winnie darlin' do your legs hurt"

She shook her head no

"Your arms, back tummy?"

Again Winnie shook her head no.

"Ok – Just you head right?"

A slow nod yes, cautiously eyeing up this stranger.

I take my time and lean in slowly, I gently pull her close to me., and I carefully pick her up. Rex tugs her leg, I did not even see him in the car, he eyes me and I eye him back. He lets go and reciprocates my nod he knows she is safe with me. I carry this broken little girl into my house. I see the crowd forming around me,

"Winnie .... W-I-N-N-I-E, Doc, Sir is she ok? Why is she bleeding like that? Where is Lucy?"

She sinks her pure body in mine, and I carry her and cradle her at the same time. I head straight for my study and lay her on my patient bed. As I turn to look at her my heart leaps out of my chest, how she looked like my wife. She is beautiful now and will grow up to be a real treat. I walk at pace to my medicine cabinet behind the bed and pick up a huge pair of scissors. Her little girl's eyes grew round like saucers. She just stares at me.

"It's OK darlin' I am gonna to cut your dress off. I need to see if anything is broken when I examine you. Is that okay?".

Again she just looked at him. She was still holding her face.

"Does it hurt to talk, blink once for yes and twice for no? OK".

With that Winnie blinked once.

"Is your nose where all the pain is?"

Winnie blinked twice

I eye her swollen split lip, "your mouth, does that hurt as well?" I asked pointing to her mouth

Winnie blinked once.

As I cut off her dress and see her brushed body I go cold. I put the thickest towel I could find to cover her, then I find another and wrap her in it. She is just a child. I notice that she is trembling beneath my touch, and it wasn't cold in the slightest, she was terrified and in shock.

What has he done to you? I start to think dreadful things that even I do not believe is possible, but... we are talking about Barrington. I am yearning to hug her and reassure this young child, but thought better of it. Carefully I release one limb at a time and gently wiped her clean.

I leave her face until last as I know she will scream from the pain. She looks me dead straight in the eyes. I say nothing to her, she blinks once and reluctantly lets go of her nose. The gushing warm red stream keeps flowing, with more force than before. I pushed my finger on the bine, she whimpers, tears stream out of her eyes, she does not move or squirm, she stays still and looks at me.

"Oh Darlin' I know its hurts but I am gonna make it okay, I am gonna make your nose better", I hold her delicate nose between my fingers and pushed the cracked bones together as hard he could. Her bones crunched beneath me. Not a sound from this little girl. Astonishing! She just screwed her eyes shut and started to shake. She was in pain and would not or could not make a sound, I wasn't sure which. I could feel my indignation hemorrhage out if me. *Keep cool son. Keep cool, he will keep, they will keep.* I head once again to the medicine counter, took out a needle and prepared it, and I gave that poor child a generous shot of morphine.

With her face all cleaned up and her right eye closed, her left eye was straining for sight. She needed to see me. I wanted to cry for her. She was just a small defenseless child. I give her the shot, to her thigh, again nothing. My voice cracks "This will take the pain away sweetie. Can you hear me?" she nods and whimpers, n

The door flung open and Mackie, his son's minder and confidant stood there with his wife in tow..

Mackie knew he needed to tread carefully, "Sir, is Winnie alright?"

"It's Miss Winnie and who wants to know?" Dr Barnett asked washing his hands without looking at Mackie.

Both Mackie and his wife took another hesitant step together, looked at one another, "We do" they both said in unison.

"Dr Barnett?" Miss Mack asked quietly "Please sir"

"So you know her?"

"Yeeeeees" she wailed.

Mackie looked at me hard. "Sir, there are many angry people congregating at the house sir. The field hands, they think Winnie is dead, please can I tell them something?"

"You tell them to mind their own business?" Dr Barnett said quietly.

"Sir" Mrs. Mack chimed in. "Lucy and Vincent are our business. Do not forget that Vincent was born and raised on this plantation. Lucy and Winnie are a part of his legacy. If we tell them that there will be trouble tonight and not just for you.

I look at the floor, the truth is that I was too embarrassed to speak to look at them. I dry my hands and walk to Mackie, I look him in the eye, he seems that I am cut up, he feels my shame. "Okay, I will be out soon".

"Sir" Mackie pressed forward. "Is Winnie OK?"

"She has a broken nose and she has lost a couple of teeth." I mumble. , "I have given her some morphine for the pain".

Crest fallen and visibly disgusted Mackie squeezed his wife's hand,

"And Lucy" he says with a force in his voice and renewed strength that not even I have heard before.

"Lucy? What about her?" I ask indignantly.

Sir, is it true what they are saying outside?"

"What are they saying", I ask, but not wanting to know the answer.

"Rex's son ran to the plantation, she's dead. Barrington murdered Lucy" Mackie said, as much as he trying to control his grief, he couldn't and started to openly cry.

I looked at Mackie and walk less than an inch away from his face "Repeat that Mackie", I whisper, all the blood drained from my face.

"They are saying that Barrington murdered Lucy" Mrs Mack chimed in, holding her husband's shoulders, trying to keep him upright.

Tears ricochet off my face, I stand there in disbelief, the room started to move. I looked at this broken child in my house, she nods her head engulfed in confirming the truth.

The door swung open and before me was my wife, impatient and annoyed at the delay I was taking to give her son, my bastard medical attention.

"Are you coming anytime soon to tend to his wounds" she scolded. She looks at me and can see from my face that I know. " I'll …. I'll come back", she tried to retreat

"Is she dead Phyllis?" I bark at her. My tone is different, it steely and filled with hate.

"Who?" Phyllis asked knowing full well who I was referring to .

I walk sturdily towards my wife, with every intention to knock her head off her shoulders, Mackie steps in front of me and restrains me. "Do not test me Phyllis?" She takes a step back and realises that the rules of engagement have changed.

"Yes I believe there was an altercation and she shot him, and he responded" Phyllis added quickly, but refusing to match my gaze. The silence between us is deafening.

I push past Mackie and grabbed her like a common tramp and threw her to the chair. Her perfect bun roused to the top of her head toppled like a pack of cards. "If I find that you had a hand in THIS ......" he pointed violently at Winnie, "I .....will...... break...... your..... neck".

Phyllis was paralysed by her husband aggression towards her. She stood up, fixed her hair and asked "Will you tend to your son? He needs your help". She pleaded.

"He is no son of mine", I scream loud enough that the whole plantation house stood still. "Miss Mack, stay with the child, find her some clothes and feed her some soup in an hour. She may throw it up, but persist every hour until I say stop. Is that clear?"

"Yes Sir ...Doctor Barnett" Miss Mack was still in shock by my violent display to his wife. She thought to herself that Miss Phyllis was a rose with many thorns, pretty but vindictive, and she could strike out at anyone at any time. This was a side that she had never seen of the Doctor, but a side that she would not want to be on the receiving end of.

"Mackie", I shouted

Mackie was still starring at Miss Phyllis, bewildered by what he had just seen. "Mackie!" I scolded.

"Yes sir,"

"Get the car; we will go to the plantation now".

"What about Barrington?" Phyllis objected,

"That son of a bitch can bleed to death if what they say is true", with that I stormed out the room. She followed me trying to protest, as he got to the door I turned back and leant into her. I could not help it something snapped inside of me, I carefully but forcefully placed my right hand around her throat "If I hear that you have spoken to her, upset her or harm a hair on her head I.....will....... punish you, do you understand me?".

Phyllis flushed scarlet, and nodded her head immediately. Miss Mack could not stop starring. Once Miss Phyllis left the room, Miss Mack jumped in the air, and clapped her hands "Thank you Jesus, he has a spine!".

As Mackie and I approached the veranda, there were over 60 workers and members of the community standing at the front of the main house.

"What did the young master do to Miss Lucy Sir?" Rex asked visibly upset and angry. Rex and Vincent had grown up on the plantations; Rex was Vincent's best man at his wedding and was still very close to Lucy and Winnie. Such was his commitment to his friend's memory that he and his other field workers would often go to Miss Lucy's plantation after church and tend to any matter that was outstanding. Miss Lucy would always cook up a storm.

"Rex, I don't know for sure, I have just been told that there is a possibility that she has been killed. I don't know the details but I am very sorry for your loss if this is the case".

"Sorry for OUR loss" somebody else chimed in" I could not identify who.

"Man shove it up your backside, this is just wicked. Wicked I say. They won't arrest him, why? He and his murderous, rapist, drunken son is above the law. We don't matter. We are not white enough to matter". The man shouted angrily. Many b=voices agreed with him.

"What about Winnie's loss?," Rex shouted. "It's bad enough that Vincent is dead, and the child's mother is gone, so what, you decided your son to finish Lucy off as well?"

"There is not a day that goes that I do not regret what happened to Vincent. Today..... I don't know what today is about. I'm sorry; it's been an upsetting day for us all, I am sure that you understand I need to get to the bottom of things."

Mackie pulled up to the house and the motor was running. Doctor Barnet slowly walked through his angry workers and got in.

"You know where Mackie, and quickly", he said, his voice shaking.

Mackie drove like a mad man, Lucy and Vincent had been like family to his family. In the big storm in 19xx, most of the village had sheltered in the big house. No-one, and I mean no one was left to weather that storm alone. It had taken Mackie's family nearly three months to get back on their feet and rebuild their homes. It was not a problem. Lucy and Vincent had welcomed them, fed everyone and made sure all the children had clothes and shoes. They were good people, god fearing, kind hearted and blessed. They had not deserved what had happened to them. None of them.

"You're quiet" I say to Mackie

"There is nothing for me to sing about if what they say is true. Lucy was.... is ....she is a good woman. I am praying that Winnie got it wrong and Barrington just wounded her". Mackie whispered.

As they drove up the driveway, Mackie's fears were indeed confirmed, Rene, Lucy's sister from childhood and her mother was being consoled by her sister Mavis. Everyone was crying. It was dusk, the moon was bright and shone brightly in the sky, and it seemed eclipsed around a million shiny stars. Through the cane fields shadows of mourners emerged, head bowed walking towards the plantation. I recognised some of the figures of the shadow people soberly walking. Many of them worked for him. They were good people and had lost a great friend and pillar of the community.

The realisation of what had occurred hit him.

"Oh Mackie, my heart is heavy" reluctantly I drag myself out of the car. Walking towards the veranda, I felt the weight of the world on my shoulders. Not only was I ashamed to the core and deeply sorry for Rene's loss. I feel somehow responsible.

He glimpsed Rene and quickly looked at the floor. He could deal with anyone tonight, but not her. She was my love, she regained my faith in women, and I loved her with all my heart, how can I reach her and tell her that I am sorry.

She watches me get out of the car. Her big beautiful eyes were swelled deep with water. If I could just hold her and tell her that it's all going to be ok. This time, he could not, he dare not. I am going to have to face her sometime, it might as well be now.

She jumps off her chair and is walking briskly towards me I know she is going to slap me.

S-L-A-P – I just need to stand there. Of course she blames me, they all do. As far as they are all concerned my family have ruined Winnies.

"Why Barry Whhhhhhhyyyyyyyyyyyyyyyy!!!, she wailed "Look at what you have done. You must be very proud.

S-L-A-P,

S-L-A-P, "Where is she, with that witch, where is she?"

S-L-A-P. I stand there motionless. Giant tears roll down my face like two crooked streams, leaving streak marks where the orange dust had settled.

"Rene", I try to reason with her,

Where is my niece she screamed?" she grabbed his lapels and shook him. I just stand there. I cannot provide words of comfort.

"Please Rene" I gently unhook her fingers from my lapels. I look deep into her eyes, I whisper "I am so very sorry for your loss", I pull her close and she collapses in my arms. "Oh my darling, I am so very sorry. Believe me, I did not know he had found out. I would have killed him myself if I had to. Darling, believe me.".

Mavis prized Rene off me, I gave her a look that said, "thank you"

The house was how I remembered it. That smell, oh ….. it took me back to happier times, Vincent, me, Rene and Lucy. That smell hitting all the right sensations, it was divine, something sweet and sugary. That's right coconuts. I strolled slowly through the hallway, that's when I see her, it's her feet sticking out over a white sheet that someone had covered her with.

Intoxicated by the moment, I am starting to feel like I am losing control. My body temperature has soared. This is not happening I try to convince myself. I squeeze my eyes shut, trying to deny the situation in front of me. It's no use, I open my eyes and Lucy is still there.

Gently I walk towards my friend, and I slowly kneel by her. I hold her hand and mutter a prayer. I pull back the sheet, knowing it's going to be bad.

"I just cannot believe it", I say out loud. I am bewildered by the trail of destruction Barrington had created again. More tears make my crooked stream, oh my, there are six bullets, holes here. Two in her head and four in the body.

My body starts to shake, I cannot contain this wave within me. I weep openly on my friends corpse, repeating the words "I am so sorry", "Please forgive me I am sorry".

The bustling room is now silent. I feel very aware that there is no movement around me. All eyes are on me. I attempt to gain my composure as I know that I am very vulnerable in this situation. Emotions are running high.

Rene stood at the door, Her eyes were venomous, I have never seen her like this before. "Sorry does not undo all of this though does it?" she spat the words out at me.

My inner spirit tells me that I need to leave. I stand up abruptly to me met by a right hook to the nose. I am momentarily stunned. I look at my assailant, its Rene. I shrink back momentarily, she punched me square in the face.   I look at Rene, my love, she does not mean to hurt me, her heart has been ripped out of her chest, this is her grief. I did not move, she lunges towards me. I will not defend myself, I just stand there numb, she claws at my face wild with mania both of her hands in the claw like clasp. She dragged every nail she had in my face. I will not move, I cannot move. I am paralysed, this is not happening to me.

95

Mackie pulled Rene off me with such force she fell into the wall. He pushed me hard to get out of myself, I look at him, not realising that my face is bleeding. Both of us swiftly retreat through the side door.

"You Ok Doc?", Mackie asked with genuine concern as he jumps in the car and drives off at pace.

"Stop at the undertaker's office on the way home?"

Mackie nods at me. I look out the window. My heart broken, feeling the weight of my grief I look out the window. Trying without success to contain his own emotions, I notice Mackie sporadically wiping the tears from his eyes.

"You seemed very familiar with the house?" Mackie enquired, and breaking the solitude of my grief.

I was breathing deeply while wiping the blood from my face and trying to regulate my heartbeat, looking into nothingness out of the window. "I used to go there after my rounds, back in the good days, after the hurricane, there were many of my patients here, especially the injured ones. Vincent and Lucy made me very welcome; we used to eat bun and cheese in the kitchen, with hot freshly made chocolate tea."

Mackie smiled "Boy Miss Lucy could bake and make the sweetest tea",

The crooked streams began to run deep. "This is not the life I wanted for me or my son. This is not how people live. This is not how civilised people behave".

"Amen to that" Mackie said. After a long pause "We ... Miss Mack and I will be moving on soon"

"Because of this?"

"Yes sir" Mackie was aggrieved that he could ask. The

irritation rang out of his tone.

"We may not have much but we have pride, loyalty, and love, as much as I love Barrington I am not proud of who is and what he represents. I cannot watch him treat my friends and family like they are nothing. Like we mean nothing. Vincent is dead because your son took something sacred from his child" Mackie was looking at me dead in the eye.

"Mackie, please believe me when I tell you that I need you"

"Sir I cannot control Barrington and I ..."

"Not for Barrington, for that little girl, she is going to need protecting in that house. Please if not for me, for Lucy and Vincent".

Mackie screeched the car to a halt, and stared at his employer. The silence was deafening,

"For Lucy and Vincent, If your son crosses the line with me I will bust his back wide open, so help me god. If that means that my actions will cause problems between you and I so be it. I will not end up like Vincent, Sir. One of us will die and on Vincent's and Lucy's memory ...... It will not be me"

"I understand" I say quietly.

"I am grateful that you do sir, as this right here" he points to his puffed up chest "is no joke business."

Mackie drove to the undertakers and waited what seemed like an eternity. The arrangements were made and I was physically tired, emotionally tired and battered I dragged my body back to the car. Rene really did rip my face to pieces, my wounds were still weeping.

"Mackie", .

"Yes Sir"

"Take me to the nearest rum bar"

"That is not a good idea ...... There will be many friends of Lucy and Vincent out tonight doing the same thing, drowning their sorrows and dealing with their loss. I cannot guarantee your safety.

I look at Mackie for a while, my eyes filled with tears and he whispered reluctantly "home *then"*.

■■■

Phyllis was waiting for me on the veranda when I returned home. She had changed and was in her white satin night dress and matching dressing gown, her hair tucked behind her ears flowing down past her shoulders, she was a vision of beauty even now.

"Will you be alright Sir", Mackie asked looking towards the veranda.

"I will, thank you for your concern". With that I reluctantly opened the car door and made my way to the house.

"Where have you been?" Phyllis scolded me. *I cannot deal with this wretched woman. Just keep walking Barry, he ordered himself.*

Phyllis was not one for rejection on any level. I could see that she was agitated and saw through the corner of my eye that she followed me through the door. She grabbed my arm and spun me around with such force I nearly lost my balance.

"I said where were you?" she screamed at the top of her voice, a few members of the kitchen staff popped their head through the door.

"Do not touch me". I yelled back and without thinking I pushed her of me. I just could not bear her touching me. She looked startled. To avoid a confrontation I walked up the stairs. Mindful of my wife's presence following me I was desperate for a bath and glass of brandy.

One inside my bedroom I started to remove my jacket. *I will be sure to have these clothes burned. I do not want anything to remind me of this day.*

"Barrington", her tone had softened, realising that she would get nowhere speaking to me in that previous fashion. "Your son needs medical attention, the district nurse and I have done what we can, but I am not a doctor", she pleaded.

Barrington stared blankly at his wife "Please Barrington" she held her head to the floor, "He's hurt and he needs you. He needs his father"

"Then maybe you should send him a telegram", I snarled. *How dare she try and use 'he needs his father line on me'. It such bad taste.*

"You have raised him as your own son Barrington", Phyllis cried.

"Well darling' that sure as hell does not make him mine does it!"

"He needs you, I know he's a little out of... out of control, but he needs you.... Please", she could not contain her emotions; she sat down and started to cry. This was momentous for Phyllis, as she never showed emotion.

"Stop that sniveling, he is injured because of his own blinded aggression and stupidities, I only wish ...."

"What?" Phyllis snapped, "What?", she screamed.

"That, it was him in the mortuary and not Lucy, that poor woman has endured enough torment at the hands of this family". At the hands of him" I yell. In need of long awaited drink I walk across the room to pour myself a brandy at the bar. When I turn around, I am rooted to the spot; my wife is on her knees.

 "Ok, you want me to beg. I am begging, please help him". Phyllis read the look of contempt and disgust on my face.

"Get up", I ay quietly. I strode towards the door, doctors case in hand. The quicker I tend to his wounds, the quicker I can get to my bed and sleep. Walking towards the East wing, of his house to where Barrington Junior resides, I saw Jeanette, his chamber maid. Fix me a hot bath as soon as possible".

"Yes Dr Barnet Sir".

The thought of offering that animal medical attention repulses me. 'I despise him; his mean and violent rages', he muttered under his breath. Phyllis pushed past me and opened the door. Barrington lay on the bed, he was pale and his skin was visibly clammy. The district nurse sat next to him.

"How long has he been like this?" I asked

"An hour maybe two at most", the nurse whispered, he could barely hear her.

I stand over Barrington and see the young broken frightened child a few doors away. Then I flashback to Lucy's corpse. I squeeze my eyes shut. Within a few seconds of seeing him on the bed, helpless, frightened and drained of life I went into professional mode and washed my hands in the bowl of fresh water by the bed and immediately set about checking Barrington's wounds. The remaining and offending bullet was lodged deep in his abdomen.

A page turns in my head, something sweeps over me. I cannot describe it. I step away from the bed slowly observing for the first time the man whom I had raised from birth, wondering who are you? Why has evil penetrated your soul?

"I knew it", Phyllis shrieked, "He dying isn't he?"

I slowly focus on my wife, for a split second I actually felt sorry for her "It is unfortunate for me that I have to tell you that the injuries that he has sustained are not lethal. This bullet did not hit the large vessel in the abdomen that is the aorta, so he will be fine. We just have to remove it. I was stood here wondering what my options were."

It took a few seconds for the news to digest and for

Phyllis to realise that her son would survive.

"Muuuuuummmmmm", Barrington groaned.

"Yes my darling, I am here"

"It hurts mumm please get him to help me", he said looking at his father. "Daaaaaaaddddd", his breathing was laboured and slow "I …..am……. sorry".

"It's not me you should be apologising to, how about your daughter or Lucy", I screamed.

Barrington was startled by my unpredictability.. "Pllllleeeesssease dad, I can explain"

"Barrington, I have just come from the plantation house, you shot that old woman six times. What exactly are you going to explain?".

Phyllis was visibly taken aback by her husband's revelation.

"She shot after me.... I just wanted my daughter.... I did not mean to ...... Then she started saying that .....And I lost my temper, I couldn't help it"

"What did she say?" Phyllis asked.

"She said……. she said that you were a whore" looking at his mother " and that I am a bastard, just like Edwina". Barrington looked hurt and helpless. .

Phyllis and I exchanged looks.

 "What?" Barrington asked "What was that look?"

I ignore the question and proceed to my bag which was situated adjacent to the bed, on the bedroom table.

"Nothing darling" Phyllis tried to sound convincing.

"Liar" Barrington groaned "I know when you are lying"

"We are just worried about your injuries that's all"

"Ahhhh found you" I had retrieved my scalpel and long prongs. He turned around and Barrington looked visibly scarred. "This is going to hurt so I am going to call a few men to hold you down."

I walked out the door, and down the stairs. I opened the front door, there was a few guys still hanging around not knowing where to go.

I need two strong men to hold sown the good master while I take out his bullets. After today's events I promise he will suffer like the son of a bitch deserves to"

Five men immediately jumped up, I allow the first three in my home. I smile as I walk up the stairs.

"Mum, was she telling the truth?" he whined.

"Of course not darling" Phyllis smiled. "Lucy was an old bitter twisted woman and at that moment I am sure she would have said anything to cause trouble". Barrington nodded and smiled at his mother. She always knew how to make him feel better.

Phyllis felt the hairs on her neck stand on edge, she turned around and I was glaring at her. She could tell by his face that he heard her pathetic excuse. I strode over with hast, Mt three new pals hands behind him.

"Hold him down, tight" I instruct them

"What's going on Barrington?" Phyllis tried to hide the panic in her voice

"I am going to remove the bullet, go and get the lamp so that I have more light" With that I rewashed my hands and started the process of sterilizing the equipment. As I head towards my patient he looks at me uneasy. I raise his night shirt and retrieved the scalpel, and smile at him.

"Wait aren't you not going to put him to sleep first?" Phyllis pleaded.

"Hold him tight" I shout at my off duty field hands. Barrington look petrified.

"Mum .... Dad no please give me something"

"Tell me Barrington, what did you give Lucy before you shot her six times, or your daughter before you broke her nose and rearranged her face. Hmmmm, Hmmmm? *I am not sure what has come over me, but I cannot stop myself. I lean into my son and grab both his ears and pull his head towards me.*

Arrhhhhh "Dad, I'm sorry .... Please I am begging you give me something". He cries.

I picked up his tools and expertly opened the wound to the bullet with the scalpel. Barrington screamed so loud the whole house heard him.

"Barrington please gives him some gas I will run and fetch it" Phyllis pleaded.

"If you move, I will leave this bullet in him and will stand by as I watch his wound being infected with the hope that he will die."

"Daaaaad .." Barrington looked shocked and hurt "Please I'm your son"

I looked him square in the eye "Well Barrington, here's the kicker boy, you have my name but you don't have my blood. You murdered Lucy for telling the truth." Barrington's eyes *grew wide with surprise.*

"Hold him down hard" I yell, my newly acquired friends smiled at me whilst obeying my instruction. Barrington tried to wriggle free it was no good. I shoved my 9 inch surgical prongs deep into his abdomen and retrieved the lodged bullet. One field hand looked like he was going to vomit,

"Take deep breaths my boy the feeling soon passes". I tell him kindly. As instructed he negotiates the air into his nostrils slowly, still gripping Barrington like his life depended on it. His chilling screams brought the plantation house to a standstill. Unsure of the horrors that were taking place, all maids in service held their breaths.

"There, you will live to destroy another life", I said as he stitched up his wound. He had passed out from the pain. Once finished, he rinsed his hand and walked out.

Once the field hands had released him, they left Phyllis tried to console her son, as he came round from his wide awake surgery..

"Let me go" Barrington said, as he was still trying to regulate his breathing. "Lucy was right, you are a whore" she spat the words out to his mother.

Crushed by her son's comments Phyllis tried to explain, "Get out now". He spat the words out; he had a look in his eyes that he did not recognise, it was hatred.

Desperate for some rest I locked my bedroom door behind me. My emotions still raw, I need to grieve in my own space in private. I take my time undressing myself, not by design, the life within my limbs diminish by each waking second. I throw my blood soaked clothes on the floor. I look at them and immediately wipe a tear from my eye. I cautiously settle myself in the hot bath that Jeanette had prepared.

Arrrrrrrhhhhhhhh, just how I like it, I thought. I look in the water and the atrocity of today's crimes disintegrate in my bath, turning my clear water a shade of pink. Repulsed by the memory I take the wash cloth and brush, soap them both up and scrub every inch of my body. Within minutes I am finished. I did not entertain my usual routine of having a soak and getting the hot water topped up. I wanted to leave that bath water as quickly as I got myself clean. I step out naked, towel free, another first, I walk over to my bureau and mini bar and pour myself a large glass of brandy.

Glass in hand, Pajamas bottoms on, I sit on my blue velvet chaise lounge chair. My mother had it especially made for me a decade ago. This was the closest thing to home I owned and I needed to be sat on it, right now. This chair was strategically placed under my patio window by my mother.

"Oh Barry what lovely sunsets you have here?" she drooled. My patio doors open, the moon was full and seemed closer than I had ever noticed before. The feeling of loneliness overwhelmed me. It was too much to bear. The one person on this whole island that loves me for me, whom I adore and love with my everything now hates me. I feel just as alone and scared as Winnie does downstairs. Oh how I wish that I was still under the guidance and protection of my parents. 'How I wish I was there now'. I tell myself out loud. I continue to observe the night yellow sun, I smile to myself. My face stings in the night air. I delicately touch my wounds and they are seeping a little. Too tired to tend to myself, with fatigue washing over me, I drift off into a deep sleep.

"Barrington! Barrington! Open this door now." Phyllis shrieked, she sounded different as if she was slurring her words.

-Bang-

-Bang-

"Barrington, open this door or I swear I will.... Just open the door"

Conscious that Edwina may be woken up by this madness I reluctantly open the door. She was clearly drunk.

"I was wondering when we were going to have a little chat about things", I say dryly. My limbs were screaming for rest, but with everything that I had I threw his ten foot hand crafted mahogany door open, "come in Mrs. Barnet, and join me in a brandy". I say sarcastically.

Phyllis stomped into the room, her silk nightdress clung to her firm and well-kept body. Her dressing gown tailing behind her as she moved across the room. She looked as if she had been crying. Her hair was slightly disheveled, her red eyes swollen and her cheeks flushed, I could not help myself. . "My my ....don't you look like you're in a state of despair darlin'".

"Shut your filthy mouth", she spits the words out to me. "How could you do that to your own child?"

"We have had this conversation before and I will not repeat it again" I try to slammed the door shut on this topic.

"He's a boy and you have destroyed him" Phyllis whined

"Correction my dear, he is a man with the temperament and the conscience of a wild boar. You know as well as I if he was a local man he would be swinging by his neck right now".

"He's just a little excitable that's all", she tried to defend him weakly.

"Wake up woman, YOU have created a monster, he is murderer and rapist and a god forsaken human being. People fear him, he is wretched, wicked and vile and he came from your loins. He is not my son"

"He is this way because he craves a father's love, your love"

"Do not try and shift the responsibility of his deviant behavior on me. He is the spurn of the devil, and has been that way from the moment that bastard was conceived ... He is his father's child. Admit it Phyllis".

Barrington's comments were very sobering and Phyllis could not contain her anger, her husband had hurt her son, so now she would hurt him.

"I opened my legs to his father because you were not m—a---n enough to do the job. I was so desperate for a real feeling that I would have slept with a field boy first than open myself up to you again. You are not a man, you're a limp fish". She glared at me with real venom. Her words caught me completely off guard, and I was annoyed that my facial expression betrayed me. This was weakness and she would go for my jugular now that she drew first blood. .

"Get out of my room you despicable whore", I snapped. "Lucy had you sussed. Is that why you order her murder with that fool" I yell at her.

"I may be a whore at least mines have a use" with that she grabbed her vagina in a vulgar way. She walked to her husband and grabbed his penis. "This worthless piece of flesh has no use to woman or beast" She laughed at me. I stare at her, not knowing what to say. I felt humiliated all over again. "I am glad that you are not his real father, he would be spineless and weak just like his dad. She cleared her throat and nose, inhaled deeply to the back of her throat and spat all of her green and yellow phlegm into my face. It handed on my nose ad chin and ran down my face like gunk.

I blink, and blink and just stare at this pig of a human being. *Nooooooo she did not just do thaaaat I scream in my head.* The heat rose from my toes. By the time it got half way up my body I felt my body language and face change. I grab her dressing gown and wipe my face, not once taking my eyes of her. Like a rupturing volcano the rage within me for the last 26 years could not be contained. *How dare she defile and humiliate you this way.* His whole household would have heard her, as well as the fields hands as his windows were wide open. He grabbed both shoulders and threw her hard to the floor. She quickly tried to recover but was winded, she had never witnessed the sheer strength of me before. I kept the beast at bay, no more. Watching her trying to recover made me smile. I marched to the door and locked it. I felt my jaws clenching, my tired limbs had renewed strength. My eyes wide open and my back is straight, she saw me for the first time in my life and knew she was in trouble.

Phyllis ran to the door behind me "Open the door", she said weakly, the fear in her voice coming through.

I could not help myself, her time has come I raised my right fist and punched her hard in the face, she fell backwards into the chaise lounge chair and bounced to the floor, he lip was split and her face burning. "Oh God" she thought, I've pushed him to far"

"Barrington please, I did not", she screamed.

109

I grabbed her by the hair before she could finish her sentences and slapped her as hard as I could across her face. She cowered and curled her body up in a ball on the ground. "Nooooooo ... Please ....." he kicked her in the ribs. She felt something snap within her, her body reacted and threw her on her back.

Towering over his wife "Your nothing. Say it..... Say It" she lay curled up on the floor, gasping for breath. "Say it"

I bent down towards her, she crawled to the opposite corner of the room , I slowly followed her and grabbed her by her hair, then I slowly drag her to her feet, Phyllis looked at the floor, she was shaking, her lip was bleeding, the right side of her cheek was starting to swell, and her ribs were on fire. *She is going to p*ay for everything and I mean everything. I have lost everything *because of her* I took my index finger and lifted her chin so that she looked me into my eyes "Say it" I whisper.

"I am" –sob "nothing" she whispered.

I let her go and she fell to the floor on all fours. I poured myself a large brandy. I felt exhilarated, joyful, and happy to be alive. Who would have thought that beating her like this would make me feel so good about myself. Had I discovered this years ago she would have left off her own accord.   I smiled at my wife who was watching me with suspicion. "You know something Mrs Barnet; I have allowed you to rule this roost for too long. You are my wife, which means you are my property. I should have treated you as such long ago. Your whorish ways has caused me much embarrassment, and I took it like a gentleman, well no more" I down my glass of full brandy in two gulps and threw the heavy tumbler on the floor. The thick glass connecting the wooden floor made a heavy clunking sound, but the glass did not break. Phyllis jumped out of her skin. "I forgive you", I tell her .

"What" Phyllis whispered?

"I forgive you. For cheating on me, for bearing me a bastard child ....humiliating me .... for tonight", now I am smirking at her. Phyllis felt uneasy.

"Barrington I am sorry. I just want to go to bed, please let me out" she begged.

"Let you out......... No ,no no nono noooooooooo. Phyllis, you have neglected me for far too long", I walk straight up to her and took her by the hand. I pick up NY soiled bath towel that was draped over the metal bath, I moistened the corner with my dirty stale bath water and wiped the blood from her face.

"What are you doing?" she asked.

"Cleaning you up and getting you ready" I replied.

She looked at him confused. "It's ok I can do that when I get to my room" she said nervously.

"You are my wife so tonight you will lay with me. I desire it." I say it like I am ordering candy. I laugh then grab her hand and pushed it on his penis "Let's see if you can find a use for me again", I stare directly at my wife.

Her eyes sprang with tears, "Barrington, No please, I beg you"

"You – are m-y w-i-f-e, now get undressed".

She ran to the door, "Please Barrington". Phyllis screamed. I walked slowly to the door, I cannot believe how aroused I am. Taking the power back in this relationship is making me feel like a confident man again. I am the King!

"It's Ok Phyllis, darlin' look at me it's going to be alright". She momentarily relaxes. I hold her hand and looked at the bed. My arousal is solid and erect I push myself onto my wife, her back was by the door, she felt him, looks deep in my eyes and recognizes that I mean business; He was going to punish her. She had taken her rage too far. I lovingly kissed her on the lips, I wanted this moment to be pleasant, and she bit me. . She was bombarded with a slap to the face, and a punch to the stomach. She lost her breath and was doubled up in pain. I am going to teach her who the boss really is.. I picked her up and threw her on his extra-large queen size bed.

"Barrington Nooooo", she shrieked.

I grab the top of her nightdress and ripped it down the middle. "You will fuck me whore, I want the same fuck you gave his father whore".

She fought hard to no use, she kicked me in the stomach, but it did not perturb me. The adrenalin was racing around my body, I did not feel pain. Not now, not after Rene hates me, it's all her fault. . I ripped open the remainder of her nightdress. Phyllis desperately tried to rolled over, in one move I rolled her back. My erection was not hearing her, it was resistant to her pleas and cries.

"Please Barrington.... No .... Not like this"

Ignoring her I forcibly parted her legs, I open them so far that I heard her hips crack. She winced with pain and tried to push her legs up but my weight was too strong for her. *Who is weak now* In one move I have placed my body weight on her, she could not move and he was inside her.

"No Barrington ...... Noooooooooooooo. Please stop" Stop Nooooo. She screamed at the top of her lungs. She started to fight me.

"Enough" I slap her harder than before. She is silenced, she stops fighting, I grab both arms and forced them over her head. All of my upper body weight is on her arms. She is powerless and I love it. His thrusts were hard, deep and angry. I want to hurt her, I need to hurt her like she has hurt me. I was treating her *like she was nothing but a piece of meat to him.*

Hmmmm, thrust Hmmmm ,thrust Hmmmmm thrust he grunted.

With each grunt I made, she would yelp in pain. Begging me to stop. The more she cried and screamed the more toughened my erection became. She started to relax her legs, as the pain in resisting him was tearing her apart.

I grabbed her hair and pulled her neck to one side I licked her neck and smiled. The smell of my brandy soaked breath repulsed her. I didn't care. I kissed her she did not dare refuse me but she did not respond.

Her slow surrender aroused me more. I pulled her buttocks to the edge of my bed and splayed her legs apart and continued with my aggressive relentless attack from the floor. I no longer needed to hold her hands; instead I just held her hips, ensuring that he had her in the right position to drive himself deep into her.   It pleasured me to see her cry and in pain. I was not going to have mercy on her until I was done. .

As the time came for me to climax I withdrew my beast, climbed on top of his wife and ejaculated in her face, she squirmed and turned her head to the side. "Whore I did not give you permission to turn your head" He grabbed both cheeks and forced her mouth open and directed to remainder of my juice down her throat. To shake off the last of my ejaculation that was remaining, I slapped my penis in her face a couple of times. I look at her and smile, I climbed off her and immediately sit in my bath; I washed myself quickly and stepped out of the bath. Phyllis lay crumpled on his bed. She was silent; she just lay in the foetal position hugging herself.

"I have really enjoyed our chat tonight, Phyllis, maybe

you should retire to your own room, hmmmm?"

She nodded; she could not look at him. She slowly got up and winced with each movement, her ribs and stomach was sore, her head was pounding, her lip split and her left eye closing. As she tried to put weight on her feet her vagina and pelvic area ached. They were under attack and on fire.

Like a gentlemen I aided her off the bed and gave her her dressing gown, he picked up his wallet from his side table and opened it. She had put on her silk gown and walked silently to the door, which I open. As she walked through it I pressed a piece of paper in her hand, it was one Jamaican dollar. "Thank you for your services Mrs Barnet"

Multiple tears rolled down her cheeks, Phyllis just starred at her hand, I knew that she wanted to say something to him, but thought better of it. Head bowed, she limped out of his room.

"Night Darling" he half sung and spoke to her. He shut and locked the door behind him. As she walked to the North wing of her house, maids were scurrying away. They clearly had listened to her brutal rape. She did not look up she just needed to get to her room. As she opened her door, her chamber maid of twenty three years Donna was waiting for her. Her own face soaked in tears. She had her Mistress Phyllis Bath waiting for her, with piping hot water and Epsom salts in it, the room was filled with steam and Epsom aroma. Donna immediately helped her lady to the bath. She tried not to show her disgust at her Lady's bruises, but her face betrayed her. She slowly peeled off her night gown and saw the blood running down her inner thighs. She helped her Mistress sit down in the bath and slowly tried to wash away the evening. Miss Phyllis did not say a word to Donna, she just lay in her bath silently crying, clutching her one dollar note.

Chapter 6

Winnies awakening

It has been four days since I witnessed my father kill my grandmother and I am weak, emotionally, spiritually, physically and psychologically. The brain is a wonderful and complex organism. I consider at length how impressive mine is, as it deleted until now, all these horrific memories, which has enabled me to live a relatively normal life.

Staying here and strong for Winnie is my priority, although she is not speaking to me. I know that she can still hear and see me. It's heart breaking to watch my younger self so frightened and vulnerable? Something died within her that day. The spark from her spirit is gone. She is no longer innocent, just damaged. I lay next to her and kiss her head and tell her that she is beautiful. All she can do is cry silently and whimper.

Mr. and Mrs. Mack have lovingly protected this child. It breaks my heart that I have not remembered any of this. For the past four nights Mrs. Mack has slept on the lounge chair in the room. She has tended to Winnie's every need and has refused entry to her father and grandmother at the request of Dr Barnett.

It was late afternoon and Mrs. Mack had bought in chicken soup for Winnie's lunch. She set it up by the table. She looked at this beautiful little girl and pity washed over her. She was crestfallen to see Lucy's and Vincent's beautiful young granddaughter battered and bruised like this. Both of her eyes were puffy and swollen, he light skin illustrated the bruise in magnificent Technicolor, illuminating the black, blues, purples and pinks under both swollen eyes, her lips were both swollen, and where the skin had been split was dry and sore. Mrs. Mack rubbed Vaseline on it almost hourly to give this little soul some ease. Her nose was tender and her neck swollen. She did not know what happened to her but she had a very good idea.

"Baby Girl, today you are going to sit at the table and eat your lunch" Miss Mack said trying to sound cheerful and happy.

She delicately picked up Winnie, and placed her at her seat. Winnie's body automatically hunched over and leaned away from Mrs. Mack, it was her upright foetal position. Slowly she fed her, and for the first time Winnie allowed her to without resistance.

Winnie looked at me, "This is as good as Mima's", she said. She attempted a smile but remembered that her face and lip was sore.

I purposely said nothing. I just smiled as I did not want to alert Mrs. Mack to my presence.

"That's wonderful Winnie", Mrs Mack said smiling. Both Winnie and I looked at each other and we both smiled weakly.

"Can I get you something else sugar?, Mrs. Mack asked sweetly.

"Some cake please and if we have any some chocolate tea" Winnie whispered.

Mrs. Mack said "I won't be long" and ran out of the room.

Once she had left, I looked at Winnie. "Honey how are you? How does your face feel?"

"It still hurts" She looked at the floor. "Is he really my father Edwina?"

"Yes Winnie, he is".

"Then why did he kill my Mima?" she whinnied, fresh

tears sprang to her eyes and she whispered " Did I do something bad?"

No Winnie, Daddy is just a bad person who is always very angry. I got on my knees so we were both at eye level. "Listen to me Winnie you are going to have to be careful. I mean it. Do not speak unless spoken to. Always and I mean always be nice to him and never ever give him back chat". I look into her terrified tear soaked eyes.

"Edwina" she whispered "can I come and live with you I don't want to stay here. I 'll be a good girl promise".

My heart broke, "Aww honey I can't take you"

Tears streamed down her face. "Please….. Please ….."

I cup my hands around her cheeks, "Listen to me my sweet darling, you are at the beginning of your little life and I am at the end. I am going to join Mima very soon and ….

"Take me with you Edwina, Please take me with you as I miss Mima and want to see her"

I firmly hold her shoulders and look at my younger self in the eye. "You have to live the middle part of your life and the enjoy your life with people that love you. I am going to sit down by a clear blue river and talk to Mima in heaven and you can't come yet.

"Why not?" she pleaded

"It's not your time?"

"Why not, I want to be with Mima?"

It's not your time, you have to stay here. Mrs Mack and Mackie, they are nice aren't they?

Winnie nods.

117

They will look after you and Dr Barnett, he is a good man, he will take care of you. Ok?

Ok?

Winnie was silent for a long time. "Edwina, can you please do me a favour"?

"What is that"?

"Tell Mima that I miss her and that I love her", she whispers.

"I promise sweetness it will be my first conversation with her".

The door opened, both Winnie and Edwina were looking for Mrs. Mack, but knew by the sound of the shoes on the wooden floor that the footsteps were too heavy for Mrs Mack slight frame.

It was my father, he looked pale but well for a man who had been peppered by a shot gun. They shared the same light caramel complexion, and the same colour hazel eyes. His face was pretty rather than handsome and his dimples in his cheeks tippled every time he smiled or pulled a serious face. His straight hair made it hard to decipher if he had any black in him, but his nose and lips were the only features that were not European in nature. He wore a white short sleeve shirt and blue khaki trousers. His shoes black patent leather shinier than any shoes Winnie had ever seen.

"Hello Edwina", he said and walked towards the bed.

Winnie searched my face, she was frozen.

"It's ok Winnie", I said "Say hello Daddy"

"Edwina, can you not hear me"? He had strolled around the bed.

"Hello dad- dad-dy", Winnie Whispered.

Barrington sat at the edge of the bed, Winnie did not notice that he had a package in his hand.

"Daddy has bought you a present", he tells her and he put the gift next to him on the bed. He stretched out his hands to pull Winnie close and she screamed and jumped back. She split her lip again in the process and it started to bleed.

"It's ok, its ok I am not going to hurt you". Barrington was surprised and hurt by his daughter's reaction.

Winnie had thrown her back by the headboard and screamed at the top of her voice everything was throbbing, she could not take any more " Mrs. Mack, Mrs Mack". Every time Barrington tried to get close Winnie broke out in her petrified scream. It was blood curdling.

Mrs. Mack and Phyllis raced into the room.

Barrington stood up to attention. "I did not do anything to her mother I swear." Barrington said anxiously. "I swear" he stood back and held up his hands. He could see that his daughter was sweating and had urinated all over herself and on the bed.

"What are you doing here" Mrs. Mack scolded.

"She is my daughter?" Barrington shouted. "I came to give her a dress"

"For what?" Mrs. Mack screamed at Barrington "Is the dress your apology for killing her grandmother and breaking her nose?" she spat the words out. Once they had left her mouth she knew that there would be trouble.

Barrington walked towards Mrs. Mack and slapped her so hard across the face she fell to the floor. He straddled her and slowly undid his belt, Mrs. Mack eyes grew large with fright. She backed her way to the wall. "What are you going to do?"

"Teach you some manners" He lurched forward and his mother jumped in between the both of them.

Phyllis held her sons chest with all her might, but recognised the rage in his eyes. "Barrington, enough...... enough .... stop! You do not want any more trouble. P-l-e-a-s-e This is MACKIES WIFE!!!!!! Phyllis pleaded. He heard her, reluctantly he stopped and gave Mrs. Mack a blood curdling stare and stormed out of the room. Both Winnie and Mrs. Mack knew that from this moment onwards she was not safe. They both had unfinished business to take care of.

Mrs. Mack was breathing heavy by the wall, trembling at the prospect of her first ever beating or worse. Once Barrington was out of the room, Phyllis turned to Mrs. Mack and walked towards her slowly. She was an inch away from her face, "I will only save you once. If you conduct yourself in that way again to the young master I will take care of you all by myself". She turned and walked to the door painfully slow, as she approached the door, she turned around "Clean up that little runt as I can smell her piss from here".

Phyllis shut the door and Winnie let out a wail. "Edwina please take me home... take me to Mima " she screamed hysterically.

Mrs. Mack took Winnie and held her close. "It will be ok baby girl, I will not leave you. It will be ok?"

Hearing my grandmother's voice again makes the pit of my stomach churn. Memories of my Grandma Phyllis are filtering their way through to me and I feel nauseous. What kind of people are they? I already know the answer. My father's blood line is sinful, dishonorable, villainous and malevolent. No wonder I forgot this part of my life. I look at Winnie with dread. I know, I know what is coming and there is nothing I can do to stop this. I look at my younger self with despondency and despair. She too is staring at me, as if reading my thoughts she lays her head in Mrs. Mack shoulder and whispers to me "save me". Mrs. Mack quite naturally presumes she is speaking to her and smothers her own grief. She pulls Winnie away from her and smiles. "I promise I will baby girl On Mimas memory I will"

I feel my body fading, fatigue consumes me. I sit underneath the window and fall into a much needed deep sleep.

"Edwina wake up ….. Edwina is that you?" I feel small slight hands rock me. I slowly open my eyes and I am somehow on Winnies bed. Dawn is breaking, the air is fresh and I smell Ackee and Saltfish, and the smoky scent of the roast breadfruit being prepared for breakfast. I open my eyes, and my younger self is looking at me. She is different, I jump up.

"Winnie what's happened"? I ask

"Nothing has happened", she says curtly, she crinkles her lips. She is angry with me.

I look at her she is different "Why do you look so different?".

My younger self looks down at herself, "do I?"

I momentarily blink, her bruises have all gone, her hair is longer, freckles are on her nose, it cannot be she is ….. older. "Winnie how old are you?"

"Ten" she says hitting me hard with her words like a blunt instrument I stand up and look at her again distrustful of her own admission. Skeptically, I scan the room and notice that the room is completely different. First there is no Mrs. Mack, second the room is softer, more girlie. I have violet drapes and bedding to match. I remember this room now. I walk to my window and pull the drapes back, the plantation is coming to life. I can behind me, the enormity of my wealth is visible, my bedroom is huge. I have my own balcony as I look out I see a small table with two chairs. My dresser is white with a large mirror. In all four corners of the room there are large chandeliers for the candles. Opposite the bed towards the door is a small white bureau and chair where I complete my studies, as I swing round I see Winnie staring at me looking less than pleased.

"Where have you been?" she shouts. She is wearing a white blouse and a purple skirt, she is at school, she looks so cute.

"Winnie, I don't know, the last thing I remember I went to sleep, and now your ten? Ten? I don't understand myself, how have you been?"

"you know how I have been as I am you?" Winnie glares at me.

"Winnie I know that you are mad, but I just can't explain it as I don't know myself. I am dying so I do not know how much time I have" I plead

"You should be dead. Your no use to me here are you. I mean, I thought that you would stay with me, but your just like the rest".

"What does that mean"

She looked at me sadly, "You'll just leave me and I will be here all alone….. with them."

"Darling I am so sorry, I am not in control of anything anymore. "Time has just fast forwarded and I am now here"

"Soooo you're not with ….. Mima" she smirks at me. Its unnerving. I am very cynical and spiteful

"Not yet darling" I pause momentarily, this is quite quantum leap and she is still with me, trusting me.

I look at my miniature self, "How have you been"?

Winnie shrugs her shoulders and walks to her queen size four poster bed. She lies on her resting place and I accompany her. I lay on the next pillow and we face each other like lovers. I feel on tenterhooks, anxious to hear her news, but already feeling the dread sweeping over me, preparing myself for whatever comes next.

123

"You know how I am, you are me, and I am in hell" she tells me.

"No Noooo Nooooooo" my body starts betraying me. I feel myself drifting. Winnie sits up, she looks horrified that I am leaving again. I am crying, *noooooooooooooo not now she needs. I awake to my family all looking at me and Alice wiping my tears. When will this torture end. I want it to end and now.*

-Click, Click, Click -

Chapter 7

Phoebe's surprise

January 13th 2005 4.39pm

"You ok dad?" I bounced into mum's room with the coffee, the break had regenerated my spirit in a small way, and I felt upbeat, even though I was already in mourning.

"I am doing ok, and mum has not changed so I suppose we are alright". With that he smiled.

"You seem different Dad?" I asked eyeing up my father.

"Phoebe, I have been different for a while now, but you would have not noticed me or that fact" Dad said looking at mum.

"What's that supposed to mean" I snapped. *All he ever wants with me is some sort of conflict. What more does he want? I bought him coffee, that is a real big step for me. What does he want from me?*

"Exactly what I said", Harold exhaled. "You are so angry with everyone that even the simplest pleasures pass you by"

"Why is that? Eh …. You made me who I am dad and you know it" I scowled at him.

Harold stood up, he was going to walk away, and then recognised the "typical" look in his daughters face. He slowly sat down and held his wife's hand. Smiling at something that he chose not to share with me, he looked at me and his expression and emotion changed.

"When you were born, I was the first set of eyes that you saw. Even though it was not PC for men to be with their wives when they gave birth, I insisted on being in the delivery room to the Matrons complete and utter dissatisfaction. When you came out you was this screaming banshee, defiant even angry. You were my activist, did you know that is what I called you for a day, but your mother was having none of it"

"Yes dad", *he had told me this stupid story a million times, and I am still not interested* I didn't mean to sound exasperated but I did.

"Yes, I called you my activist Annie PP, that was short for Punchy Protester. As I held you, you doubled both fists and punched the air. You may not believe me, but I loved you the moment our eyes met and I promised you then that I would protect you from all harm. It was my job as a father to ensure that you always felt safe. Harold had a proud grin on his face.

"But you didn't did you?" I snarled

"I ensured that my children wanted for nothing" Harold looked hurt by the suggestion.

"Love is not buying me dresses, its listening to me. Like you said dad it was about keeping me safe. I did not feel safe around you; we didn't know who was coming home, what mood you are in, and which one of us would receive a slap, punch or kick. I remember dad, I remember. I remember when your broke Jon's arm when he was 8.

"That was an accident you stupid malicious child" Dad was indignant.

"I remember when you slapped Maddie so hard her nose bled for three hours, she was ten. I remember you ripping my nose ring out of my nose and using my head like a ball with the radiator. I remember you, and who you are and what you did to us. Do you wonder why I hate men? Why I am angry all the time? Why I can't be with a man more than a few weeks as I have real intimacy issues, why Jonathan is with a man? And yes it's to spite you. Why Maddie is an alcoholic? Do you not wonder?

"It is not all down to me. You have to take responsibility for the life that you lead." Dad snapped. "I cannot be held responsible for all your wrong turns. You are all adults, and yes we make mistakes but we cannot be responsible to anyone else apart from ourselves."

"Have you taken responsibility for the lives that you have impacted upon" I barked.

"Don't you have any happy memories?" he asked with his tear soaked eyes.

"Yeah I do but I just don't think there enough happy ones, you know" Phoebe said.

"I hear you" dad said crying. "I hear you"

There was a knock at the door, which forced them back to the present moment.

They both straightened up in their chair. "Come in" Harold said.

Completely taken aback, Harold could not believe his eyes. "Thank you Jesus" he said

Is it really you? The last time I saw Maddie was six years ago and she looked terrible then. This woman looked ….. well she looked like my sister, sober, clean and well presented.

"Mad –dieeeeee" I squealed, "Look at you, you look great"

Sheepish and nervous Maddie stepped into the room. "Hi Dad, where is Jonathan?" Maddie always called her brother by his full name. She looked around the room.

She did not acknowledge her sister at all.

"He's with Jack, he will be back soon". Harold got up and hugged his daughter. He kissed her hair and whispered "Welcome h-o-m-e honey, welcome home. You look fantastic. Are you…. Well?" He peered deep in her eyes for the answer. Maddie matched his gaze and nodded with deep affection for our dad.

Phoebe was hit with a pang of jealousy that she could not explain. Her father had not embraced her like that ….. ever.

"Where have you been? We've been trying to get hold of you for days" I enquired.

"Dad I have been in rehab for the last 90 days, and I only received my personal possessions back this morning. I rushed over here, thinking….. I was too late", Maddie whispered.;

"Why didn't you call" Phoebe snapped

"Well that did not take long?" Maddie looked directly at her sister

"What?"

"For the bitch in you to come out" Maddie's words sliced through me like a samurai sword.

"I just meant .. " Phoebe tried to explain

"I know exactly what you meant. I did not call because I knew that you all had to see me to believe that I AM sober, which I have been for over 163 days now. I feel great, energised scared and vulnerable, but I am here." Looking at her mother in the bed Maddie started to tear up, "Dad how long have we got"

"Not sure but it's not long" I said, still no acknowledgement, she was just stayed transfixed on mum.

Maddie pulled up a chair, sat next to her dad and held his hand, "Oh dad for the record, I did not drink because of you, I drink because I was unable to deal with the heartbreak of….. well I am an alcoholic and have an addiction. You were not my trigger, never have been" With that statement Maddie threw Phoebe a filthy look.

Suddenly feeling hot, I stood up, it's like that is it sister dear! "I'm going for some fresh air guys, give you two some space."

"You do that my love", Maddie said sarcastically and pulled her chair closer and put her arms around her father's shoulders.

"Oh Maddie" Dad rested his head in her shoulder "I am so glad that your back, I need you, I need my girl I can't shoulder this alone."

Stomping down the corridor I could not reconcile my emotions. Just what did dad mean " I can't shoulder this alone". He's not alone, granted he is not my biggest fan but I'm here aren't I? I'm even talking to him. I even bought him a coffee. How typical is this? Betty Ford walks in and all is right with the world. I continue to stomp towards the stairs and before I knew it I was outside. I decided to sit in the grassy verge on the bench. I just needed air. I exhale slowly and deliberately *as if I am* practicing yoga. My thoughts are all over the place. I need to center myself and gather my thoughts, Life was easier when Maddie was drunk. Sad but true. The truth is when Maddie is sober she is on her game and brilliant. Me on the other hand am not brilliant. She is beautiful, funny and very intelligent. Me not so cute, well maybe a little, not funny and mildly intelligent. It's all an act, one that I do so well and Maddie knows it. She was always her authentic self, even when she was drunk she was real. Me ….. I am just the fake.

I search my bag for my packet of emergency cigarettes. I just need some nicotine. I get it, it's not PC now that I am at a hospice, but I need something to get me through the night. I light my cigarette and was about to suck this cancer stick dry when I hear Jack and Jon. I look up and across the small grass verge was the car park. They could not see me as there were rose bushes separating the verge from the car park.

"What have you been telling him?" Jack yells .

"N-o-t-h-i-n-g Love I promise" Jon says desperately trying to appease his irate lover.

Then why did he lay into me, threaten me? Jack screamed inching closer to my brother in a manner that bothers me.

"What?", Jon was stunned,

Jon …. Look, darling I promise I have not said a word.

Said a word about what? What is going on and why is Jon acting so… so….. passive.

Jack pushed my brother violently on his car, and clasped his jaws with one hand so tightly that Jon lips were pushed out he was unable to move them. Jack was saying something to Jon in his ear, his face changed it was menacing. I could not hear, but Jon …… he looked terrified.

What the hell was happening? I started to feel sick. No, not Jonathan, he was so ……. So…….nice. I start to think back at all the snidely remarks he has made over the years. I just put it down to his warped sense of humor. My brother was different around him, I thought it was just nerves, you know being with his family and his gay lover. Then it hit me. My brother was on edge, not because of my family but his nasty abusive boyfriend.

Jack pulled Jon off the car and threw him to the floor like he was dirt, he jumped in the car and left my brother on the floor.

Once Jack was firmly out of site, I ran through the rose bush, scraped my arms and back even though I had a thick polo neck on, but I did not care. "Jon … Jon are you ok?" I started helping my brother up. He could sense my anger and concern.

Smiling through his pained expression, "Yeah I'm fine". He swiftly wiped a tear from his eye and tried to regain composure.

Jonathan looked devastated. I was not sure whether he was upset that I had witnessed his attack or by the fact that he had just been attacked in a freaking car park. "Phoebe please don't say a word, it was just a petty argument"

"Jon it looked like a domestic and not the first one that you've had", I yell accusingly.

"Phoebe", Jon tried to keep his voice low to placate me "this is just a dispute between two people that love one another, he loves me ……. you know that; this is just stressful for him".

"Love – What is stressful for him", I grabbed my brother broad shoulders and tried to shake them with no luck "For him", I repeated myself, sounding incredulous. "He is not the one whose mother is dying of cancer how this can be difficult for him I don't know. Mum couldn't even stand him".

"Really? He's a bit jealous and possessive and likes to be in control and for once in our relationship he's not as I have to be here".

Jon you are with your mother where else would you be?"

"He just needs reassurance", Jon protested.

"Reassurance of what, will my foot planted firmly in his arse do it? He needs a right hook Hun, maybe two." I try to sound calm and compassionate but it's not working. "How long Jon?" I was not in the mood for him to fob me off.

"What?"

"What? Do not play with me, How long has Jack been knocking you around?

Jon looked around the car park to scan who was in ear shot. Phoebe you are such a comedian?" and tried to laugh off my suggestion.

"Listen to me, I saw what I saw. You can try and blow me off, but I saw Jack hit you" I hiss furious that my brother who could most probably take on most Fijian rugby players is getting beaten and battered by his Spike Milligan look alike boyfriend. If Jon wanted he could snap his spine like a fish bone.

Jon looked at me "Don't look at me like this?"

"Like what", I snapped

"Like that, Like that", he cried silently and look away far away into the sky. "Like I am weak and a pathetic victim. Like I am useless".

I ran to my brother and hugged him, he sobbed for what seemed like an eternity and in between hiccups, he mumble "I'm sorry"

"For what", I said,

"For being weak, for allowing him to do this to me. I deserve this", he mumbled with his head down.

I grabbed Jonathan's face, "No John, you don't and deep down you know that".

Islington High Street has always been Phoebe's most favorite place in the world. Even when the grey clouds loomed over it, these streets glistened with a scintillated haze. It must have been the affluence of the area, the large shops, the idiosyncratic alley ways, the kitch boutique and restaurants falling out of the narrow lanes onto intrigued tourists, and local residents anaesthetised to the historic marvelous surroundings foraging through the crowds, trying to get on with their day to day lives. Islington did not smell of London, on any sunny day you could have been in Paris or Milan. It's a part of London to be celebrated with its diverse richness, admired for its flagrant opulence and humbled by the legions of thespians, dancers and actors roaming the street, making their way to the world famous saddlers wells and beyond. It's a place where Phoebe felt safe, wanted and at home.

"I love this high street", I tell Jon gripping his arm to show my support.

"Yeah" Jon muttered dejectedly with his head bowed.

"You OK?" I asked *Oh God please be ok, I need you to be ok. What has that Bastard done to you?*

"Look Phoebe, I know what you're trying to do. I am not discussing it. And I am especially not discussing it with you?"

"What is that supposed to mean" I snap yanking his arm back and physically stopping my macho man brother. I stare at my brother full of rage. "Well?" I yell, passersby momentarily break their routine and stare at us.

"No offence, you are a nightmare. You can't hold water if you tried, and this..... well ......it's a private matter".

I stare at my brother incredulously. "First of all I can hold water very well. Secondly, and more importantly when your arsewipe of a partner physically attacks you in a public car park for all to see, that rubbish is not private, it's very public. For god sake I am y-o-u-r s-i-s-t-e-r!"

"It's none of your business we just need time to work it out"

"Jon, I saw what I saw, so you can act like the battered wife who pretends that her husband is not battering her, but we" I point to Jon and I, "know different"

"Are you for real, battered wife, is that the best you can do?

"What?" I stare at my brother. "Are you seriously getting upset over the fact I have called you a battered wife, like really Jon. I saw Jack hit you and you did nothing. I saw him …… and you ….. did …… nothing".

We came to a natural stop at the pedestrian crossing. I looked at my brother who is completely transfixed on my favorite eatery on the High Street, Browns. He is deep in thought somewhere far away. I too concentrate in his gaze, and for the first time since were out can feel the cold air on my nose, which is stinging from the cold weather. The mahogany furnishing and fancy Victorian esq chandeliers are inviting.

Let's get a coffee, Jon sighs.

"Ok Sounds great".

I am so fatigued from the emotion of it all. It has just been too much. First with Dad, then Maddie and now this. What else? I sit twiddling my thumbs. I am nervously observing my brother at the counter. My mind is racing, there are so many questions that I need answers to.

When did the abuse start? How often does this happen? Why is he still in this relationship? Who else knows? I know that I am going to have to tread carefully.

My mind races bask to Beeches Primary School, when we were kids Jonathan always looked out for me. I was proud that he was my brother. He always protected me. At the age of eight when Adrianna FitzJohn punched me in the tummy and pushed my face in the muddy puddle; it was Jon who ran across the playground and kicked her as hard as he could in the arm and dragged her off me.

When my first love at thirteen dumped me for my so called mate and broke my heart, it was Jon that waited for him at the bike sheds and gave him a whopping black eye. Even as a teenager boys thought twice before approaching me as I was always Big Jon's little sis. What happened to that guy? When did he go from being this mammoth tough guy to such a sniveling wimp? It's not right, none of this is right. I start to feel my skin tingle, my mind as racing. I could feel that I couldn't control myself. Try and be sympathetic, say nothing. Gold your tongue sister dear. How dare he treat my brother that way? Tears swell in my eyes. I am going to make him pay for this. The question is how?

For the first time in a long while I see my brother. I mean visibly and emotionally see and read him. He is tired, I cannot decipher whether this is due to mum dying or whether he is brow beaten literally by that maniac of a boyfriend of his. A pang of remorse sweeps through me like an electric shock. I feel the energy race through all corners of my body. I see him for a first time in a long time, he looks tired, vulnerable and in need of someone to hold him through this time. A large tear rolls escapes from my right eye. I look down and swipe it from my face before it barely catches my cheek. He is at the bar and I see that our coffee has gone out of the window and a bottle of Malbec and two glasses are making their way towards me. Jon face illustrates the picture, he needs

Dutch courage.   I know that I will hate every word of what he is going to tell me.

Chapter 8

Confessions

This is not happening; of all the people to witness my mess it has to be my undiagnosed bipolar narcissistic sister, who has always had the ability to find drama on a tranquil day out to the country. How could I have let that happen? It was my fault. I shouldn't have made him angry and now he's lost it, and mouth almighty is here looking at me like I am sodding Tina Turner. Christ, how am I going to explain this without looking like a complete tosser!

"Well?" Phoebe whispers, her eyes are full of pity and disappointment

Well? Well? Well what, well mind your own business and get a life, better still find yourself a man, preferably one that does not abuse you. Find yourself someone to occupy that perfectly honed and toned body. Someone to appreciate your precisely filed manicure, pedicure, and fantabulous weave. A man to kiss your sweet heart lips and to love that hard to love exterior which we all know is an act.

Jon, what is going on? She begs

The cat is out of the bag, so what the hell. If I don't tell her she will just make it all up as she always does.

"You know what's going on, you said it yourself, my boyfriend is knocking me about" I say sarcastically. I could not keep it out of voice, what is wrong with me. Why am I upset at Phoebe?

Phoebe looks disgusted by my frankness.

"Duchess you said that you want the truth, here it is"

137

I see her try to temper her annoyance "How long?

"How long what?", I scathe. I look the other way as I just can't face her anymore.

"Jon", she whispers and edges closer to me, she touches my arm and when I look at her my defensive armour dissolves. I am visibly touched by her emotion. It was real, there was no agenda just genuine concern. Her eyes are searching my face, and I hate it. She sees me wince away and pulls my face close to hers. Her warm tears wet my cheek.

I cup her head in my hands and push us apart. I take her hand, when I look up she is still crying and searching my face for answers. I sigh,   "It started shortly after that…. that Christmas babes"

Really, she shrieks. Other customers look over. "That long" she looks visibly shocked. She is right a day is in the life of Jonathan George is far too long.

"Shhhhhhh yes!", I whisper, the embarrassment rushes through me I blush uncontrollably.

"That's been like years Jon, decades"…… she wails "rea-llllllly??"

The two women at the next table give me the filthiest look.

Phoebe notices the awkward glances and tempers her tone to a whisper, "Why do you ….. you know, put up with it. Babes you could really hurt him if you wanted to, look at the size of you". "How could you …. You know"?

No I don't know, what?, *what is she accusing me of. This was a bad idea..*

Phoebe held her head down

"What Phoebe?" I am starting to get agitated

She looks at me and can see that I am angry

"Look at me?" I shout "Like what?"

The two women look over at Phoebe and ask in an aggressive manner. "Are you alright love?"

"She fine" I yell back starring at my sister and visibly showing my annoyance "Now if you don't mind, mind you own bloody business" I snap

The both look at me, wanting to take the matter further, but can see that I am in no mood for rubbish. They mutter under their breath, finish their last swig of wine and leave. On the way out I wonder if they are reality stars as they both look super imposed, wearing the latest fashion, botox up to the hilt with their pretty Frankenstein stares. Their unnatural jet black hair, fake boobs and high gloss make up represents the glamour model look or dare I say it expensive hooker glam but I could be wrong. I turn back at my sister. "Like what?" I ask in a quieter voice conscious that I am causing a scene.

"How could you allow him to do this to you?" she whispers looking anywhere but at me.

The emotion rips through me, my eyes swell and burst their floodgates. "Is that what you think?" I ask in disbelief. "You think that I allowed this? Want this? Deserve this? Enjoy this?" I point to my new swelling above my right eye.

"No Jon" she whispers regretting the words as they come out. "No No Jon, it's just that physically your more .... Stronger than Jack. You could easily ...... you know, kick his arse"

"It's not me and you know it, I hate violence"

"Screw violence John, this is self-defense and you know

that".

Why? Why do you stay?

I Love him, I say, *it sounds pathetic and I hear myself for the first time. I am a battered husband*

I put my head in my hands and let out a few sobs, I wipe my eyes, embarrassed that I cannot keep my emotions in check. I discretely scan the room with my puffy blood shot aching eyes. No one is looking, no one cares. I feel the intense gaze of my sister and know that I am going to have to disclose this part of my life once and for all.

I sigh. "Ok babes" the tears roll down my face. My life is a lie, I am not this confident strong man. I am weak, battered, tired and lonely. I have not felt great about my relationship for the past 15 years. "It's just so awful" I whisper "I mean just awful." I sniff. "Do you know I can live with the physical abuse" *I register the look of disdain she throws at me.* "No Phoebe I can…... I can, it's the verbal and physiological stuff that is harder to recover from.

"What do you mean?" her eyes are filled with pity and sorrow, she squeezes my hand.

"He is a terrorist, when I step out of line, he punishes me", I cry

"Huh?" Her expression turns to rage.

 SOB …… SOB he punishes me SOB. *For the first time in twenty years I say the words out loud and it offends me.*

"What like a child? What do you mean?" Phoebe looks at me in annoyance, I am not sure if it's at me or what I am telling her.

"If I do anything that offends him, he will either attack me, sometimes he even takes my allowance away" I chuckle but can see that she does not find this funny.

She cuts me of abruptly "Wait.... wait Jon, what allowance?"

"My wages go into a joint account, but Jack controls the account, he checks all my transactions online every day. If I take out ten pounds he wants to know where I spent the money. I can't do anything without his approval. He buys my clothes, tells me how to cut my hair, what food to cook, even down to the underwear that I wear", My eyes automatically connect with the floor.

I was surprised at the ease that I disclosed my hideous life to my sister. Just seeing her face and listening to me made me realise that I was living in a living hell.

"What happens if you disobey him Jon, I mean how bad has he hurt you? *Wow she is really concerned.*

"He has really hurt me in the past babes" Yet another tear breaks free as I say the words.

"How bad Jon?"

"What does it matter?" I whisper my eyes find the floor for solace.

"You're my brother of course it matters", she snapped angrily. "What happened to you? She let go of my arm and distanced herself from me. Her spine straightened and she tilted her head at me. *I knew what this meant. The ice queen is back.* "You were such a hard nut at school, how can m-m-y-y-y brother be reduced to this? She waved her arm at me like I was a plate soiled mussels from her favorite restaurant The Pont de la Tour. The disgust in her voice was recognizable and cutting.

"What?" I ask wounded. *I cannot believe that she is being like this*.

"Look at you, you're pathetic. This is just utter bollocks. Are you telling me how you're sick looking fragile boyfriends beats the living crap into and degrades you at his leisure? And you do nothing about it, nothing to defend yourself ......You sound like a......like a"

"What Phoebe, what tell me?", another disobedient tear sashes down my cheek.

The real Phoebe emerges like a phoenix, ready to cast what little self-respect that I have left under the bus. Her eyes narrow, she sucks in her breath and stares me square in the eye. She spits her words out like an ex con in the prison yard, "Like a little snivelling bitch. You disgust me. You could have defended yourself, but instead you've chosen to take this crap".

Aghast I stare at my sister, all I could do is blink in her words. "You don't mean that?" I whimper. *The last of my confidence shatters into a million pieces. Each word delivered with its poisonous venom was like being attacked around the heels by an angry cobra. Her words are in repeat in my head. You are a pathetic sniveling bitch. You are a pathetic sniveling bitch. You are a pathetic sniveling bitch.....The feeling sweeping across my spirit takes me back to my childhood. She is my little acid tongue sister, who always pulls me in and strikes straight for my heart in battle. I am that powerless eleven year old, who is different, vulnerable, frightened and homosexual. I am weak, I feel weak, I am useless, I feel worthless and I am nothing. Once again, my family is right, there is no point to me. I am pathetic.*

"Thank you for your support as always Phoebes" she rolls her eyes and I walk out of Browns. This time my tears are on free flow and no one or nothing can stop then. My wound is open and it's critical.

Beneath the Love of a Woman

Chapter 9

Maddie is Home

January 13th 2005 7.09pm

Father God help me to stay safe from harm. Keep me strong during this time, as I need to be strong for Mum and Dad. Purge my impulses away and curb what I say and do. I have been hiding through the darkness not realising that my family is my truth and the light. I need to deal with my demons. I have to confront me fears, make my peace and hold my enemies to account. With you I am strong, do not let evil enter my life again. I have committed to you my life and will make it better for all people who are suffering without a voice

I have wasted so much time and as a result I have lost so much, but I am back now to say my goodbyes. I have to make things right with mum and dad. I know that they are disappointed in me. But I am now on your path and the change in me has been a miracle.

Father God I ask that you welcome my mother with open arms and take her to your bosom. I know that you will look after her, and she will like you to watch over us. Give us all strength to deal with the loss to come. In particular, give my father strength to carry on. I promise you that I will help and protect him, love and nurture him through this time.

"I didn't know you became religious" dad said

"Oh my gosh daddy you frightened me", I said with a start

"I am sorry love" dad look so apologetic.

"No sweat pops I'm good" I say. I smile. My father looks

so old and unkempt, which is totally not his thing. In fact, you can tell that mum is unwell. She would have read him the riot act. I look at my dad, he seems so sad, so very alone and scared.

"You ok dad", I ask

"Hmmmm I am trying to take this thing minute by minute, it's so bloody painful though. By far this is the most humbling experience I have been in. I still cannot believe that she is leaving me. That is the hardest part. I feel that she is ready, but she was waiting to sort out some things first."

"Like what dad"

I'm not sure" he laughs out loud. "Maybe I am just talking rubbish, you know me", with that Dad walked from the door and sat down next to me by mum. He stroked her hair and kissed her forehead, and held her hand and sat down. I watch him intently and can see the awkwardness all over him. I cannot remember a time when he kissed her face or held any part of mum's anatomy. Mine were not the parents to show affection to one another. They were warriors, soldiers at war, if they were not fighting one another they were fighting the world. It was never easy growing up in our house, but despite everything, there was a sense of love and home. They may not have expressed this, but as I have grown older, I have appreciated that what we have as a family is not broken or fragmented. We all have our demons, we all have our drama, and we may even from time to time have wars. What we believe that divides us does not divide us at all. At the end of it all we are still family. My father had his issues with depression which made him respond to us the only way he knows how. I did not feel neglected or abused, just different at school. Being an addict opens you up to a world that you believe exists in the movies. It shows you how wretched humanity can be, how thoughtless and loveless we are and the depths of the gutter that you sink, believe me there will always

145

be someone lower than you lying on their stomach, stinking in their own stench ready to pull you down into their pit of sullenness. I have seen the best and worst of people these last seven years. Some days we may not act like family, even at our worst we are not as despicable as some of the characters I have met along the way.

I too stroke mum hair and rest my hand on her shoulder. I look at dad who is now crying silently. He is trying to be stoic but it's not working.

"How have you been dad?". My voice is low. I recognise my nakedness in my father's eyes. He sees me all of me. My pain, my sorrow, my fear. I cannot hide.

"Oh you know …. Half right and half left", he said with a wry smile.

He clears his throat and wipes his eyes like an errant child. "Maddie, how have you been? *He searches my face looking for clues. I lower my gaze, fearful he will see what had become of me. Knowingly he changes the subject, to hide my shame.*

"Knowing that your child is homeless, makes sleeping a luxury". *Again that glare.* "I drove around this city to the most undesirable of places searching for you. I nearly got arrested for curb crawling, can you image that". Dad chuckled.

I giggle, "No dad I can't imagine, you don't even like driving at night"

He smiled tight lipped, "When your baby girl is out there doing god knows what with god knows who then of course I pounded the streets looking for her. In fact both your mother and I would take a drive most evenings after 11pm. It broke her heart to see the real London at night. It's not a safe place if you don't know what you're doing"

146

"Dad what do you mean dad 'doing god knows what and god knows who?"

"We heard that you lost your job, and you know, in order to make ends meet you were doing …. Night work"

"What" I stare wide eyed at my dad, "Night Work" my voiced cracked from the emotion.

"Yes" Dad said looking to the floor clearly embarrassed by the whole ordeal.

"Dad" I say softly "look at me … please daddy look at me"

Dad raised his eyes but his head was still sunken into his shoulders "I never … ever…. sold myself, and especially not for alcohol! Where did you hear such trash?"

"Really, you were not a prostitute?" Dad asked confused

"No dad" I say with authority I may have been an alcoholic, but even we have standards"

"Maddie" dad said straining to keep his composure, it was all too much he cracked and burst into tears. "I – SOB- -SOB- am so SOB very pleased to hear you – SOB- say –SOB- that". He takes a long pause and clears his throat, drinks his water and pulls his handkerchief and dabs his eyes   "Very pleased indeed. Do you hear that my darling" Dad bends over to kiss mum, he slightly raises his voice so that mum hears "She wasn't on the game after all. Phoebe got it wrong love. Isn't that good news? Eh Winnie, Good news". He strains a smile through his happiness and grief.

The pressure is my temple feels like it is going to explode. Why would my sister dearest tell my parents that I was a hooker. Oh she has a lot to answer for and trust me I will make sure that she answers for everything this time.

"Come on Maddie calm down. This is not the time or place". I kneel down next to my father who is seated next to my mum and hold his hand.

"How long as she been like this?" I ask

"Like this, a couple of days" dad whispers. *It's as if he only wants mum to hear good happy conversations. I smile inwardly, as I know that she is hearing everything.*

"You look tired dad, do you want to stretch your legs or something?" I ask

"No love, I'm fine. I will just get a drink and come back"

"Dad, stretch your legs you could do with the walk and call the family and let them know how she's doing, when was the last time they had an update". I ask

"That's a point, you always think of everything. I will call them outside"

I smile as dad leaves the room. He closes the door in slow motion so not to make a noise when the door creases align. "Finally, I have you all to myself" I say in my most cheerful voice. My mum looks old and small. She is off colour that is the only way to describe her. The shadow of death is looming and I can see that we don't have much time. I hold her hand and squeeze, praying for the miracle that I know will not come.

"Where have I been I hear you say? Truth Ok, I have been in rehab for the last 90 days, before that I was living with my artist boyfriend Franco in Italy, he lived in a little village outside Lake Como, lovely man mum, he really was lovely when he wasn't drunk." I laugh. I feel the emotion of the moment wash over me. "Mum if I could turn back time I would have handled so many things differently. I can hear you now, you have to stop running from yourself Madeline, learn to feel life as its happening around you and to you. Stop suppressing every emotion and go with it". Tears roll down my face. I carefully place mums hand in mine, and I kiss it lovingly, not wanting to disturb her I place her tear soaked hand on the bed. I feel her presence and look up and see her looking at me. She looked thinner with her eyes closed.

"W—a—t—e—r", she croaked. Startled by the weakness in her voice I momentarily froze. I grab the bottle of water with a straw and carefully raise her neck so that she can drink. "Hi Mum", I say as if the last seven years haven't happened.

Mum raises her eyebrows at me, searching for signs of my alcoholism.

"I am clean mum, and you are not dreaming, I have finally sobered up, its taken me seven years but I am clean" I am humbled in this moment. When you are dying you command the truth, it's the least the person who you require it from can give you in this moment. I have not spoken to my mum in over six years, and considering that this is our first conversation, it is filled without judgment and wrapped in the gloves of sincerity and integrity. I can sit here shameless as I have overcome my demons and this time it is not a lie.

"A-m I d-e-a-d? she asked with her new dry raspy voice.

I smile broadly "No mum you're not dead as I am alive". I reply in my chipper London accent..

Mum smiles "Gooooood", my heart swells with pity, I can see that its taking a lot of effort to talk.

"Oh by the way I was never a prostitute" I blurt out through the tears. *Maddie, happy face, normal voice, the last thing she needs is you falling apart. I take some prolonged deep breaths"*

P.D Lorde

Mum looks at me and nods her head once as if to tell me that she already knew.   Maybe she heard the conversation.

"I asked god to let me see you again ………… and your …….fine" mum smiled.

I am so glad that I made it back in time, to see her face and for her to look me in the eyes and know that all is well. "For sure mummy, I will not go back to that place again"

"yoooou p-r-o-m-i-s-e" mum asked searching my face with her eyes

I start to cry, mum looks upset as well. "I promise mummy, I promise you that I will not have another drink as long as I live"

"You need to ….". her chests heaves and her throat wheezes as she tries to breath. "You … need… yo ….forgive…. yourself I L-o-v-e- y-o-u" Mum smiles, "I'll see you"

"What?"

"I w-i-l-l   s-e-e y-o-u".

Its ok mum I am not going anywhere. I tell her. She looks at me annoyed with disgust, she knows that I understand her and I am sitting in this moment which belongs to her and I make it about me.

"But …. I …. Am".   She says then looks out of the window.

Hold on mum, for a little while longer. I need you. She looks at me pained as she knows that she is needed, but there is nothing more for her to do. Her time is running out.

She mouthed "L- o –o- v v- e – e   y- o- u" and closed

her eyes.

I sat there crest fallen. Why did it take me forever to figure stuff out. I could have been here with my family. They needed me, and I was out there being needy and dependent on the bottle. I stand up and smell the peachy fragrance in the room. I look out the window, past the gardens, and see people walking about their daily business. Young woman arms looped laughing with her boyfriend. She seemed carefree and genuinely happy. "Are any of us genuinely happy?" I ask

What was that love?" Alice said. I spun around and Nurse Mckee was taking mums vital signs and completing her chart. "Are you family, it's just that I have not seen you before?"

"Yes I am", I smile "Are you mums nurse then?"

"I am one of them. my name is Alice. I would shake your hand but I need to administer more pain relief to your mums drip"

I nod appreciatively, "How is she doing?" I ask looking at mum.

"She is where she needs to be on her journey"

I motion Alice to come over to the window, "What does that mean, she just told me that she is leaving. You know, like she knows that she is going to die soon. Is she close?" I whisper.

Alice looked at me, "Give me a minute please and we can talk outside". She looked at mum and then at me. I nodded as I understood the need for us to have this conversation outside of the room.

Alice completed her checks and stroked mums arm. "Are you alright my love?"

Mum liked her, she smiled at her, not wanting to be a burden and points to her chest.

Alice leant down, "Is it burning or just aching my darling"

"Buuuurrrrr"

"Its burning Ok I will ask the Consultant to come and have a listen. We may need to alter your pain relief" she said sweetly. I just want to ensure that you are as comfortable as possible hun. Are you happy for stronger drugs?"

"Nooo" mum said defiantly. "I need to say goodbye". Alice took mums hands in hers and said with compassion. "I understand poppet I am going to place your mask on so that you can get some more oxygen in those lungs" she nodded whilst she spoke.

Alice walked out the room. "One moment love, I just need to talk to the consultant and we can have a quick chat" I nod at her, and sit down next to mum.

"Well you have her trained" I say. Mum did not open her eyes she just smiled and raised her eyebrows. She clicked her machine a few times and drifted away.

The Consultant returned a few minutes later with Nurse McKee. They spoke quietly and he listened to mums chest and reviewed her chart. He looked at me not with pity or sympathy, but in the knowledge that my mother would soon pass away. I read his face, he could see it and removed his gaze. He despised this part of his role, I could tell. He walked towards me. A tall chap, mid-thirties, quite handsome really, with his thick brown hair and blue eyes, he was in fact striking. His lips were thick, his jaw rounded. He was quite lovely.

I understand that you are a daughter, your family?" he asked unsure of my status or relationship to his patient.

"I am her daughter yes. I arrived this morning".

My name is Mr York, Oncology Consultant.

"I see"

"Where are the rest of your family?"

"Taking a break" I mutter

"I am sorry to report that your mothers condition has worsened. I would strongly recommend that you contact your family and tell them to be close by". He patted my arm "You will need to brace yourself"

"How long?" I ask mortified.

It's not an exact science Miss George but I would predict that she may pass away within the next 24 -48 hours.

"That quick", I snap, tears form immediately.

Mr. York nodded apologetically.

Chapter 10

Rock Bottom

January 13th 2005 7.54pm

"Are you alright mate" a older woman asked me as I wiped my eyes

"No I'm not, I have had some bad news, but thanks" I say.

Bleeeeeep Bleeeeep, I look at my phone and it's the hospital.

"Hello its Jon, is she …."

"Jon its Alice, where are you?

"On the High Street, is she.." I try to suppress the emotion from my voice

"No love" Alice informs me

Gratefully I exhale loudly.

"Edwina's health is declining and you do need to be here, get back here as quickly as you can"

"I'm on my way" The moment she hangs up I look around franticly for Taxi or a number 21 bus to take me down the high-street

"I don't mean to be rude but you look like you've had a shock can I help" my random stranger asks.

"To tell you the truth. I have had a hell of a day. My mum is in St Augustus, and my sister has just witnessed my long term boyfriend attack me. She has proceeded to tell me that I am nothing more than a sniveling victim amongst other things. I am sorry I should not have said all that I need to get back" I tell her. I see a black cab in

154

the distance "Taxi" I put my arm out. The driver took one look at me and drove straight past me and his light was on. Frantic with fear I swear out loud and shake my fists at him.

"I have a car, and you don't seem like a serial killer. I am just parked less than one hundred yards away. Let's go"

I hesitate, "Its fine, I can run there"

"You can but I will get you there quickly, let's go it will take a few minutes at this rate"

"Thank you, you are very kind, and you too do not look like a serial killer" I smirk at my good Samaritan.

She smiled. "Sam" she stretched out her well-manicured hand.

I look at her, mid-fifties I would say. Very polished, old money, maybe an actress, definitely a thespian of some sort. "Jon", I reciprocated I suddenly became very conscious of my state of dress, hair, breath and general stank demeanor.

My good Samaritan glided through the traffic in the latest model of her Land Rover Range Rover sports estate within minutes. As promised she delivered me to the hospital in only a few minutes. "Good luck Jon" she said kindly.

"Thank you, I will always remember your kindness" I smiled at her and left her car feeling that my faith had been restored in mankind.

My limbs are weighted with grief, and it's becoming physically harder and more laborious to walk and to keep my body upright.

I walk into mums room, she looks peaceful, her night

gown has changed. She has her post sky blue satin and lace number on.

"What's with change of bed clothes" I ask quietly.

"Mum left me strict instructions to ensure she said goodbye in a decent nightgown" dad said his lips quivering.

We all smiled "Trust mum" I laugh quietly.

Dad, Phoebe and Maddie all give a pity stare.

"What"? I ask demandingly, already knowing the answer from their stares. I look at Phoebe who averts my gaze.

"This is not the time" dad said "I am so sorry son, I should have been a better father to you"

"What… " I try to laugh it off "dad what are you talking about?" .

"I told them". Phoebe cut me off "They all know that you are a battered fag hag"

"Eeeeeek" I slam my hands to my mouth, and felt my knees buckle. My father and sister Maddie run to my aid.

"I got you son. I got you. I had no idea. It my fault my pride got in the way of me being your father. I should have been there for you. I should have protected you and I was too interested in protecting my image in the community. I am going to make him pay for what he's done to you. " My father kissed me over and over again on my cheek. My beautiful, beautiful child of mine"

"Jon we are here for you, I am here for you" is all that Maddie could say. "We will get through this, you have to leave him and I will help you, your better than this situation and you know it" she could barely speak through her tears

I hold them both close to me, my eyes are closed and my head is throbbing. The love that I have for them both in this moment is greater than anything that I have ever experienced. I look up and Phoebe is smirking at me. My mother is awake and is looking pained, as if she has experienced the whole thing. Maybe she has. I let go of them both and walk towards my mother. I kneel down and take her hand.

"Mum I am ok, do not worry about me, look" we both look at Dad and Maddie "they are going to help me get through this. It needed to come out. I needed to be free of the shame and guilt. Do not worry mummy. I am going to be ok" I kiss her hand, she smiles at me, tears streak her face, she looks at me lovingly and blinks slowly. "I love you mum, when you're ready to go you just leave, we are going to be fine"

Mum looks at Phoebe.

"Its ok I tell her, we are going to take care of her as well". Mum looks at me and nods slightly and slowly closes her eyes.

My sister looks at me and feels the burdens of her behaviors and shame. She raises her handkerchief to her eyes, and runs out of the room.

Maddie makes her way towards to the door.

"It's OK Mads. I'll go stay with Dad and Mum" I say calmly.

I chase my sister to the corridor, and drag her to the stairwell. She looks at me full of regret.

"Jon I …. I don't know why"

I slap her so hard she falls into the wall. She holds her cheek, and gives me daggers. "Now you find your backbone, shame you can't demonstrate this level of aggression with Jack", she snarled

That wasn't for me" I say quietly. I point to the room "Your mum is dying Phoebes, get it, she is in the last stages of her life and even now all you can think of is getting one up on me. In this moment, you have tried to make her death about you. Have can you be so selfish?"

"No I didn't, I told the truth and look everyone is in love with St John so why are you complaining" she yells

I look at my sister with renewed eyes. Even now she is contrite and unapologetically cruel. "I just had to give her comfort right now, so that she can die in peace. Have you no conscience?". I yell. "Why? What has happened to you that you feel like you can act like a poison cobra in everyone's life?".

Her face softens again. "Jon I am sorry. I didn't mean to. I don't know why I do"

"Bullshit" I interrupt. "You a grown woman, you're not a child anymore. You swore to me that you would not say a word. You offered me support then you do what you always do, you kicked me as hard as you could when I am weak. I met the most delightful human being, a stranger. She offered me more compassion and understanding than you."

" I am sorry" she whined like a child. "Its just happens I don't know why but it does, I don't mean it"

The door to the stairwell swings open and slams into the wall. Its Maddie. She is looking at Phoebe with a hate filled glare.

"Oh get lost Madds no one invited you to this party, it's between me and Jon" Phoebe snarls.

My perfect little sister, so pretty and sweet, who would

believe that she slept with my Pete". Maddie said in a childish rhyme like chant.

"What?" I exclaimed. I looked at Phoebe for some sort of confirmation that she has gotten this seriously wrong, but her face said it all.

"What gives you the right to out Jon like you're a saint. You should have outed yourself first. Your real good at telling other peoples secrets and a master at keeping yours to yourself, or so you thought" Maddie says quietly.

"Madd I …. I ….."

Maddie walked up to Phoebe and I was convinced that I would have to drag them apart. "You ruined me. Its taken me seven years to get over what you did, to deal with my broken heart to acknowledge that you went out of your way to wreck my relationship with the only bloke that I have ever loved." Phoebe was crying silently, just wiping tears from her eyes leaning against the wall. "You did that. What did I ever do to you sister dearest?"

Phoebes was really sniveling "It wasn't like that. At the time, I I …I know it inexcusable, but I thought that he …. Loved me"

"He was not yours to love" Maddie screamed at her. She then threw her hands up in the air, angry at herself. "Today cannot be about you. Jon is right. I am here for mum, dad and Jon. You can jump off London Bridge as far as I 'm concerned. You are so dysfunctional, all this" and she pointed at us in the corridor "is just another day in paradise for you. We will have our day babes and yours is not going to be today, but its coming"

I look at my sister, I am speechless, my mind is racing. I am aware that she was very competitive and jealous but not to this extent. This was just foul even for Phoebe.

"Madd's why did you run out on everything three days before your wedding"

She looks at Phoebe "Go on tell him what you were doing with Pete in our flat"

"What?" Phoebes eyes were wild

"Tell him", Maddie responds angrily.

"You were there?

"Yes I was and I heard everything." Maddie informs my sister who is looking grey and all colour has drained from her body. I was in the loft, that's where I hid his wedding present. I heard you laughing at me, both of you. What was it that you called me. Poor pathetic maggot Maddie, thinking Peter will be her child's daddy"

Phoebe shakes her head, Look I'm sorry we were high.

I could not take it in. I sit on the stairs and put my head in my hands.

"Madds you left because of her" I say with venom

Maddie nodded. "You know what bro, I have missed the last seven years with my mum because of her. You know what I know now. They were not worth my exile. I missed out on my family because of you and it was not worth it. You and Pete you're the ones that are damaged. Your both worthless and you have the integrity of a worm, but I owned it and for that I won't forgive myself, as I am here wishing that I had the strength at the time to confront you both. Today is not about you it's about mum. Your nothing to me". She looked at me and Phoebe. "We are done" With that she left.

I sat there in silence. I Look at my sister. "This is the worst day of my life so far." I shake my head still trying to process the last few minutes,

"Jon I can ex…"

"Forget it Hun". .I abruptly interrupt. "That ship has sailed. We are meant to be family, but your actions make me place you in a different category. To hell with you. After the funeral I am done with you. Truly. Be spiteful, bitchy and wicked to your cats. I chose not to be bothered. Your energy taints all that is pure. Deal with that." I looked at my sister and walked out of the stairwell and back in the room. Maddies right. We have to focus on mum and dad right now. This bullshit has no place in my reality.

"Alright son" my dad embraced me as I walked into the room.

"Yes dad. It needed to be said. Now let's just concentrate on mum".

My father nods.

"Here Here" Maddie chimed in.

We sat quietly praying with her.. She was somewhere else now, we could see that. Her colour changed, she was slipping away, I could feel her spirit leaving us. I wanted to scream, make a pact with the devil or god, the universe anyone and anything. But I know its fruitless. It was all fruitless. This was her time and I have to just grow some balls and accept it. I thought that there are not many things in life that one has to accept as there is always an element of choice. Today is different. This moment is bigger than us and we need to embrace it for what it is. Mum is leaving us to start a new life elsewhere.

I look up, Phoebe is sulking by the far wall. By herself alone and bitter. That was her choice.

P.D Lorde

Chapter 11

Revelations

She is beautiful. I lay in my bed lifeless but perfect. How I wished I had the vision to see how beautiful I was then, to appreciate the freshness of my youth. I have been gone some time as I must be at least 15 years old. My hair is on my shoulders, my nose has healed, and only to the trained eye you would notice the slight imperfection on the bridge of my nose. My limbs are lithe and sculptured, far more than I recall.

It's early, the fragrance of dawn creeps through the open window. I sit on the window ledge, This room has changed since the time I was here. It's fit for a princess. The colour scheme was lime and cream, not bad grand mama, Good Housekeeping would be proud. My Balcony doors are shut, the extra-large king size four poster bed represented opulence, the floors were a deep red mahogany polished to perfection. When the sun started to rise I saw the reflection of my face looking up at me. I look terrible my burdensome body looked ragged and unwell, my skin has turned grey and I feel weaker than I ever been.

"Winnie" I whisper

My younger self sucked in all the air in the room, and sprang up to the perfect right angle, breathing heavily, eyes wide open desperately trying to focus on what or whom was next to her. After a few seconds she realised that I was no threat to her, her eyes narrowed, "Edwina?" she asked in a muffled voice.

I smiled at her "Hey kiddo it's been a while"

I thought that you were a figment of my imagination", she pinches me hard. "Are you dead yet?"

"I don't think so".

"Where have you been", she barks at me angrily.

"I'm not sure", I say apologetically.

"Why are you back here?, it's been five years. Why now?

"Five years" I say, although I guessed the length of duration it still takes me back.

"You're like all the rest", she said with venom

"The rest. Who?" I ask, my little self was real feisty back then.

"Mima, my mother and now you. You all leave me in the end, all of you abandoned me and left me in this hell".

I want to cry but am no longer producing tears.

" Am I expected to feel for you? Look at my life, its miserable. I am in this big and beautiful home without anyone that loves me. Tell me that my life gets better, that I am happy and loved.

I stare blankly at this young girl, not knowing what to say, she searches my face for clues relating to her future like I am so old gypsy woman"

"Tell me", my younger self yells.

"If you insist, your life is wonderful, you meet your husband and have the most wonderful life. Your life is filled with love, laughter and three beautiful children. Voila, I stand up and take a bow.

My younger self stares at me. "Then I …. Am…. Happy", she eyeballs me as she asks that question.

"You are, we are" I smile hoping that it will hide the doubt in my eyes.

"You're sure", Winnie self asks with a poignant glare

I nod and swiftly change the subject. "Where is Miss Mack?"

What do you mean where is she? Don't you remember?

"No", I snap

Winnie looks pained at my shortness. She went to see her sister one evening in Trinity Ville, November 6th 19xx, and never came home, both villages searched for her, it was like she vanished into thin air. Tears filled Winnie's eyes, but none fell out. "She protected me and he killed her for it"

Who did, I whisper. I started to tremble, fear washed over me.

"You know who~?" she said in a low voice, she was enjoying torturing me. I cannot recall being so spiteful as a child.

I close my eyes a torture type pain surges through my spine whilst injecting all of the abominable, bloodcurdling, execrable memories of my childhood, back to that part of my brain that carefully locked them away in a vault. Lying on her bed next to my younger self, I feel her glare on me. Winnie stretches out her hands and clasped them in mine. I open my eyes, and she looks at me with sedate sobriety. "I can see that you're remembering aren't you?

The pain was too intense, I do not know whether its from the cancer or being here, but its too much. I Open my eyes, I notice that my face is moist. I am hot and clammy, I know that my time is coming soon. I focus on my mini me and for the first time have nothing to say. Everything aches.

"Our father is a loathsome son of a bitch isn't he? Winnie

whispers in a voice so deep it was bare audible. I let go of her hand and turn my back on her and gently nod my head. I have the familiar feeling of giddiness. *Hhhhh Noooooo not now, she furious with me as she thinks I have abandoned her. As I travel through time multiple* memories *flood through my mind's eye.* My body begins to feel light, I am floating on the ceiling, its no longer a liberating feeling, I can't go back, Lord take me now but do not let me go back. I float through the years, and am sat in the same room five years earlier. Mrs Mack is making my bed. She is talking to me I am sat on the window ledge looking at the plantation. Her voice is so high with excitement that I cannot help but tune in.

"Oh Winnie my darling, I am so excited, my sister Sarah has given birth to a lovely boy. Fit and strong just like my daddy. I cannot wait to meet the lovely sweetheart"

Feeling her joy Winnie, clasped her hands together "That's great news Miss Mack, when can I come and see the baby?"

Hmmmm not sure I will speak to Dr Barnett about a little visit later on in the week.

I am sat on her white bureau chair looking through her school books on the table. Winnie looks at me, she gave me a look as if to say "What are you doing here?"

I raise my finger to my mouth to remind her to be quiet. She nods silently.

"You OK sweet pie?" Mrs. Mack enquires.

"Yes Ma'am I was just wondering what name you will give to the baby, please can I come with you. I don't want to stay here by myself, also Grandpa is not home so they will be mean to me."

Miss Mack picked Winnie up off the bed, her hair was in perfect ringlets, with four yellow stain bows tied evenly where her hair was equally parted into four group of ringlets. Her cream knee length dress with accompanying kremlin petticoat, was a site *to behold.* She looked stunning and a child borne to wealth.

Mrs. Mack placed me on her lap

"Listen Sweet Pie, I will be back in the morning. Ok?. I will prepare supper and cook will help you this evening at bedtime. She lovingly kissed my head". My heart skipped a beat. I felt the love but also could see the adoration in her eyes.

No one heard daddy enter the room. He stood at the doorway looking exceptionally distinguished yet smelled like a well fermented vineyard. The atmosphere within the room plummeted even though it was November and well over 30 degrees. Both Mrs Mack and Winnie both jumped to their feet and stood to attention by the beds. The once defiant Miss Mack was no longer around, she was trembling. She held Winnie's hand to reassure her but her display of reassurance did not fool either of us. Winnie looked at me pleadingly as if to say do something.

"Child come to daddddddy and give him a kiss", he said slurring his words. He not only smelt unkempt he look like he had been in the same clothes for the past week.

Winnie looked at me pleadingly again, wishing that I had some magical powers to strike her father dead.

"CHILD!!!!" Daddy screams,

"Go on Winnie, give your Daddy as kiss", Mrs Mack instructed her.

As Winnie gets closer to daddy, his demeanor changed. Daddy raises hand high, Winnie stands still anticipating the blow, he delivers a hard slap with the back of his left hand, her poor little head is thrown back. He grabs her hair with his right hand and pulls her down as he drops to his knees.

"Daddy No" I scream, what type of monster is he?

Winnie lets out a blood curdling scream. The whole household comes to a standstill. He moves to punch Winnie but Mrs. Mack grabs his fist and her skirt engulfs the punch, she pushes daddy hard and he loses his balance so is forced to let go of Winnies hair, they both topple over on the floor, and daddy hits the floor hard, as Mrs. Mack's weight falls onto him. Mrs. Mack grabs her skirt to make a run for it, even though daddy was drunk he was on his feet first.

He swings towards Miss Mack head but she jumps backwards.

She raises her hand, "Calm down Sir..... she is just a little girl, Hasn't she been through enough?"

A sensation of fear dominated us all, for each of us knew that it would not end well for Mrs. Mack. Winnie ran to her bed with her hands at her ears.

"Daddy please no" she screams tears streaming down her face. "I'll be a good girl I promise, please don't hurt her, she's my only friend. I 'll be a good girl daddy"

I ran to the bed and put my arms around her. After last time I knew I was powerless.

Both Daddy and Mrs. Mack looked at Winnie, his face softened momentarily, we all silently prayed that Mrs. Mack would get a warning, even Mrs. Mack. Suddenly with raging vengeance daddy punched Mrs. Mack so hard she fell to the floor out cold, Winnie leapt of the bed to run to her "Mrs. Mack she screamed". Daddy turned his head, he face was unrecognizable with rage. "GET AWAY YOU LITTLE BITCH!!!" he screamed at Winnie. she stopped running, rooted to the spot with fear.

Within a matter of seconds Mrs. Mack started to come round, she raised her head slowly "Win... Winniiiiieee" she held her head, blood was dripping from a cut under her right eye and both her nostrils were filled with blood.

Daddy walked towards her and was laughing. No one here to save you now you old hag"

"You only beat me because my husband is away with your daddy. Please….. Please sir" Mrs. Mack pleaded. "I will not say a word".

Daddy looked over at Winnie, but I would have sworn he was looking directly at me on the bed. "Get on the bed", he snarled. Winnie ran as quickly as her legs could carry her and jumped on the bed. She went into the foetal position, please don't she whispered over and over again.

I cradled my younger self, its ok I cry. It will be ok I promise. Don't turn around ok?"

What is it about you, always meddling in my business" he yelled.

Mrs. Mack still dazed was on all fours, "Pleeeaaaassseeee" she whimpered.

Daddy grabbed her hair and pulled her to her feet, "You think that you are better than me, but I am a gentlemen, a man of position, I am respected here, but you, a common bush girl, a daughter of a slave whore think that you are better than me, don't you?"

"No sir, No No No No" She pleaded tears strolling down her face.

"Yes, Yes, Yes, Yes …. He pushed Mrs. Mack to the wall, he pushed himself up against her. He leered at her, "you know something woman, you are passable, there is something about you, I am not sure what it is but its passable", He glanced over to the bed and saw that Winnie was sat on the bed with her back to him. "Winnie Get out".

Winnie turned around and starred at her father, she shook her head defiant.

"Winnie I will beat you black and blue today if you disobey me, Get out"

Winnie looked at Mrs. Mack. Not wanting to abandon her friend. She looked pleadingly for her not to send her away.

Mrs. Mack looked at Winnie reassuringly. "Its ok darling, daddy and I are going to have a little chat. Ask cook for some lemonade and pineapple cake, I soon come"

Winnie cautiously walked out the room, as she was about to go through the door, "You promise?"

"I promise baby" Mrs. Mack said, her voice breaking through her trying to sound reassuring.

"Why have you turned my only child against me?"

Mrs. Mack said nothing, she just looked at Barrington with hatred.

Daddy pulled her skirt above her waist, Mrs. Mack tried to save herself but was greeted with a hard punch to the stomach.

"Arrgggghhh" she gasps for breath.

I watch my father punch my only friend repeatedly until she is gasping to fill her lungs with oxygen, he rips off her panties. She doesn't cry out, she no longer struggles, she lies lifeless on the floor. My father's fumbling attempts to enter Mrs. Mack become laughable. She lies there waiting for the unwanted intrusion, and nothing. He tries again repeatedly with the same response. Mrs. Mack lies there motionless, with each failed attempt she smiles.

The ferocious aggressive attackers is no more, instead there is a drunken, unstable hesitant young man. He rolls on the floor, silent and panting. Mrs. Mack did not move or say anything. She lay silent, crying and smiling.

The situation in the room seemed explosive yet sedate. My father got up off the floor and went over to Mrs. Mack, she did not flinch she still had that smirk for a grin. My father walked toward her, he lent out his hand, remarkably she took it and he pulled her to her feet, she winced all the way up, but she was standing, thank god. Upright holding her ribs, she just starred at my father with that same smirk on her face, and hatred exuding from her eyes.

He apprehensively walked towards Mrs. Mack. She puts her hand "STOP!"

"Keep your mouth shut and we can forget about tonight" daddy says.

Mrs. Mack is silent.

Daddy walks to the door, Miss Mack I mean it if you don't want a repeat performance of ……

Mrs. Mack burst out laughing, "Repeat Performance of what?" she looked with disgust at his private area.

Daddy looked fatally wounded "I mean it say nothing to Mackie"

"I could never tell Mackie any of this, he would hang if he knew what you TRIED to do" she was angry and defiant.

"What did you say?" Daddy demanded.

"You heard me the first time, maybe I am just too old for you. After all we all know how you like then young"..

"Shut your mouth?" I could see the vein bulging in his forehead. I sit on the bed, hand over my mouth trying not to scream. Even though they could not hear or see me, I wanted to be sure.

"Or what sir, you going to tickle me with your broken bamboo stick" Mrs. Mack starts to laugh heartily, she fell so far in her own joke she did not see the aggression reemerge in daddy's face.

Daddy walked towards Mrs. Mack, she did not flinch, he head-butted her so hard she careened to the side of the bed.

"Nooooo" I scream.

The emasculated man had gone, the barbarian rapist that I had become accustomed to who always delivered his punishment was back, he threw Mrs. Mack on the bed, raised her skirt above her head and raped her.

I feel weightless, I am on the ceiling, before I had time to turn I am spinning in a vortex, lights are flashing, I can hear multiple voices, I cannot make out what they are saying. I land with a thud on Winnies bed.

"Edwina are you feeling alright? You don't look too good?" Winnie asks as I open my eyes.

"I am dying child, I should look terrible", I tried to smile at my younger self, but could not muster the energy to do that.

"You've been asleep for a while. I was wondering, what's it like"?

"What?"

"Dying, Are you ready for it all to end?"

I look at my younger self, "I am not sure that I am, it's funny really, my body is ready for the journey, but my

172

mind, it's still as sharp as ever. Mentally I am still 21 years old, but with more wisdom. Does that make sense" I ask

"No", Winnie giggled" No it doesn't."

"It will. Do you remember Mima?"

The sound of her name pained her face. "No I don't". She whispered.

"Then let me tell you what I remember. Our grandmother was a strong beautiful woman. She was married to Grandpa Vincent for many years. They were so in love, even after all those years".

"What was he like?"

"I don't know, I never met him Mima would tell me a story about him every day and it was funny, she was gateway to his life and the connection between the both of us. I know I was young, but she kept his memory alive so vividly, it did not feel like he was dead sometimes. He lived on through Mima".

"How did he die?"

"I don't know." I lied

"Why are you lying to me? I am you remember so I know when you're lying."

"Drop it Winnie, I said that I don't know how he died."

"It was him wasn't it"?

"I honestly don't know". I try to sound as sincere as possible.

"Look Winnie, there are experiences and things that you need to learn in your own time. I cannot rob you of that, it would not be fair"

"Ok well answer me this". She looked so serious

"Honey if it's about how Grandpa died that is not going to happen".

"Why?" She looked really annoyed. I gave her the I am your mother don't mess with me look.

"Ok… I am not impressed with your reasoning but ok" I was so serious back then. "So what about Mrs Mack? How did she die?"

I inhaled hard, then held Winnies hand. "Don't ask if you can't handle what I am about to say Kiddo"

Her eyes became red and moist almost immediately "I can handle it" she whispered.

"When I went back to sleep, I saw what happened. Daddy raped Mrs. Mack, although I did not see him kill her you and I know that he did it. He could not risk her telling Mackie. He just couldn't".

Winnie closed her eyes. "Thank you for telling me, we … I need to get ready for breakfast"

There was a beautiful porcelain bowl on the dressing table with cold water in it. Beside it was a face cloth. Winnie methodically washed her face, she stripped and wiped down her whole body with the coconut soap as her aid. I sat back and watched my mini me dress herself, the opulence us was staggering, even for that time. My curly ringlets nestled snuggly by the nape of my neck. My curly corkscrew fringe was bade with a green headband. I put on my undergarments that looked hideous and a light cream sleeveless over shirt, with a bright green skirt that matched my head band with an under starched white under petticoat. I slipped into my channel pumps and opened the door.

"Morning Miss Edwina", the maid said. Holy flip. The

maid was stood outside her door.

"Good morning" she chimed in her cheerful voice. I watched her with suspicion. I have just told her that our father raped and murdered her one and only friend and she doesn't flinch.

"Breakfast is served Ma'am, are you ready? Your Grandma and Papa are in the breakfast room"

"I will be there in a minute". She replies politely.

The maid looked surprised by this.

"Yes Ma'am".

Once the door was closed Winne looked at me. "Tell me" she said with brute force as if she was talking to the help, "Do I fall in love, am I happy? Do I have an amazing life, is this hell worth it?"

"Well I'm here at 70 so what do you think?"

You have not answered my question

Taken aback by her tone, I say gently "Winnie it's worth it, trust me"

She smiled, "Ok let's go to breakfast"

I walked across the circular landing, and was taken aback by the beauty of the handcrafted mahogany staircase. The grandiose oil paintings were of past ancestors on both sides. As I walked down the stairs, I watched slave owner from each generation bid me Good day. I suddenly felt clammy, to be back in this house, knowing all the pain that it had caused my family, let alone the poor slaves of centuries gone by. I was the decedent of slaves and its owners. I not sure how I feel about that. I sat on the step to catch my breath.

Winnie stopped and looked at me. She gave me a

concerned glare. I waved her off "I'm ok?" See you in a minute"

"Good morning darling girl" I heard a rapturous deep southern voice behind me.

Winnie grinned wider than a Cheshire cat. "Grandpa, good morning and how are you on this beautiful yet illustrious morning"

"Darling, now that I have seen you I am just fine"

He propped his elbow out and Winnie took it and the headed down the wide beautiful mahogany staircase with the Ming rug stapled in place perfectly.

Feeling well again I followed them into the Breakfast Room.

This room was the size of my downstairs house. I counted six double doors which led to a balcony, that could oversee the whole plantation from each direction.

"WOW" I say.

"It's beautiful" Winnie bellows.

"What is?" Grandpa enquired.

Grandma Phyllis's and my father momentarily look up from their papers

"The day Grandpa", Winnie looks at me awkwardly then smiles.

Winnie walks to the food station, there are three maids dressed immaculately, just waiting.

"Good morning", Winnie says to them all. They all smile, they like her. "I will have some salt fish and ackee, breadfruit with avocado, thank you" Winnie walks to the table.

I laugh, "Winnie I forgot just how much money we all have".

What are you smiling at girl? Grandma Phyllis's barks.

Winnie lowers her eyes and her smile disappears "Good morning Grandmother".

"Well?"

"Grandmother, I just felt like smiling for a change. Aren't you tired of my frown?"

The room stood still. There was a defiance in her eyes.

My father starred at Winnie. "What did you say Edwina?

Winnie looked at her father cautiously and like a sweet piece of plantain said. "Daddy I asked Grandmother whether she was not tired of my frown?"

"Well I for one am pleased that you are smiling", Grandpa said, "It brightens up my day that's for sure".

"Thank you Grandpa".

"What do you have planned for today", he kept my gaze as he knew that the others were seething at my mini self's impertinence.

"I thought that maybe I could go into town to do some shopping", I look at my father and ask "is that ok daddy?"

"It's out of the question you have your riding lesson this morning?"

In her sweetest voice Winnie says, "Yes daddy, I was hoping that I could go afterwards, with you, we don't spend any time together and I was hoping that he could have some father daughter time".

My Grandmother dropped her spoon on her plate, as we

only ate out of the finest china, and all cutlery was solid silver, it was quite a clash. Daddy was caught off guard and starred at his daughter. I could not help it, I just laughed. Winnie my little actress was perfect, she kept a straight face. The silence prolonged for a few seconds more.

"It's ok daddy, I know that you are very busy", she lowered her eyes and continued to eat her breakfast head bowed.

Barrington rarely showed his emotions. He was choked for a few seconds. Barrington Senior looked at him, and was nodded to his Granddaughters direction. Even Grandma Phyllis's appeared to thaw.

"Winnie, I would be honored", Barrington said, his voice was soft and tender. "What did you have in mind?"

"Anything you pick will be just perfect Daddy" Winnie smiled, eyes wide with a devious twinkle.

"Ok….." Daddy was caught off guard for a second time. "Ok I will surprise you" he smiled. A few seconds later he swiped a stray tear from his eye.

Seeing my father like this, vulnerable and kind was a rarity. For the first time in my life I realised, all my father wanted was unconditional love from his daughter. Nothing more. As he continued to eat his breakfast, he would glance over at his only child, there was something else there that was not annoyance. It was love in his own twisted way.

What I did not count on was another emotion at the table. That was my grandmothers. Hers was not one of happiness, it was one of pure jealousy.

I smiled to my younger self. "Well played my love".

Winnie looked up and starred at me. I knew what that

look meant. She was going to make them pay.

I sat to the West of the plantation, cautiously observing Winnie and Daddy on horseback in a slow canter across the paddock area. My tension soon wains as I notice that my father is actually talking to me. He does not bark, slap, punch or kick me. He appears to be interested in his daughter; Winnie is talking to Daddy, waving her hand around, a trait that I did not lose. I smile, the warmth of the sun radiates across my body, and somehow neutralizes my aches and sever pains. I stroll slowly to them both. Winnie observing me from the corner of her eye.

"Daddy who taught you ride?", Winnie asks

"Grandma Phyllis's", he smiled when he said it.

Winnie gives a shocked expression "reeeeeaaaallllllyyyyy?"

"Yes", Daddy says with hilarity in his voice "you know she wasn't always this uptight, cut her some slack Winn.

Winnie lowers her eyes. Startled by her reaction daddy immediately interrupted her thoughts "I was not chastising you, so take your eyes off the floor," he said gently. "I am just trying to point out that Grandma is quite cool when she's ready. I know that she can be a bit mean. But it all comes from a good place".

"A bit", Winnies whispers, her eyes to the floor.

"Listen, I have not been the perfect father, and your Grandma had not …… always been very grandma-like, but that does not negate how much we love you. I …..

"What daddy?".

"Nothing Winn", he looked away.

"Then why does she hate me then daddy?"

179

"She doesn't Winn I promise you". Daddy had to crunch hard on his teeth as his emotions were getting the better of him

"Then why does she treat me like an animal?"

Daddy looked wounded "she does not do that Winn"

Shhhhheeeee does and you knooooooww it", my poor younger self sobbed uncontrollably.

Daddy jumped of his horse in one move, he was quite the athlete, and pulled Winnie from her horse, and hugged her. He pushed away from his chest and cupped her face, "You are my blood, she could not hate you if she tried"

Winnie had her eyes firmly closed. "Look at me Winnie", he said with authority, "My mother does not hate you. Her blood, my blood runs through your veins. Hating you would be like hating herself. It just is not possible"

"Then why does she behave the way that she does daddy?"

"It's complicated, she was not always like that. I promise you that."

The horses trotted to the corner of the paddock where there was a bale of hay and water. Both stallions rehydrating seemingly bewildered by the conversation around them.

Daddy took Winnies hand and led her to the house, as pulled her close, she rested her head on his chest, and my father did something that I could not *recall until today,* he kissed me on the head and held me close. He was being my parent.

Daddy are you sure that I can have anything I want? Winnie asked eye wide

She had never been to the Crystal Hotel in Morant Bay. It was the nicest hotel in the district.

"You are a Barnett so yes my darling you can have anything you choose?" Winnie smiled.

She looked stunning, her hair was free from ribbons and any hair band or debris, and her curls just nestled with grace and sophistication on around her face. She was wearing a beautiful lace two piece that her grandmother had ordered from her dress maker in the United States. The colour was rose which complemented her complexion. The sleeves ended just past her bicep, and the shirt was fitted, showing off her curvaceous figure. Her skirt was long and greeted her leg in between her knee and ankle bone. Winnie has a white Chanel bag, accompanied with Channel Kitten heal shoes. I was beautiful. I looked like a movie star.

My father had impeccable manners and that came to the fore front on this day. I think it took both Winnie and I by surprise. He was waiting at the bottom of our beautiful mahogany staircase. In a lovely Navy Blue suit, with a crisp whiter that white shirt, no tie, and a white silk handkerchief in his pocket.

"Daddy you look very handsome", Winnie said.

"You look beautiful", Daddy whispered in my ear "Now I hope you're hungry", with that he looped his fingers in mine and walked pride fully out the door.

The Crystal Hotel restaurant was delightful. The waiter approached the table. As Winnie was familiarising himself with the menu, he was familiarising himself with Winnie. Daddy starred at the poor young chap so hard, he became clumsy"

"Winnie. Drink? What will it be?"

"Oh Daddy there is too much choose from, you choose for me please".   My father was touched by this and softened his stance momentarily.

"Alright," He looked at the waiter and became acid "Boy! Two Mango and pineapple juices for us please"

Startled by his approach the young man looked at Daddy "Y-Y-eess Sirrrr"

"You alright boy, do I need to write this down for you?" He snapped at him like an aggressive alligator.

Embarrassed by my father's etiquette, Winnie lowered her eyes to the table cloth. The boy scurried away like a field mice.

"So" Daddy reappeared all smiles. Winnie looked at me. All I could do is shrug.

"Daddy why did you embarrass him like that?"

"That boy was salivating and undressing you with his eyes".

Daddy, Winnie said genuinely aghast.

"Winn I do not mean to be so crude, but I know what these peasant boys are thinking?".

I look at Winnie and say flatly "That is what all men are thinking?"

"Daddy that is what all men are thinking?" Winnie says looking directly at her father

"What do you know of such matters?" Daddy snapped

"I read about it", Winnie says indignantly trying to hold her ground.

"Really?" he asked sarcastically.

"Yes".

"What have you read that describes men in this fashion?" he asked smiling at me now.

Winnie smile broadens, "I am reading Tess and Derbyvilles"

We all laugh. Our drinks arrive by another waiter. I look at Daddy and say" See you're a bully"

They both smile.

"Winnie, thank you"

"For what?"

"For handing me the olive branch".

"Daddy I have been handing it to you for many years you were just too … preoccupied to notice"

Daddy eyes filled with tears, "I am sorry".

"Anyway Daddy this is a fathers and daughters lunch. No sad talk".

They both smiled and daddy grinned "Agreed"

"I have to tell you Daddy, most of the women in this room keep glancing over to you" Daddy laughed so hearty. "Seriously Daddy …. Look" Winnie whispered.

Daddy smiled with such heartfelt happiness. "They are not looking at me my child, they are looking at you. You are Beautiful".

"Really". Winnie asks needing approval

"Yes really".

Blushing, Winnie took a sip from her juice. "Why have you not married, you are a very handsome and eligible bachelor"

Daddy spat out his juice with laughter. "What?"

"It's a question? You are".

"Erm. Well. I I I suppose that I have not met the right woman yet?" he was grinning from ear to ear.

"Oh.. What about my mother?" My father's eyes grew wide.

I chime in, "Winnie ask him if he loved her"?

Winnie looked at me annoyingly. "Did you love my mother?"

Daddy cheeks flushed red.

"Winn. I…"

"Please Daddy".

He lowered his eyes. "In my own way I adored her?" he said very quietly.

"Why did you not get married then?"

"It was complicated, parents, families, it was just not meant to be?"

"Why? Was it because she was poor?"

"Come on Winn, Lucy and Vincent would not be described as poor, but it was just complicated. Also I was not in the best place. To answer your question, I loved her. If I could go back and change… change the way.. I behaved I would"

Wide eyed, Winnie asked "What does that mean Daddy? Did you hurt her?"

"Winn I have the tendency to hurt everyone."

She ignores his response "What was she like?"

"She was a lovely girl. She had shiny black ebony skin, so dark it was smooth to touch. Her eyes were large brown, shaped like almonds but large one. She had beautiful lips, and the whitest teeth I have seen on any woman. He hair was like yours, but afro, it was soft and thick. She was a very sweet person. I did love her. Sometimes I am unable to show my affections."

"Daddy what did you do?"

"Winn, it's not important it was such a long time ago".

"It's important to me.", she looked emotional and daddy could see it.

"I did not treat her well".

"Why?", she asked sharply.

"I was young and arrogant and foolish"

"Did she love you?"

"Yes, Winn if I could change the outcome I would. To answer your question. I just do not think I am the marrying type."

"You are Daddy, when your loving you are loveable."

Daddy starred at Winnie, "Thank you"

"You're welcome." She smiled and showed all her teeth.

Daddy laughed. "Daddy I think that you should meet a nice woman who will open your heart and give you more children, maybe a son. I think this would be good for you"

"And you're ok with that?"

"Daddy I am 15 Years old, In a few years Grandma will have be paraded to all the suitors in Kingston. I am confident I will be married and a mother by 21 years of age."

"Nonsense", Daddy Barked

I laughed which made Winnie laugh, then Daddy laughed.

The laughter came to a screeching holt. A woman in her last twenties walked towards my father. She was had a light skinned complexion, light brown eyes, peachy skin and thin reddened lips, that drained the colour out of her face. She had straight hair that flowed either side of her parting.

"Barrington, who is your new whore?" she demanded in her lady like demeanor.

Daddy stood up with such force, his chair fell backwards. Clinching his fist, the woman flinched as she recognised that she had just run over daddy's line, let alone crossed it a mile ago. I too thought that he was going to knock her head off her shoulders. "Winnie do something quickly"

Winnie stood up and stroked daddy's arm. Then turned to face the rude woman. She walked around the table, towering above the woman. She stretched out her hand, not leaving her gaze.

"Who are you?" she asked with a regal type curiosity.

"Who am I ?" This woman was clearly one of daddy's floozies.

"Let me tell you who I am. My name is Edwina Barnet"

Horror crept over the rude woman's face.

"If you are too ignorant to work it out, I am the Granddaughter of Dr Barrington Barnett, and" she looked at daddy, "the daughter of Barrington Junior. Now ..... who has chosen to address a Barnett so disrespectfully?"

Oh Barry I am soooo sorry", she looked at me "Let me apologies my dear I had no idea"

"Clearly" Winnie said with a streak of her Grandmother in her voice. "What's your name?"

My name is Sylvia Edwards, I I I'm am friends with your daddy

"Oh really Sylvia. I could have sworn I heard jealously in your voice, which in my estimations, would have made you one of his whores".

Sylvia looked pained, "Barry ..I"

"Would you not agree Daddy" Winnie asked without removing her gaze from Sylvia, who had diminished to a sweaty mess"

"I would", Daddy chimed in confidently.

"Now Sylvia, under different circumstances I would have asked you to join us, however, having met you, I choose not lunch with whoremongers. You may go" with that Winnie waved her hand.

Daddy looked at his daughter with bemused astonishment.

Sylvia gave daddy a begging plea, "You heard the young Miss Barnett, leave us to dine in peace"

Once out of earshot, "Daddy, is she really your lover?"

My father looked poignantly at his daughter. No I go to her when I want the company of a woman. After today that will never happen again. Edwina you are more like your Grandma than you realise" He laughed out loud "Whoremonger"

Winnie giggled. "I heard Grandma use the term once"

They both laughed. "well after all that excitement my child I am ready for lunch. You?"

"Yes Daddy"

My life was being played out to me like a soap opera. Anyone observing them would have thought they were a strong family unit. How wrong they would be. This relationship was as fragile as broken glass, and as sharp too.

After tucking into their pumpkin soup for starters, Chick, rice and peas for main, both were sated by the delicious food. It had been a lovely afternoon and they had talked like old friends from school.

Daddy, can I ask you a question without you getting angry?

I don't know if I can promise but I can try

Why do you drink so much?

Daddy exhaled. " Winn I cannot answer that"

You can Daddy, you choose not to answer

Its complicated

Alright.

Edwina, it is complicated. I have been drinking heavily for nearly twenty years. I have not had a drink in over five years and I feel great. Sometimes..... Sometimes..... I regret my behaviors after being so drunk that I lose control. No good can come from it.

Winnie and I both look at each other, nothing is said but we come to the same conclusion. After he murdered, my only friend, he knew that he had to stop. The conversation moved onto other topics. I had stopped listening. Instead I was watching the young man, eyeing up my younger oblivious self from the bar. It was Harold, he was our awkward waiter. Bless him, he was really handsome and so very young. Fresh faced with whole life ahead of him..... with me.

I have drifted into a deep deep sleep, I am back at the plantation, its evening. I hear the sounds of crickets echoes the sounds of the night garden. The sweet aroma from the apple, lemon and lime trees encase the lining of my nostrils.

"Edwina wake up" Winnie gently rocks me

"Hmmmmmm......."

"Wake up, where have you been"? Winnie was excited about something.

"I have been here"

"No you haven't I have not seen you in weeks" she snipped.

"Really?"

"Yes. Where were you?"

"The last I remembered we went for lunch, which for me was like yesterday, actually it feels like that occurred earlier today"

"Well you here now. There is so much to tell you".

"Like what?"

"I met a really nice young man".

"Really who is he?"

"Remember the waiter that Daddy was really rude to?"

"You mean?"

"Yes at the Crystal Hotel, its him."

"Daddy is going to lose his mind when he finds out", I warn her.

"He's not going to find out, is he. It's not like you will tell him. Nothing is happening I just like him that's all. We have talked a few times"

"How is that even possible?"

"Daddy and I have lunch there every Thursday. There are some places not even daddy can follow me to."

"Such as?" I arch my eyebrow with disapproval.

"The Powder Room"

"You meet in the Powder Room?" I laugh

"Nooooooo there is a small store cupboard and we sneak a few minutes each week with each other. We exchange letters and he kissed me yesterday. It was just..... scrumptious, his lips were so soft. He really cares about me. I think he might even love me."

We did not hear the door open "Who might love you?" Grandma Phyllis's said with a quizzical glare.

"My daddy" Winnie spat out the words with such venom both Grandma and I was taken aback.

Grandma walked towards the bed where Winnie lay, suspecting that her Grandmother may take this as an opportunity to beat her Winnie jumped of the bed and stood her ground by the four poster bed.

"So you think your daddy loves you?"

"I know so"

"you gullible naïve child"

"You father is incapable of love, he is damaged goods, you can thank your mother's family for that?"

"What does that mean ?

Realising that she had sad too much. " Nothing"

"My father loves me and you can't stand it can you?"

"You know nothing of love".

"I knew the love of my grandmother before you all killed her, that was real love"

"Lucy was a ……"

"What Grandma???" Winnie was shouting at my Grandmother

"She was a lying deceitful old peasant who deserved to die like a dog"

"Noooooooooooooooooo" Winnie lurched towards her Grandma fist raised

"Mother!" Daddy screamed, "Get out"

"Barrington darling thank god you're here, this insolent little street urchin,"

"ENNNNOOOOUUGGGHHHH!!!!" Daddy screamed at my Grandma. She stop dead in her tracks and backed away.

Winnie was lying on the all fours her head on the perfectly polished mahogany wooden floor weeping her soul out. Daddy grabbed his mother by her shoulders and walked her forcefully out of the room. He sat down on the floor next to his daughter. He held her close, Winnie pulled away and slapped her father hard. Grandma is right. You murdered my Mima like a dog" Winnie spat the words out.

"Edwina …" Daddy was crying

"Get out! Winnie screamed, "Get out" they were both on their feet, Winnie fist clenched, was driving them into her father's chest "Get out, Get out, Get out!" Daddy walked out and slammed the door. Winnie sobbed on the floor for hours. I tried to comfort her, it was no use. Grandma Phyllis had just ripped the scab of this wound and it was bleeding heavily.

.

Chapter 12

Barrington Barnett Junior.

What in the world possessed my mother to be so rancorous. Come on Barry how can you make this right? I run down the staircase, through the corridor and out of the house. The night air is warm and pungent with the smells of the plantation. Too angry to confront my mother I walk towards the main road. It's at least a mile, this should give me time to think. I look up, the moon is full, a light breeze washes over me and proceeds to cool my temperament. My initial stomp has been traded for a rhythmical walk to the melody of the swoosh and churn of miles of sugarcane enveloped either side of me.

I shake my head, not knowing how to mend this fragile bridge between my daughter and myself. All of my emotions swell around my body, yet I feel the heftiness of my burden in my chest. The pain is indescribable, but this is the closet I have been to heartbreak. How could my mother inflict a wound so deep into her only grandchild? It's just so …..Cruel.

I arrive to the main road and am surprised that I have travelled so far in such a short space of time. Well Barry, this is progress, five years ago you would have shot your mother in the face. I smile at my sick sense of humour, although it is not humorous, I have to laugh at the situation. I have travelled an arduous emotional road to get here and do not wish to return. I turn around to walk back I see the plantation, unable to face the confrontation which lays ahead of me,, with a heavy heart I walk deep into the sugar cane fields. I find a spot in between the perfectly manicured rows and lay down, gazing at the clear night sky. It was truly magnificent, each star that I focused on seemed to shine and twinkle brightly for me. I think fleetingly of the spirits I have released from their waking bodies, Angeline, Lucy and Mrs. Mack. I cannot help it, nor do I want to control this, I weep for all the pain that I have caused. I weep for displacing the only person that I have loved without fear, but most of all, I weep for myself. As I look into the night's sky, I feel god's presence over me. This is bigger than me, Edwina, my mother and all the others. I can do better. I will do better.

I awake with a start. Its deep into the night and I am cold. It's been raining and I am soaked through. I walk to the house and see that most of the lights downstairs are on. I walk with haste, fearful that something awful may have happened in my absence. I open the door and my father, mother and Winnie run out of the drawing room.

"Oh Barry you're ok" my mother exclaimed with sheer relief in her voice.

My anger cannot be sustained. She runs to hug me and I *push her away, hard, she nearly topples over.*

"Barry!" She yelps, as she steady's herself on the paisley armchair by the wall.

My father steps forward, I put my hand up and look at him "Don't"

"Have you been drinking?" my father's asks annoyed looking at Winnie

"No father, I am sober". They all looked relieved.

"I just …. Needed some time away. I was angry and did not want to do or say anything that I would later regret", I look at Winnie who looks tired.

"Are you angry with me daddy?" Winnie asks in a shaky voice, she looked beautiful in her white night dress, her hair all unruly.

"No Winn. I have no issue with you. You were being human, reacting to information delivered by your

Grandmothers acid tongue. You were ….are wounded, I accept that. It was the perfect reaction, nothing more than I deserved under the circumstances."

Winnie looked pained as she searched her father's face for clues as to what he was thinking. "Daddy I am going to bed now that I know that you are safe….. Goodnight", I could tell that she thought about kissing me, but decided against it. Things are awkward between us. The swell in my chest rises. There was only one person to blame for all this pain.

Before she leaves the room she looks at mother, she smirks I think. I am not sure if I am over tired. We all watch my beautiful child as she disappeared around the corner. I cannot contain my anger. I look angrily at my mother and father and walked into the drawing room.

"Barry, look I am so very sorry for my indiscretion" my mother quickly walked around the armchair in the opulent room. She was fidgeting with her hands, and both my father and I could tell that she was nervous. "It was thoughtless and …and …and "

"For a woman with so many words I am surprised that you are finding it difficult for find the right one. Cruel is the word that you are looking for", my message is delivered with authority I am no longer the puppy led his throat. I am a man, my own man, and tonight she will see this,

"Yes" she mutters almost inaudible, she barely looks at me. She senses the sea change in me, she feels my new energy with her. The relationship has shifted. I am in the driving seat.

"Sorry mother what was that?" *I can't help it. I need to see her squirm.*

"Yes. It was …. Cruel and I am truly sorry". She is searching my face wondering whether this pathetic excuse is enough.

I stare at my mother for what seemed like an eternity. I did not realise that I had started to cry again until the tear fell off my cheek.

"Barry, I am so".

I put my hands up and my mother stopped in her tracks.

"You are a deceitful, treacherous, conniving, miserable, cruel wicked old bitch mother. That is what you are. You have manipulated me for far too long.

Both my parents look aghast at my disrespect. I am the way that I am because of you. I have committed hellish acts because you are my mother, you have been able to wind me up and I foolishly have created havoc in your name. You said those things to crush my only child. Your only grandchild. You said those things because you are jealous that we have fostered a relationship through the odds.

"Nooooo Barry"

Shut up and do not interrupt me. You said those things because you my friendly serpents prefers me drunk, and wanting, in need of your assistance. Were you trying to get me to throw myself in a bottle again? I will never forgive you for this mother. You have taught me that I have misplaced my trust in you. A mother who loves her son does not behave in this way. A Grandmother that loves her Grandchild would not dream in hurting them like this.

The room fell silent and my mother was wiping her eyes. She looker old and small.

My father looked at me and nodded. "I am sorry for you son", he had not called me son in many years. " I don't say this often, irrespective of what you have done in the past, I am proud of you and the way you have turned your life around. Man to Man, you have my respect. At least now you can see your mother for who and what she is" My father looked at his wife. "I expect you in my room in the next five minutes. I suggest you go and prepare yourself"

A cold chill ran down my spine. I knew how my father kept my mother under control, I did not like it, but now see that it was perhaps a necessary evil.

It has been a long time since I have craved for a drink like this. The pull is so strong that I know that if I stay I am going to fall off this ten year wagon od sobriety, and I may never get back on it. It's been a struggle every day. Some days are better than other. The last twenty four hours have been the absolute worst.

I just need to get through tonight and tomorrow is a new day. I laugh at myself and with myself. I relay the evening in my mind. My heart is overcome with emotion. My father is proud of me, the man that I have carved out of the gutter. I momentarily flash back to whom I was. I push the old Barrington away. It's safer for my sobriety that way. My eyelids are like iron clads. I cannot keep my eyes open any longer, and I fall into a deep and peaceful sleep.

Its dawn, I feel the warmth of her soft naked skin next to me. I turn and Jeanette is tucked under my arm. She is plainly beautiful in her own sort of way. I find her enchanting, loyal and ruthless. Had she had been from different stock I may have married her. She has been my sole stabling force for the past five years. She was my savior and salvation and I will love her to the end of time.

I lay awake restless looking aimlessly at the ceiling.

The night sky was slowly creeping away.

"Good Morning Darling", she whispered and kissed me on my forehead. This was how she greeted me every morning for the last ten years.

"How are you?" She asked her face full of concern. Her big brown eyes searched mine for a sign, any sign.

"I am hurt sweetheart, really hurt". I scrunch close my eyes like a child.

My lover entwines her body around me and my head lay in her full breasts. Comforted by her womanly curves I hold on to my love.

"Barrington, it will get better. This is storm and it too will pass. We will all get through this". She delivers the message like she always does with conviction and sweetness.

I look at her "How?" tears wet my eyes. "How can you be so sure, she hates me, and so she should. I am a wicked vile human being". My voice cracks "I have done unspeakable things".

"That man had now gone, you are a different person. It's your mother who is vile and wicked" she snapped.

I look at her cautiously.

"Darling this is not your fault. This is not …….. on you."

"How can I fix this?", I nestle my head in her chest, she holds me tight.

"You can't Barry. You just have to give her time and space."

"I don't know how. We have come so far. Finally she is talking to me, and now its ruined." I close my eyes and roll over.

"Then go somewhere, take a break you deserve it, a

199

break may just cool the temperature down, for everyone". Hmmmm? What do you think?

"I will only go if you come with me?" I tell my beloved.

"That could not happen, as well you know"

"A break will do us good, it's time to stop with the charade. Let's be together. I need you by my side as my woman, my wife" I say quietly

"Your mother would have be strung up" she laughs "no thank you"

"Why?", I ask insecurely "Do you want rid of me?"

"Never" Jeanette proclaimed with delight. Never" she whispered again. With that her hot mouth reached mine and she sedated my quest for alcohol two successive times.

Chapter 13

The Blooming of flowers.

Our plantation library was a place of wonder. The fourteen foot walls were covered from wall to ceiling with deep oak wood shelves that glossed and sparkled. Every inch of this room housed classics, from Pruce, William Shakespeare, the Bronte sisters and Tennyson. I lay on the 60 foot oriental rug, so opulent you would be forgiven thinking that it came directly from the Ming Dynasty. I feel so very sober. These years that I have blocked out, erased all memories, irrespective of whether they were happy or not. How I robbed myself of the core of me. Like it or not, this was my legacy and I gave it up for love? Or did I? Was I an unruly teenager in the throes of puberty? Or did I make poor choices? Now that I have seen my father, I can see that he is truly remorseful for his crimes. I have filled my heart with hate for this man when all I feel is love for him right now. Maybe I could have made this relationship better. He was right Harold was not good enough for me. This love has taken all that I have to keep this marriage together. Why? Why did I just not leave? I could have had a different life with Courtney. I have never longed for, yearned for and loved a man with more passion, than I did him. Yet I stayed. I was a coward.

No ...... I was a wife and mother. I chose Harold all those years ago. My choice nearly cost him his life. My family made me indebted to him, trapped like an animal at times, and here I am. Full of regret that I did not pursue that love of my life.

"Edwina what's wrong?", Winnie asks

I roll my eyes. There is not much to say, "Nothing I am fine" I tell her with dejection in my voice.

"You're not" Winnie chimes in

"No Winnie I'm not. I am dying of cancer. Three weeks ago I was diagnosed with Terminal Stage 4 Malignant Melanoma, which has metastasized to my brain and chest.

Winnie looked scared "What does that mean?" she whispered wide eyed.

It means that the tumors have spread from their original primary site in my breast, and have developed in my brain and chest." My younger self look crushed. "Winn I am only here because I am dying. This is not a figment of your imagination its real. I am here when I should be with my husband, beautiful children, my friends and I cannot understand why I am here reliving this, this painful chapter in my life. I shut this out a long time ago and never thought that I would revisit it. Now I am here. I cannot do this. I cry but no tears fall. The pain in my chest seizes me and my body becomes rigid.

"Edwina…Edwina, please don't die, you're not ready" Winnie falls to her knees and holds my head in her lap. She kisses my forehead. "You are all that I have. Please stay. As her tears wash over me I feel ease through my body. I look at her"

"I cannot do this anymore. I want to die, its tooo tooo much Winn. I just need to go" I plead to her and god, wanting them to take me to a place where I am pain free.

"You cannot leave yet. There is much that you need to do first. It's not quite your time", she said, looking very mature and grown up.

At the corner of my eye I saw a figurine at the door. "Winn", I say looking at the doorway.

Winnie swung around.

"Who are you talking to child and what are you doing on the floor" Grandmother Phyllis's asks. She hesitantly walked into the room and look around the corner, the closet and under the bed.

"Answer me, who were you talking to?" she cautiously walked towards the drapes and pulled them apart, to ensure there was no stranger lurking in the room".

"I will not tell you?" Winnie wails. "Please don't leave me" she looks deep in my eyes. Not now"

What?

"I will not tell you" she sobs openly as her loss.

"What is it child?", my grandmother looked shaken by my display of emotion.

"YOU would not u-n-d-e-r-s-t-a-n-d!" Winn was still hunched over cradling my head.

"Get up", Grandma Phyllis's commanded.

"I can't Grandma, she is dying can't you see her?"

"Who?" Grandma turned pale, "Edwina there is no one here?"

"I am here, look harder, it's me and I'm dying"

"Ed… Edwina please get up dear", Grandma is really concerned" she kneeled down next to me and pleaded quietly with me to get up. Fear washed over my grandma, she ran from our room "Barrington she yelled, Barrington come quickly, Come quickly, her voice became shrill and high.

My miniature self, on the cusp of womanhood, whose primary emotion since the age of five has been grief and loss, looks at me desperate to give her advice. This cancer is ravaging my insides, the fight is nearly over and I am starting to feel relieved. She helps me to her bed lovingly. I want to reassure this young girl before me but I just can't. She looks at me "Don't die, who will I talk to". I weakly squeezed her hand, she looks at me. "Listen Winnie, do not tell them about me. They will think that you are mad. Please stop talking. Ok?

Winnie just nodded.

Lying on the bed did not ease my pain, but enabled me to feel better. I could feel myself drifting back. No I need to stay I willed myself.

"Winn …." I could hear Daddy shouting my name as he ran up the stairs taking three or four steps at a time. Grandpa was next and Grandma Phyllis's a few seconds behind.

Winnie sat on the floor leaning up against her bed. Daddy immediately scooped her up and sat her on the bed.

"Winn darling talk to Daddy. You Ok? Who is here with you?

"No one" Winn sobbed.

"Barry that's not what she said, I swear". The words tumbled out of her mouth.

Daddy picked up Winnies hand and kissed them." Baby tell daddy, what is it? What's going on?"

"Daddy please don't ask me?", she threw head in his lap, he stroked her hair trying to reassure her.

"It's ok. No matter what you say, I promise I won't get mad. I will not react, is that what you're worried about."

"Pleeeeaaasssseee"

Daddy held his only child as if she was about to die any

moment.

"Tell me Winn, what is it?"

She looked at Daddy. "They are here with me?"

"Who is darling?" Grandpa asked and stepped forward.

Winnie threw her head on her father's shoulder. The others looked at each other confused.

"Who Winn? Mothers says you were crying and saying that someone is dying. What is going on?" he sounded desperate.

Winnie points to the lounge chair by her balcony. "Mima is sat right there". Daddy's eyes grew large and all three of them stood with open mouths. On the bed is Mrs. Mack"

"Mrs. Mack", Grandpa exclaimed. "What?"

Grandfather walked cautiously towards Winnie, daddy took at least four steps back, both hands ran through his hair. He clasped his fingers and locked them at the nape of his neck. He starred at Winnie, incredulous at what he had witnessed. Both Daddy and Grandma Phyllis were locked in the same shocked gaze.

Grandpa sat down on the bed. "Princess look at me"

As Winnie looked up she saw the disgusted look on my face. She smirked at me.

"Princess how long have you been hearing voices". Grandfather asked.

"I am not hearing voices Grandpa, they are here. I can see them"

"What are they saying?"

Mrs. Mack is asking me to tell Mackie that she is ok? She found peace." I look at Daddy "She has a message for you do you want to hear it."

Simultaneously Daddy said "yes" and Grandma Phyllis screamed "No"

"Tell me" Daddy demanded. He was pale and looked like he wanted to vomit.

"Mrs. Mack says that to this day she will never understand why you had to rape her, she did not deserve that. She would never have told Mackie, the shame would have killed her. You did not have to kill me she says, I would have killed myself sooner or later as I would not have been able to live with what you did to me. She says that you will rot in hell and no peace will follow you until you die"

"Enough Grandma Phyllis screamed. Daddy ran to the corner of the room and threw up his breakfast. He was on his knees.

"Barry really the girl is delusional, it can happen when ones had a shock," Grandpa tried to explain.

Grandpa took a moment to soak up the emotions in the room. It was thick with fear. "Barry, Barry……. This is just…..Barry, Phyllis. What aren't you telling me?" Grandpa voice became quiet.

Grandma Phyllis walked to the balcony.

"Father….. I …… what Winnie says is true, I did those things and"

"No Barry … No…. No …..How could you do this to her, to Mackie? You are an animal" Grandpa stormed out of the room and slammed the door with such velocity that the field hands could have heard it.

"Tell Mrs. Mack that not a day goes by that I do not regret that night" Daddy said, "and" his voice cracked "your Mima, tell her that I am so very sorry for all the pain that I," Daddy pointed to Grandma Phyllis, "That we have caused you"

"What did Grandma do Daddy" I ask feeling sick before he could answer.

He looked at me. "I am sure Mima will tell you at some point. She killed your Grandpa Vincent, it wasn't me"

"No ……" Winnie sat on her bed looking at her Grandma with sheer horror.

"How?" I whispered?

"The how does not matter, what's done is done and cannot be undone". Grandma Phyllis said quietly.

"Oh Winnie, what have you done" I ask her. "You have unleashed the Pandora's Box and I do not think that even you can put this right"

"Grandma, she has a message for you"

"Who?"

"She says that she knows that you see her in your dreams. She wants you to know that you will never have peace, not even in death you both will not have peace.

My Grandmother complexion drained away from her skin. She looked ashen and my father walked out the room and quietly shut the door.

"Winnie", I exclaimed "What were you thinking?"

"Me….. You have sat here with your booo hooo depression talking about how terrible it's been. I am doing something about it. I am going to make them all pay. All this family does is destroy people".

"Well you definitely fit in now don't you"

"What? Do not remember how he killed Mima. You told me that he raped and murdered Mrs. Mack, remember she was OUR only friend. What do you expect me to do? Do nothing? Not going to happen. I will destroy them as they have destroyed me, how they destroyed you. How can you live your life not remembering you childhood? How can that be possible?

"This is not the answer, Daddy was distraught", I snapped

"So was Mima, so was Mrs. Mack and the countless others that he has killed, raped, destroyed" she shouted. "They are both culpable and I am going to make them pay for it. You blocked it all out as it was too much to bear. It is too much to bear I know I am living it"

"I am too weak Winnie to fight with you. You have to be prepared. This will not end well my dear. I roll over and fall into a deep sleep"

"Edwina don't go, what am I going to do. Edwina …..
Edwina"

The sun rises and sets on my lonely heart. It's been weeks since I have seen Edwina. I don't know whether she is dead or alive? Oh Lord please don't take her way from me before I have the opportunity to apologies. She has to understand. I have to make them pay for what they have done to me. They robbed me of my Grandfather, and Mima. The only woman outside of my family that loved me enough to nurture, sing and play with me was Mrs. Mack. What did my father do to her? He rapes her, and then he kills her. I am going to make them regret the day they snatched me from Mima.

The last few months have been glorious with Daddy, but a few months cannot put right all the death, pain and hurt he and my Grandma Phyllis has caused me. The math's just do not add up. I should not feel like this. I have done nothing wrong. It's them. Grandpa had avoided everyone. He is staying in town at his flat above the surgery. I heard the maids whispering that daddy has started drinking. I didn't want him to drink, he is nasty drunk, and when drunk he is unpredictable and ...... dangerous. I wanted him to hurt him. If he cannot control his demons that has nothing to do with me. Grandma Phyllis won't look at me, she wearing her crucifix. It's not avoidance, its terror. I am more alone than I have ever been. Maybe Edwina was right. I have unleashed the madness. Loneliness and solitude is something that I have been used to. The difference between then and now is that I had conversation, even snidely conversation is better than this. Now I have nothing. I did not think that it was possible to feel any more alone with so many family members around me.

My oversized closet is every woman's dream. I dress as a lady should. I put on my lime dress, I wet my hair and crunch my curls, and slip a matching ribbon around my curly bonnet. I wear my Chanel white heals. I look at myself in the mirror. I look tired, but then I feel really warn out. This emotional conflict that I am experiencing is taken its toll on me. I may not have the maturity or the strength to see this through and I am really scared. I have unhinged them. I look at myself in the mirror again and apply some pink lipstick.

"What would Edwina say? I ask myself out loud. "Hmmm she would say you started this. So finish it. Be strong, decisive and honest". I smile to myself. "On my god, how can I be so foolish. It's you Edwina. I am you, I make it. I actually make it and that won't change. Edwina is living proof of that. I review my image in the mirror. Give them all hell. I can, whatever is to come I survive" I laugh loud and smile at myself.

I run downstairs as I was positive that I heard voices. I put in my best act as I bounce into the breakfast room.

"Morning father, Grandmother"

"Morning" they say at the same time.

"You look nice" Grandma Phyllis says in a sweet voice. I actually think she meant it.

"You Ok?" Daddy asks me. Looking for signs of life outside of me around the breakfast room.

"I will be when you stop drinking Daddy" I say. The maid in the corner of the room, looked up from arranging the papers and looked at me.

"What.. How do you know that", he asked alarmed.

"Don't worry daddy" I giggle, I whisper "I did not get a message, I overheard one of the maids last week if I look tired it's because I am worried about you. Besides. You're a mean drunk".

"I slipped once" daddy explained quietly. "Its … It's been hard to process these last few days, there's been a lot to take in."

I felt a huge pang of guilt. I look up and see Grandma Phyllis smiling at me.

"I was thinking that maybe I will go away for a few weeks" daddy tried to play it down.

"Really, where?" I am surprised but hide it well.

"Anywhere except here" Daddy muttered. His light was gone.

"Barry you need to be here for.. for… Edwina, you can't leave now" Grandma pleaded. "What she meant was that you cannot leave HER with me. Not now.

"Daddy I will be fine. I am ok, I promise. I think Grandpa was right as I have had no more visits." I smile at them both, desperately trying to reassure them.

"How long do you think that you will be gone?" I say too bubbly for everyone's liking.

"Not sure, maybe a month", daddy tells me eating his scrambled eggs.

"Ok where will you go?" I ask more sedate this time.

"I was thinking going to see some of Daddy's family in the United States?

"Daddy that would be great. Please go, besides it will give Grandma and I time to actually have some girl time". I look at my Grandma who looks disgusted at the prospect. "How does that sound?"

She looks at Daddy, "It sounds divine"

I smile at Grandma, she can see that I know that Daddy needs this time. "Settled then"

"When will you go?"

Daddy hesitantly looks around the room. " Tomorrow"

 "Daddy can I go into town?" I ask

"What for?", Grandma snapped, I eye her like a swordfish with my curt side eye. "To see Granddad. I have not seen him for a few days " I look suspiciously at the maids trying to choose my words carefully. " So can I go please?"

"Of course …. You know Winnie, I am constantly in awe at how thoughtful and kind you are. Always thinking of others. Who would have thought that I could have such a lovely daughter?" daddy smiled

"It's easy daddy, I have all your best bits and mummy's good bits", I got up and kissed him on the head. "Thank you Daddy"

"You're welcome Winn"

Grandma, do you have any message or would you like to take Grandpa any fresh clothes.

"No dear, thank you" my Grandma eyed me suspiciously. I smile to avert her gaze.

"I will ask Mackie to drive you" daddy said

"Is that wise, Grandma chimed immediately after he said it.

"Hmmmm"

"Daddy its fine". I leaned in and whispered in his ear. "I am your daughter and your secret is safe with me. I am a Barnett after all." Daddy looked at me and smiled. He looked proud.

He cleared his throats "It's fine mother"

"But Barry" she exclaimed

"It's fine mother.   Mackie will drive her.   "Besides, ironically I trust Mackie with my life. He will take good care of my little girl"

I flash my Grandma a big smile. "Grandma can I get you anything from town?"

"No dear" she looks at me with hateful caution.

"Ok Daddy I will be ready to leave on ten minutes. That Ok."

"I will call Mackie now" and he left the table.

As soon as Daddy was out of earshot. "What are you up to little girl?"

"Wouldn't you like to know Grandma?"

"Careful now that is my son you're playing with". She stood up and walked towards me.

I straighten up and looked at my Grandma in my face. "I am not playing, believe me" I say quietly as we have given the maids quite a show already.

"Just because you have your daddy wrapped around your finger, do not think you can do the same to me" my grandma told me through her smiling face, and gritted teeth.

I laughed and deliberately throw my head back "I do not want   you   wrapped   around   any   part   of   me Grandmamma". I snapped spitefully.

"You become more like Mima every day" she says quietly.

"Then you should watch out".

Me….. Tut Tut Tut "I destroyed her ….. Remember". Grandma suddenly became aware where she was and that we had an audience.

I stretch to the sky and cock my head at a right angle, "That was then Grandmamma. There is new, young, energetic fresh blood in the house old woman. You will find it hard to keep up". We both stare each other down. "Have a nice day Grandma, I will give your regards to Grandpa"

The morning sun hazed my view, to the extent that I had squint to see Mackie. He was stood by the car. Over the years his body had thinned,, his chin appeared closer to his chest than I remembered.

"Good Morning Miss Edwina", Mackie said with a smile.

"Good Morning Mackie". I avoided eye contact as I felt choked with guilt at what my father had done.

"You look a vision this morning", he said quietly blushing as he opened the door.

"Thank you", I reciprocated in the same whispered tone as his.

We sat in the car, I look out and the plantation was luscious green, yellows and honey. It was rainy season and everything felt as if it were in bloom. We drove slowly along the dirt mile road. I sigh aloud.

"I know it's beautiful this time of year", Mackie broke my train of thoughts.

"How did you know."

"Miss. Look at this", he waved his hand across the windscreen to the view behind it. "Only a blind man would not appreciate the beauty", he chuckled..

"Mrs. Mack used to say that to me all the time.

He smiled, "Yes, sounds about right, she was the one that taught me that saying".

"I miss her", I say gently and quietly

"Me too my darling. Me too" he looked out the window for a few seconds while driving. Mackie's shoulders drooped and he frowned. He wiped his eye quickly and cleared his throat and inhaled with speed.

"Mr. Mack, I am sorry I just didn't think. I did not mean to upset you. I just wanted to."

"No Noooooo, its ok. I get like this sometimes, It's the time of year. It was Maggie's favorite time rainy season".

I giggle. "Wow"

"What?" he asked looking at me.

"All these years and I never knew her name?"

"Really?" He sounded surprised.

"Yes." I smile broadly.

I mist up. I can't help it. "I loved her you know, she was …. Is my only friend in the world."

"I know how you feel, she was the only person I could rely on." He tells me and means every word. "I just wish I could either find her or figure out what happened.

"With what?"

He looked at me. "Something happened to Maggie. The pain each day for me is that I have no closure. I have no peace. When someone dies you say goodbye. I have not been able to do that. I am stuck in the not knowing".

"Are you sure that she is dead?"

"I know it", he tells me with conviction. "We have never been apart not one day and it's just not her style to go off. We .... Loved each other. It's not like some of these people who are married that had to stay together over duty, I only wanted her. I only loved her. That has not changed."

"Is that why you have never moved on?" I ask

"Yes and no. I cannot move on as I am stuck in the past. I have no closure. It's not fair for me to bring all the hurt, anxiety and fear that I have about Maggie's death into something new."

"What about you, you are such a nice looking man. I know that you are good and kind as Mrs. Mack would tell me so all the time"

"Really?", Mackie smiled.

I nod smiling at him "I often wished you were my father instead of .... Him"

He looks at me through sad eyes and nods. "That sounds like my Maggie. She would always praise the good in a person."

"You can meet someone else. You can find love again, marry have children. Mackie if I was older I would marry you." I blurt out.

Mackie laughed out loud, "You would, would you?"

"Yes I would. Mrs. Mack told me what a great person you are. She was hoping for a child one day. She was soooo good to me"

"Darling, you were our child, you are still my child and we loved you as if you were ours. Especially ....when you first arrived. You were so ...wounded."

His words seep through my pores like sponge. I look at

Mackie, he pulls into the highway.

"You Ok Miss?" he enquires.

"No" I whisper.

"Now it's my turn to apologies. I should not have said that to you. I am sorry."

"Mr. Mack you tell no lies so don't apologies. You have done nothing wrong. My father is the culprit here and he is to blame."

Mackie's eyes fall to the gear stick. "Miss Edwina, I loved your grandmother with all my heart, she and your Grandpa Vin, they were goooooood people. Whenever I go to town, people, neighbours stop me and still ask after you all this time "How is Mars Vin and Miss Lucy granddaughter? Do you know how many warnings I get for you," he laughed. "Warnings I kid you not"

"I don't understand", I giggled

"This person and that person says make sure you look out for her in that house." For poor Maggie it was worse. He laughed

"What was she like?" I ask

"Who Maggie?"

"No. I mean yes but I was referring to my Grandmother Lucy."

He smiled. "Your Grandmother was a pioneering woman, she was wise before her years, and she was talented with a sewing machine. Oh my lord knows that I tell the truth, she used to make Mrs. Barnet dresses and gowns that was when your Grandma was a looker. She could turn a blind man's head."

"Really?"

"Yes she was beautiful." Mackie nodded

"No not about that. Mima made Grandma's dresses? Really I did not know that." *Hmmm Mima worked for Grandma.*

"Yes Mackie" said realising that he may have said a little too much.

"Mackie don't stop, this conversation is between us. No one talks about her, them, and it's really hard. I know that I have this love for all of them, but do not know why and my childhood memory is so limited."

"Your Grandpa Vin was an amazing man. He was a good friend to my father. They were neighbours, at the plantation.

"What O-U-R plantation?"

"Yes, his father was a slave as was my great grandfather"

"Then how did he get to the big house?" I was fascinated by my family history.

"It was largely due to your Grandmother, she was a wealthy woman at one point from all her dress making. She made a lot of money from Wedding dresses, christening and that sort of wear. Her clients were wealthy whites in Kingston. There was a war on, so imports from Europe and the US were nonexistent, and your Grandmother could sew. She worked hard, and made enough to buy that plot of land. Vincent was not happy. He wanted to be the provider, but he soon came around. They represented that dream of every slave., and plantation worker. Ownership of land, meant ownership of your time, ownership of you the man. Do you know what that means for a black men like us. It meant everything. Your Grandmother when she started to build that house some people did not speak to her, as they felt that she wanted to be better than them. Miss Lucy put them right. She started to tell them, the white house was not just for her and Vincent it was for the community. When your Grandfather discovered that Vin owed land with his wife, he evicted them.

"What?" I asked shocked

Mackie's voice changed, it was harder" Yes Miss. People like us in their minds must always be subservient and grateful".

"Mackie I had no idea. I always remembering her being so capable. How did my Grandfather die Mackie?"

Mackie starred at me as if I asked him to sleep with me.

"Mackie, how did he die?"

Miss…. I am not going to lie to you. I know exactly how he died, but it's not for me to tell you the ….how?

"Then who?"

"Miss ….. I think we need to get going Miss."

"Does it involve my father?" I ask.

Mackie eyes were dead straight on the road.

"My Grandfather?"

"Miss it does not matter how many times you ask, I have told you my stance on this position and it will not change, he said gently.

The rest of the journey was in silence. On arrival Mackie got out and opened my door. As I got out of the car he helped me out the car. He looked at me, "You look like her you know?"

"Who Mima?"

"No darling your mother"

Tears sprang to my eyes "really". I don't know what she looks like. I have not seen a picture of her."

"Miss she was very beautiful person and had the kindest heart. Your Grandpa Vin called her his butterfly. She was delicate like Lucy, but she was strong."

I hug Mackie. "Thank you"

Mackie gently pushes me of him, looking around to ensure that gossiping mouths do not get the wrong idea. "What time shall I pick you up?"

"I would like to spend the day so do not rush back please." I ask "Any Mackie"

"Yes Miss"

"Do not ever call me Miss anything again, Its Winnie to you, Ok?"

He smiled, "Ok Winnie".

In all the years that I lived with my Grandparents and father I had not once visited the Barnet's Medical Centre. I had driven past it, waited outside of it with my Grandma Phyllis yet we never entered. I walk up the steps and knock the door. There is movement inside thank goodness or I would be stuck. A tall, thin beautiful mature woman walks towards the door. She has her hair in a bun, and a lovely pale blue mid length skirt and matching short sleeve shirt. She looked very sophisticated.

She opens the door and stares at me.

"I am sorry to disturb you, I am looking for my" before I could finish she cut me off.

"Grandfather, she says, her eyes were misty "I know

who you are, come in Winnie". She took my hand, it felt so familiar to me that I did not withdraw it. I allowed her to lead me to through the surgery, up some stairs, once at the top of the stairs was an enchanting open plan room. It was so simple, Beachwood floors, open shutters, a sea view in the distance. Sophisticated cream lean furnishings, it seemed so modern. The bed overlooked the window and the view of the village with the blue sea protruding out of the tree tops was enchanting.

"This is breathtakingly beautiful" I exclaim.

"Yes it is" my mystery woman agrees with me.

"Now I understand why Grandpa spends So much time here. It's delightful. Where is he?"

He is out with a patient, she is very unwell and may not survive the day, so…"

"I see, well I can leave".

"No …No this stranger woman says, please say". She looks at me intently drinking in every element of my presence.

I was about to make lunch. Can I get you something to drink? Juice water anything cool Winnie",

"How do you know my nick name?"

"I know you, my name is"

I abruptly interrupt her. "Rene, is your name Reneee, Auntie Renee".

"Yes Winnie darling" she leapt into my arms and we held one another kissing each other for a long time. She kissed my face, neck and the backs of my hands. All the while her wet tears caressing my skin.

"My darling, my beautiful sweet honey pie….. my sweet darling. How I have longed for this this moment. Look at you? Perfection just like your mother.

My Aunt Rene, made us iced tea, we sat in the living area.

"How are you?" she enquired.

"I am well thank you?" I say politely.

"Are you?"

"Aunty Rene I think you used to come to Mima's. Is that you? Have I remembered the right person".

"Yes, Mima and I were sisters, not blood sisters but sisters none the less"

My heart skipped. I feel weak. "Today is a strange day?"

"Why?" My Aunt Rene looked concerned.

"Mr. Mack and I were talking for the first time about Mima and Grandpa Vin." I smiled

She smiled, How is Mackie?

"He is well, I love that man so much"

"He and Maggie were …. Are good people." She corrects herself.

"Hmmm" I nod whilst fidgeting with my fingers.

"Winnie, as I said your Grandmother and I grew up as sisters. Your Grandpa Vin and I were like brother and sister. I am the closest family that you have here."

I snap at her "Then why am I not living with you?".

Surprised by my rude outburst she explains "I tried to

take you, to raise you, but your father had rights. He was the father. I tried everything but they were too strong for me." She says regrettably.

"Who was" I snap

"Your Grandmother, your father"

"Hmmmm", I continue to fidget, I am feeling very warm all of a sudden. *Rene keeps staring at me which unnerves me.*

"You are such a stunner, I heard that you had blossomed, but this is, you are lovely" she smiles

"Hmmmmm", I look out of the window.

"Are you ok?" she asks.

"Aunt Rene Why are you here? I mean in the private residence?"

"The Truth?" she sighs.

I nod. "Yes please" I want to be suspicious of her but I can't she seems so familiar to me.

"You Grandfather and I have been lovers for twenty five years"

"Really???", I gasp. I am annoyed at my response. I am momentarily unnerved, but intrigued, there are so many gaps for me. I intend to get answers, and I think she can close them all.

"Aunt Rene, this is a lot to take in.", I chuckle whilst reeling from my shock.

"I know, but it's wonderful for me." I missed you, she says quietly.

"There are so many gaps that I have with events,

people, and reasons why things occurred, can you help me?"

"Sure," she says.

"Aunty Rene I need answers not platitudes, I look at her seriously "Will you help me?""

Aunt Rene got off her chair and came and sat next to me, she cupped my face in her hands and looked me in the eyes. "If you ask it. I will tell the truth. All of it. Even the bits that are hurtful. I will not leave any of it out. I promise you."

Tears starts to roll down my face "Tell me everything. I want to know about my mother and how she died. I want to know what actually happened between her and daddy. I heard today that Mima and Phyllis's had a relationship. I need to know why Grandpa Vin died at the hands of Grandma Phyllis' and finally how did Mima injure her arm. I mean if she was a seamstress that was her income. Can you do that for me?

She sighs hard "Yes I can" My aunty got up walked to the bedroom, opened her dresser drawer and took out two white handkerchiefs. She then walked to the kitchen and took out a bottle of rum and two tumblers.

"I hold my hands up, "I do not drink"

"No. But after I tell you all that you have asked you will need one." She says seriously.

"My head is pounding Aunty Rene. I cannot take any of this in. I am decedent of pure evil. My father raped my mother. My Grandfather Vincent goes to rip my father's head off quite rightly, and end up dead because Grandma Phyllis stabs him. As if that was not bad enough my father on the same night hacks away my grandmother's shoulder with a machete. My mother then dies in childbirth, then years later when they find out

224

about me my father kills my grandmother. Now that's a family tree to be proud off". I look at Rene "You must really love my Grandfather?"

"I do" she says quietly.

"He is really pure". She beams.

"Really, he threw my Grandfather off his plantation when he discovered that he bought land with Mima. That's terrible?"

"Yes he did those things, but regretted that decision and made peace with your Mima and Vin. Who do you think delivered you?"

"Grandpa?" I gave her a questioning glance

"Yes, and he kept that secret, he never said a word. He would visit you every week."

"I …. I don't remember. I had no idea?"

"You had a lot of protectors." She says proudly.

-Bang –

-Bang- Bang-

"Is that the door?" we both jump out of our skin.

"Yes, it must be Mackie", I say

I notice the time. It's after 6pm, I look outside and it's dark.

My Aunt flies down the stairs and returns with Mackie. I am still lying on the sofa, looking ruined.

"Miss Winnie you alright? You feel unwell?"

"No Mr. Mack I am fine, just exhausted with my family. I

know the truth, all of it. I do not want to go home tonight. I will not go home tonight. Tell Grandmother whatever you choose but I will not go home. I need to speak to Grandfather. Please tell my Grandmother that I will be home tomorrow".

"Miss Winnie, she will not accept that" Mackie says with a worried frown. He looks at Rene with disdain.

"I do not care about that. If she wants me she can come and get me. I will be home tomorrow after I have spoken to my Grandfather." I say with annoyance.

I fall asleep after 8pm, my aunt was right, I needed the rum, it definitely took the edge of the emotion. Deep in an alcohol induced coma, I hear my Grandpa calling my name "Winnie, princess wake up" he says, he looks tired and concerned that this day had tipped me over the edge.

"Princess…. Come on, how much rum did she drink he yells angrily at Rene. He quickly understands that I have lost the use of my limbs and am clearly nit in control.

"She had two glasses", Rene told him.

My grandfather shakes me hard Winnie wake up. "She is not a drinker" he says scornfully at Rene.

I sit up then throw up all over the beautiful beach flooring. Grandfather hand me a handkerchief, Rene *runs to the kitchenette for water.*

"I am so sorry" I moan.

"It's ok Winnie, your drunk this is a natural reaction. I must get you home." He tells me as he attempts to move me.

"Noooooo" I moan.

"Yes", he shouts at me angrily.

"I need to talk to you, please Grandpa"

We can talk in the car, he gave Rene a filthy look.

"Barry she can at least stay the night, poor dear is unwell." My aunt tries to reason with him

"And whose fault is that?" He yells at Rene.

"Barry!", Rene exclaims

"Shut your mouth", he shouts back. I was shocked to hear my grandfather speak to anyone like that.

"Please Grandpapa your scaring me". I had never seen this side to my Grandfather and I was starting to worry for Rene.

She mouthed to me "Its ok, see you soon" and waved bye.

My Grandfather pulled me off the chair. I had the water in one hand, he had a bowl in the other. We enter the car, "Please don't be mad she was just trying to help me"

"I can see that," he snapped. He sees that I am fighting the tears and looks at me. "I hear it's been an eventful day for you" he asks softly.

"Yes, it's been pretty awful". I wail.

He pats my knee, I would have told you everything when you turned 18 years old.

"Hmmmm", I give him the look of liar. "Grandpa, I need help. I don't know how long I have left in that house with them, but I will need a money. I will get a job and look …

My Grandfather cut me off. You will not get a job. No matter what I will take care of you. I will make arrangements, you will never want for much." He said in his southern accent.

"Thank you". I smile " I like Rene"

My Grandfather smiles. "She is impossible but I love her."

I will tell you know, your day cannot get any worse. I plan to divorce your Grandmother and I am in the process of changing my will. They will benefit from nothing. I leave this all to you and Rene. Mrs. Mack, it was the last straw. I cannot continue to pretend anymore. I love you, but I am fearful. It's the lies and secrecy that kills me. Your Grandmother is your fathers coconspirator, she should never have helped him bury the body.

"Oh Grandpa, where is she? She deserves a Christian burial. If not for us for Mr. Mack, he is stuck in time, it's cruel."

"I don't know where she is. I am still trying to understand how and why." He look at me with say eyes. "I will have an account set up for you by the end of the week. Ok?"

"Thank you". *I leap and dance inside*

Also, now that you are aware of everything. You inherited Mima's estate. I can arrange a =n appointment with my lawyers and we can meet to discuss how you proceed. You are already wealthy. Your aunt Rene has been managing the farm, plantation and overseas all the sugar contracts. You can leave tomorrow and be independent. You don't need your father, or me.

"Really Grandpa?"

"Yes Winn. You don't need any of us, that's why they have been trying to control you. They need you,"

"No matter what I will always need you." I tell him.

Chapter 14

Circumstance defines you.

It was June 1955, and the piercing Jamaican sun beat down on Harold's neck and back, his skin the shone like a precious onyx stone. Now 19 years old, his body was sculpted and his muscles rippling with every movement he crafted.

Winnie watched her man in the field. She smiled at the thought of him. My butterflies creep into my abdomen and my man friend awakens in longing. I love this woman and one day she will be mine, all of her. Harold was so proud of his beau, she left her Grandmother three years ago, and never looked back. Restoring the big house to its glory with Mackie at her side, her farm, was the most successful business in these parts. She even out planted the plantation. She was happy, we are happy and one day she will be my wife.

"Harold you want some water boy?" Mackie offered. I take the copper cup and drink my fill, this was thirsty work.

"Hey boy, stop looking at the missus. You see how she is in the house and you are in the field. It's not going to happen," Calvin my jealous younger brother joked.

"Shut up fool," I snapped

"It's been like forever, and you are still in the shade, its like she is embarrassed to have a man like you as her man." He twisted the knife.

"Calvin, you would not know as you have never been with a woman" I jibe, the other men laugh

"Well you have not been with the grand duchess over

there so we are even". He jabbed back. The men laughed louder and harder at my situation.

"E-N-O-U-G-H," Mackie bellowed, and immediately commanded quiet. "I have known many of you a long time, some of you all your lives. The next person that makes a dirty remark about the mistress will not be able to work this farm ever again, nor will they work any other farm in this district. Understand. I expect you to respect her, not only when she is in front of you, but also when she is not. Understood?

Murmurs of compliance from the men were received.

"Good" Mackie said with finality. "Harold, a word", the remaining men looked at Calvin who bowed his head from my gaze as I walked past him as he knew yet again, that he had crossed a line. I followed Mackie out of the thick of the cane field for a few minutes onto the road. It was clear that whatever he had to say to me he did not want any one hearing us.

"What is wrong with you?", Mackie demanded

"Mackie, I … look" I stutter.

"Do you feel that insecure that you have to talk about her like that to them foolish boys", he barked

"Mackie" I try to laugh off my embarrassment, "listen, my brother he's"

"I am not talking about your brother boy, Mackie stepped towards me and I feel the fear in my gut rise to my throat, he was serious, his eyes narrowed, muscles flexed and he was looking straight through me. "I am talking about you", his lowered his head to my face, I could feel his warm breath. I cautiously step back, everyone knew that Mackie was not a man to be trifled with.

"Mackie, you know that I love Winnie" I complain.

"That's it boy, I don't know. How can you allow those fools to even put her name in their mouth like that and you not slap it out", he yelled at me. I am grateful that he led me away from the flock as I would never live this down.

"Listen Mackie" I try to interject but Mackie had not finished with me

"You say that you love her but you do not honor this woman. Just look at what she has done in the last three years. She has restored this great house, he points aggressively in its direction. "You now have work, so does most of your family and village, and this is how you repay her".

I look at Mackie, he is boiling hot, and I start to appreciate how remote we are. "Listen Mackie" I plead

"It's Mr. Mack to you Boy, until you start acting like a man you do not refer to another man by his name boy. Do you understand me." He stepped forward and every muscle from his jaw to his toe flexed. I feel his restraint. I sense his rage, I do the only thing a man who wants to see tomorrow could do, that is, I put both hand up. "Mr. Mack, I am so sorry. I can do better, I will do better. Your right". I step back again, I am trying to get as close to the road as possible.

"She is a Barnet and for thirteen years, she has lived in privilege and comfort. Before that Miss Lucy treated that girl like a princess. Lucy and Vincent are like our motherlands Royal Family. There are so many expectations set for her, where she will live, to whom she will marry, how many children she will have. Half of the wealthiest families in Jamaica seek her hand in marriage. Yet, she is here, entertaining the village idiot, who is not man enough to command respect from his peers let alone his family. Boy, if you love her, let her

231

go as you are not man enough for her. If you insist that she is the one for you and you truly want to be with her. Earn her!", with that Mackie stormed through the sugar cane field from where he came from. Breaking and spiking many of the canes as he ploughed through.

I look up in the sky, the sun penetrating through the cloudy haze onto my skin like blue flames on a fire. I look at my feet, my shoes are battered, I did not even own them when they were new. Every piece of clothing that I own is as a result of a family member purchasing something new. Why would she choose me? I wouldn't. I am the son of a field hand. I have plans to move to England and make my fortune, but I am in love with a woman who has inherited a fortune and is managing her successful business, without me. I am not worthy, she is a Barnet after all.

I walk back, my heart heavy, filled with fear and hopelessness. I hear Dexter Winnies beloved dark brown thoroughbred neigh in the distance. I know that damn colt don't like me. As she canters towards me I notice the horse saddle and blanket, even Dexter is dressed better than I. She jumps down and leads Dexter my way.

"Hello stranger, are you ok? I wanted to see if you were ok"

"Why wouldn't I be?" I snap. *My god she is beautiful. Dressed in her blue khakis and white shirt. Her body is firm, her breast swelling with innocence.*

"Winnie smiles at me. Well I saw Mackie and you go off in a storm, and now Mackie is marching to war in my cane fields shredding my profit with his thighs as we speak. Everything alright between you."

"Did he say anything?" I try to enquire without sounding too desperate for the response.

"That's the funny thing, he has said nothing. Is everything alright between you both?", She looked beautiful when she was concerned.

"It's good, man talk you know". I tried to sound like a man in authority.

"Really, Ok", she giggled.

"Why you laughing?" I ask annoyed, "You don't think I am a man? Or because you have this plantation and your grandparents are the richest in St Thomas, do you think you are the man?

Winnie dismounts, with such athletic prowess, she swings her right leg and pushes her body out of range, then jumps out of the her foot holding with her left in one move. "What?" She enquired more than annoyed but not enough to temper anger.

"You heard me." I shout at her now.

"Harold I am not one of your street girls", her acid tongue appeared.

"Well if you think I know street girls I must be nothing more as a street boy."

"Harold my job is not to make you feel better about yourself.

"Look at me, I am in rags working for my woman's plantation like a farm hand. I am a joke. I should be with, running the place, not working like a dog for you" I was right in front of her. She just stared at me.

"What are you suggesting Harold?" That you … you move in?

I nod, my confidence waning as I see her expression.

"For what?"

"I am your man and I should be with you. Winn look at it from my perspective, I am your man and I am in rags. I have no status and everyone takes me as a joke".

"I see", that's all she said.

"You say you love me, but my life has not improved because of this love. I am not better off. I am just here working for you, seeing you when we can, hiding from your father and grandmother. I am a laughing stock. Your house is big enough that my family and I could be living with you in comfort, but no, the man you love and his parents and siblings, we are still out in the cold.

"Well we cannot have that can we?", she replied sarcastically.

"Don't talk down to me?"

"What?", she was vexed now I could see the vein in her forehead popping out

"You heard me", I yelled.

"Me… You are the one doing all the talking". Winnie glared at me.

"Well, what are you going to do about it. I am your man and you need to treat me as such." I demanded. *She need to step up. If she wants me she needs to make my life comfortable. She is worth a fortune, we … all could have a nice life. My mother could move in and run the house, my youngers could give up working as kitchen help and we could send them to school."*

She stared at me "My Man, Ok what does that involve?"

"What?" I did not understand where she was going with this.

"You being mmmmmyyyy man, what does that involve?" she was being funny now and I did not like it.

"I am here for you. I help you with the business. I take care of you." I tell her. *Why can't she see that she needs a man around.*

"Hmmmmmm is that so", she glares at me again.

"I look down. Look at me Winn I dressed like a beggar. I do not even have any decent clothes, and here you are looking like Princess Elizabeth from blasted England", I was started to show my annoyance and impatience.

"So", she said with the spite in her voice, "This is about money"

"No, it's about respect. If I had all the money you would not have to suffer like this." I tell her,

"So your suffering now." She looks to the sky and crosses her arms.

"Yes" I look at her how can she not see this.

"Horse shit and you know it" she screamed.

Dexter, her chocolate brown Colt grunted and bolted up right.

"Winn", I try to explain, as I can see that she is angry.

"Shut your filthy mouth. How dare you try and manipulate me. You clearly think that I owe you." She scathes at me,

"No, that's not what I meant", I try to appeal to her.

"Yes that is exactly what you meant. I owe you. I live in the house that my grandfather am grandmother built, and am running their plantation so that means that I am responsible for making your life better.?" She looked at me tears in her eyes, but no tears flowing.

"I'm just saying," *I feel her hurt, what have I done*

"I heard you Harold, I should be taking care of you. You who have had no input, have not slaved to build this house or plantation should just be able to sit in Grandpa Vins chair because what, Oh yes, because I claim that I love you. You believe that you are entitled to all of this this. In the name of love. If that is not enough, You also think that I am now responsible for your whole family, , and because you have told me that you love me, it is now my responsibility to feed, clothe and house all these people as I have so much space."

"You make what I said sound cheap."

"I didn't do that my love, that was you?"

"Whilst I was falling in love with the man, the man was falling in love with my fortune, and counting the days that I would share it with him."

"No Winn, No!" I walk away from her my hands on my head.

"Yes Harold. I have had to endure a lot and"

He interrupts me "Endure... what have you had to endure Princess Winnie. You have never gone hungry. You do not know what it's like to be poor."

"No I have never been poor, but trust me when I tell you I have endured. My grandmother was murdered in front of me. I have no mother, she too is dead, until recently I lived in a house with my alcoholic abusive father". Winn grabs my hand and puts my finger on the ridge of her nose. She looks me in the eye, "Feel that ridge, that's where after my father shot my grandmother in her head, he then punched me so hard, he broke my nose. I was..." *her voice broke* "I was six years old." Her tears started to flow

"Winnie, Baby love", I try to pull her close to me,

"No," she screamed and wrenched her body from my grip. "No Harold. I thought that you were the only person that wanted to be with me for me."

"I Doooo" I explain *Oh no look I didn't explain myself well.*

"Harold, I would rather of been dirt poor but with a family that loved me like yours. Any day. My father did things to me that were unspeakable. My grandmother is a hateful hag and hates me to this day. I just wanted to recreate and live Mima's dream, I wanted to provide her and Grandpa Vin legacy for me, you and our children." She looks in the distance.

"Winn, I just feel that you treat me like a farm hand." I say quietly.

"You are a farm hand. I cannot promise you what I cannot give. I don't want to give you what you want." She tells me her works like acid is burning my skin.

"Why not?" I cannot believe she has said this. She is ashamed of me.

"The moment you become visible to my father, you, your family are all dead men walking. My father will hunt you down and kill you. He's dangerous Harold."

"I can take your father"

She slaps me hard. "I cannot believe that you hit me?"

"Wake up Harold. You are not the Lone Ranger, this is real. My father will destroy you, he will destroy us and what's left of me. Is that what you want?"

I raise my hand, Winnie steps back. There was not fear in her eyes. It was war. I run through the corn fields, frustration and anger resonate through all pores. My tears are hot with fury. People like me never get what they want. Maybe it's time I become the man. Maybe I earn her, just like Mackie says.

Chapter 15

Awakening

I cannot believe that fool. Who does he think he is? Why would I take care of him. His family. Lucy and Vincent worked hard for this land, they spend years building this house, and he thinks that I am just going to give this to him. His family and whoever he feels is deserving just because he is my boyfriend. We have not even been intimate yet. This is crazy.

"Brrrrhhhh" I pat Dexter,

I know Dexter, I stroke his neck, thank you for agreeing with me. I smile, and start to gallop. Thoughts are racing through my mind. This cannot work. I have been kidding myself for quite a while. He's right we are still the same virginal teenagers that met three years ago. He should understand that if I commit to him, like that he will be have to be my husband. I do love him. He is so sweet, but he is naïve, stupid at times. He is a dreamer, he does not have a clue how hard it is to run this place and what's involved. He thinks that he can get a seat at the table, just like that, contributing nothing and earning this. He is a fool. .

"Arggghhhh" I scream out loud. Dexter slows to a canter, as if he can sense that I need more time in this field to work these thoughts through. I yank the rains and gallop in the opposite direction from where I have just come from.

I ride and ride around the plantation, dusk is upon me and I still am no closer to a resolution of this anger that I feel. This position that has been burdened on me. I have to make this work as without it I am back under the wicked watchful gaze of grandmother. Also, having my own business provide me with an income, so I am not reliant on anyone and that includes any man. I fear the future, he is not quite ready to be a man of mine, and is no match for my daddy, that's for sure. I dismount Dexter and gently hold his reigns to show him that we need to keep walking. Dexter stops. I look at him and stroke his nose. He leans his neck on mine. I look deep into his eyes. Dexter snorts through his nose, "Your Right honey, It's time to go home". I rib and kiss his nose.

"Where have you been?" My Aunt Rene yells at me as I walk into the back door of the kitchen.

"I have been riding, I tell her calmly

"You have been gone a while?" Mackie eyes me suspiciously.

"Oh I just needed time to think on things". I say trying to be casual

"What things"?, Rene walks over to me and immediately wraps her arms around me. I shrug her off aggressively

It's too much. The emotions of the day erupt and I cannot keep this to myself. I felt like crying but I can't. I am so disappointed, but more importantly, I am furious. How dare he. I shake my head. I walk to the cooler and take out a bottle of ginger beer.

"Winnie what's happened?" Rene asks concern written all over her face.

I look at my aunt, "nothing I want to discuss"

I did not ask you whether you wanted to discuss it young lady. What is wrong? She asks, there was no messing in her voice.

"I think Harold and I are over." I gulp the remainder if the ginger beer. Sweat beads were on my head, I wipe my brow look at my aunty Rene ,who is just staring at me.

"Why?" she asked quietly.

"He …. He is just a free loader. He telling me that he wants to be running this place with me". I start pacing in Mimas kitchen. I notice the door is open. I walk briskly and close it. I look at Rene, who is now sitting in my Grandpa Vins chair.

"Is anyone else here?", I enquire.

"No my sweet darling it's just me." I smile, she always reminds me of Mima when she calls me that.

"I love him, but I am not sure whether it's enough for him. He wants and needs so much more than I can give". I tell her

"Like what?"

"Well he thinks that he should be here with me, full time". I look down as I am embarrassed by what I am about to divulge "you know"

Aunt Rene looks at me suspiciously, "no I don't"

"Like man and wife."

He asked you to marry him, Aunty asked confused.

"Nooooo, he says that he should be with me in the house. He is upset that he is a field hand, he wants to be running the place with me".

"What experience does he have with such matters". Rene asks angrily.

"That's it I say.

"Does he think managing a business is easy. What skills does he bring to the table?"

"Exactly" I exclaim.

Does he think that marriage is his way in? she asks.

"Well, he did not ask me to marry him", I say with embarrassment. "He wants us to act married."

"Oh… You mean that you're not already?" Aunt Rene ask surprised. Her eyebrows arched and she tried to hide amazement.

"No I have not. I just wanted to wait. You know for marriage."

My aunt nodded her head apologetically, I could see that she was still reeling from the information received.

"It's like…" I hesitate

"Yes… It's like what darling". She was all ears.

It's like he wants me to take care of him and his whole family. He started to tell me how his whole family could come and live in this house and there still be space. He tells me that he is suffering and I am here looking like princess Elizabeth. I mean it's like he wants me to …. Save him. I am just not prepared to make such a commitment. Everyone thinks this is easy and it's not. I honestly thought that he would be happy, grateful even that I have given him and his family jobs. Instead, he resents me. He seems more worried about his friends and brothers' opinion rather than recognising that I am just trying to do my best. This is Grandma Lucy and Grandpa's house. I am just babysitting it. I cannot just open it up to him and his people. I love him. I really do, but he is making me responsible for him. I just cannot do it, can I?" I look at my aunt for reassurance.

"No, you can't", my aunt said quietly.

"If you do not feel comfortable then you will have to do

what your gut is telling you. If it does not feel right, then Baby it's not right."

"Rene, I do not have the energy to save him. I am just learning how to save myself. I feel … I feel so … so.."

"Trapped", Aunt Rene asked

"Yes" I gruffly whisper. There was so much sadness in my voice.

"That's ok. If that's how you feel then you should end this now."

"But I love him", I say, the emotion building in my voice.

"Do you?"

"Yes" I snap.

"Then sacrifice everything and do what he asks of you" she said quietly looking at me.

I can't believe that she is asking this of me. "Aunty I love the way he is when he is with me, he's"

"What about when he is not with you? When other people are around?" she asks.

"Huh?"

"When there are other people around? What is he like then?"

"What are you getting at?" I ask.

"When it's you and your friends, how is he?" She asked very matter of fact.

"I don't know what you mean?" I look at her confused.

"Do you feel that he loves you when he is with his friends

and brother? Does he hold your hand, kiss you? Touch you?"

I look down, "Well you know he's shy?" why is she doing this?

"What does that mean?. Are you saying no?"

"He is attentive". I protest.

"OK", she is staring at me and I am now very hot.

"What is this? I snap.

"What?"

"This, interrogation, coupled with your questions. I love Harold" I tell her, but neither of us believe me.

"Oh sweetie I do not doubt your affection? She said. "Your dinner will be ready on an hour", she said trying to change the subject.

What is this woman trying to do to me. She knows that I love him. Harold means everything for me. I just can't be rushed. I won't be. He needs to live his dream, make his way. I cannot give him my way, he's not earned this. I do love him, but I am no fool. I know that I may be young, this forever thing is not all that it's cracked up to be. I don't want to end up like MY Grandmother Phyllis's in a loveless relationship, awaiting only her freedom of the death of Grandpa and her liberation through widowhood. I have to be sure.

"Aunty this is unfair. I know that you don't feel that he is good enough for me, but I make my own money and am capable of making a living for me with the business. I am not reliant on him or anyone. That does not mean that I need to save him." I stand up, not knowing what else to do.

Aunty Rene stepped away from the stove, "Do not put

words in my mouth. I never said that, Aunt Rene bellowed. You need to be honest with yourself. This is your beau? Right? Yet your Beau has not touched you, caressed you, he works on your farm. You have no immediate plans to move the relationship along at all. Ok I understand that the young man is reaching, expecting to run this, and have his family up in here. But"…..

"What?" I interrupt her, raising mi voce more than I expect.

"It appears to me that you are the one full of doubt. He's ready to be part of you and your business. He wants to integrate you with his family." Rene tried to defend him

"No he wants to live off me" I tell her curtly.

"You're sure of this?" she asks.

Of Course I was there not you. whilst I was busy falling in love, he was busy falling in love with my fortune. Your wrong. I have not got reservations. I love him",

"Then what is stopping you". I tell her exasperated.

"You know what", tears fill my eyes and fear swells my chest.

"What?" My aunt looks confused.

"My father. You know that when he realises that Harold is my beau, he will kill him, just like he has destroyed anyone and everyone else that loves me" I say

"Then why put him through this? If you love him as much as you claim, end it." Rene looked pained by ny revelation.

"What?"

"So you are comfortable with the idea that Harold may

be murdered in one of your fathers jealous rages?" anger started to swell in her chest..

"No of course not."

"Then if you love him, end it."

"Your twisting my words".

"Me… No I am trying to show you that you are not as serious about Harold as you claim. He is your security blanket, your play thing nothing more. Stop being cruel, drown the puppy, club it but for god sake put it out of its misery. If you don't, this puppy will follow you everywhere and will continue to shit in your shoes".

"That's hideous, your hideous, now who is being cruel?"

"It may be hideous, but it's true and you know. Just think about what I have said."

She's wrong. I love him. Harold has been amazing to me. I don't have to want to give him my everything for this to be real. I just feel like I am being pushed into a corner and I cannot have that. I am not responsible for him. So why do I have to be his everything. He is not mine. If anything happened to Harold I would die…….Or would I?

I want a man who is strong in his love for me. A man who would declare to anyone and everyone that he is mine. That's not Harold. Harold lives for his family. He is directed like a puppet and dances to their tune. This is why I am in this situation. It's not his doing, it's his family's doings. They crave to live a better life, yet they are not prepared to work damn hard for it. I will not dig out my gut for him. He has not proved his worth to me for such a sacrifice.. A man should be able to stand on his own. Not expect his woman to give him the world. If only he was more like Mr. Mack, he is strong, courageous and his own man. Even though people

246

thought he could better than Mrs. Mack, he loved his wife and was in love with her …… and she loved him.

I love Harold, but not enough to be his everything. I have responsibilities and need to take them seriously. Being a wife and mother is a luxury. I need to be a successful business woman like my grandmother. My father controlled my every move up until now, I just about have financial and psychological freedom. I am not the slave of this plantation. I am its Master

The plantation has turned into a well-oiled machine. I have the right people, in the right roles, doing just what I require them to do. My vision over the next two years is expansion and to become the supplier of choice in America. The village is thriving, I have hired over eighty percent of the population. The church has a new roof, and for the first time the children in the village have a school building, rather than a rundown shack. My grandparents would be proud of me. Even Grandma Phyllis's congratulated me in my efforts. Daddy, I know he's proud. He has not told me so, but he will tell anyone who will listen. "Have I told you that Edwina has just completed building the School. Fine work I say fine work".

Life is good and God is great. My father and I are on the firmest and strongest ground. We talk every other day. We dine twice a week in Morant Bay. He is a shrewd business man, and even though we are competitors he wants the best for me. I see it now, through his narrow lens, he love me with all his heart, and I know that he will do anything to defend me and my honour. In a strange way, I do find that sweet. He loves me and wants to protect me. I have come to terms that he is a different man to whom I first met, but I cannot and will not forget our history.

We talk now, I mean about everything. He is my best friend. He even told me about Jeanette. I am trying to convince him to bring her from the back of the closet to the lighted dressing room. I think, he could be considering this, he loves her and radiates every time he mentions her name. It makes him vulnerable, like the rest of us. I had contemplated telling him about Harold. However, Aunty Rene and my Grandfather advised strongly against it. Deep down they are right, he still has the capability of being unpredictable which makes him extremely dangerous.

It's been at least two weeks since I have seen Harold. I

have played this evening in my head and just need for it to be over. Harold left me a note asking to meet me. When I left him a note to say that I and he agreed, my heart sank. I need to be brave, he has to recognise this, whatever it is, is just not working. My Aunt is right I have to let him go.

It Saturday, my field workers have left early and have gone home for the day. I have bathed and am ready for bed, but need to reorganise my thoughts for my conversation with Harold.

I put on my beige khaki skirt, and blue cotton over shirt. I look at myself in the mirror. I am tired and have lost weight. I smooth coconut oil through my hair and pull it back into one ponytail. I slip on my pumps and sit on the veranda waiting for Harold. I go into the kitchen and boil my kettle. There is a medley of fresh lemon, lime and crushed ginger in a small muslin bag in my teapot. I pour the hot water in the cup and when I turn around, he's there looking dapper with a pair of new black trousers and a crisp white shirt and flowers.

"Harold, you startled me". I jump back.

"Sorry baby", he looks embarrassed as he can see that I am taken aback by his demeanor.

"No its fine, I was not expecting you so early." I relax a little flattered that he made such an effort.

"I couldn't wait to see you, and its warm so did not want my flowers to wilt". He beams at me. "Here", he thrust them at me.

"Oh thank you". I blush "What's the occasion?"

"They are a peace offering. I behaved ..... badly", he said his eyes on the floor.

I smile, "its Ok, let's go on the Veranda and talk".

As we walk through the kitchen and long corridor to the front of the house, Harold smiles at me.

"What?" I fix my hair. "Do I look ok?"

"You look perfect", he smiles.

I sit on the large hand crafted wooden chair with bullet holes in the arm ledge. it is still here after all these years with my grandmothers cushions, we both sit down and look across the veranda to the plantation.

"This is beautiful Winn?"

"I know I smile. This is my home I feel safe here" I smile at him, and notice that he is melting under his new Sunday best attire. "Oh Harold I am sorry where are my manners, do you want a drink?"

"Oh Ok, anything cool"", he wipes his brow embarrassed.

I rush in and pour some warm lemonade in a glass. As I walk back to the veranda, Harold is on his knees with a small red velvet box in his hand. I stop at the doorway, and the bile in my stomach pushed its way up to the back of my throat.

"Edwina, I …"

"Stop Harold, please stop." I feel sorry for him, he's so nervous. I rush over and put the lemonade on the table.

"Edwina" There is a brow of sweat prickling its way to the surface. "Will you ..

"Harold stop, I grab him under his sweaty arm pits and wrench him up to his feet. He looks at me completely crushed. "What are you doing?" I barely whisper looking around the plantation to see if anyone was watching this spectacle.

He glared at me with wounded pride "I was trying to propose to you baby", he barely mumbled.

"Why?"

"Why?", he snapped, "Because that is what men do when they want to declare their love for their woman. Why, because that is what you want? Why? Why? I love you stupid?"

"Oh" I look out to the plantation. This evening was not going how I had it planned in my head.

His body language became defensive. "Why won't you allow me to ask you?"

"Because tonight I only agreed to meet with you so that I could end things between us." I was trying to be kind, but my words sounded so cruel.

Harold stepped back, he put his hands to his eyes. "No …. No baby you don't mean this?"

"Harold look I have had time to think and were not ready? I am not ready." I try to explain.

"I'm ready, that's all that matter and I love you, and only you".

"That's the problem Harold. I am not ready. I don't want to be married right now, and I don't want to be married to you. I have so much to do here. I have responsibilities to the community, myself my grandparents who built this place."

"Your grandparents are dead Winnie, they would want you to live your life."

"Yes they would. Harold being married to you would not be living my life. I don't want these things that you talk about. I just want to be Winnie, living her life without restriction. Not answering to anyone. I am free spirit and I want to remain that way for as long as possible. I have been a prisoner for far too long."

"What?"

"I don't want you. It's not you" *he needs to know the truth.* "I love you but I am not in love with you". I stand back and watch him absorb the news my aunt was right I needed to let this puppy go free.

Harold's eyes brimmed with tears "I heard you but I cannot believe what I heard. Wait, do you think I will keep you prisoner or something. You make this proposal sound like prison", he yelled. He was angry now.

"No that's not what I am saying. I can't marry you".

Harold walked towards me and grabbed me by the waist, "Why?" He pushed himself on me. "Maybe I should have treated you like them gully girls.

I push him off with all my might, "Harold", I scream "No! It's over. I will not feel guilty for my life, my wants ,my dreams. I am not responsible for you. I cannot be responsible for your family. That's not my job" I tell him curtly.

"Is this what this is about? Hmmm I am your big black buck, but my family is too black for you."

"No that is not what I said."

"You want to marry a light skinned man with money right. Hey. Some man with class, standing. A man who does not work in a field, A man who has a name

"I will marry the right man for me. Harold I don't need to marry for money. I have more than I require and you know that. I just cannot marry you. I'm sorry."

"I walk to the house and feel him grab me and push me inside the door. We are in the foyer of the house. His eyes are wild, he looks like he wants to hit me but is thinking real hard about it.

"What you gonna do Harold, show me what a man you can be" I point to my privates, is this what you have become. Some field hand rapist..

"Maybe?" He grabs my neck and forces me to kiss him. *I need to get away, or else who knows what he'll do. I have pushed him too far.* I turn my head "Nooo No get off me, this is madness"

"I love you Winn, after all this time you can't just walk out on me. There is no me without you. Please don't do this. Let's talk.. Let's…"

"Noooo" I push Harold off.

"You don't know your own mind", he grabs and pulls me me again and I struggle to push him away.

"Enough!" an woman stood in the corridor by the kitchen.

She was youngish, I would say late twenties. She was well dressed, jeans and a t-shirt. Her afro was short, her curls soft, her face familiar to me somehow. We both froze. She walked towards us both brandishing her machete towards Harold.

"Boy, I think you outstayed your welcome, don't you?"

"Leave this house. This is private business and I want you to leave", Harold yelled.

"Well the way I understand things this" she points to the house and plantation "does not belong to you. I heard the Mistress tell you to leave and your still here, so the way I see it, you byoy is the only person who has outstayed any welcome. I am a reasonable woman. I will ask you once more, and if you are still here in when I start to move, tonight one of us will meet a relative we lost a little while ago." She meant business.

Harold looked at me and sucked his teeth.

"Winn", he looked at me. What did he expect to do, throw her out.

"You heard her. Now leave, and never come back. You and your family find some other fool to hire you and take care of you. I am done!"

Harold walked out of the door and slammed it behind him. I ran and locked the door, then ran to the kitchen and locked the back door. I turn to my young warrior. "Thank you", I say, "He's not like that, I have driven him to this"

"What? You have driven him to abuse you?", she snapped

"No you don't understand I have just broken his heart, so he is hurt". I explain. I walk to the cupboard and take two cups, "Tea"

"Do you have something stronger?"

I shake my head no.

"Yes please, tea will be lovely" my young warrior answers.

I turn around and she is sat in my Grandpa Vins chair, shoes off crossed legged as if she had been there her whole life.

"Comfortable" I look at her slightly annoyed.

"Very" she exclaims laughing at me.

"What's your name?"

"Just call me Saint"

"Saint", I laughed "is that really your name?"

"Yes, my mother named me Saint, think of me as your female, living 'Saint Christopher'".

I laugh out loud, "You cannot be serious?"

"I am," her face was stern

I give her the tea.

"Thank you Miss Winnie". For a machete wielding vigilante she was incredibly polite, and familiar. We drink in silence for a while.

So, what's your story Miss Winnie, Saint asked

"You know me, have we met? I enquire.

"Maybe, though everyone knows you Edwina Barnet."
She says sarcastically.

"You seem so familiar to me, that's all, I tell her".

Hmmm she smiles broadly. "I knew your grandmother
when I was a girl and would play with you as a child."

"OK" I smile.

"You" she points at me "needs to meet a nice man. Not
someone from round here. Broaden your horizons, you
can do better than the village idiot."

I laugh, "you sound like my Aunt Rene", Saint smiled.

"Maybe … your Aunt Rene is a wise old bird", she said
"you should listen to her"

"Who told you she was old?"

"Winnie, I'm from round here so I am familiar with a few
of the villagers", she smiles

"OK?" I look at her trying to place her face and voice.

I hear a car in the distance tooting its hirn, he must have
found out, he was driving like a mad man. I look at the
clock on the wall.

"Who's that? Saint enquires looking uneasy.

I think it could be my daddy" I walk to the main door and
spot his black Chevy. "Please do not tell him about
tonight, its complicated", I say as I walk into the kitchen.

"Oh," the door was open and Saint was gone. I close and lock the door. I start to panic. I do hope that someone did not see Harold attack me.

The bile in my stomach reached my throat again. I feel hot.

BANG

BANG

BANG BANG BANG

Winnie, my daddy screams, "open this door". I run to the door, preparing myself for the full velocity of my father's temper.

"Daddy calm down I can"

"She dying", he sobs, "She is dying"

"Who daddy, Grandma?"

"Noooooooo, Jeanette, she dying and I cannot save her". He wails.

I stand in the doorway and hold my father as tight as I could. "It's going to be OK Daddy"

"Nooooo he sobs, it won't nothing will be the same again.

My Life has changed quite dramatically over the last two months. I miss him, I really do. Harold has always been my security blanket. He was the only person to stabilise me. The man that I loved was my best friend and I feel so bereft of him. My Grandfather has been so sweet, although he did not approve of us, he could hardly insist that I give him up. Not when he's with Rene. It's strange, they seem so more suited than he and Grandma. He's is so much more relaxed with Rene, and is so funny. I mean he is a hoot. His stories of a childhood Mississippi, sounds like another world. I understand him now, more than he realises. He is more focused as a human being here. He is able to stand freely in the personality that God has given him. He loves all people, regardless of religion, colour and wealth. My Grandfather is a true humanitarian. He recognises that he cannot be his true self anywhere else in the world. Aunt Rene would be raped and beaten to death in his world back in America. Here, they can love and be loved by their friends and family, free from judgment.

The night that Harold proposed weighs heavily on my mind. I am so disappointed that it, we, did not end better. I have not seen him, he has not written to me and won't reply to my letters. Grandfather says that its better this way, even though this is messy its clean.

The same day that I broke Harold's heart, Jeanette was diagnosed with lung cancer. Grandfather tried, he could not soften the impact of the devastating news to them both, but in particular to daddy. He immediately started to grieve her, however, when her physical condition altered, it reaffirmed his worst fears and he became inconsolable. She suffered more than any of my animals on the farm would be allowed to. In the end, she begged grandfather for death, and the humanitarian within him, did what he knew to be kind, and obliged. On the 24th October 1958, Jeanette Grantham, who was forty years old, held onto my father's hand, and told him for the least time that she loved him. She promised him that she would be with him forever and she was honored to be the only woman in this life, and will be waiting for him. My father had moved her out of the service quarters to his bedroom suite where she had slept every night for the last eight years. Grandma Phyllis was not impressed by this display of compassion, but soon realised that the subject was off limits and would be a fight that would shatter the relationship, and would leave deep shards of glass in both of them to fester, My father insisted that the room was filled with purple and pink hibiscus flowers as they was her favorite. Jeanette insisted in being bathed and oiled, she instructed her nurses to put in her finest church dress, and to tend her hair to make her look presentable. Withered and ravaged by this cancer, she wanted to look and smell nice for her Barry. That day, all her friends and family came and said their last farewell. Kissing her and tearing up at the sight of this once vibrant and spritely woman being reduced to a shell of her former self. That was the tragedy. With dignity she smiled, cried and where she could said her goodbyes, all the while my father was at her side, holding her hand, stroking her face, telling her that she was beautiful and he would love her forever.

I sat with my father for ten long days and nights. I prayed with him, stayed with Jeanette when he needed to get air, eat and smoke his tobacco. He was such a rock for Jeanette, yet, when he left the room he would diminish into a heart broken man. I saw him humbled and quiet for the first time and felt that my own bereavement could not compare to what daddy was going through.

My Grandmother watched from the corners of the room, taking in all the activity. She had loved Jeanette, like the daughter she never had. Jeanette started work at the plantation over twenty years ago when she was still a child herself. She had been Grandmother's chambermaid for the last fourteen years. She held secrets for my grandmother, that would die with her. She was more than my Grandmothers maid, she was her friend, confidant and in the latter years, both women became very close, especially when Phyllis's realised that it was Jeanette had effected change in her son. Although, it appeared to everyone else that Phyllis disapproved, in fact, it was Phyllis who sent Jeanette to my father's room. For years she observed the young woman's love my father, and watched as she blushed uncontrollably when Barry was in the room. Jeanette had Grandmothers blessing, and the first night that she spent with my father it was grandmother who sent her to be my father bed maister, which turned into something far more meaningful to both their lives.

Two days before Jeanette died, my father left to bathe, sleep and rest. He was exhausted. Jeanette insisted that he take a break. My grandmother ordered me out of the room, and when I returned, she was on the bed, Jeanette head was in her lap, and my grandmother was stoking her hair and with one hand and body with the other. Both women were crying, yet the room was silent. I felt the grief and sadness, and backed out silently unnoticed.

That evening was very somber, the air was strong with the scent of death, coconut oil and lavender. Both my Grandfather and father was at the corner of the room and she talked quietly for some time. Both men look drawn, but my father was thin, he was tired, he welcomed the news with a somber nod. The pit of my stomach churned and I could feel the bile creeping to my throat. I could see that she could not suffer like this no more, and death was a welcomed friend to Jeanette, and for those that loved her. The nurse summoned my mother, and Jeanette grandmother was present also. She opened her eyes, and smiled at my father, "thank you for the flowers", she told him weakly.

Daddy delicately put her hand into his and kissed it repeatedly, then looked at his love and smiled with her.

"You're welcome darling", he said. They both smiled. "You look beautiful," he whispered.

Barry, she smiled shyly. My father tears rolled down his cheek, he swiped them away like unwelcomed pests. He sat next to Jeanette, lay down and he maneuvered her head into the crook of his arm. "Are you sure he whispered and looked at her"

She nodded weakly. My Grandfather took the morphine viles and put them on a tray. He informed them both that he will inject her in her thigh, and soon afterwards she will drift off into a deep sleep. Jeannette smiles at Grandfather. My Grandmother who was stood at the corner of the room, ran over.

"Wait" she held Jeanette's head in her hands and whispered something that made my father cry. Jeanette expression was pained . My Grandmother kissed her sweetly on the lips and left the room. My chest felt full with emotion, my temperature was rising and the bile was back in my throat.

My Grandfather stoked her leg, On the tray were 4 needles filled with morphine. He mechanically administered them one by one, Jeanette told my father that she loved him, and they smiled. She became sleepy quickly and then she fell into a deep sleep, her face relaxed, pain free and she was smiling.

One by one we left the room, and my father and grandfather stayed. I walk into my old bedroom, and my Grandmother was sat on my bed.

"Is it done", she asked

"Yes" I say

"He is going to need you more than ever" she tells me.

"I know"

"She was a sweet girl, so young", grandmother says wiping her tears with a silk and lace white handkerchief.

"I know, I say….That's what I want" I tell her

"What?" she asks quietly

"Love. Grandma I want love, to be loved to feel love, that's what I want."

"Then find it" she tells me as if she is ordering shoes.

"I don't know how?" I tell her without shame.

She smiled, "I do and I will help you. You are beautiful. Clever, Smart independent and a business woman, men between Jamaica and China will walk on broken glass for you"

I smile at her. "Leave it with me. I need to rest, both my heart and head are heavy.

When the heavy door closes I lay on my bed and silently cry. My thoughts are of course with Jeannette, but they are with Mima, Grandpa Vin, my mother and Mrs. Mack.

Chapter 16

Butterflies

Its dawn, and the plantation alarm clock crows to yields the morning sun. Life as we know starts for the day. I am tired mentally, my muscles are sore and I genuinely feel fatigued. My life is not my own. I am a young woman with far too much responsibility and I am starting to feel the strain of it. On top of that my father is drinking again. Not as much as before, but he has slipped and its noticeable. There are flashes of the old bastard and I don't like it. He unnerves me, and I don't like the feeling of vulnerability that I have when he is in the room. I am older and more able to deal with old behaviors, but his acid tongue burns old wounds and opens up new ones.

The familiar sound of crunching gravel on my drive way startles me. I jump out of bed, rub my eyes and head for the window. It's Grandmothers car. I look at the clock it was 5.15AM, something must be wrong. I grab my jeans and pull a cotton shirt over me. As I open the door, the morning sun peeking through. The air was cool and fresh, and felt refreshing on my skin. Also, the cool air helps my unaided breast stand to attention.

Grandmother parked the car by the front of the house, "Morning Edwina" she said authoritatively and walked straight past me to enter my house.

"Come in Grandma" I say sarcastically.

"Edwina, I am concerned" she says looking at me, "your father has not returned home, in fact, this is the second night he's been absent. Have you seen him"

"He stayed here the night before last, but I am not sure

about last night?"

"You look tired?", Grandma asks, but it felt more like a statement.

"I am?" I sighs looking around my kitchen, trying to avoid her gaze.

"Then take a rest, this place is doing well, you can leave Mackie to tend things.   You need to rest, your looks won't last forever, and you will not be able to find a suitable man if you looked tired and old.   A young woman as beautiful as you should maintain her looks, not diminish them because your determined to work like a field hand."

My father walked into the kitchen from the back door. "Mother she is not a field hand, and does not need a husband. She has me now".

I look at my daddy, "What does mean?" I asked worried at what his response will be.

"You do not need to rush into anything, you have plenty of time, mother I stayed here last night.   It was closer and I got in late".

"You mean you were drinking?" I ask.

"Winn, I had a few but I wasn't drunk" daddy said without apology.

"Daddy, this is becoming a habit again. I hate it when you drink, you are nasty, violent and unpredictable.   I cannot be around that again. I just can't. You have to find a way to get over this. Until then you can stay out of my house"

"What?"

"You heard me, stay away."

"You can't talk to me like that? He looked at me that vein rearing its head,

"Why not? The last time you were drunk in this house my Grandmother died. I am just making sure that we understand each other". Once I had said the words I regretted them, that said, they needed to be said.

My father starred at me " Last night ….that was my last drink."

I walk over to daddy and look at him. "Don't make promises you are not prepared to keep. There are too many things riding on this"

Daddy picked up his hat and wallet and left without a word. He got to the backdoor, turns and looks at me and nods and leaves.

"Coffee Grandmother" I now ask in my stern voice.

"Yes dear, why not" she replied with a half-smile on her face. She looked lovely, in her lemon two piece skirt and blouse. Her hair was in a chignon, very stylish indeed. Her grey strand looked like high lights.

Under Phyllis watchful eye she observes me as I make her coffee. I have some bun in the larder. Would you like a slice.

"That would be lovely" she says quietly.

I pour the coffee in a pot, set out my finest cups and saucers, I have a selection of Hard dough bread, cheese, ham, tomatoes, and cucumber dressed in lemon and oil.

"This looks lovely Edwina", my Grandmother is genuinely surprised.

"Can I be candid Grandmother?"

"You may" she eyed me suspiciously.

"Why are you here today? You could have called me, you didn't need to drive all the way here.

"Yes I could have, but wanted to tell you that I have booked us a box at the races and thought that you should attend with me."

"Ok", sounds nice I think to myself we could use some sheeting up.

"Yes it would be nice and the islands elite will be there. You may meets some new friends. I worry that you are not enjoying your time.   You need some friends like you, and your own age group".

"That would nice", I smile "maybe that I am a little too serious, you know for my age but I just want to make a go of things"

"You have done that already. I don't want you miss out on your youth. Once it's gone, it's gone"

"Ok when is it?".

Next week. I thought we could go to Kingston this week to buy something nice, what do you say?".

"It's sounds good, Mackie can hold the fort for a couple

of days".

"That's the spirit"

"Grandmother what else are you up to?" I enquire still not convinced of her reason for visiting.

"Nothing, it's just a nice day out". She smiled to herself.

"Hmmmmm" I watch her like a hawk.

"This is lovely but I must dash. Lots to do. By the way, good for you."

"Good for me?" I enquire.

"Barry needs a firm hand, and now Jeanette is gone, you may need to be it.

The back door flies open. "Morning" Rene bound's through the door, chirping away about her day ahead. She looks up and stops dead in her tracks. "What are you doing here" Aunt Rene asked through gritted teeth.

"I am leaving, the air distinctly smells of rotting fish" grandmother says.

"Get out" shouts Rene, her body lurching forward like she was ready to pounce.

"Temper temper whore, I see that you are still an alley cat".

Aunt Rene drops her bags and picks up my solid wood rolling pin. I jump in front of her, shocked at how she is carrying herself.

"Ladies" I nervously laugh, my voice is at least three

octaves higher than usual. "Ok Grandmother you are leaving and Aunt Rene, the books are in the office. There will be none of this" I point to both of them "in here. ok?"

My grandmother turned around and look directly at Rene. "Whore you and I have unfinished business. The next time you pick up a weapon, be prepared to use it". Grandmother looked at me and smiled and walked out of the room towards the front door. Rene was rooted to her spot, heaving like she wanted to rip off my Grandmothers face. I escort Grandma to the front door, still in shock with what I have just witnessed.

In the kitchen, Rene is seated head in hands. "What was that about?" I ask genuinely interested in the response.

"Why is she here?" Rene was visibly upset.

"She was enquiring about daddy that's all, and she has arranged for us to go to the races"

"Really?"

I know I thought that was quite sweet".

"Sweet…. Winn don't be an idiot".

"Excuse me" I was put out how dare she call me that word.

"Seriously are you that naïve and stupid? That woman does nothing unless she benefits somehow. Be careful that's all I'm saying She has most probably prostituted you off to some high faulting family. I am saying be careful".

"Are you sure that you're not jealous?" I could not help it.

"Of her" she shrieked. "Winn I know your grandmother personally, she is not one to be toyed with. Be careful. That's all I'm saying" My Aunt walked towards me and kissed me on the cheek. "I am sorry for calling you stupid", she said in her normal voice. "Winn, I know what I am talking about…. Be careful." With that she walked back to the office.

Once out of sight, I smile broadly. My grandmother was pretty damn awesome. Not that I should be impressed but she ripped into Rene without even breaking into a sweat. Now I don't know what issues they have, what I do know is that it has nothing to do with me. I for one plan to stay well out of that.

My Grandmothers organisation of us all regarding this one day at the races is so excessive. Our trip to Kingston embodied numerous trips to "Sally's" Boutique. Sally was the only Boutique in town who catered for the elite. I had three outfits for Lady's Day. My Grandmother conveniently did not tell me that there would be a Charity Ball that evening, followed by a picnic the following day, and Gala dinner that night.

"Its three days" I moaned.

"So, what is the issue" she asks.

"Edwina, you made a commitment to attend are you going back on your word?".

"Yes … No, Do I have to go to all these events, I need to be back at the Plantation" I exclaim with annoyance.

"You have Mackie who is more than capable of handling

business whilst you are away. Also you have at least one hundred and fifty field hands working, so you can and will take three days. You yourself only last week agreed that you needed a break. Have one and stop complaining.

The day before we were due to leave for the races, my Grandmother surprises me. "I know that you're busy Edwina, but I wanted to drop off your luggage"

"Luggage really I have bags".

Ok this is your holdall dear, the young boy Colin who worked in our house jumped out of the car to give and gave it to Edwina It was beautiful, Black shiny leather case.

I have been bullied into going to Kingston the day before the races, so that I can rest. Although I have been resistant to this idea, it is a worthy one. The moment we arrive at the hotel my body aches with exhaustion. After a delightful shower, I drink what appears to be a gallon of water and fall promptly to sleep in the king sized Bed. To my surprise I sleep all afternoon.

"Winn, come on its time to get ready for dinner. We are meeting your Grandmothers friends from Manchester" my grandfather gently tried to nudge me out of my sleep.

"Grandfather I am so tired." I moan "Tell her I am unwell, I just need to rest, my body is aching and I just need sleep".

"Winn I am not her biggest fan, but I know that she has put a lot of effort in these few days away"

I look at my Grandfather apologetically. "I am sleeping.

I am tired and need to lie down. I really don't feel well. Grandmother will just have to understand. In fact", I yawn, "she was right I do need the rest. I just need sleep, I will be better in the morning".

"Winn....."

"Please, I have been working so hard and just need some space to sleep and recuperate. Tell her that I have a temperature, anything but I am not going" With that I slam my head into the comfortable pillow, My curls are thrown into my face.

My Grandfather sighs, knowing that he is for the high jump. "Sleep tight we will see you tomorrow"

A few minutes later I heard muffled voices, and by the tone of my Grandmother I knew she was furious. I smiled. I did not care, and that was that.

I opened the windows and went back to bed, after a few nonsense thoughts I was back in a deep sleep.

"Good morning sleeping beauty" My Grandmother barks like a sergeant major, and in one swift move, she pulls the blankets from me.

"Heeeeeyyy what" I moan.

"It's time to rise my dear. Lots to do"

"Mother, give her a chance" my father walked into my room. "Morning Winn he keened over and kissed me.

"Morning Daddy" I hold on to his neck and pull him close, he hugs me back "Help me Daddy", he laughs out loud.

"Breakfast is on its way, then the hairdresser will arrive

at 9.00am"

"What time is it?"

"7.30",she replied

"What?"

"Beauty takes time to cultivate", she said with a smile.

"What?"

"We have work to do now get up" she barked.

I looked at my father who was thoroughly amused. I then looked at my grandfather who put his hands up in surrender. "You better do what she says. She's serious. Barry, we have time for a quick round of golf"

"Sounds great dad" Daddy looks at me and mouths "Sorry" as he walked out of the door.

My grandmother Phyllis looked at me. I slowly realise that today is about her. "Ok. I will be compliant, what's first"

My grandmother smiling. It's funny, that's not a side to her that I see very often. She looks radiantly beautiful when she is happy. In fact today felt like we were family and I loved it.

Tap

Tap Tap

"Ah breakfast is here."

I eat saltfish and Ackee, plantain, and boiled green

banana with chocolate tea. I look at my grandmother fully satisfied. "I was sooo hungry"

You should be you slept for nineteen hours. Are you feeling better?

"You know what, you were right I needed to rest", I tell her.

She smiles, "well sleep agrees with your complexion"

Thanks I say as I slip off my bathrobe, and walk into the shower, I shower and wash my hair. I then hear a knock on the door. "Yeeesss"

"Monique is here" Grandmother shouts

"Who?"

The hairdresser"

I slide the shower curtain over and wipe the soap from my eyes. Who I say blinking trying to avoid the soap suds from stinging my eyes..

"The hairdresser so hurry up. I will go to my boudoir dear as my lady is here too."

"OK" I shout my voice echoing of the walls of my bathroom.

Now, she is very experienced so try something …. New.

"Hmmmm Ok?" I finish off and wrap a towel around my head.   Monique is beautiful, her skin is dark and her features petite like she is. Her hair was rolled tightly to her head.

"Ok Ma'am I have strict orders so we need to get started?"

"Strict orders for what and you can call me Winnie". I goggle nervously.

"Ok Miss Winnie, you Grandmother would like you to have a natural drop curl style if I can achieve this."

"Oh she does, does she".

Monique smeared a serum on my hair wet, and combed my locks through. She then took large rollers and adequately partied and rolled my hair. Then I was instructed to sit under this blistering heat on my head and scalp for one hour. I was a hot sweaty mess afterwards.

I took every precaution to cool off. I went to the bathroom and put a face towel underneath the cold water. I wiped myself down and awaiting the next gruesome installment.

Grandmother walked into the suite from time to time to see inspect her handy work. There were no protesting, she meant business. Whilst I was cooling down with a coco cola on ice Monique then went into her bag of goodies and produced at least twenty bottle of nail polish. I chose a blush pink, which was not to my Grandmothers taste, however, I did not care, it suited me.

"Ladies are you ready", Daddy asked impatiently.

"Stop fussing, we will get there in time Barry. Meet us in the bar we will be no more than ten minutes".

"Ten minutes and no more" Grandfather bellowed, muttering some nonsense about women making him late.

Monique looked at me. "Miss you look sensational, you look like a movie star." I chuckle, and look in the mirror. I was unrecognisable. I did look like a lady. I smile, "WOW".

My hair has soft large curls that fell obediently with body and shine all over my head, I had a side parting and fringe. I looked so grown up.

My dress was off the shoulder, this was the most flesh I have ever showed. The top was lace and fitted with a sheet satin slip underneath to give me the modesty that was required; the skirt was embodied with both lace and satin. When I saw it in the shop I was not sure, when I tried it on, I knew it was made for me. The colour was off white with a hint of pink. I wore pink matching suede shoes, with the highest heels I have ever worn, and a pink clutch bag to match. I wore a solitaire large diamond necklace, with diamond drop earrings. Altogether it look very nice.

Grandmother smiled. "You see, you are a pretty girl, with a little more encouragement you are a superstar" she smiled "Now let's go mingle with our people, the elite of the elite, more importantly lets have fun".

We leave the room and the bell boy who was in fact a man was staring at me so much Grandmother had to remind him to press the button. The lift arrived, we walked through the doors and was greeted by knowing stares. Grandmother walked into the bar first, my Grandfather and father either did not see me, or did not recognise me. Both men were dressed in their Black morning suit jackets, white shirts grey cravats and trousers, and impeccably shiny black brogue shoes.

It was Grandfather to spot me first "Winnie… " he sucked in the air, Is that you?"

I giggle with embarrassment.

"You look sensational", he said.

I walk over to my father who was at the bar rooted to the spot. "Well daddy, how do I scrub up"

"You do more than that, you look very very very beautiful," he crooked his arm out, "May I escort you Miss Edwina Barnett to the races"

I giggle, "you may Daddy,

"I need to be here, to protect you from all the men that will be trying to talk to you."

"Oh Daddy, I doubt that", I tell him.

He stopped and looked at me. "You are beautiful, don't forget that and I can assure you today I shall be beating these men off with a stick"

On the approach to the races I now realised what all the fuss was about. Even the palm trees looked well watered and opulent on each side of the road. Their barks immaculately groomed. Ladies day was more than I could have imagined. Everyone looked well groomed and superbly polished. It was here that I recognized the world to which we derived from. We were not just Rich, but we were wealthy, and people knew it.

We approached in a large black Rolls Royce. The concierge opened the door "Dr Barnett, Mr. Barnet, both men stepped out of the car. The concierge looked at me Mrs. Barnet may I help you, he stretched out his arm. His uniform was immaculately pressed and starched. He wore black trousers with a British racing green strip down the outside of the each leg. His Jacket had the same design, and his shirt was crisp white, with matching white gloves. I was busy placing this monstrous hat that grandmother brought for me. It had a broad rim which was covered in feathers, however, with my whole attire it just worked.

Miss Barnet, the concierge said," Can I help you?" The voice was distinctly familiar, I look up my heart stopped. It was Harold. His face desperately trying to stay fixed, I am unable to move.

Daddy asks him to move and stretches out his hand, "Come on darling, Its ok, don't be intimidated, this is your world" I crawl out of the car and glimpse Harold. I see the look on his face. I look great, and he knows it. I smile. "Ok Daddy lets go have fun"

"Atta girl"

We walk through the plush doors and I feel his eyes burning in my back. I shake it off. Harold is the past, this is my new life. I am going to show him that I made the right decision. He does not belong to me or my world.

Daddy takes my hand "Your shaking Winn, are you ok?"

"Daddy I'm fine" I smile" its excitement." I whisper.

My father smiles at me, "you are so sweet"

I look over, my Grandmother and Grandfather are surrounded by people that I have never met before. My grandmother motions to me and Daddy, Daddy waves over and they all wave back eyeing me suspiciously.

Daddy smiles "they are all wondering who this beautiful woman on my arm is?"

I smile.

"You look absolutely lovely" Daddy said.

"Yes she is, I hear a loud polished accent bellow".

Daddy spins around "Jackson, how are you man, it's been what ten years?" Jackson hugs my father and stares at me.

"Who is this delightful creature" he enquires "your wife, you always had great taste in women you lucky dog you".

My father looked at me embarrassed, cleared his throat, "Jackson please meet my beautiful and talented daughter Miss Edwina Barnett" . The older man looked visibly shocked.

"Barry I never knew that you had a child, when did you marry, have I met her?"

Daddy looked at me and smiled. "My wife died nineteen years ago in childbirth."

"Oh … I am sorry Barry I didn't know", he looked at me, "You my darling are delightful and he held my hand and kissed it" My father threw his friend Jackson a warning glance.

"My son Courtney is here from Miami for the week, you kids should meet", he said looking directly at my father as if to say cool down papa.

"That would be nice I say". *I smile at my father for protecting my good name. I was touched, he called my mother his wife.*

Excuse me Barrington" My grandma Phyllis leaned in and literally pulled me from the men. I turned to my daddy who mouthed to me for a second time "Sorry". Admittedly I loved that attention and smiled.

"Dear" I looked hard at my grandmother, she never, ever, called me dear!. "Meet Jackie Boullier, she is an old friend of mine". I smile. Jackie and my grandmother were the same age. Her son Bradley has just graduated from the University of West Indies as a lawyer and has joined his father's firm in Kingston. Bradley stepped forward. He was a pleasant looking man, with thick eyebrows, and nice lips. He too kissed my hand. I look at Daddy who was watching every male interaction I was having. I smiled. He did too, he looked a little sad.

I spoke to Bradley about the weather, races and my plantation which he already knew that I owned.

There were at least nine or ten such introductions. I was talking to a boring young man Royston Northgate, whose father owned the construction company who is building all the roads hospitals and government buildings in Jamaica. Again he was lovely, knew all about me and was dull.

"Edwina Dear" , my grandmother called me, it's time to

go to our box.

Ok I wave, "Excuse me Royston"

"Can I escort you to your box Miss Edwina", he asked politely.

"Sure" I say wishing I had the courage to say no.

We walk towards the box corridor, which is carpeted in a thick royal red colour. The thickness of the carpet made my heels sink so I had to lean on dear Royston for support which he loved. As we get to the reception area of the boxes Royston mother, Marcella Northgate comes over and introduces herself.

"Oh my what a handsome young couple you both make"

I look at Royston and immediately unloop my arm. Royston gives his mother the death glare. "Er thank you Mr. Northgate, as we are stable ground, I no longer require your assistance"

"Oh my darling, I did not mean to embarrass you both" Mrs. Northgate apologises for her foot in mouth. Clearly realizing that she had overstepped herself in the situation.

My father touched my shoulder, I smile relieved to see him. "Mrs. Northgate, it's always a pleasure to see you"

"Thank you Barrington, she blushed "likewise". I suspiciously look at my father.

"Royston, my haven't you grown" Daddy said confidently looking this young man in the eyes.

"Well thank you for the escort. I can manage from here

on in.". Daddy loops his arm around my waist and shuffles me towards our box, once inside we both look at each other and fall about laughing.

"Daddy did you and Mrs. Northgate have a thing?" I ask.

"A gentlemen never talks, and as I am no gentlemen yes I did", he smiles with a twinkle in his eye. This is the first time I have seen it since Jeannette passed away.

"Is Royston my brother?" I whisper in Daddy's ear, he bellowed with laughter. All the other boxes looked at us. By this point I too could not control my laughter.

Our box was on the balcony, we were in prime location to see all that was going on. The paddocks could be viewed from our box, and in the distance I spotted at least thirty or so horses being groomed in the distance.

Our chairs were leather, the carpet royal blue, we had an amazing buffet, a selection of lobster, crab, chicken, salad, and an assortment of alcohol.

"You ok Daddy" I ask concerned,

"Yes I am having a great time" he responds automatically.

"No I mean with all this alcohol around" My father looked at me, took my hand and kissed it "I am fine"

"Ok just checking."

He looked at me "What is with that hat" he laughed

"Ask your mother, I say apologetically.

I have an idea, and he took my hat off, and out it in the

adjourning table behind us. Daddy then punched his fingers up my nape and ruffles my hair. "I love your hair like this" he smiles

"Thanks" I giggle.

"I hate the pink lipstick and nail polish", he says seriously.

"Well daddy I love it and so does all these young men, I laugh. I look up, and notice the royal crest. "Daddy, are we in the royal box"

He smiles "Yes we are"

"How?"

"We are royalty baby, do not forget that. We are goooooood stock", he laughed. " You are royalty.

Harold walked past me with a tray of champagne.

"Boy come here" Daddy said.

"Daddy its fine please don't make a fuss" I look down. I could see that Harold was humiliated.

"No princess it's not ok", he snapped and starred at Harold.

"Daddy please …. Don't" I plead. Without acknowledging my pleas daddy took two champagne flutes and passed me one. I took it and smiled. Harold just stared at me.

My father smirked at Harold. "You can stop starring at my daughter right now. Boy hasn't anyone told you that you should not hang your cap too high, she is out of your league"

"Daddy!" I shriek

Daddy laughed. "Oh Winn, I am just playing". He said unapologetically.

Harold looked at my father. "Yes Sir I am aware of the saying"

"Good", daddy chuckled and winked at me.

"The young miss is not my type Sir. I have a beau and am very happy Sir". Harold informed us with a smirk on his face. *What do you mean you have a beau I wanted to scream. It was as if Harold hit me in the stomach. I looked at my father glad of the cap too high comment.*

"Hmmm I see", Daddy smiled, I think he liked his cockiness.

"Winn are you OK, Daddy enquired.

"I am just hot, Daddy where is the powder room".

"To the left, are you sure you are ok?"

"I just need a minute." I walked briskly to the ladies room. Once inside I felt immediately better. I look around, this was the most impressive bathroom I have ever seen, and it was cool. A few middle aged ladies eyes me suspiciously.

"Are you alright dear?", a tall dark skinned woman, with an thick perfect chignon and aqua blue dress asked. Her features were pretty but appeared pinched.

"I am, it's just very warm."

She smiles. There is some cool water over there shall I get you some, she seemed concerned.

Thank you. I replied "you are most kind".

She puts the glass in front of me. I am standing in front of the largest mirror I had ever seen, it was wall to wall with a thick chrome finish. The wash basins were white and grey marble with sparkling silver taps. I smile. A young maid walks towards me with a face towel that had been soaked in cold water.

"Here Ma'am", she smiled

"Thank you". I sit down and put the cool towel on my neck.

"Arrrggggghhhhhhhh". I close my eyes. Both women look at me and we all giggle.

"It's so hot" my new friend tells me. "My poor horse she whined.

"Your horse is racing?", I asked impressed.

"Yes", she smiled proudly showing off her perfect white teeth.

"What is his or name", I enquired genuinely interested.

"Her name is Carousel".

"Well that is whom I am going to bet on, I smile. I stretch out my hand, "My name is Edwina".

"I know, we are all talking about you. No one knew Barry had a love child, let alone one so beautiful", she gushed without thinking.

"I and look down, immediately caught off guard by the comment.

"Oh no don't do that…. I 'm sorry I did not mean… My name is Lynnette the klutz with a big mouth. She looked genuinely sorry for her gaff. *Come on Winn toughen up I command.*

We both laugh. "It's ok, truly" I say.

"I am sorry Edwina, I was not trying to be unkind." Lynnette meant every word.

"Call me Winnie, all my friends do. Its forgotten."

"Well Miss Winnie have you cooled down". Lynette asked in a very assertive manner.

"Yes". I smile at my new friends looking her squarely in the eyes.

"Good, Carousel will be racing soon and I want you to come to my box. We can cheer together." Lynnette looped her arm in to mine and off we went.

On the way back to the VIP enclosure I spotted Harold in the corner of my eye pouring champagne is more flutes with other waiters. He momentarily looks up. I look away as I recognise that expression. He is annoyed with me. How dare he? He is the one that has moved on. Clearly I meant nothing to him. Tears momentarily wet my eyes, but I am determined not to cry. Not over him, not anymore.

I walk past our own box and my Grandmother gives me the eye suspiciously trying to place my new confidants face. I smile, elated at the fact that Grandmother dearest will not be introducing me to the son of this whose fathers owns that.

"Hurry Lynnette" I hear a male voice cry out. "Were starting"

My new friend dragged me into her box and races to the balcony area, she expertly scoops a pair binoculars from the table and immediately steady's her focus on her horse.

"Crack" the gun snapped and the horses galloped to cue.

"Looook", Lynette squeals "Carousel is number seven, my jockey is the one in blue and purple".

"I see him" I scream over the cheers in the box.

"Come on Carousel" I chant with the others. I have to say that horse racing was a hoot. Carousel was like lightening, clearly the best thoroughbred in its class, she eased his way through his opponents and won with at least four lengths between him and the second rider.

Everyone was whooping and screaming. I turned around, and Lynette was gone, she had run down with her father to the paddock to give Carousel a big kiss and a much needed drink.

I felt the presence of someone behind me, I presume it was daddy.

"Hello" whoever he was his voice was deep and silky.

I look round to a divine set of lips and teeth smiling at me.

"Courtney" he said stretching his long, thick hand to me.

"Hmmm" was all that I could think of to say. He was a man mountain, with lovely square jaws, white teeth, wide brown eyes and dimple in his chin. I just stare at him, besotted.

"My name is Courtney, I spotted you earlier, and could not believe my luck when Lynette brought you to my box"

"And Lynette is …."

He smiles "She is my sister … and you are?"

"Her new friend" I smile back "Pleasure to meet you, Its Edwina Barnett, My friends call me Win, though you can call me Miss Barnet".

"Nice to meet you Miss Barnet", with that he delicately kissed my hand, which sent shock waves through my body. "It seems I have much work to do if I am to call you Winn.

"It appears so" I giggle. *Play it cool Winn. He seems too good to be true.*

"Champagne", he snapped his fingers and Harold appeared. I look at Harold, and smile

Feeling awkward I ask, "May I go to the paddock I would love to meet Carousel?"

Courtney held my hand, which was very forward, I pulled it away. He looked at me with regret. "I apologies Miss Barnet. May I accompany you to the paddock?"

We both smile. "I would like that. Please don't get the

wrong impression I enjoyed you holding my hand, it's just.

"Edwina, its fine. I am teasing you".

He stretched out his arm and I took it, he was tall, much taller than Harold, His morning suit was made for a man with his broad and muscular physique.. I could tell that he had a fine hard physique underneath all those clothes. *I start to blush, and not just in my cheeks*. On arrival to the paddock, Lynette runs over.

"Sorry for leaving you like that Winnie, this is just so wonderful".

"It's ok your brother has been taking care of me".

"I can see that", she says sarcastically.

They both smile at one another. I catch his gaze and he gives me a wink. *He seems so confident I really like that and I am finding it a very attractive quality.*

"Come and meet the horse", Lynette asked.

"Actually I should go back to my box".

"I will escort you" Courtney replied smiling. My heart skipped a beat and I had flutters in my base of my tummy.

"Ok" *I try to sound cool* .As he escorts me to my box, we fall silent. I could not believe that I was tongue tied over this man. Are you kidding Winnie, he is delicious. Not just nice but adorable. He changes course as the last minute and leads me to the bar.

"I have a confession. I don't want to let you out of my

sight. Can you please have a drink with me?"

"Alright, that will be nice" I smile.

He motions over a waiter, "A lemonade for the lady and a water for me".

"So.. Courtney, what do you do and who are your people?" I ask with an air of Phyllis Barnet about me.

"Are you serious?" he exclaims, I am not sure if he was genuinely surprised or offended.

I look confused.

"Edwina do you not know who I am?" he asked bemused

"I'm sorry, I blush "Should I?".

"No …. No", he was the one who is now embarrassed. "Miss Barnet I am Courtney Du Pille the third, My father is Courtney Jackson Du Pille the second, known to his peers which includes your father as Jackson. He is …. We are the founding owners of Jamaica First National Bank"

"Ok then" I say with sarcastic humor, "no need to tell you who I am as you already know".

He laughed, "Yes, my father and your grandfather are acquaintances."

"I learn something new every day" I smile.

He stares at me for a few seconds. "You are very enchanting Edwina Barnet" he said quietly.

I blush and look down, Courtney out his index finger

under my chin and gently raised my chin so that I was looking in his eyes. "Don't be embarrassed, you are lovely, this is how god made you so embrace this face, body, mind that you have been given. We are made in god image, revel in it".

I smile, my heart quickens, to my surprise I feel my panties moisten, and my nipples harden. I look at Courtney, he too is lovely. "You are a very handsome man Mr. Courtney Du Pille the third" I say quietly, as I did not want to be overheard. He steps into me and brushes his body on mine. The flutters in my stomach are somersaulting.

"Then its settled", he says in a low voice "we will make beautiful babies".

I burst out laughing.

"What's this?" I hear my Grandfather interrupt our intimate flirting. He gently tugs me away from Courtney that I am forced to take a step back. Courtney did not move.

"Dr Barnet sir it's a pleasure to see you again", he said staring at me.

"I can see that" my grandfather replied annoyed. Embarrassed by my Grandfather I look to the floor only to be greeted with Courtney's large feet looking at me.

"Golly you have boats for feet" I gasp.

"Well when you sail me you will never get wet" again I laugh uncontrollably. Courtney too is trying to suppress his laughter as he can see that my grandfather is less than impressed with him.

"Edwina come along". My Grandfather curtly pulls me in the opposite direction. As I walk away from him I mouth "sorry", and he winks at me. My heart skips a beat and my panties are soaked for a second time today.

"There you are?" Daddy whines. "I thought you got lost. Where was she?" he asks Grandfather

"In the bar", he said disapprovingly.

"With?" Daddy asked curtly suspiciously eyeing me up and down for clues.

"Du Pilles son "Grandfather said raising an eyebrow. My father was silent and cracked a shy smile.

"I see" he said quietly, then looked at my grandmother with approval. She too raised an eyebrow and smiled. *I on the other hand dance inside, I saw it for the first time ever. Its approval. I plan to go full steam ahead.*

This day has exhausting, there were so many highlights, but the most impressionable, has to be that beautiful man, Courtney Du Pille. I cannot stop thinking about his chocolate cocoa smooth skin, his shapely lips, white teeth and fine clothes. Who are you kidding Edwina, it was that body under the clothes. He was the whole package and more, and I cannot wait to see him again.

Riding back to the hotel.   "Good day darling" my Grandmother asked, trying to be noninvasive about my meeting.

"Yes, it was lovely", I smile "Thank you for forcing me to come out and have some fun" I say.

"I see that you met Lynette, very accomplished like

yourself. I can see you becoming quite friendly."

I smile, "I think you could be on to something there Grandmother" I note that grandmother and father all exchange looks and smile. My Grandfather looked grumpily out of the window.

It 8pm and there is so much commotion next door. Monique has pinned up my hair. I have on a Chanel dress which make me feel quite exposed. However, my Grandmother is insistent that this is all the rage. I am wearing a pink chiffon dress which is strapless with a sweetheart bodice to cup and corset my bosoms. I have cupped shoulder straps off the shoulders and they sit perfectly on the upper part of my biceps. To break the dress up is a diamonded sewn in belt, then the skirt is pink chiffon to the floor. I do look very different. I look so grown up and aristocratic compared to my usual day to day plantation look. The door separating our bedroom opens and my father stands there looking at me.

"Daddy don't just stand there daddy pass me my necklace". I snap.

"You look sensational", he smiles, walks over and kisses me on the head.

"Twice in two days" I say.

"Winn you look better without anything at all, you don't need a necklace. You look lovely"

"Earrings?"

"Show me?" daddy asks.

They are grandmothers drop down diamond earrings", I

hold them to my ears

"Bingo" daddy said. "Courtney is going to have a heart attack when he sees you"

"That's the plan" I tell him. Monique was fussing with my hair smiled at me. I look at my father who is stunned by my response.

"Do you like him?" he asks quietly, his expression becomes very serious.

"Daddy he has a lot of potential and I do feel drawn to him, he's nice and is not intimidated by me"

Daddy smiles, "I see, well you look beautiful. Enjoy this evening. Can I give you some advice?"

"Hmmmmmm" I say applying more lipstick.

"Be a little unavailable, men like a challenge" He smiled. I look at him.

"How do I do that without turning him off?" I say.

"Do nothing, make him chase you and do not make this easy for him."

"Ok I will try" I smile to myself. My daddy was a sweet heart when he tried.

"The Royal Kingstonian gala dinner" was held downstairs in the Paul Bogle Ball room. Daddy escorted me through the doors and I was taken aback by the sheer size of the room. There was George Lewis and his Ragtime Jazz Band.

"Awww daddy is that?.."

"Yes baby, its George Wallace himself. Daddy's face lit up at my excitement.

"Awww Daddy I love him" I squeal.

"We all love George", Daddy said trying to contain his excitement. "Well I hope that those pretty shoes can dance as I plan to wear you out". He then showed me some of his dancing moves. My grandmother barged her way between us.

"Edwina you are the prettiest woman here, I want you to have fun and commit to no one. You have the pick of the room, choose wisely dear." she stretched out her arm for two champagne flutes.

I blush and smile. I cannot believe she is being so nice to me. I must say that my grandmother seemed more relaxed with these people, than she did at the plantation.

"I am not sure Champagne agrees with me" I confess.

"Nonsense it's an acquired taste. You will get used to it." She jabs me back into position.

The evening was rapturous. There was an explosion of good looking women in luxurious beautiful dresses, handsome men all looking important with their brandy glasses and shiny sleeked back hair filled with brill cream and coconut oil. The banquet was fit for a king. I have never eaten so much at once, even my grandfather asked if I was ok. The conversation on our table was delightful we were sat with Bradley Boullier, his excruciating annoying mother Jackie and his father Ken, otherwise known as Boxer to his friends. The champagne made it all so bearable, and Bradley and I discussed plantations, politics, love affairs marriage and babies. In all accounts anyone who was observing would be forgiven for mistaking us for a courting couple.

Jackie and my grandmother were deep in conversation, yet observing our every reaction. The evening sailed past me and we were already at the coffee and mints.

"Edwina darling, let's go freshen up"

I look at my grandmother undecided whether this was genuine or an intentional ploy to prize me away from Bradley. My father and grandmother momentarily paused their conversation with Boxer and Jackie. My father raised his eyebrows, so I was pretty sure it was an intentional ploy.

"Excuse me Bradley" I say politely. He looked disapprovingly at my mother.

"Of Course ladies, with that all the gentlemen stood up." I smiled enjoying the etiquette shown to me.

"Come along dear" Grandmother chimed with the broadest grin in her face.

We walked arm in arm to the powder room. We both used the cubicle as if it were some sort of penance for leaving the table in the absence of actually wanting to pee.

As we stood at the mirror my grandmother fixed my fair. "Dear apply more lipstick, your starting to fade".

"Oh Ok," I say with a smile. In all the years I lived with this witch, this was the first real attention she paid to my appearance. It just made me feel nice and wanted.

"Do you like him? She asked reasserting her sharp assertive tone.

"Who?".

"Bradley?" she said exasperated and raising her eyes to the ceiling.

"He's nice" I giggle.

"Nice. Tsk".

"Yes Grandmother Nice".

"Hmmmm well he's not quite to our standard but he will do".

"Whhhhhooooeeee Grandmother!" I exclaim.

"Yes dear", she turned and looked at me.

I like him as a friend I did not realise that you expected me to court and marry him at the same time.

"Oh so you don't like him" she looked at me confused.

"He is a nice man, but….I would not call him a suitor. Why would you ask me that, we have just eaten dinner, I was being polite".

"Well when you did not acknowledge Courtney?"

"What. When?" I am momentarily panicked that I slighted my honey in waiting.

When you were talking to Bradley he walked past on at least four occasions and you did not even look up once.

"Really I did not see him". I say mortified.

"Oh OK, I just presumed that you had lost interest". She informed me.

"No I must find him , he cannot think I am being rude." Panicked I started to leave the bathroom.

My grandmother tugged my arm. Firstly apply your rouge. Now if you do not listen to another word I say. Be cool. He loves it. He is boiling over for you and whether it has been by design or a genuine mistake your being embroiled in conversation with Bradley, has him wanting" my grandmother said with a spark in her eye. For a second she was reminded of memories in her prime. "Play it cool, if you chase him now, you will be chasing him forever."

"But.." I try to protest, wanting to wear my heart in my sleeve.

"No buts, be interested in Bradley, he needs to know that he is not the only bull in the steed". With that she laughed mightily, clearly enjoying her own humour.

I smiled broadly and raise my eyebrows, "Grandmother" I say and smile. As instructed I applied my rouge. I look at me in the mirror. I momentarily see Harold's in my mind's eye. I shake him off. I lean in survey my face and hair, yep perfect now time to have fun.

Back at the table Bradley and I pick up from where we left off.

"Edwina, do you think that we could have dinner sometime, my cousin Evelyn can chaperone it would be most proper" he asked.

"Umm I am not sure, I may need to speak to my father." I

smile politely.

"Arhhhh yes, of course", he smiled. "So you would consider it?

"I will ask him"

The band piped up and I let out a sigh of relief. "I love this band" I shout over the southern dulcet tones of the percussion.

"Who are they" he shouted back.

"What are you serious that" I point aggressively "is George Lewis". As I point I spot Courtney at the corner of the room, he was talking to an elder gentlemen and they were both looking at me.

"Dance" Bradley shouted.

"Pardon".

"Would you like to dance?" he shouted not realising that the music was softening and most people close by looked over and smiled at us both.

I smile, desperate to save his embarrassment. "It's Ok" I smile, I turn to my father, "Daddy can I dance with Bradley?"

"You are your own woman, don't ask me, do you want to dance with him?"

I nod. He smiles a little too wide for my father with gratitude We sway to the music and Bradley cut loose. He was really quite good, we danced for what seemed a small age, but it was delightful and one of the best evenings that I had ever.

An announcement was that George Lewis band were taking a break so another band came on. They looked like one of the American linidpop bands that was all the rage. The guitar started and I immediately felt like I too had to cut loose.

The hairs on my body arose at his presence. Courtney slowly walked over towards me, smiling at me and locking my gaze. "Excuse me Bradley"

Bradley looked suspicious, Courtney stretched out his hand to shake Bradley's hand and pulled him close and whispered something into his ear, Bradley looked at me apologetically and said "Sure"

Courtney looked absolutely edible in his tuxedo. His hair was slicked to one side, and his face had a glow to it, he stretched out his hand, which I immediately grabbed, kissed the back of my hand, he looked at me which made my nipples harden immediately. "Let's dance " he shouted. The rock and roll beat took over and we twisted and skanked, and piroeted around me like an old pro. He could tell that my gown was in part a restriction and also that most of the room was watching us. After the third rock and roll song, I mouthed "I need a break".

"You ok", he asked.

"Hmmmm I think so, I need air and lots of water. My mouth is dry".

Courtney grabbed my hand and led me out to the bar. It was outside and the pool water shimmered aqua blue in the moons ray. The evening was warm , and there were many party goers outside sat down on the patio furniture.

"What does the pretty lady want to drink?" asked the barman.

"Madam" Courtney said sharply "shall have a water with ice.

The barman nodded compliantly. "Yes sir" and continued with the task at hand. I walk away embarrassed and walk towards a vacant table and sit down, the arch of my right foot is aching.

"Here baby" he says, putting the drinks down and pulling out my chair.

I look up, grinning from ear to ear.

What? He smiles.

"I like the way you said that. A lot."

"Good, as I loved saying it" He sips his water and I stare at his lips. "I better get you back inside before Bradley comes and gives me an old fashion beating over his girl".

"What?" I giggle".

"I am nobodies girl" I laugh.

"Not even mine?". Courtney enquires with a confident smile.

"Well you have to earn me I am a powerful wealthy business woman, I am not just going to quiver at your feet just because you call me baby".

Courtney looked at me, his face deadly serious, he pulled his chair close to mine, he positions his face a nose width from mine I smell the brandy on his breath. I read the intensity in his face. There is a connection between us. It feels needy. In his low gruff deep voice, he says, "When I have earned you, I will make your body crumble and quiver underneath me", with that he leaned in and kissed me closed mouth hard and quick. I look at him, his head in the same position. I then leaned in I wrap my arms around his broad muscular neck and kissed him soft and slow.

This courtship has been undeniably unexpected. It has only been three months but I do love him. It's not infatuation but love. I find him attractive in all ways and I am finding it difficult to keep my hands of him.

Courtney is everything that Harold isn't. He's really tall, at least six foot six. An athletic build. He has a perfectly sculpted upper body, each muscle is pronounced and cut to perfection, complimented with a high round muscular bottom, and strapping legs so muscular that his thighs remind me of the well-honed muscles of my father's stallions.

I adore the fact that he loves me, and is open and gallant and unashamedly bold about it. This is the man that I need. Someone who is willing to show up for his woman. He turn ups to the plantation, and he will get stuck in with any task that we are involved in. The other week Bertha my cow, was having a difficult birth, Courtney my banking city trading boy, helped us hold her down, he even assisted Mackie in pulling out the Calf, both men were elbows deep in Bertha.

"Mackie we have to get it out, it's been too long" I wail desperately. The two men carefully tugged and pulled the calf out of her mother's womb, this life was hanging in the balance and we all knew that each of us had to do all that we could to help her to live. Struck by the enormity of the moment we all were desperate to set her free and I with two plantation hands, did our utmost to hold Bertha in place, through the pain of calf birth, and having two large men with their hands in her womb, trying to negotiate her stubborn calf to come out into the real world.

I look at Courtney, I could not contain myself.

"Please save her". He could feel my anguish. He pushed deeper into Bertha, she let out a huge wail and pushed her leg free, which caught me on the cheek. I saw a flash of yellow and orange in both eyes. I catapulted to the floor

"Winnie!" Courtney screamed,

"I'm ok", I lied, the instant swelling rising like bread on the left side of my face. Dazed I grabbed her leg and pushed it down through the stars and choir echoing in my ears.

My grandfather and father ran into the barn, "How long has it been?"

"Too long, Daddy she can't die." I wail, tears of grief, and the pain from my head streamed down my face.

My father stood behind us, Courtney, Mackie in the count of four I need you to pull down. The two field hands hedged round to make space for daddy and Grandfather. Both men were on their knees and their elbows was in the middle of Bertha's body, It was Daddy who first pushed as hard as he could towards the top of Berthas stomach, She let out a wail and thrashed around. "Moooooooooooooooooooooooooooooooo"

"Keep her still boys "Grandfather yelled to both field hands, he counted us in "One Two Three Four" and repeated the exercise.

Bertha screamed at the highest pitch I heard a cow moo. It was excruciating. Both Courtney and Mackie tugged hard and set the calf free, she was limp and lifeless.

"She can't be dead" Courtney screamed at us angrily.

"Help me" my grandfather shouted. All the men lifted the calf and had her perched over the half stable gate, the field hand grabbed a bucket of water and was washing away the mucus on her face, nose and mouth. My father rubbed the calf's back vigorously, and Mackie pushed through the mucus glue and blew into her mouth. The poor calf's airways were so blocked that when Mackie blew in its mouth a mucus bubble popped out of its nose. Courtney took over the mouth to mouth when Mackie needed to catch his breath. Finally the bubble burst, he kept blowing and a few seconds later the was a splutter from the calf. She took her first breath.

They lay the new born her next to her mother. She looked at her baby lovingly, licked her face, and closed her eyes for the last time. Her duty complete, her daughter saved, that is all that mattered. .There were no words in this moment. All of us was drenched in sweat, blood and mucus wiped down the calf, daddy helped Courtney and we brought Bertha's daughter to the big house.

"How are they? Rene ran off the porch to me with her lantern in hand, it was after 10 o clock at night. She looked at me and knew that she didn't make it. In the distance she saw the men and the calf.

"I have a large dog bed under the stairs, Lucy made it for Daaaag. She pulled it out, ran upstairs, and came down with spare blankets.

Courtney was in the living room, the calf was shivering. Mackie took the blankets and wrapped the calf. Courtney still held her in his arms and stroked her head. "It's ok little bird, he said softly".

Unsure what to do Courtney came in and took control of the situation. "I will sit with her, Rene warm some milk for me. Winnie go get a bath and get Barry to look at your cheek"

"No I'm fine" I protest. I want so stay with her.

"Winnie, my grandfather put his hand, on my shoulder, go bathe, and take Courtney with you. Let's us help, you look exhausted. I will come up in a while and look at your face. Does it hurt to blink or talk?

"No it just hurts" I tried to smile, but the muscles in my face were in protest and refused to move.

I show Courtney to the main bathroom on the landing. Rene had been a dear and had the hot water running. The bath was filled with Epsom salts and there was some imported lux soap on the side.

Courtney entered the bathroom and shut the door. He look crestfallen by tonight events. As he shut the door he weakly smiled.

Come on Rene beckoned me from my room door. Your bath is ready. I undress and slowly enter the bath. All my muscles were aching and sore from the evening restraints. Rene takes a jug of bath water and wets my hair. She finds my shampoo and washes it, whilst humming. I scrub the evening off me mechanically. I had an overwhelming feeling of regret. I could have done more. I lie back allow the water to absorb me and dunk my head under the water.

As I surface Rene is gone. I did not want to tell her to leave but I am glad that I was alone. I get out, pick up my large fluffy towel and wrap my body twice. I find my short hair towel and wrap my hair. I walk through to my room, to find Courtney sat on my bed half naked with a towel wrapped around his waist.

"Baby I don't know about you but I need a hug" he tells me. I run to him and push my face deep into his chest. He peels the towel off my head and strokes my wet hair. The more he stroked me hair the harder it was for me to control my feelings. I fall into him and cry. He holds me firmly in his arms.

"Winnie I am so proud of you. You are like no other woman I have seen. Today you were truly remarkable".

I look up, my face is swollen from Bertha's kick, my eyes are red, and there is snot falling out my nose. Is he serious. I pick up my towel and wipe my eyes and nose. He pulls me close and kisses me, My face hurts and I moan in pain.

"Oh baby I'm sorry how is your cheek, he then turns me to inspect it". Courtney eyes grow wide and his face becomes very serious.

"What, what is it?"

"Honey how you feeling?" he asks with a hint of panic in his voice.

"I'm ok, my head is throbbing why?"

Courtney picked me up and put me on the bed carefully. "Don't move I'm going to get your Grandfather".

"What I sit up" looking puzzled at the situation.

"Winnie" I said don't move, she shouted at me for the

first time in our courtship. It really frightened me.

I lay back and feel water trickling down the side of my face. I realise that the has trickled to my collar bone. Hang on something is not right as my hair is only damp not wet. I look at my crisp white pillows, it is covered in blood. I gasp, it's my blood. I begrudgingly inform my fingers to investigate. I look at my finger tips and do what I always in any bloody situation I pass out.

Chapter 17

Mr. Lover Man

We run in the room and she is very still. *Dear God do not let this woman die on me. She is my everything.*

"Why is she naked and why were you in here" her father yells at me.

I look at him incredulous. "Sir with the greatest respect, I think we need to concentrate on the blood that appears to be seeping out of her head" I say more assertively than I wanted to. He glares at me, I stare back. He does not frighten me. *I know this son of a bitch thinks he's in control but he's not. Far from it. I see the way that he treats others around him, but I will not allow him to treat me this way. I plan to marry this woman and when I do I plan to leave this island with Winnie for good.*

"I'm serious" he barks as he walked around the bed.

"So am I" *Stand your ground Courtney.* "I am neither intimidated nor bothered about you and this. I just want to be sure that she is ok?"

"Winnie" her grandfather says gently, he gently rubs her forearm. "Winnie honey can you hear me?" he checked her pulse, went to his bag and got a small light and checked her pupils. He shook her more vigorously "Winnie"

"Hmmmmm" she lay there dazed.

"Winnie I need you to open your eyes..... Winnie", he started to shout at her.

Both her father and I look at my beautiful woman lying lifeless in the bed.

"Winnie" Grandfather shouted

"Dad what's going on, what's wrong".

"She's had a blow to the head it could be a number of things" the old man looked concerned.

Winnie slowly opened her eyes. "My ear is bleeding?"

"I know my darling. I just need to examine you to determine why?"

"Ok", she whispered. "I think I fainted when I saw the blood"

"Hmmm Hmmmmm" her grandfather said

"What can I do to help?" I ask feeling completely useless.

"How about you put some fucking clothes on" her father snaps.

"They are dirty remember". *This man is such an arse hole. What does he think happened here? I heard about him, the women, his bullying nature, his unpredictable temper. I will not be toyed with. He does not control me.*

Right on que Rene came in with a pair of work trousers and a short sleeved shirt. To provoke him I slowly dress myself.

"What's the prognosis doc?"

"Not sure, but what I do know is that my granddaughter needs privacy so please all of you leave the room.

We walk down the stairs in silence.

"Everything alright" Mackie asks, he looked concerned for her. He really loved her.

"I shrug my shoulders, the truth is we are not sure". I say feeling even worse than losing Bertha.

"Sit guys, have some tea" Rene chimes. Barry is a great doctor, he will find out what is wrong with her.

Barrington takes the hot tea. He looks visibly worried, which reassures me a little. I am not sure why. He looks old, tired, like life is wearing on him. As he sits down he looks at me with peppered intensity.

"Why were in my daughters room without your clothes on boy", he said in his most menacing voice.

Stand down old man. You have no idea who you're playing with. "Firstly B-a-r-r-y I am not your boy. To answer your question I was pretty shaken up by Bertha so thought I check in on Edwina. I was consoling her, she was upset.

"Are you sure that's all you were doing", he asked.

"For god sake man have some respect that's your daughter we are talking about. May I remind you that she has a nasty bruise on her face. I … I just wanted to make sure she was ok? I look him square in the eyes.

He backs down "Well I just needed to hear it", Barrington snarled. I don't want anyone taking advantage of my

311

daughter".

"Barry not everyman likes there women battered and bloody" I say sarcastically. The moment the words leave my lips I know it was a mistake.

Barrington leapt off his chair and grabbed me by the throat. I push him off. Rene jumps in between us

"No. No No No Nooooooooo. You are not here for this. Take this macho melodrama out of here. She is upstairs with god knows what injuries", Rene was fuming, realising she was shouting, she lowered her voice "she loves you both. There is enough room in her life for you both, so stop this now."

I look at the old man, he was panting hard. I step away. I feel sorry for him. She is all that he has in his life.

"Sir, this evenings events have taken me by surprise. I apologies for any comments that may have caused you offence." I stretch out my hand.

Rene looked at Barrington as if to say "well?"

He steps back, stretched out his hand "I apologies Courtney, this evening has stirred up unpleasant emotions and I would like you to know that I regret my actions".

Rene smiles. "What you both need is a beer. She walked to the cooler and pulls out two redstripe beers. "Go on, go outside, walk and talk. Your family now, sort this out properly, she cannot choose so don't make her.

We look at each other. For appearance sakes we knew this has to be done. Rene would tell Winnie exactly how we behaved so we knew we had to end the story on a positive note.

Barrington strides ahead, he throws the beer to the ground. "She knows that I don't drink?"

"Why not?" I ask knowing the truth.

"I just can't it's a long story". He shuts me down.

"I heard that you were sorry drunk, but you have turned your life around." I look him squarely in the eye.

Barrington turned around and looked at me " Listen Kid, for whatever reason she likes you. I think she could do better but she has chosen you" he looked directly at me.

"Like you I do love her Barry. I know what it looked like, I would never disrespect her. She is too special to me for that. I want it to be special? Us … you know".

"What your first time?" Barrington said sarcastically.

I smile "Yes, I wouldn't do that to her. Look we have not had the best relationship but we have to try for her sake"

"Why" he snapped.

"Because we are going to be married. I love her. I would have asked her today but Bertha dies then her ear, now you".   Barrington is just glaring at me. I nervously drink the beer.

What makes you think she'll say yes." He asks.

I shrug, "just a feeling". I smile.

"Have you asked her the question?" he enquires.

"Not yet? I'll do it soon. I don't want to wait. Not after today. Life…", tears well up in my eye. Its fragile and I just want to be with her.

"Well" Barrington said cheerily "Welcome to the family" he opens his arms to me and walks towards me. He bear hugs me which throws me off guard, then he cups his hands around my face "If you hurt her in any way, I will kill you".

"Gentlemen" her grandfather shouts suspiciously eyeing us up, trying to decipher whether this is friendly banter or whether we have entered enemy territory.

"She's going to be fine. The kick to her face ruptured her eardrum. She will need to rest and keep it covered for a week, as she will be prone to infection, but the sight of blood frightened her so she will be a good patient" .

"Can I go and see her please? I ask politely.

"Of course son".

I run up the stairs. She was lying on her bed in a white night gown.

"My poor darling, Bertha brutalised you" I laugh. I lay next to her, Winnie looks me up and down and smiles. "Baby what are you wearing?" she asked me trying not to smile.

"Rene clearly does not like me. Can you sit up for a bit."

"Yes" she looked confused. I help her get up and prop her pillows around her so that her head and neck are covered.

"Baby I need to ask you something very important." I kneel down next to her, the bruising in her face is horrendous, and her complexion illustrates the iridescent spectrum of bruising in all its hues. The whole of her left jaw is swollen, her cheek bone was burgundy and black, her eye was swollen and the rest of her jaw was black and purple. I smile.

"You look awful" I whisper, she wants to laugh but can't. "I need you to know that you are the most extra ordinary young woman I have met in my life. Today has made me realise that if your heart tells you to you jump, you should jump". She looked confused. I gently hold her hand, "I need you with me baby, not just as my girl but as my wife. Will you marry me?

"She smiles, then winces, then smiles. "Yes baby, now get in here and cuddle me to sleep. "Grandfather gave me some morphine and I am woozy as hell", tears trickle down her face.

"Are these tears of joy Winn? I ask.

"Yes baby", she smiles through the pain.

"Then I am the luckiest man in the world."

Chapter 18

The Making of the Man.

Our seven bedroom beach house in Negril is the family retreat from the city and we all love it. Directly on the beach front, this house has fond memories for me. It belonged to my grandfather and once he had passed away my mother gave it a much needed make over.

Stretched over three floors with decking on each floor, there was no area of this house that did not represent a sun trap. My adorable finance loved it and I for one loved her even more for that, as we will be spending so much time here. My bedroom is located downstairs as I love the sound and smell of the sea. As a teenager I kick up an almighty fuss to have my own way, and smile each time I sit in this room with the patio doors open, my landscape for as far as the eyes can span is cloudless clear blue skies and aqua blue water. Breathtaking!.

Sitting on my beach wooden decking looking at to the unknown and sipping some mango juice, my intimate thoughts are interrupted.

"Court I am so excited for you. You're going to be married in a month, are you getting nervous?" Lynnette bounces in my room with her red bathing suit on.

My sister literally did cart wheels in our living room when I informed my family that Winnie and I were engaged. With immediate effect my mother and Phyllis moved into action and between them have planned the biggest society wedding Jamaica will ever see. It's indulgent, extravagant and opulent, and over the top, hell it will be a great shindig, and I for one am very excited.

"Hey there loved up byoy, did you hear what I said". She pestered me.

"I did Lynne?" I say with exasperation and roll my eyes at my sister "and yes I am excited about married life, but this wedding is all about mum and Phyllis, you do realise this right?"

"I know, I know", she said apologetically. "Courtney, You are the heir and only son to one of the wealthiest men in Jamaica. You are marrying the bastard heiress of one of the wealthiest families in Jamaica. This has to be celebrated". She giggled.

"Lynn don't let me warn you again. That's not funny" I smile, even though my sister was offensive she did not mean anything by it.

"It so is funny how mum and dad have made such allowances for the Barnet Princess, if she was one of your local common round the way island girls this would not be happening. Admit it."

"Lynne enough" I bellow " She is my choice and that is it"

"Bruv I know, she is a lovely choice, you will be enjoying her for years to come" she laughed.

"I sincerely hope so", I wink.

"So what's the plan for tomorrow tonight?"

"Barry, dad and I are going to some old club in Morant Bay, this is the pre amble to the stag party. It should be a hoot."

"Who else is going?

"Ronnie and Jeff are flying in from Miami." My sister tried not to look too interested but she was real sweet on my boy Ronnie.

"You going to spend time with Barrington now are you? Lynne said sarcastically and raised her eyebrows.

I laugh "I am, now that's progress for you"

Just you make sure that you don't get in a punch up with him. Or this fairy tale wedding is over. You hear me". We both laugh and Lynn heads out to the beach for a swim. I lay back allowing the sun to warm my skin.

Edwina Barnett's loves me to the point she scares me with her intensity. I am genuinely mad over heels in love with her. No question, but I am fearful. I just don't want to hurt her. My father adores my mother, but he still has women all over town. Will I burn with desire for my wife in ten months, ten years. Suppose the sex is terrible, then I am trapped.

I immediately shrug off this feeling. No Court, you may be your father's son but you are not your father. She is the one, and you felt that from your first kiss. The quality that I admire the most is that she is completely independent. If I acted like a fool, she would not be dependent on me or my family, she is her own woman. I am not sure why I find this so attractive, but I do, she is so young yet so capable.

My wanting to be married is not just about sex, but I'd be a liar if I said that I was not looking forward to undressing my beautiful virginal bride. I know what pleasures awaits me. I have restrained myself many a night. The urge to rip her clothes off and have her mount me has been my fantasy for months. Now in one month, she will be mine completely and I have a promise to deliver. I smile remembering that I told her that I plan to make her crumble and quiver. I remember the first night that we kissed, it was magical. Since that week, I have locked off all my lady friends. I am completely committed. .

I have laid it all out to her. There is nothing that she does not know about me, and there is nothing I will not do for her. I have never been so committed to one woman, and so honest. My parents have seen the change in me. For years father has pressurised me on a date when I will join the Bank. I gave him one the day after I proposed. I know that I don't have to provide for her but I want to.

I will finish my masters at George Town university. Then I will move my wife and I to the capital and learn to be the next CEO and owner of Jamaica National Bank. I have it all. The wealth, the family, the career now a very accomplished and beautiful wife. As the sun beats down on my naked body, I smile.

"Hello son, you look like you got the cream" my dad asks.

I laugh out loud. "You think?"

"So you're sure then?"

What is with everyone. "Of what dad, I try not to sound too annoyed.

"Marriage?" he looks at me seriously.

"Yes Sir 100% pop, she is just adorable, and I don't

319

mean the obvious. She is the whole package."

If your happy with her then I am happy", he smiled. He looked pensive. "Courtney, I am not in the habit of delving into your business, but I have to ask. Have you…….. well?

"What Dad?" *is he serious? Do we need to do this now. I mean, he knows that I am his son in that area.*

"You know what I am trying to ask?

"Dad are you asking whether we have we slept together?" I ask him directly.

My dad nods apologetically.

"No dad, she is a lady and you know that" I reply annoyed.

"Even ladies like to chew sugar cane from time to time", he smiles broadly. "Also she is a country girl and they are hot. Believe me.." We both laugh out loud.

"Wait do you think she is knocked up?" I laugh and point at my father as if he is crazy. "Come on dad, wash you filthy mouth out with soap".

He slaps my back. "Well now I know that she is what I hoped her to be, I am satisfied"

"Why dad?, What difference does it make? You know that I am not a virgin. I am intrigued by this train of thought.

"You are a man. You need to feel that you conquered

the mountain first. No man wants to walk on another man's beaten track." He looked at me when he said it. I am not sure that I am that bothered. I don't want the town tramp but I would have preferred some experience. Although I can teach her everything she needs to know.

"Listen it's important to me too so even though I should be just as virtuous I am happy that she is a virgin". I say to placate him. We both laugh. "Now what do they have in store for us tomorrow night"

No idea son, but if Barry as anything to do with it, it will be fun, he was the original wildcat in his day.

Ronald Whole and Jeffery Finch have been my best pals since elementary school. We met in the playground on our first day. This fat kid called Carl was picking on Jeff and pushed him to the ground, Ron and I stepped in and that was the last day that Jeff got picked on. Since then we have been inseparable, we went to the same boarding school and we all travelled to Miami to go to university. These guys were not just my friends they were my brothers. Both men ran into my room in there swimming trunks.

"Hey man why so glum" Jeffrey asked concerned as he saw me lounging on the deck.

"I'm cool man. Just chilling and contemplating" I say

""What how you're gonna make your wife to be screeaaammmm" Ron crudely chimed in. We all laughed. I stood up and pulled down my linen trousers, my trunks were underneath.

"Nah Brother" I say seriously. They looked at each other and sat down next to me.

"What's going on" Ron said "Cold feet"

"No…., I am just conscious of the magnitude of what I am doing. This is for life and I want to be sure in myself that I will not let her down in any way, she means that much to me"

"Man you are one of the wealthiest men in Jamaica right now" Jeff came back amazed that I was thinking so deeply about such matters.

"Jeff being a man is not about money"

"Tell that to most if not all of the women I know" we all laughed. "I mean that, and start with my mother. I get what you are saying, but you will not have the same issues that face millions of married couples today. You will never have to worry that she is with you for your money, as she has money and lots of it. You do not have to scrimp and save to buy your house as you have one already. It's not that bad for you guys. You just have to love her. That's it. That's your job. Everything else, and I mean everything else is already taken care of."

"I hear you but"

"There are no buts" Jeff retorted angrily. "C-A-N you love this woman? Simple. Yes or No?"

"Yes" I say smiling head down.

"Then that is all that we have to talk about, let's go and get you married. But before that, can I take a swim in that gorgeous Jamaican water please. Come on, the last man to the water is buying all the drinks all night.

With that challenge ahead of us we all sprinted to the sea. The boys night was a treat. Barry and his father went all out. We had the private dining room, there were beautiful waitresses everywhere. Jeff and Ron were in their element and had spotted a few country girls that they would definitely get close with very soon.

The humidity in the air was stifling. We all wore loose fitting linen shirt and slacks. The Morant Bay hotel was nice, but lacked the finesse that we were used to. That said there was everything we desired. Booze, card table, Roulette table and women.

"Thank you Barry and Dr Barnet, this is some shindig" I smiled..

Even my dad was delighted at the welcome and I had to keep his roving eye under control. Barry and Dr Barnett invited their friends which included Mackie.

"Court can I get a drink?" Mackie enquired.

"Sure why not" I had had enough but wanted to be polite. Mackie was not just a plantation foreman. He was Winn's rock, she loved this guy, and I think he's pretty cool.

Mackie returns with the drinks, "So how are you my young brother?"

I laugh, he always made me feel part of the family "I am cool, I am looking forward to married life"

Mackie smiled, he looked behind him, the barman a tallish medium sized man was listening intently.

"You know Mackie, you don't need to worry, I will take

care of her. I love her you know, she is the best thing to happen to me.

"More soda sir", the barman chimed in and interrupted our flow.

"Er No thanks" even though I had said no the waiter took my glass and diluted my neat aged Wray and Nephew Rum.

He slammed the glass on the bar. I glared at him, *what was his problem.*

"Now that you have ruined my drink, make me another one, and don't take your time about it" I snap at him.

He eyeballs me, like I know him. "Yes Sir" he says sarcastically.

I hear him crashing around behind me. "Hey, do I know you?"

"Harold cut it out" Mackie warned. Mackie gave the young man a stare that I would never want to be on the receiving end off. All background noise calmed down. Harold gave me my drink and Mackie motioned that we go outside.

"You know him?" I ask.

"Yeah he's a mixed up kid, pay him no mind."

"Why is he upset with me, I have never met the jerk"

"Look he used to work at the plantation and we fired him about six months ago"

"Really why?"

"It didn't work out" Mackie said quickly.

"Is that all?" I ask

"It's complicated, you know what they say brother you can't please all of the people all of the time. We dealt with it" Mackie said reassuringly, but now I am aggrieved. I look towards the bar.

"Let it go young brother so tell me again, are you ready for this?."

"By this you mean marriage? " I smile remembering my gorgeous bride to be.

"Absolutely. Like I said before we were rudely interrupted, she is the one. There is nothing that I would not do for her".

"That's good to hear, she is a diamond. A rare treasure and you must ensure that you treat her like that. Defend her always, Take care of her, honour her and always ensure that's she safe.

"Jeez Mackie you make it sound like she's in mortal danger". I laugh.

Mackie laughed nervously. "No man, I just want you to take care of her. I have been in her life since she was 5 years old. She is like a .. a.. daughter, My wife and I love that little girl".

"Your wife. I didn't know that you were married".

"She died some time ago" Mackie said quietly.

"I am so sorry to hear that man, what happened?" I asked. Mackie looked pained as he talked about this.

"I just don't know" he said his voice gruff, he looked to the stars and exhaled. "That's the worst of it you know, I have no peace, she was on her way to her sisters and went missing, she never turned up and I have not heard from her since. She's dead though"

"How can you be so sure?" I asked. An ache developed in my chest. I would not be able to function if that was me.

"Mackie pounds his chest, with his fist. "I feel it in here every day" his voice broke. I did what any human being could have done, I hugged this man and told him how sorry I was for his loss. It was real and raw. I so wanted him to have peace.

We both pulled away and drank our rums. "Another one?" Mackie asked wiping a tear from his eye. We both acknowledged that he needed something to do.

"Sure" I nod looking in my glass,

Jeff and Ron walked onto the patio "Hey you alright man" Jeff asked concerned.

"I am just fine" I say quietly.

"Why so glum?"

"Nothing, just talking"

"You're not having cold feet again are you Ron asked, a little too loudly. We heard a crash of glasses in the distance. It was Harold, he just glared at me.

"You Ok man" Jeff asked.

Harold did not answer him he just sucked his teeth and

put the broken glass in the tray. Another waiter came to help him, they looked similar to me, he was just slightly younger and shorter.

I look at this Jack ass, he too starred at me. What is his problem. Let it go Court.

Harold walks past and looks at me and sucks his teeth again.

"What?" I shout at him. I hear the other waiter tell him to keep moving. .

"That's right man, listen to your friend" I shout again.

"What's with you" Ronald asked.

This guy has been a complete arse all night man" I say loudly.

Harold throws his tray on the floor and there is an ferocious crash. He storms back, the other waiter trying to pull him back. I immediately stand up my adrenalin pumping angrily around me veins.

"What's your problem boy" I spit out the words.

"Your my problem rich boy" Harold says squaring up to me. Other waiters run behind Harold. Mackie comes rushing out and immediately gets in between us. He pushes Harold away and whispers something in his ear. Harold looks at me hard. I see my father, Barry and Dr Barnet walking swiftly towards the fracases

"I heard you", Harold shouts at me.

"Heard what?" Ronald chimed in aggressively.

"I heard him say that he has got cold feet" he snidely bellows looking in Mackie's face. All eyes were on me. I immediately shoot Ron a look.

"No what you heard was me asking him if he has cold feet?" Ron chimes in like a good friend and foot soldier.

"That's right" Jeff said. It was like we were all five years old again, ready to fight and protect one another to the end.

Daddy stepped in, he looked behind him and could see some of the other men were crowding the scene. "Listen fellas, please go inside, this waiter is clearly thinking that he can join the party rather forgetting that he should be working for the party," the guest smile and some chuckle already half drunk. "Please go inside, we will sort this. Can you get the Manager someone". Dr Barnet helped daddy and them in and shut the door.

Dr Barnet walked towards the us "Harold go home", he ordered.

"Dr Barnet I heard him, he is not worthy of her. How can he have second thoughts. She is a wonderful person" Harold said.

"She is". I tell him.

"What?" Harold said.

I see Mackie giving him a look. I could not out my finger on it. "Who are you?" I ask not wanting to know the answer, "and why do you give a shit whether I have cold feet or not?"

The younger man next to Harold, looked at us all and

laughed. "Let's just say that he knows your wife far more intimately than you do"

Barrington stepped in and hit him hard with the tumbler in his hand.

" Good god man was that necessary?" My father shouted.

"Barrington" Dr Barnet screamed at his son. The poor chap was writing on the floor, two older waiters rushed to his aide

The humidity in the air became suffocating. I felt that I had been hit in the face with the tumbler.

"Ken!!!" Harold screams, Ken staggers back to his feet blood seeping from his eye. One of the waiter's pressed a napkin on his eye.

"Shut your filthy mouth or I will shut it for you permanently" Barrington screams. A single vein in his head was protruding and throbbing as he was about to step in for the kill when Mackie grabbed him and whispered in his ear. He stopped and looked at us all.

"I do not know who he is or why he is saying this to you, but I assure you that it's not true. My Winnie is not that kind of girl. And you know it"

"You think that you have all the power, but just remember no one is invincible. You must think that my brother is Lucy. Hmmm." Harold looked at Courtney' and his family "Are you sure that you want him for a father in law? Hmmmm. Look at him, he is a murdering rapist. This man murdered Edwina's grandmother, he killed her grandfather, and although we have no proof, "we all know that after he brutality raped her mother he killed her too"

Barrington lurched forward to grab after Harold. Mackie thwarted this attempt.

"She was my girl for three years. Just ask your father, Mackie or Rene" we all look at Dr Barnet. I stagger back as I read his expression. He's telling the truth.. Ron and Jeff are on either side to me. Ron immediately props up my shoulder.

"Dr Barrington flushed, he looked at Mackie "Get them out of here" The manager runs over. A short dark man, with round glasses, he was sweating and nervous. "Harold, Ken get inside and wait for me" He looked at us all standing there "Gentlemen, I am sorry for his insolence"

"I think the actual word that you are looking for is his honesty. my father said looking at the Mackie, Daddy and Dr Barnet who were all stood together.

"Courtney, Jackson " Dr Barnet walked forward me and held my shoulders "That man" he points towards the bar paints a dishonest picture of my granddaughter, she is virtuous, yes they had a friendship but that is all it was. I swear to you they were no more than friends. Close friends we admit, but friends none the less. She would never have spoilt herself, not with him. That why she ended it, she could not give him what he wanted and that was her."

I look at Mackie "Why did he leave the plantation?".

Mackie looked me dead in the eye, "She told him that there was no prospects for them. "He wanted more and she would not give him what he wanted, so he left, and as you can see he is still wounded"

"Sounds like a relationship to me" my father chimed in.

"Gentlemen, we have heard enough, we bid you goodnight" Jeff said trying to spare me the details.

"Yes Jeffery you are right, we need to get back" Daddy told them all.

"It's only 11 O'clock" Barrington said "This can be explained I'm sure"

"Can it" I say. "Really …. Some field hand had just told me that he knows my Edwina in ways that only a husband should experience. Explain that" I yell.

My father held my arm and squeezed it. He could sense that this could turn either way. "I am a simple man Barry, I do not condone violence, but understand that I am not totally against it in the right circumstances, and that was not the right circumstances. I would like to thank you all for your hospitality gentlemen. It would not be presumptuous of me to say that Courtney needs time to digest this evening, also I think that we can agree that he needs to talk to his betrothed at once"

Barrington, Dr Barnet and Mackie all nodded, they respected my father, but feared him also. He was a powerful man, far more powerful than any of them. They had heard the stories about him. He was ruthless and not to be challenged or underestimated.

We got into our Chevy, the driver was waiting for us outside the hotel and looked surprised that we arrived so early. He immediately put out his cigarette and jumped out of the car and opened the door. Once inside I ordered my driver to take me to the plantation. The thirty minute journey took forever, all I could do to retain my anger was to look out of the window. On arrival, the lights were on.

"Son I think you should have this conversation tomorrow once you have time to reflect on the situation Hmmm?"

"No dad, the time for talking is now. Besides I will not be able to sleep. I need to look at her. I need to hear her explanation."

I walk onto the veranda and Lynne opens the door, I can hear Rene and Winnie singing, but I could not tell you what that was.

"Hey party poopers" Lynn chimes. I push past my sister "Winnie" I scream.

She sobers up immediately. "Court what's the matter?" she looks at me worried. My father pulls her aside, with Jeff and Ron and they talk in hushed tones. My bride to be comes out of her living room, she has had a few"

"Hello Courtney, I was just telling my friends how much I love you" she says trying not to slur her words. I push her away hard and she lands on her sofa.

"Hey Rene" screams.

Court what's wrong with you? Baby" she stands up confused. "What's going on, why are you so mad?"

I have two questions. I look and the in the doorway is my father, sister and two best friends. I walk toward the door and close it. "Rene please leave" Rene does what is instructed as she could sense this was a serious moment. "Who is Harold?" The colour from her cheeks drain.

She inhales deeply..

I repeat the question unable to quash my temper. "Who is Harold?" I scream at her.

My dad opened the door "Court" my father chimed him. I gave him a warning glance and he read the message. "Stay out of this"

She glances to the door, "can we discuss this somewhere more private" she pleads

"No when Harold informed me of your relationship he chose to do it in front of everyone at the club"

Winnie looked horrified, "He did what?" she asked tears rolling down her face. "Harold and I met when I was sixteen years of age. We talked for three years. He wanted more than I was prepared to give. I ended it the night that he proposed. He got ugly and I asked him to leave.

I stand there relieved. I believe her, my heart softens. "How ugly?" I ask

"It was nothing". She said defiantly

"I asked you a question?" I snap

"He pushed me around but we kicked him out".

"Who did?"

A friend of my grandmothers her name is Saint, she was

wielding a machete and was passing, she came to my aid and helped me.

Harold informs me that he knows you intimately?

Winnie gasps, "That is not true baby. I never. Not with him. If you need proof before the wedding we can find a doctor to confirm it, but I N-E-V-E-R slept with him, or allowed him to do anything to me other than kiss me. That is all. I swear it.

"Court this looks like a misunderstanding" Lynn ran towards me and hugs me. I stare at my beloved who is weeping silently shaking her head. She can see that this has hurt me.

"Maybe you need some privacy" Rene pipes up.

"No" I say "I've heard more than enough for one night" and I walk out of the door pushing past my father and friends heading towards the car. I hear Edwina sobbing, then hurried footsteps up the stair. I sit in the car, followed imminently by my father and friends. We drive back to the hotel I sit with my head in my hands, disappointment in my heart and doubt creeping through my consciousness. Why? I begin to feel angered by him, Harold, why would he do this if it was not true.

"Wait!" I shout. "Let me out" I say "I need to stay, pick me up tomorrow"

"Like hell" my father's says

"I'm ok dad I promise" I try to explain.

"It's not you that I am concerned about. If what that boy said was true I am not leaving you here."

"Nor I" Ron chimed in

"Nor me" Jeff said.

"And I don't plan on going anywhere " Lynne told us all.

I walked to the house, knock the door, Rene opened it wide and looked up the stairs. I walk to the bedroom.

"There is some food left over from our feast, anyone hungry?"

"Yes Miss Rene", Ron pipes up.

The follow me she smiled and walked them to Lucy's kitchen and fed them until their bellows stretched.

Chapter 19

Father and Daughters

The men walk out of the club I start pacing the patio. I look at Mackie who looks to his feet. My father walks into the club house main room and inform all guests that the groom has fallen ill and has retired, and the activities will cease. All the men groan and moan, and slowly trickle out of the club house.

My father walks towards me, disapproval all over his face. "What in god's name was that about" he asks angrily.

"I couldn't help it you heard what he said" I explode at him.

"Yes, we all did, but no one else tried to gauge out his eye?" Daddy said stood over me.

"He cannot speak about my daughter like that" I tell him.

Why not Barry, people say things all the time about one another. We could have dealt with this. We could have shrugged this off, but no, now he has gone and exposed you to Courtney, his family. Don't you see, this was her chance to be …… someone normal, with ….. normal people. Why could you not have laughed this off. You have ruined this for her",

"No …"

"Yes, I know Jackson more than you do and he is ruthless, especially when it comes to his reputation and his money. You could have managed this so many other ways. If this is unsalvageable she will never forgive you.

I mean never"

It will serve her right for going behind my back"

"Shut up you buffoon. You have no idea what you have done do you?" Dad asked

"What?"

"You have exposed your daughter to heart break" Dad tell me.

"Well if it's all rubbish, Courtney can get over it" I say.

"You are such a fool, "if they withdraw the offer of marriage it will not be about Winnie, it will be because of you" Daddy said quietly.

"This is a union of families, your rage has time and time again, got you in hot water, and you tonight showed your ass. Why would they trust their only son with us ..... in this family ..... with you. I wouldn't if the shoe was on the other foot. You are a loose cannon. Someone to be wary of."

"That's nonsense" I say. *Deep down my heart starts to sink. He is telling me truth. Goad what have I done. He's right. I have ruined her opportunity of happiness.*

"Is it, really. There is only one person who will be responsible for her broken heart and that as always falls to you." My father said with disgust " well done".

"I don't think.."

"Yes I do, where are they, they have gone to consider their position. Jackson is the head of the First National Bank in this country, he cannot and will not be linked to scandal. That much I know". With that my father walked out.

"Where are you going?" I shout after him.

As far away from you as possible" he responds.

"Get me a drink someone, anyone. I would like a rum now". I shout. Within a minute a waiter was walking towards me with a glass of neat rum, I know its weak of me, but I can't help it. I am ashamed of myself, my father was right, but it's like a switch goes off in my head. I just can't help it, and here we are again in a pickle and its down to me. She will never forgive me.

"Bring me a bottle of rum" I shout, there's no point in fighting it, I just need to blow off steam. Mackie walks towards and slaps the drink out my hand. "Barry look how far you have come and you seem like you want to self-destruct all over again."

"You don't understand she is going to hate me" I whine.

"Grow a backbone man she will hate you more if you come back drunk" Mackie was really shouting at me. "Do you know how lucky you are to have a daughter like Edwina. She loves you, even after everything."

I lower my head. Mackie was now standing over me, I knew that if I took another sip he would beat me where I sat. I poured the contents of the rum bottle on the floor.

"Thank you Mackie" I say ashamed of myself.

"For what" my friend smiles.

"For sticking with me and having the balls to tell me

when I am being the biggest jerk around.

Mackie smiled, well we are stuck with each other now aren't we. Beside you have an engagement to salvage. Don't let her down.

One question, I ask standing up. "Why didn't you tell me about that little field hand touching up my daughter" I ask

"There was nothing to tell" Mackie said

"Really that's not what it sounded like today, it sounded like a three year love affair."

"It wasn't like that?" Mackie eyes grew wide, apprehensive of me,

"You was meant to be my eyes and ears", I snap

"I was always".

"Then what the hell happened?".

Winn and Harold was on a need to know basis. She was in need and you just didn't need to know" Mackie said indignantly."

I could feel the vein throbbing in my head. "What?" *is he serious.*

"Have you considered what that little girl has been through. She lost her mother, her grandmother and my wife, if I had told you about them she would have lost her only friend too. She grew up before you like any other neighborhood kid, happy carefree and playful. You knocked that out of her. She's insular, isolated and alone. I just wanted her to have a friend her own age. She needed him more than you realise.

"It wasn't your decision to make" I say through gritted teeth. You had no right Mackie no matter how well intentioned.

"Well I did and it's done and were here. He did not take advantage.

"How do you know" I ask quietly. .

"Because I know your daughter and she is no fool. It was only ever temporary." Mackie said quietly trying to control his own rage. "We all could see it why couldn't you."

"Who the hell is we?"

"The doc, Rene and …"

"Who?"

"No one. We just knew that's all".

Well you took that from me didn't you.

No more than you deserve you selfish son of a botch. Have you considered what you have taken from her. This is not about you. It's about your child and her happiness." Mackie chastised me.

"You know what make your own way home. I gone. I don't even work for you". Mackie erupted.

"You only work for her because I allow you to. Remember that"

Mackie spun around. "So what you think you own me?" Mackie pushed his chest into me.

"I own you, I own everyone here" I tell him.

Mackie laughs at me. "You own nothing all you do is just take because you own nothing. You have no natural authority. Jackson, now he is a man who commands respect, you don't. people fear you. No one respects you mot even your child".

I own you and everybody in this village. I can have any woman, anytime whether she wants me or not. It does not matter what I do, or how many women I take, hell I have taken them young and old. I do what I want as I am the privileged one".

Mackie looked at me with renewed eyes. It was as if he could really see me. "It was … you wasn't it?"

"What?"

"Did you rape my Maggie, then kill her?"

"Noooooo" Mackie you've had too much to drink. *How does he know? I have said nothing to give myself away. It must have been …. No she said that she would keep my secret. After everything I have done for her she does this to me. Traitor!*

"As far as I am aware you only raped Angeline, she was young, so who is the old woman that you abused. Hmmmm. Who?" Mackie stood still, though every muscle was flexed and his eyes were wide. "Don't tell me no lie, did you hurt my Maggie?"

I tried to style it out and flatly deny it. This was my friend. He knew me better than anyone even when I was lying. I try to laugh it off "Come on Mack let's get out of here?"

"Your face says it all. It was you. I could not for the life of understand why Maggie would up and just leave me. But it was you. I suspected, we all suspected but I did not want to believe that after everything I had done for you, that you could do anything to her. I suppose I always knew, but listening to you tonight, you really believe that you are more superior to the rest of us, don't you.

I can't lie anymore "I'm sorry" I break down. "I was in a different place than where I am at now. You know that"

"Did you rape my Maggie?".

I cannot answer. I will not lie and cannot say the words. I look at my friend and he is standing above me crying hands on his head. *I am being a good friend. I have released him. He can move on now finally.*

"Where is she?" he asks

"We buried her under the water well by the stables", I tell him. My burden lightening my spirit almost immediately.

"Why?" Mackie asks, his face soaked in tears.

"I don't know, I was drunk, I honestly cannot remember" I tell him truthfully, "No a day goes by that I don't think about her, you, Winnie, all of them. Not a day"

"Bullshit, then how come you did this tonight. You are thinking very hard are you" Mackie told me.

"I am sorry Mackie, truly I am very sorry".

Mackie ran up to me and kicked as hard as his leg would allow in my shoulder, I roll over, "Get up" he screams.

All the waiters including Harold and Ken come out. I stand up looking at my friend, he comes closer and punches me hard, I stagger back and stand again, he punches he even harder I fall backwards onto the patio furniture, my blood sprays the immaculately clean white patio furniture. Mackie runs in for the kill, but Harold tackles him to the floor.

"No Mr. Mack. He is not worth it." He shouts. You will hang, despite all of his crimes, it's you that will hang. What would Mrs. Mack want?" Mackie stepped back and looked at Harold. He was right, Maggie would not want him to do this in her name, she was a kind loving and good woman. Mackie walked to the bar jumped over and picked up the first full bottle of liquor he could find, it was gin. He came back to me, opened it, knelt down and grabbed my cheeks and starting pouring.

"Earlier I stopped you from drinking as I been under the illusion that you were my friend. Well had I known that you were my enemy I would not have stopped you. Now I know that you are my enemy, have this drink on me.

I spit out some of the contents, Mackie tilts my head back and I am forced to drink. The poison hits my senses quickly. *Oh how I have missed thee, my naughty mistress. I need you, I have been a naughty boy, make me forget these feelings of fear that I have, take away my pain.*

I pass out, I have no idea what tie it is. My intention is to wait across the street until the police arrive and I will hand myself in. I see my car across the road. Some rodent has vandalised my wheel, my passenger side window is smacked to pieces. I immediately check the glove compartment, my revolver is still there. I put it in my jacket pocket for safe keeping. I triple check that the safety catch is on. The last thing I need tonight is to shoot off my nuts. That is all that I need. I laugh quietly to myself. I drive to the plantation and stop the car at the main road. I don't want them to seem I am going to walk.

I have to ask her, why did she tell him. She promised me, why did she betray me, how could she do this to me. I am approaching Edwina's Plantation, memories of the past come back to me. I wipe my eyes every so often, wondering what's wrong with me, why I am like this. I know. I have buried this secret so deep that when it resurfaces it turns me into this…this animal. I close my eyes, the same film is playing in my head. I am back in Mississippi and my uncle Mason is on top of me and inside of me. Ravaging me, raping me, the more I cry the more violent the attack. Every summer since I was nine years old, without fail he would take me fishing, and it was there that he stole me away. The real Barrington is dead, he killed him when I was nine. He would tell me, "Shut up boy, you think because that you are light skinned that makes you kin, it don't. In Mississippi you are one hundred per cent nigger boy. That means I own you, you are nothing and you are nobody, your just black. It was my Uncle that gave me my first drink at the age of fifteen. "Drink this boy and sleep?". I have tried to forget but I just could not control my rage. Apart from Jeanette, every sexual experience that I have had with a woman has been when I have been drunk. I just did not know how else to be. It was Mason, he killed me, he did this and now I am stuck with this guilt, I walk every day with the shame and in order to feel, as I find it hard to love and to be intimate, I inflict pain. An angry reaction is better than no reaction right. I will sort this. I will pay the boy some money for his eye, give Mackie the equivalent of a year's salary, then I will travel to the united states and spend some time with Uncle Mason, I need to pay my debts all of them.. My first priority is to make things right with Courtney and his people.

I hear a sugar cane snap. There was someone there. I stop look around and nothing. I stay rooter to the spot. I try and concentrate on my breathing and listening. How are there? My senses tell me there is more than two. I listen again. Nothing. I get a bad feeling about this and start to quicken the pace. The lane was pitch black. I start to jog and I hear at least three or four canes snap, my jog turns into a run, I take the gun out of my right pocket I have my lighter in my left hand, ready to provide me with light.

-Crack- I am dazed I am seeing stars, something or someone hit me in the head with something real hard. I feel another lash across my back I am on my knees. There is more than two of them. One is breathing heavy, I slip off the safety catch with my thumb and flick the lighter, it did not light and I aim the gun straight ahead of me and shoot anyway.

-Bang-

"Arrrrrrhhhhh" a young man screamed. I aim the gun to the steps to the west of my left ear.

-Bang-

-Bang-

Something hard hit the dirt just yards away from me. My lighter finally worked I see two or three men running through the cane fields. Ken the man I glassed was

345

bleeding from his chest, he had ceased breathing, another man, much older was dead his eyes were open, with two wounds in his head. They look related. I want to vomit but am too petrified to stop. I sprint as fast as I could to my daughter's home, I did not stop running until I got to the last two hundred yards. My father, Jackson, Courtney and his friends are on the veranda looking into the darkness. Winnie has lit the lights in the house and is holding a fully loaded rifle with Daddy and Rene and Mackie. All four riffles are pointed at me.

"Who goes there?" Mackie screams his voice menacing.

"It's me, don't shoot" I hold my hands up.

"Barrington throw the gun on floor, but ensure the safety is on first. Jackson pulled his children and their friends inside.

"Who were you shooting daddy?" Winnie sounded frantic.

"Oh my god, those dirty little field urchins tried to kill me I say shaking" I walk around the room like a mad man, too absorbed in my own fear that I did not notice that all around me was still and silent"

"Mores the pity they did not succeed" Jackson's tone was icy.

I ignore him "Winn you don't understand, they attacked me and I had to defend myself". I run my hands through my hair and sit on the leather armchair by the window, I look out the window as to face them would have been worse "I think I have just killed two people, Dad ....it ....it was the man who I glassed with a tumbler and an older man, I didn't recognise him but he looks like a field worker" I momentarily look at them all.

My father just dropped his head. I could not read his expression at first, I thought it was anger, but it wasn't. It was indifference, fore in that moment I understood that there was nothing that I could do to disappoint them. It had already been done. This was yet another scenario that I had caused someone pain. I saw it for the first time, this night. They no longer cared. Who could blame them. I was a poor excuse of a father, son and human being.

"Winn let me go out and look to see who it is. It sounds like Ken, maybe Baxter George?" he said quietly.

"Noooo, I'll come with you?" Winnie said her voice shaking.

"The hell you are?" Courtney screamed, anyone could be out there.

"The men that may be dead out there its Harold's brother and father". I say, "We need to see if they are still alive and if so we need to help them.

Grandpa got his doctors bag, Mackie, Jackson, Ron, Jeff and Me all had lanterns. We see a light in the middle of the field. Saint my savior is already there. She has sheets under her arm and has wrapped Kens blood soaked body into the first sheet. I look at Baxter on the floor, I kneel down and close his eyes. I say a prayer and help them to wrap him up. I notice that Courtney, Ron and Jeff move towards the main road, they don't need to say it, they are sickened to their stomach. They see me, my people who we really are. It's not for them, this is not their world, nor should it be.

We get to the house, Courtney is still in shock, he walks over to me, he hugs me, but it's different. He is withdrawn, my love is altered.

"Edwina, it's time we left" Jackson said, this time none of them protested.

I silently cry, my hand still soaked in the blood of these innocent men, I go to touch Court, all he can do is jump back. I see the distain in his glance. He looks at my father, no words appear. The look said is all.

They walk to the car I cannot leave it like this "Courtney" I shout he turns around. I walk towards him. I am so sorry for this.

"It's not your fault" he reassures me.

"Here" I give him back the engagement ring. He looks at me grateful for my courage. "I release you baby"

He smiles, "I love you. I am just not sure that you will be content with boring old me. What I do know is that I cannot live with all of this. He is a liability Edwina. This much death and destruction will not go unnoticed. People will rise up against your family, you are his child, you must leave here. I fear for your safety. I fear for you. He does not deserve you, any of you. He is unwell, there is something wrong with your father. To hold so much rage is not healthy and definitely not good for the soul". He stepped close to me and kissed me on the mouth. If you need me, call, I will always come running".

"Courtney" Jackson bellowed "Let's go son" he snapped curtly. He tipped his hat to me, Lynnette waved goodbye, Jeff and Ron said nothing, and within a flash they were speeding down the dirt road.

Chapter 20

Pressure Burst Pipes

Rene tries to console me. What can she say. There is
nothing. I stand up drenched in my own sick, I survey
my surroundings as if it's the first time I see this room.
It's so lovely, the long white drapes the white soft sofa
with large green flowers, the fresh scent of mango's and
limes throughout the downstairs, as by window around
my property sits a lemon, lime or orange tree. This
house, my home was truly beautiful and the three years
that I lived here, I have loved it and my freedom. Today,
I have learnt that freedom comes with a price. I was
never going to be free of him, his name or his past. My
father could not let me go. He knew that I would leave
him, and he has done everything he can to tarnish me,
ruin my life, my choices, my happiness. I walk up the
stairs slowly.

"Winnie are you ok?" Aunt Rene asked.

"This will never be ok aunty. I need to rest I am tired. I
walk into my bathroom and turn on the shower. The
putrid smell of vomit, blood and death is pungent. I take
a scrubbing brush and scrub my skin to free myself of
this shame. My flesh raw and bleeding I repeatedly wash
my hair and body over and over again. Praying that I
would feel clean, hoping that I could redeem myself
somehow with my cleanliness. I tell me myself over and
over *this was not down to me*; *It's not your fault*. The
harder I scrubbed I slowly realised the simple truth. My
father no matter how much I loved him, or forgave him
was nothing more than savage murderer. The revelation
hit me like a sledge hammer, the remaining strength in
my limbs evaporate. I felt withered, like a dying shriveled

up flower that has had no light. My legs no longer able to support me, I collapse in the shower, the water bouncing of me looking for a way out.

"Baby" he says quietly.

I stir, my beautiful sleep interrupted.

"Baby, .wake up sleepy head" he says softly. I feel a soft kiss on my head, I open my eyes. Startled by what awaits me. I jump up disorientated.

"Courtney" my voice is gruff and my breath strong like a toilet pit. I leap out of my bed and run to the bathroom, wash my face and scrub my teeth and tongue. I look up in the mirror, I look awful. My eyes are sunken, my hair was slumped across my face and head likes clumps of clay in a mound. I close my eyes, and pull my hair back in a bun and rub some coconut oil on my face. I dampen the towel and wiped under my arms, and my lady garden, and change into my navy blue house dress.

"You look lovely Winnie" he said. He looked worried.

"I feel like rubbish Court", a stray tear leaves my eye.

He grits his teeth and nods. "How are you?"

"Not good"

"What happened?" he looks at me accusingly.

"Well when you left I asked Daddy to leave. I told him that I am done with him, his antics. All I have wanted since my grandmother died was to be in a happy home, you know. I know that I would have had that with you.

He smiled at me.

351

"It's my fault, all of this is down to me. I should never have gotten involved with Harold, you have to believe me" I wail. "Do you blame me?"

"Never" Courtney shouted at me "You father is a mad man. Two things will happen, either the Lord or a man will take care of him. What is clear is that you have nothing to do with this. Baby, he is your father, you do not control him or his actions" he came over and pulled me into him hard. "I just want us to be married so that I can take you away from this all" he said.

"Really ….. you mean after all this you want to marry me?" I whisper.

"Yes, I want to marry you. Who else would I love, who else would I marry" he pressed his lips into my temple.

"But my father"

"He is y-o-u-r father. That does not mean he is you".

He pulled me away "Baby, I think my parents would have preferred that we never met, they know I love you, but they are concerned about your and my welfare. You father…. he's unpredictable." I look at my fiancé, he looked tired.

"We should leave here, you're not safe?"

"My father would not hurt me?"

"It's not your father I am worried about. This community is tight. Your father killed two local men. There are murmurings. I think you should come to Negril with me".

"I can't". I protest.

"Edwina!" Courtney was shouted at me "There is no discussion, you will pack your things and come with me tonight. It's not safe. I will not, cannot leave my wife here. Now pack!" *I smile, your wife, he still loves me.*

I stare blankly at Court, he was not taking no for an answer.

-Tap- Tap-

"Come in" Courtney demands. My grandmother, grandfather and Rene, entered the room. My grandmothers appearance startled me, She looked drawn, her hair was not up in her perfectly manicured bun, her long grey and brown wavy hair was freely scooped to one side of her neck. Her rims of her eyes were red, her skin was blotchy and she had no powder or make up on.

"Are you ok?" she asked me.

"Me … I am fine, it's you that looks like you have been through the wars".

My grandmother starred at me with a steeliness that I have not seen in a while. "Edwina I want you to leave with Courtney". She said sternly.

My grandfather stepped forward and thrust a white folder in my hand.

"What this?" I ask, I open the folder, there is my passport, at least three thousand pounds, keys and a UK bank account in my name"

"Here is keys to a town house in Islington, London .It was going to be my wedding present to you both. When

I was last there I set up a bank account for you. The rest is all the sterling I could get my hands on. Your father has proven ..... unpredictable, which has led the behaviors of others to be ......unpredictable.   I have booked for you to fly to Miami, then in a few days you fly to England, your travel begins the day after tomorrow." Tears sprang to his eyes. "I can protect you from your father, but I cannot protect you from rogues in the village".

"But".

"It's for the best" my grandmother says she walked over to Courtney and held his hand "Thank you, please take care of her. Promise me"

"I promise ma'am".

"What about the wedding?"

"We can come back and marry later" Courtney reassures me.

"Baby get ready, pack do what you need to do. We will be downstairs. I promise you, we will marry, just not now, I was thinking that we could get married in the UK. He smiles weakly as he and my grandfather left the room.

Once the door was closed, Rene and my grandmother started to go through my drawers. "Phyllis what will she need I have not been to England?" Rene asked.

My grandmother picked out all my matching skirts and pullovers and jackets. *Hang on when did you two become bosom buddies.*

"It's summer over there so this should work for now, as the season changes she can buy whatever collection she chooses", she said. She was emotional. I look at her and notice that her dress was new.

"New dress?" I ask

Both women stop and look at me " Yes dear. I had it a while and thought that I should try something new". In unison, they both continued.

"Get showered my darling, you need to get on the road soon" My aunt Rene says gently.

As instructed I entered the bathroom. Closed the door.

This is all happening so fast. England was never in our plan. There is so much that I do not understand. I need to talk to them all. They are treating me like a child. Why is that? And why is Rene and Grandma such best friends all of a sudden, they hate each other. Something has happened and they need to start being straight with me.

"Winnie there you are?" My grandfather said, his voice still strained.

"What's wrong with your voice?"

"Nothing my throat is sore", he replied.

"I am going to be in England in a couple of weeks so I will pop in." he informs me.

"Since when?" I ask shocked by this news.

"Since my only grandchild will be living there". He smiled, which in turn made me smile. I walk up to him and give his a tight squeeze and a big kiss on the cheek.

"Look I don't want to be rude but you need to travel before dusk" Grandpa instructed quite sternly. They all looked at him and nodded. Both Rene and my Aunt started to move quickly.

"Why?" I ask them and they all ignore me.

"Edwina it's a long journey and I am thinking of the driver." Grandpa finally responded. Again there was the knowing glances

"What is going on" I snap"

"Nothing ….." Courtney could see that I was not buying it. He sighed heavily. "Actually there is a lot that has happened, I will explain it all to you in the way", Courtney looked at them, "is that ok?"

They nodded silently at him, avoiding my gaze.. Courtney held my hand, "we have to go, baby please trust me".

I embrace my grandfather, he was shaking "Are you ok?" I whisper.

"I am fine", he whispers back.

My grandmother and Phyllis hug me hard, they both kiss me, and each cheek. "Good luck, Be safe, I love you" is all I could hear.

Fear has gripped me "What about me, suppose I don't want to go". I hear myself and sound like a whining child.

My grandmother stood forward, "You are a woman now,

you have to act like one. We all have to do things that we don't want to do. Its life. Your life is with Courtney. You will be a wife soon, with responsibilities. You have to be brave."

Courtney tugged my hand, we walked to the car, and I noticed there were two cars either side of our vehicle, with men that I did not recognise.

"Who are these people?"

"They are my father's private security personnel from the bank"

"What's going on Courtney" I ask, a queezy feeling in my stomach made me feel unstable.

He opened the door, "Get in darling I'll explain everything".

The cars drove off into the orange sunset. I looked behind me at the plantation. Rene was hugging my grandmother and my grandfather was sat on a chair on the porch. I roll down the windows and exhaled deeply and close my eyes. The sweet smell of the sugar cane, filled my nostrils. I cry silently as we approached the main gates to my property.

"You alright?" Courtney asked.

"No……. I can feel it" I say so quietly it was hardly audible.

"What?"

"The fact that I will not be back here for a long time".

We sit in silence. My head hurts. All I could do was

close my eyes. As few miles later the aroma all around us changed. The air smelt smoky, I close the windows, as it started to tickle my throat. The closer we got to my old home, the stronger the aroma and thicker the air. My throat started to get real dry.

"Here" Courtney handed me a bottle of water. This will make it better. He then took a handkerchief out of his pocket and gave it to me. You'll need this" he said. He puts his handkerchief over his nose and mouth.

I stare out of the window, the visibility was compromised. I know what this means but don't want to connect the dots in my head. As we turn the corner, with the orange sun setting over my grandparents plantation, my old home is burnt to a crisp, it barely standing, and is smoldering. The whole frame of the house appears to be leaning to one side. I view the sugar cane fields, they have been withered by the heat. The crop is ruined. I flash back to my grandmother earlier this day. She has lost everything. Her son, her granddaughter and now her home. All the pieces are slotting into place. This is why Courtney and his father's security were escorting us to Negril.

"Am I in danger" I ask

"Yes" My beautiful finance kisses my hand, thinking that his lips would pacify me.

"Who did this?" I asked shocked.

"It was your field workers, people who loved Mrs Mack, Harold family who knows, the list is as long as your arm darling."

"My poor grandmother, she must be devastated, why

didn't you tell me".

"It was agreed that we would not say a word to you. We all knew that you would not leave, so we made a pact" Courtney could not look at me and was left with no other option but to lower his eyes.

"Driver turn around please" I command. The driver looked at his rear view mirror and continued on his journey.

"Excuse me please can you turn the car around now"

Nothing. I look at Courtney, his face was pained and desperate "Courtney I need to go back" I plead.

"No Winnie" he said quietly, He shook his head and held my hand. My lip started to quiver.

"You don't own me. I am my own person."Stop this car now" I shout at the driver. I look at Courtney and try to get to the door, he is too quick for me, he grabs my arms and pushes me to the floor.

"Noooooo please, they are not safe. I need to be with them".

"Winnie please I can't let you go back there"

"Geeeeettttttt oooooooffffffff me. I want to go back. That's my family" I cry through my screams.

I struggle and punch Courtney in the face, it catches him off guard, he grabs both my hands. "Stop it Edwina". I kick him in the stomach, he flies back on the door. He grabs me by the shoulders and shakes me hard. He grabs my hands and throws them above my head and keeps hold of them. To ensure that I don't attack him further he lays on me. "Please Winn, darling stop".

"Why" I ask panting like a crazed locked up animal.

"They have threatened to kill you, the plantation was a warning. It is you that is not safe" he says

I stare at him blankly, he should have punched me it would have been kinder.

"What?" I stare at him wide eyed.

"They want *you* dead" he shouted. All the strength in my body drained away. I felt weak, suddenly the heat was unbearable and the weight of my fiancé started to crush my lungs.

"Courtney I can't breathe" I whisper. He jumps off me cautiously, and sits on the seat. He looks at the driver. "she's ok" he nods. Perspiration runs freely through my pores.

"Winnie, sit up, here let me help you" Courtney pulls me off the floor and seats me next to him. I stare at him Blankley.

"We are going to be alright?" he whispers. "I am here, and I will get you out of here I promise".

"Who wants me dead?"

"We think it's the family and friends of people your father killed"

"You're not sure?"

"They didn't leave a name, but it's pretty certain that the

two events may be connected". I hold his hand and gently lay my head on his chest. His heart beat is strong and quick. He is anxious. Courtney rubs my arm, strokes my face and kisses me. I drift off into a deep sleep.

A few moments later the car comes to a screeching halt.

"What is it?" Courtney yells panicked.

"Trouble ahead Sir" his driver yells back. I bolt upright, its pitch black outside, there is debris in the road blocking our path. The cars behind us and in front of us are forced to stop as well. Three men step out of each car, all carrying shot guns. They watch each other as they remove the debris, I am looking deep into the night for signs of foul play. In the distance I see a group of men with machetes and clubs making their way to the car.

"Look to the east", there are too many of them. I close my eyes.

"Hurry up" Courtney screams.

A rock is lobbed at us and it hits one of the security guards hard in the head, they all panic, and cock their guns, *no more bloodshed please.* I hear Dexter galloping, I swing round and see her, its Saint, she is riding Dexter like an old pro wearing all white, the security detail take aim to shoot her.

"Noooooo" I scream and run out of the car.

She rides up to them, "Don't shoot" I scream. A stray rock flies past her she dodges it. Mackie is behind her on Daddy's jet black colt, she jumps off the horse and addresses the crowd. They stop, they listen. She holds up her hand, Mackie cocks his gun at the crowd. She speaks again. I glimpse the security men moving the rubbish from the road. Its take a few minutes, they are still holding off the angry crowd. I want to get close but Courtney is pulling me back to the car.

"Thank you" I say loudly, Mackie turns and nods at me. We drive off into the night.

"Who was that?" Courtney asks, I hold his hand and feel that he is shaking.

"Saint, she is the woman that saved me from Harold"

"Hmmm Saint by name, Saint by nature" he smiled gratefully, "I will be sure to ask the lord to bless her".

I hug him tightly and we are both exhausted but are far too anxious to sleep.

"Baby, Baby" Courtney gently shakes my shoulders. "We are here?" I look around,

"What time is it?"

"It's around ten thirty", he says.

"This is not Negril" I step out of the car. We were in Kingston at the Pegasus Hotel.

"I'll explain later". He says " We're tired"

Two concierge walk towards us. Mr. Du Pille have been expecting you. Your father's suite has been prepared". We walk to the elevator, Courtney did not look at me once. Once the door was opened a long marble hallway awaited us. At the end of the hallway was a light airy living room and dining area, towards the far end of the room the patio doors led out to the balcony. The concierge put our luggage in the closet, Courtney paid him and went straight for the mini bar.

"Drink baby"

"Yes whatever" I look for the bathroom, and shut the door, the bathroom was huge. The shower could fit at least four people in it. I slowly take my clothes off, my limbs feel tired. I look at myself in the mirror.

"Tomorrow will be a better day?"

The warm water flowing from the shower was inviting, I walk into the cubicle and let the water work its way over me. I masterly lather the bar of soap on my wash rag and gently scrub my body. The scent of the soap and warm water tingle of my nostrils. I turn up the temperature, and stand under the water. It felt good on my breasts and back. The shower door opened. I opened my eyes, it was Courtney stood in front of me naked. I stepped back, he smiled and walked in. He starred directly into my eyes, my nipples hardened.

"Court"

Her turned me around, lathered my wash rag and started to rub me with it. His hands were large, thick with broad fingers. He rubbed my neck with the wash cloth with his right hand and gently rubbed my breast with his left. He hands expertly explored and rubbed my back, buttocks and the back of my legs. He turned me around and used the soap with his bare hands to lather me. His left hand and the soap circled my body and his right hand rubbed and explored my torso and thighs. He abruptly pulled me into the water, smiling at himself and me that he had aroused me. I then watch him use my wash cloth on himself. I laugh.

"What" he smiles

I snatch the wash cloth. "Why should you be the only person to have all the fun" I rub his groin, moving towards his penis, which was rigid I look down at this unsavorily looking piece of equipment. I drop the rag and take the soap bar and lather my hands, I gently hold my fiancé with both hands and rub and explore him, he smiles at me.

"Having fun?" he asks

"You're the first … I have never seen one of these before, you know on a grown man that is" I continue to fondle him. I feel the blood pulsing in his man friend, Courtney pushes me hard against the wall and kisses me hard plunging his tongue into my mouth, and kisses me passionately. I let go of his friend, he pushes him on me, and holds my head. I push him away. "I need air" Courtney smiles at me and continues to shower. I grab my towel and leave the bathroom. I gaze at myself in the mirror, I am flushed. I sparingly pour coconut oil in my hands, and rub through my hair and body, I find some white panties and a white night dress. *I laugh to myself as the last thing on my mind is being pure. Oh he is a delightful man, his chest is high and proud, his neck thick, his abdominal muscles chiseled and defined. I blink my man is naked in my mind's eye. I shrug off the feeling, the sensation inside my lady garden, she is ready. My nipples harden under my shirt. I squeeze my thighs tight and think of my new life with my soon to be husband.*

Courtney enters the living room, his body is glistening as the waters slides down his smooth dark chocolate skin. *This man is here to tease me. I squeeze my thighs shut again and scrunch my eyes.*

"Would you like a drink" I leap off the chair. I feel his gaze and I know, I just know this is going to be too much for me to bear.

"Thank you baby, fix me a scotch and soda"

I look at him, gosh he is beautiful. I stare a little too long, he catches me. I walk to the white bureau and slowly lift the bottles to identify the scotch. I feel him behind me, the heat from his body pierces my skin. *Hold off Edwina, the deal is not signed yet. Do not let him touch you, you cannot trust yourself to behave. I look at Court and he has a look in his eyes that I have not seen before. He pulls me close, my heart is exploding out of my chest.*

"Court", before I could finish my sentence, he pulls me close. He strategically put his left hand around my waist and loops his right arm behind my neck. I 'm trapped and I love it. My fiancé lips touch mine softly, at first, then more wanton and needy. His hand start to explore my body, he runs them down my back and cups my buttocks and squeezes hard. I pull away he continues to kiss me, I wrap my arms around his neck, he feels strong. Courtney pulls me off the floor and leans back, my feet are off the ground, he then lifts me by my hips and rests my legs on his hips, kissing me tenderly throughout. *This is it, as hard as I try I cannot stop my body responding to him. My man excites me. I want him.* As we lay on the bed his hand explore me and I let him, he pulls my nightgown over my head. The reality of the moment sets in. I must have looked scared, he holds me and kisses me some more. "It's Ok baby, I promise it will be ok. I will not hurt you" he whispers.

"No Court I can't please stop. This is not right, we're not married"

He kisses my neck, "why not, you're going to be my wife within a week or two" we both giggle. "Do you want me to stop" he asked. He stops kissing me and looks at me seriously.

I look at him and pull him close. My small hands work their way to his towel which was still wrapped around his waist, I tug at it and the once secure knot unfolds, he is exposed to me. I look at his beast and nervously smile

"No Court, don't stop" I kiss his neck, he rolls me on my back and pulls down my knickers and throws them over his head. We both smile. I feel my heart in my ears. "Relax baby" he tells me.

I stare at his beast and feel queasy, it is erect, and it is too big for my lady garden. Courtney parts me legs and with his thighs and lays on top of me. He is heavy and I push him off, "I can't breathe" I pant.

He alters his weight, kissed me neck, and moves his lips down to my breast, he licks, sucks one breast and cups the other. There is an explosion deep in my lady garden, all I can do is moan out loud, he looks up, pleased at his accomplishment. I arch my back and he caresses my other breast, He raises his hand to my mouth and shoves two finger in it, I suck them obediently, he races them back to my nipple that is exposed and fondles her. "Ooohhhh"

He resurfaces and kisses me again and again, "Baby are

366

you ok. I can stop whenever you want me to" My mind is elsewhere, it's with body parts in heaven. Courtney leans down further and kisses my stomach my thighs, he then parts my legs

"No Court waiiiiiitttttttt," it's too late, his lips and mine meet, his tongue becomes his beast. He does things that I did not know was possible, I moan and pant, the feeling intensifies and I try and wriggle from his grasp. He clamps down on my thighs with his hands, and my body reacts to him, the pleasure is unbelievable, man I had no idea the tongue had more than one use. The volcano within me unable to control itself, erupts with an intense explosion, and that sets off other eruptions within me.

"I told you I would make you quiver beneath me" he smiles and kisses me deeply, plunging his tongue deep into my mouth. I taste and smell myself for the first time. Not bad. I smile. Courtney kisses me again, not giving me time to recover, I groan in the back of my throat, and I feel his manhood twitch on top of me. He part my legs once more, and gently positions himself at the gate of my lady garden, he looks at me

"Trust me" he commands. I nod, his tongue dances around my mouth once more, more intensely than before, he curls his hips and pulls my left leg out of the way in order to open the gate further, he starts to push, I shudder and tense my thighs, he stops "It's okay baby, breath and don't tense"

I look at him, smiling nervously. He kisses me once more intensely than the last, he pushes deeper I gasp, he rests his forehead on mine, intently starring at he "Push your hips up", he instructs. I obey dnd he hurls the rest of his beast into my garden. I close my eyes, my seal is broken and the gate is open. I yelp. Courtney ignores me and expertly and slowly maneuvers himself around. This is pleasurable and painful at the same time. He raises both my knees and thrusts deeper, his beast is locked him , he groans and I feel the sweat on his back, boy he's working hard. Something is happening to me. My toes are curling the sensation in my garden hardens my nipples, I clench my gate to try and stop the beast, "Arrgghhh baby you feel so gooood", Court responds breathlessly. His pace quickens, my heart is ready to beat right out of my chest. I feel the it mounting, "Court" I cry he moves faster and deeper, I can't control the eruption. Its larger than before, Courtney stops suddenly, his chest raised his arms straight his eyes closed shut. His explosion is deep inside of me. I am his, he has released me.

Oh this ache of mine feels sweet and tender beloved. I look at my husband to be, he is beautiful whilst he sleeps. He's strong, kind, loving and he loves me for me, and not who he thinks I can be. He loves me not for what I bring to him, but for what I can enhance in him. He loves the good, the bad and the downright sad. Fore he is my king.

Courtney opens his eyes, "good morning my precious"

I smile and stretch "Hello".

"Hungry baby? You worked up an appetite on me"

"I could eat a feast fit for a king" I smile

"Then a feast you shall have". Before he jumps out of our love nest he kisses my head. I too jump up from the bed, but my body ached with vengeance, my lady garden is battered and sore, and is in need of an ice bath.

"Ok" he asked concerned I look back and saw the red blood stain in the bed.

"Oh Court is that normal?"

He is genuinely shocked and laughs, "you'll live" embarrassed I ran to the shower, the water was warm and lovely. I gingerly washed myself and my tender parts. As I turned the water off I heard voices. "It must be the maid" I dry myself off and put on the bathrobe.

"Edwina so nice to see you" I stop in my tracks it was Courtney's father Jackson

"Morning" I say and scurry to get my clothes and run back in the bathroom. Whilst I put on my underwear I hear Mr Du Pille shouting at his son.

"How can you be so irresponsible? she is not one of you gals, she's a Barnet"

"I could not help myself dad, she it was…."

"Spare me the details he snapped. I smile to myself, his father is just old school, we are going to be married in a couple of weeks. I put my dress on and walk back into the room. That when I heard him

"I mean it, you are in your own. I forbid it, put an end to this now"

I look at Courtney who is sat on the bed with a white towel around his waist. My lady garden twitches at the sight of him I look at Courtney's face.

"End what? What do you forbid Sir"

They are both started to see me so soon. Mr Du Pille walks towards me and kisses me on the head " Goodbye dear".

"No sir please tell me what is happening here, I will be your daughter in law in a few weeks. Sir please tell me."

"This was not supposed to happen. The agreement was that he would bring you back to Negril, we would watch over you, he" and he looks at his son, "he was supposed to let you down gently, and you would travel to England tomorrow. That was the agreement".

I look at Courtney puzzled, he looks like he needs to be sick.

"What is your father talking about, agreement?." I start to get angry "with whom?"

Darling come and sit down, he motions to the bed. "my parents have forbid me going to London with you".

"Sooo you will come later then, will I travel on my own?"

"Yes, were connected now. You are my wife and nothing and nobody is going to get in the way of that" he says looking at his father.

"I have made my decision, it's nothing personal Edwina, it's just that, you…. Your father, it's all do complicated and ….. beneath us. He said looking at me. "In the beginning you seemed so suited, but it's clear that we are different people."

"My parents want me to call off the engagement," he tell me looking at the floor. He looked up "Dad I think you should leave now", Jackson looked at his son pained, nodded and walked out of his suite.

I stand up "Why?"

"Winnie you know the reason why." Courtney tells me calmly. "It's him your father, what he represents, my father does not want to be connected in any way to a scandal. People entrust their life savings with him, his image is everything", he said defending his stance

"What do you think?"

"Well I told him that I would marry you come what may, and this morning he turned up to tell me that if I go ahead with it, he will cut me off"

"Cut you off?"

"Financially, I will not have a penny to my name"

"I have money" I scream. "We're fine, you don't need his money"

"What kind of man lives off his woman" he says.

"The same man that can live off his father" I snap

"I am not giving you up" he says seriously. We leave tomorrow as planned. *I smile and feel an queasy feeling in the pit of my stomach. I feel it. My happiness will be short lived.*

Courtney.... I do love you"

P.D Lorde

"Me too the soon to be Mrs. Du Pille"

Chapter 21

January 14th 2005 8.36pm

Farewell

It was evening I could tell. My bright winter sun has disappeared and in its place is the most beautiful well lit full moon I think I have ever seen. It's a cold night as the skies are clear. My body feels oppressed with this unmanageable cancer. I look at Alice, she reads me. I am uncomfortable, without asking she props up my pillows and adds another behind me so that I am lifted higher. She can see that I am having difficulty breathing. Lying here watching my family, I feel sorrow for them. I know that I need to leave this body here, I am withered old and diseased. Most of all I am damaged and at 69 years of age, I am still ashamed of him, my father and all that he represent. I suddenly feel sorrow as I can feel his pain, he was not all bad, he loved me in his own way, but was a relentless tyrant.

My lights in my room are dimmed, the TV is on in the background, it's my favorite TV soap, coronation street.. Harold looks awful, he has strategically positioned himself to the right of me, just staring ..... I am not sure if he sees me anymore, or whether he is consumed with this disease. My sweet pathetic Harold, how he needs to cope and keep the children together. He must. I am relying in him. He needs to be strong.

Dr. York takes my vital signs again. He scrutinises my face for signs of something, I am not sure what. Now, I just don't care, I will take what comes. We are all fearful regarding what is to come. Me.... I am petrified of the unknown. I pray that it's as I believe it to be and on the

other side, that I am happy pain free and with people
who love me. No matter what, death has to be it has to
be better than this suffering.

Mr. York speaks quietly with Alice. She shakes her
head and they look at me, Oops there it is. The pity
stare.

He walks over "Edwina" Mr. York says softly. "Alice tells
me that you don't want any stronger pain relief is that
true?"

I nod and close my eyes.

"Things may get rough later so I will see how you are in
in twenty minutes or so. I motion for him to come closer.

 "I need to be here" a tear leaps from my eye.

Dr. York clenched his jaw and nods his head. "Whatever
you think is best", he holds my hand with a firm but
gentle grip and looks me deep into my eyes. We
connect and we both know it's for the last time.

"I just want you to be a comfortable as possible" he
forces himself to say. I blink slowly and give him a half
smile.

"Hmmmmmmm" is all I could muster.

I look at Jonathan, my first born, my heart and soul and
best friend. I smile to him, he comes over and strokes
my face. Harold holds my hand, and kisses it, I feel his
damp tears on my hot skin. He is his father son, tall
broad and strong, he even had his head for numbers.
There were so many times I wanted to tell him.
Courtney wanted to see him long before now, when I

374

told him that he was gay, those requests stopped overnight. I have left Jonathan a letter explaining everything. His father, well he will soon be aware. I emailed him for the last time two weeks ago with Alice's help. All my secrets will soon be free. I just hope Jonathan forgives me, and his biological father accepts him.

"How you feeling baby?" Harold mutters

"Nooot gooood" I whisper. " Waaatttteeerrr" I take a sip of the cold liquid which instantly refreshes my mouth. "Its... up ....to you". Harold looks at me, something has happened to me, it's as if a switch has been turned off. *I don't have the energy to speak to him. Take care of my flock my darling and for the record I love you. Tell Ange to come quickly I need to see her"*

Harold nods "I go and get her, she is next door, she needs to say goodbye" he says. I look at him astounded. He heard my thoughts. *This is just crazy. Typical! I am dying and this is the first time in my life that he understand me. I smile. If I had the energy I would laugh.*

I stretch out my hand to Phoebe, I cough slowly and deeply, my lungs explode. Alice is all over me, she sits me up and injects something into my drip. This is take the pressure off and it will help with your breathing. She puts on my mask. I pull in as much air as possible for the next few seconds. I hear my heart beat in my ears and its slowing down. My eyes start to twitch and my vision is starting to become hazy, like sun rays zig zagging across the room. The back wall is no longer there, instead of the wall is a garden. It's my front garden and porch at the plantation. How I missed that place. It is absolutely beautiful, the sun is shining and there are people there. I can't see them clearly, I just see their shadows and outlines. Whatever is going on looks like a party. Maybe it's a welcome home party. I smell Mima's cooking. Its coconut cake. I smell the jerk chicken and rice and peas. This is going to be a real homecoming.

"Mum", Phoebe sits next to me. I look at my child, confused, angry and bitter. "*Enough of thhhissss. Those that know better, do better, and you was raised. I say crossly in my mind's eye.*

She nods. Tears roll down her cheeks she is trying to be strong. I feel her fear. I want to tell her that its ok, but I have lost my voice. I feel so light headed.

No, god damn you. I need time. Give me more time I scream in my head. Finally she is listening to me. There is so much more that needs to be said.

The lights in the room start to dim and the colors in my garden are more vibrant and iridescent.

My spirit is starting to descend, I look up and she is there. I feel better knowing that she is here. She is beautiful just as I remembered her all those years ago. She is not old, she is my mother, and I see her youthful face. I cannot help but acknowledge her, all eyes in the room are watching us. They feel the something magical is happening. I close my eyes and start to feel well again. She has to hear me say it. I breath in hard "Muuuuummmmmmm" She falls back into Niall and my brother Phillip. We look at one another and both cry, she leaps towards me and holds me.

"Don't try and speak Edwina, concentrate on breathing"

Alice tell me.

Harold is sobbing uncontrollably by the bed. Maddie and Jon are supporting him. *I look at him, he knew didn't he. All these years, he's known. Unbelievable, if I wasn't dying I would rip him a new one. Now I know why God sent me back, it so I can remember you. Its so I don't die alone. You were right you are my Saint. Thank you Saint Mum. Thank you.*

"Help me I need to hold her" Mum says.

Alice turns to say something and I hear those words I have longed for my whole life

"I am her mother please help me raise my child. I need to hold my daughter now". Her sobs are uncontrollable but she pulls it back. She does not want her last moments to be consumed with this, she can cry when it's over. *No Noooooooooo, I need more time this is my mum, there is so much that I need to tell you.*

My children are rooted to their spots confused to the point of disbelief. Somehow, my beautiful 84 year old mother slides behind me and holds me. All of my memories of her flash before me, playing with me at the plantation, rocking me to sleep as a child, shadowing me at the Morant Bay Market, protecting me from Harold when I broke off our engagement, making sure that I got out of Jamaica alive, being my friend, neighbor and protector for the last 50 years. My half-brother Phillip and step father Niall walk over to the bed. They both kiss me on the head. I always loved them both. My brother looks at me with renewed eyes. He has travelled from New Zealand, Niall insisted that Ange came clean and he is glad that she did.

"Forgive me. I am so sorry my darling" she sobs "I had to protect you and this was the only way I knew how. Forgive me. I am failed you. you still ended up with him. I tried to get you back, they were too strong. Forgive me my darling."

 I turn and look at my mother lovingly and smile. I hold her little finger and gently squeeze. It means the world to her, she knows that I have no malice. She squeezes me and kisses my face. I look at her for the last time, my ears start to buzz, she hums the same song she sang to me as a baby and toddler. I remember it. I look around the room, my family is with me. I feel love and acceptance. I feel my mother's embrace and I feel complete. All my life I have yearned for my mother to hug and kiss me, to hold me and tell me that she loves me, and today, she is here, and I feel her love running through me, and see her love in my children.

Wiiiiiinnnnnnnnnnnie, I hear her. I would recognize her voice on a room filled with a thousand voices. My heart skipped a beat.

"Yes Mima"

"Come on baby its time to go, I have your dinner waiting" she tells me. "I have baked your favorite Coconut cake".

"Mima I need more time" I say "Just five more minutes".

"Winnie you have had a lifetime, it's time to say your goodbyes, and be sure to make it count, we only get one shot at saying goodbye". I feel sad, but grateful for my journey so far. I see the other side and I like it. I am no longer scared but excited.

My breathing slows, she sees that she is losing me.

"Love you" I say to her. She smiles through her pain. My mother strokes my hair, the only way that a mother can.

"I got you baby girl" she whispers "Mummy is here, Don't be scared honey…. The lord is going to protect you".

The pain is gone and I am free. They are my past. My body reforms, I am young again, beautiful, energized and healthy. I laugh out loud, no one can hear me.

"Noooooooo" Mum cries out. Niall immediately runs to his wife and holds her.

"Mum, Oh god she's gone" Maddie cries.

I hear them crying, but its muffled now, the room is getting darker, I hit the ceiling with a thud, I roll over and look down, they look so sad. Dr York stand close by and strokes Alice's arm. This is so hard for everyone. My mother looks in shock. They have noticed I have left them. Mummy holds me tightly and kisses me repeatedly. *I am here I want to scream. I am still with you. Please don't be sad, its fine. I 'm fine and so will you be, just fine.*

My mother starts to pray. "Yeah thought I walk through the valley of the shadow of death I shall fear no evil. For you are with me, your rod and your staff shall comfort me.

Harold bends over in his chair, his head in his hands, he is rocking. Jon and Maddie cry on each other. Phillip holds Phoebe's hand. But my mother is still talking to me.

"I know you're here baby girl. I still feel you. Mima is

going to take care of you she tells me. Don't be afraid she will not leave you. You need to get there and make it comfy for me"

Dr. York looks at Ange "She is gone Madam".

"Young man I have waited 65 years to hold my daughter. You will not rush me. I am her mother." She said and stroked my hair. He immediately backed off.

"Winnie" Mima shouts.

I look at the plantation and see them, I am shocked. Its Mima, Grandma Phyllis, Aunt Rene, Mrs. Mack, Mr. Mack, Grandpa Barrington and daddy, they are all there. I see a beautiful man, he is dark and tall in the distance, he is sanding down that beautiful wooden chair on the veranda. It was Grandpa Vincent. He looks up and smiles at me. I turn to my family and smile.

Grandpa Vincent walks over to me "Mima has told me much about you, young lady, I have waited a long time to meet you?" he smiles.

"As I" I laugh. I love him already.

I look at them now and shout to them all "I will be with you all each and every day. I have to go now. I don't want to leave but I have to. It will be well. We will meet one day, and always remember, that I love you."

THE AUTHOR

P.D LORDE is mother to three beautiful boys and live in the East of England with her husband and children. She has been writing poetry since the age of eight years old and short stories and novels since the aged of eleven. As a young child she has been surrounded by energetic and passionate storytellers within her family. Her early influences were Dr Maya Angerlou, Beatrix Potter, Terry McMilliam, Barbara Taylor Bradford, Steven King to name a few. After graduating with honor's degree in Law in the late 90's she pursued a career within the legal field. Only since her forties has she gained the confidence to share with the world a collection of her poetry "Laid Bare", this novel which is a trilogy. The sequel "The Journey will be available in the summer of 2018. Thank you for your time and energy in committing to read this story.

18078407R00227

Printed in Great Britain
by Amazon